THE QUEEN OF SHARDS

BOOK I

THE CHRONICLES OF LILITH

JENS C. BÜDINGER

THE QUEEN OF SHARDS

THE CHRONICLES OF LILITH SERIES – BOOK 1

Developmental Editor: Susan Barnes.

Line & Copy Editor: Clare Ashgrove

Cover design art: Dave Arredondo.

Special thanks to Michelle Dawn (critique partner and dear friend).

Trigger Warning: This book contains themes and graphic situations of violence, abuse, sexual encounters, suicide & adult language.

This book forms part of a series and ends on a cliff-hanger.

First Edition.

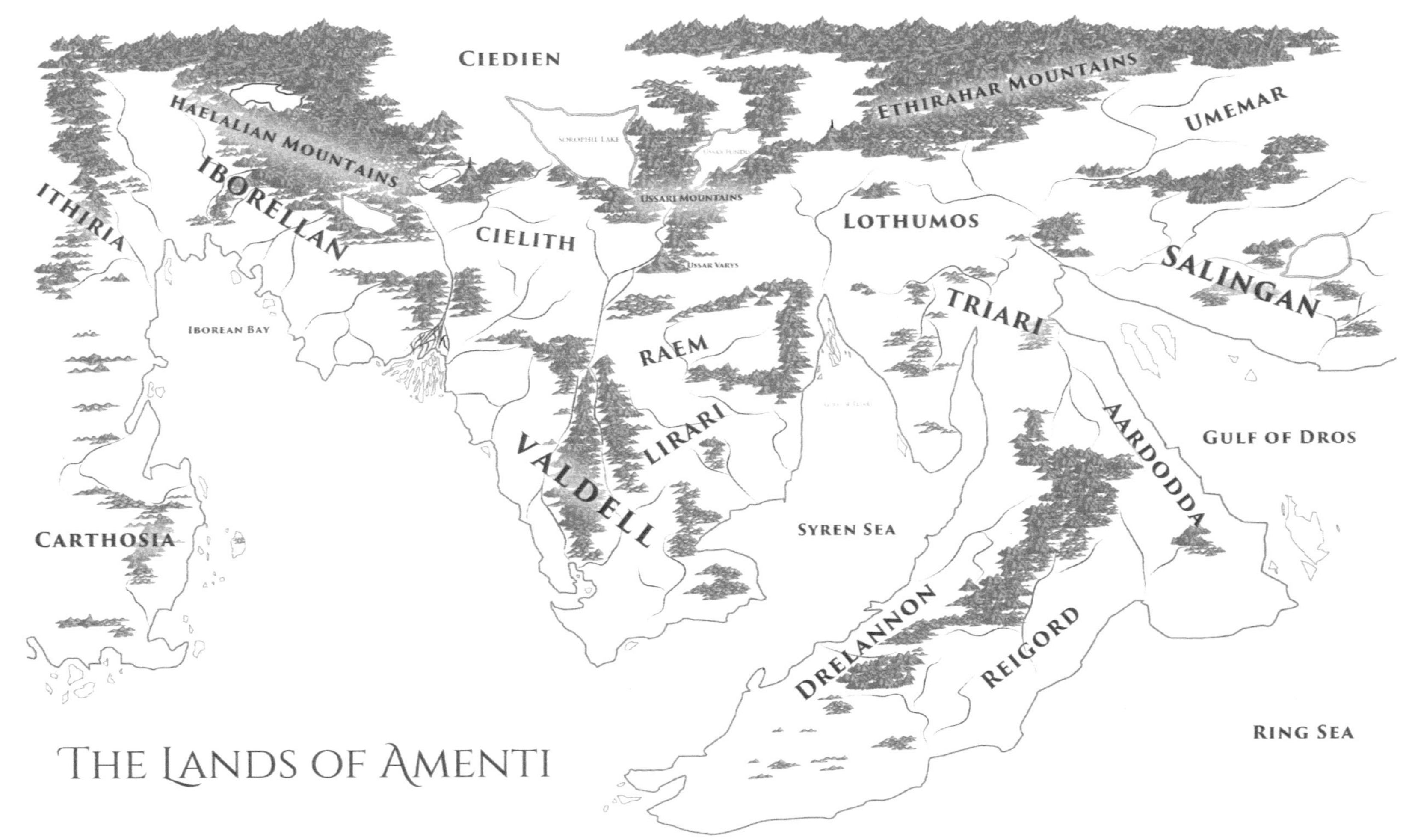
CIEDIEN
ETHIRAHAR MOUNTAINS
UMEMAR
HAELALIAN MOUNTAINS
IBORELLAN
ITHIRIA
SOROPHIL LAKE
USSARI MOUNTAINS
USSAR VARYS
CIELITH
LOTHUMOS
SALINGAN
IBOREAN BAY
RAEM
TRIARI
VALDELL
LIRARI
AARDODDA
GULF OF DROS
CARTHOSIA
SYREN SEA
DRELANNON
REIGORD
RING SEA
THE LANDS OF AMENTI

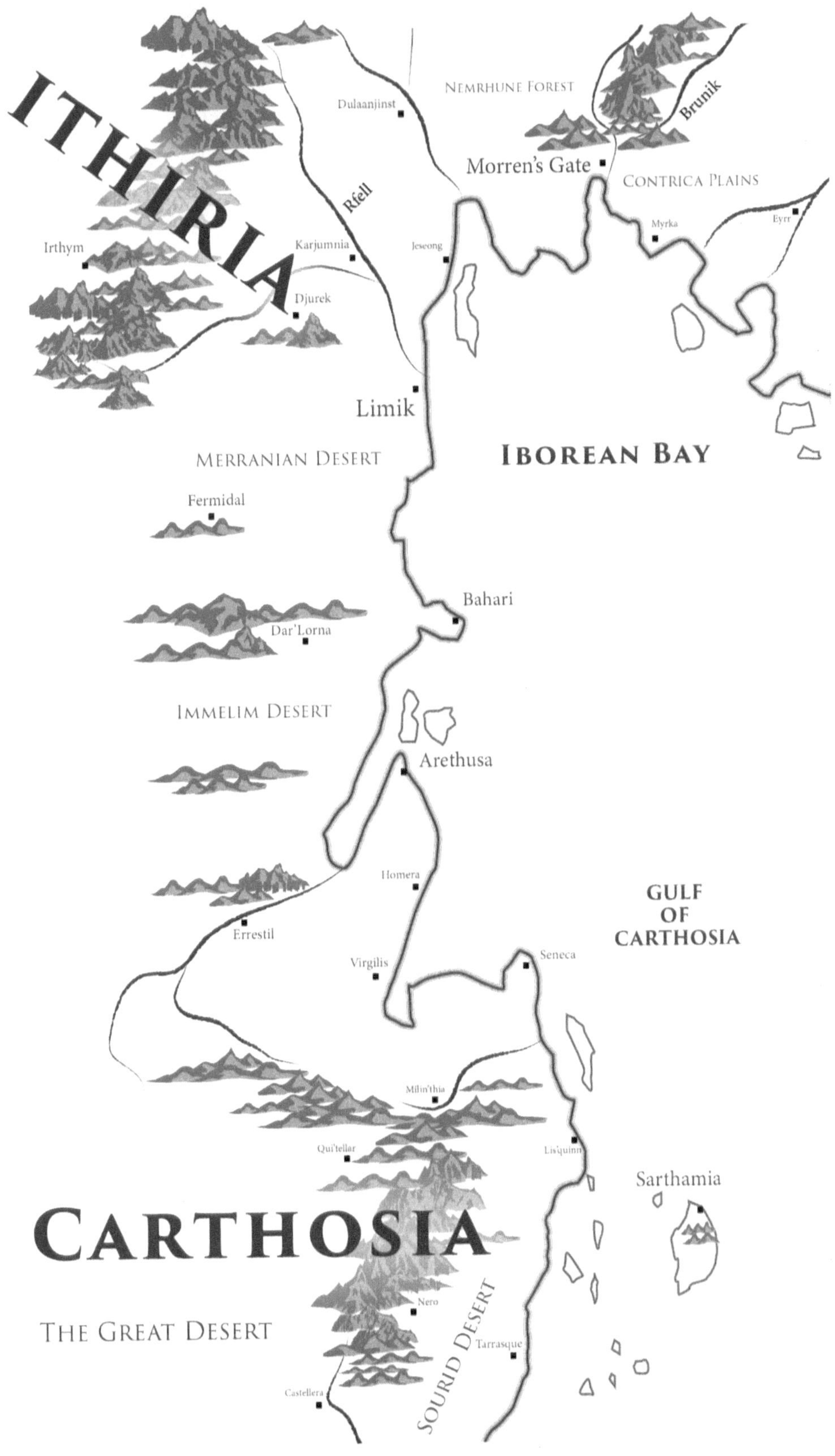

ITHIRIA
CARTHOSIA
NEMRHUNE FOREST
Brunik
Morren's Gate
CONTRICA PLAINS
Dulaanjinst
Rfell
Myrka
Eyrr
Irthym
Karjumnia
Jeseong
Djurek
Limik
IBOREAN BAY
MERRANIAN DESERT
Fermidal
Bahari
Dar'Lorna
IMMELIM DESERT
Arethusa
GULF
OF
CARTHOSIA
Homera
Errestil
Seneca
Virgilis
Milin'thia
Qui'tellar
Lis'quinn
Sarthamia
THE GREAT DESERT
Nero
SOURID DESERT
Tarrasque
Castellera

CARALIS FOREST
SOROPHIL LAKE
The Last City
CALANTIS JUNA
Rhyns Land
CAELIS LAKE
Leptis Mines
Ryn Mines
ILLONTRIS FOREST
RHYN FOREST
Lerrem
Serinnelle
CIELITH
Shena Asari
Karankal
Wylmanas
Quitain
Siensell
ERRELIHM FOREST
Myalthas
FRONFERRE FOREST
THRELIS FOREST
Eterras
Illyum
Sylmaris
Ungsol
Yammimer
WHITE FOREST
Threlis Manor
Vinesse
Reffa
SORELL
Avern
Verdosa
Aratiwa
SALMIS
PLAINS
Peretus
Lantima
Cadrid

BALUR SEPHIT
USSAR FUNDIS
The Eternal City
Gates of Dos Narak
RED WASTES
Legris Khari
USSARI MOUNTAINS
Lesrak Tarh Plains
Morirua
LOTHUMOS
USSAR VARYS
Great Lumath Steppe
Black Pass
Maniver Forest
Prandarii
Barrannario
Harlot's Hold
Rakshir Plains
SILVERHORN
Sillum
Strait of Jox Novia
Blackrock
Lonlina
Orestil
Norfolk
SILVERHORN PLAINS
Moorvish
Flemingsway
Solomi
RAEM
Dill Candor
Hill Top
WISP WOOD
Orensway
NOVIAN PLAINS
Raemsburh
Ascope
Kirkburh
Novania
GULF OF TRIARI
Gari
Ceseglie
LIRARI
Lirari
Lergamo
Aveicedo

Peretus
Cádrid
Lantima
DRESL WOOD
Valdor
Taire
VALDELL
Este
Constance
Hillburn
Maribell
Legnamola
Valendria
Vidian's Citadel
West Valendria
Vrilisteri
Larnes
Prabia
Prasso
Palaga
Salagona

To all lost souls in a lost world.

'Fate hath spoken unto the Greater Immortals,
commanded they struggle in the worlds left by the Will.
For the Will of Existence had failed to deliver
the secret to life and the reason within.
For only through living can an answer be given
on whether existence should cease or not.'

Canticle of the Greater Immortals 2:23-28

PROLOGUE

AWAKENED ABSTRACTION

"If you want to truly kill me, you're going to need to do a lot more than that," said Zain in gasps through the black bag over his head.

The bright lights buzzed overhead. The night was cold, and the wind found its way through the distant dark corridors. The winds of winter softly hummed around the never-ending halls, punctuated by echoes of grunts and the smack of skin to the cold, hard floor.

"Get him up. Make sure he's locked in, secure," ordered the commander sternly, failing to mask his exasperation. "I hope she knows what she's doing, tinkering around with this freak."

"Oh, thank y—"

One guard punched Zain in the gut, sending him once again to the ground.

"Are you sure it will hold him, sir? Can he even integrate with it?" asked another guard.

"Once you're in the Abstract, it is impossible to get out." The commander groaned. "Though with his type, there's no telling. But right now, there's only one way to find out."

Zain was thrust against the walls and a series of chains and bindings were latched to his arms, legs, and neck. He kept quiet, breathing deeply through the bag.

"Ready?" said the commander.

"He's in," said a feminine voice.

They snatched the bag from Zain's head, and the cell went dark and silent.

"Finally, some fresh air." Zain clutched at his chains, bound tightly to the floor, struggling to brush his long black hair out of his face. "So unnecessary."

The commander narrowed his eyes, observing him closely.

Zain groaned as he slowly found his smile again. "I was about to say thank you, sir, lord, commander, sir—"

The guard kicked him. "Stay down!"

Zain groaned as he lay down, struggling to right himself with his bindings. "I'm afraid I don't think I'm going to be of much use to you soon. I'm going to presume you aren't too familiar with the nature of the Eldaresh... a Vampire."

The commander looked to the other guard and nodded.

"Listen. I'm dying." Zain breathed long and deeply. "I mean, I know I can't die, at least not the way you do. But if you can't find me any, and I mean *any*, blood that I can drink, all you're going to find is a shrivelled corpse. And I'm quite sure I will become far less entertaining than I am right now."

"You truly believe so?" asked the commander as he drew closer to the moonlit window, hands behind his back, revealing his long white hair, silver-grey skin, and menacing deep red, eyes.

"Do I look like I'm joking?" asked Zain, raising an eyebrow.

The commander paused as he observed his perfectly trimmed fingernails, his other hand behind his back. "Fine, then I'll see to it that you get what you need if indeed it is blood that you want," said the commander as he walked out of the door, followed by his escorts. "Perhaps you might prove to be useful after all."

The door shut.

Zain sat waiting with his bound, raised hands, seeking alms. "Well, I guess it's not the first time I've gone to bed without dinner," he said before lying back in his corner, wincing, and curling up to continue the rest of his sojourn.

He closed his eyes, waiting for silence to invite his sleep. The soft wind trailed over his slightly pointed ears, sending the chill of winter right into his spine. He took a long, deep breath, drawing in the cold air, filling his even colder lungs. Breath by breath, growing longer.

His descent into darkness felt like an eternity.

"Do you remember who you are?" whispered a voice.

From within or without? he thought, with his eyes closed.

"Who are you looking for?" asked the voice, now more feminine. "Where have you been?"

"What?" He stirred. "What!" he exclaimed as he awoke, shuddering, looking for the source.

"I said, where have you been, Zain," said the voice from behind the moonlit shadows.

"Krea!" said Zain, startled, as he looked around, attempting to orient himself.

"Surprised you didn't catch me in the dark, Vampire?" She smiled.

"Nonsense," he said, sheepishly looking away. "I knew you were there."

"Let's continue from where we left off last time, shall we?" asked the tall, sharp-eyed Drae'shï. "But first I heard you were hungry. This should keep you going for the time being." She threw a sack of live rats before Zain.

"Eek," he said as the squeaking, rumbling rodents desperately sought to escape their fate.

"Is that not to your liking?" asked Krea, feigning genuine concern in her tone.

"Yes! Yes, it is!" he said, shuffling to grab the sack laid at her feet. "Holy Mother of Light! Finally." He dug into the bag, fishing out rat after filthy rat and draining their blood as if in one of the drinking contests he so used to enjoy and also cringed at. "Ah! I'm alive again. Pity, though, that the company leaves much to be desired."

"You've proven to be a rather unruly guest after all," said Krea calmly. "I understand we should make some progress today since you're satisfied." She pursed her lips.

"If your idea of extracting information from a Vampire is to bludgeon him to oblivion, I can assure you it won't work."

"I know where to prod and twist to get the information I need out of you," said the slender Drae'shï as she strutted towards him.

"I've given you everything I know. Why do you insist on knowing my entire life's bloody story? What is the point of all this?"

"Because, Zain, we oft reveal our darkest secrets, unbeknownst even to us, in the most uncanny of ways. You say you have lived for hundreds of years. I'm sure you won't disappoint." She bent on one knee before him, narrowing her gaze, shifting her sight from Zain's left eye to the other. His icy blue eyes were reflected in her red. Her hair was white and cut short, giving her an air of superiority that rivalled Zain's earlier visitors.

"I'm tired of this. Please just tell me what it is you want to know," he said, recoiling from her scrutiny.

"Fine, let's get back to it then." She snapped back up to her feet. "Who's 'The All?' We know it's someone close to you."

Zain sighed. "This again. I don't know what you're talking about, and I have no one."

She mused for a moment. "Truly? No one? What about a wife, children? Significant others then?"

"Why? Looking to bag yourself a dashing Eldaresh? I'm the last of my kind, might I add," he said, flashing a sarcastic smirk.

She kept looking. Her expression had not changed.

"Fine. None. All dead."

Krea took a deep breath. "Whether you're aware of it or not, you're proving to be more uncooperative than I thought, Zain. But worry not. We know you have the answers buried within your mind. We'll extract them one way or another."

"Good thing you're all tickles and giggles then."

"So, let's begin. Back from when you first encountered Lilith, when this all started," she said, ignoring his unnecessary remarks.

"Fine! But can you at least unchain me? This is not the kind of bondage I'm into, you know," he said slyly.

"Tell me your story, and perhaps I'll tell you how a man escapes the bonds of his own creation."

Chapter 1

The Loneliness Of Death

Zain hopped off his horse, landing in mud and possibly also pig dung. "Charming," he said, shaking his boot before tying his horse to the nearest post. "Don't worry, my friend, you'll have plenty of garbage thrown around for you to eat." The filthy dew-draped town went about its daily business, congregating around an outdoor marketplace where all manners of wares, women, and wayfarers gathered. Orestill was one of the few old townships left in Raem that still resisted the bitter winters of the north, long after the ancient Eldarï of Ciedien migrated south and took the eternal summer with them.

Still, Zain kept a certain skip in his step, self-amused, entertained by his cultural exposure. He walked around standing tall amongst the townsfolk, occasionally picking up the randy smirk of a local prostitute coming his way over her cold bare shoulders.

"I need your largest room, your best wine, and most unbesmirched whore. Thank you," he said as he burst into the first questionably decorated inn he found.

"Payment upfront, friend, and there be no unbesmirched whores in this house. There's nothing quite not besmirched around here, actually," said the innkeeper through his dirty, thick whiskers and runny nose, sniffing every few seconds.

"Enough?" Zain asked, dropping a heavy purse on the table.

"Most definitely, sir!" said the semi-congested innkeeper, before wiping his nose on his forearm and then on his apron, eager to claim his earnings.

Zain's cringe quickly shifted to a smile as the man met his gaze again and nodded wide-eyed before swaggering away into the chatter of the inn's barroom. It was small and dingy yet packed with patrons, all crammed around their beer-soaked tables. A roaring fire raged in the back where a cauldron bubbled and oozed quietly, filling the air with a nutty scent of sage, mushrooms, and venison.

The day passed in what seemed like a couple of hours, and as the streets quieted, the chaos of the market now retreated into the tavern. Zain was already entertaining.

"And so this poor sod is standing there, mashed snail in his hand, looking at what he believes is some new aphrodisiac from the untamed lands of Ardodda."

The crowd laughed hysterically.

"Wait! Wait!" said Zain, panting as he sipped clumsily from his flagon. "It gets better! It gets better!"

All were eagerly awaiting.

"Come on," cried a man.

"Shut up," screeched a woman.

"He then proceeded to smell it." Zain mimicked the movement.

The crowd could hardly contain itself.

"Before sticking out his tongue to taste it."

Half the crowd roared, and the other half cringed whilst Zain kept whipping out his tongue like a wriggling worm to his audience.

"More ale!" he said, shaking away at his flagon, spilling its contents all over the place.

Music broke out once again and the crowd cheered in unison.

Zain reclined, letting out a grunt as he stretched out.

"I hope you will not leave us unattended to." A red-headed tavern wench slid across the ale-drenched bench to lean and swoon on the handsome taleteller.

"Obviously not, my darlings," said Zain, as he also turned to the approaching blonde.

She promptly claimed his lap as he wrapped his long arm around the redhead.

"You see, someone who's seen much and travelled so far and wide develops a certain stomach for alcohol and a keener appetite for the finer things in life," he said, slurring in his most chivalrous voice whilst moving closer to her lips, almost hypnotizing her with his seductive gaze.

The redhead jealously turned his chin back to her, stroking his face. "And how come such a charming, handsome, worldly man never settled in one place?" she asked as she then trailed her finger across his open shirt.

"Or in one person?" asked the blonde as she turned his face back to hers.

"Oh, that was many lifetimes ago, my dearies. Now my heart wanders the world, chasing the ghost of a love long lost, outliving every single romance since. A pointless existence is a life without love," said Zain in his more hopelessly romantic tone.

Both girls moaned sympathetically. "I'm sure we'll make you forget about her."

"Oh, I'm sure you'll try," said Zain, pausing for a moment. "But first!" He stood up, almost dropping them both to the floor. "Piss!" he claimed vigorously and marched his way out of the homestead and into the crap-ridden back alley.

As he relieved himself against the wall, Zain gazed at the moon, enamoured by its soft light. His night's beverages continued to intoxicate him further. "It's been a while since I've been this sloshed," he said, pausing as he swayed in his haze. He stared blankly as his drunken grin slowly dimmed. "Forget you." He falsely smirked. "I miss you." He sighed, shaking his head. "So much, Sarail. It's been such a long life. Alone. What's the point?" He raised his head, closing his eyes.

A subtle shade crept from the corner of the alley, brushing against the wall.

Zain narrowed his gaze to straighten his vision. The soft step of a cloaked figure, slouched like a hag, dragged her feet through the dirty alley.

"If you're hoping to rob me, believe me, there's nothing left that's worth taking," he called out.

The figure ignored him, slowing its pace as it dragged itself against the wall.

"Are you alright?" he asked approaching cautiously.

The figure collapsed.

"Whoa!" He swept in, catching the figure in his arms.

The moonlight revealed the face of a woman. Zain stopped for a moment to observe her luminescent grey complexion and dark lips. The moonlight further accentuated her foreign features. She was a Drae'shï; a dark eldarï. Her features were distinctly contoured, her skin light grey and her hair white as snow.

"I haven't seen the likes of your kind in quite some time, and home is definitely not in this direction."

The Drae'shï groaned in pain. Her cloak fell open, revealing a long deep cut along her hip. Dark blue blood soaked through her black leather garb.

He let out a snort before regaining his composure and sobriety, looking around before cursing under his breath. "Well, whoever you are, we've got to get you out of here. You're not exactly the kind of traveller these folks are expecting."

Zain wrapped the Drae'shï in her cloak and lifted her, sneaking his way back into the inn and up to his bedroom under the curious eyes of some of the drunken patrons. Soon his bed was host to the unexpected guest.

The following day, Zain woke from his sleep as the midday sun also kissed the Drae'shï's face.

She stirred slowly, gradually opening her dark red eyes. She attempted to rise, but cried out and held onto her side before she collapsed back in bed. Again, she raised her head, looking down at herself. Her waist was wrapped in bandages, and her hands and feet were tightly strung to the bed frame with sheets. Her struggle intensified with the realisation of captivity.

"Calm down, or you'll need another set of sutures," said Zain, sitting cross-armed across the bedroom, rocking on a rickety chair, now less inebriated and far less amused. "And after the look that cleric gave you, I'll be buggered if I have to do them again myself."

"Unbind me. Now!" she snapped in her raspy voice, tugging violently at her ligatures.

"I can't understand you. Calm down," he said, but his pleas only provoked her further. "Alright, shut it," he snapped as he attempted to cover her mouth.

She snapped back at him with her teeth until he finally fed her a bundled bed sheet to silence her. He pushed down at her mouth and raised a finger to his lips. She let out a long huff and nodded reluctantly.

"Never learnt your bloody dialect, so many ughs and ghuhs and kehs. Alright, let's try this. My name is Zain. I am Eldaresh," he said slowly, pointing to himself and his slightly longer canines, before releasing her mouth.

She spat out the sheet.

"I can understand you, you blithering idiot," she said, struggling once more. "And aren't the Eldaresh supposed to all be dead?"

"And there I was hoping you'd greet me with some of that Drae'shï charm and gratitude and join me for breakfast on account of my display of chivalry last night."

"Your assistance was not needed or requested. Release me. Now." Her patience was evidently wearing thin.

"Well, I couldn't let a damsel collapse on her own like that even if I tried. So how about that breakfast now?" he asked, completely ignoring her.

"Release me now!" Her temper surged. She once again tugged at the sheets that bound her. "What do you want from me? Who are you?"

"Ah, yes, that's the question!" he said, flipping the chair right before him, sitting at a safe distance.

"I have to go. Now!" she yelled further.

"All right. All right. Shut up, or soon you'll catch more than just my own attention," he said as he edged his ear close to the door.

She understood and quieted herself again.

He began to stroll the room. "Now, I'm not from these parts, and I don't know how someone like you ended up wandering out of that big mountain of yours you call home, but I'm pretty sure that you're not supposed to be here."

"They're after me. I *have* to leave. Now!"

"Yes, I'm pretty sure they are by now."

The din outside the room, sounding like a scuffle, drew her instant attention. Zain looked over too. Laughter ensued below.

"Yes, they definitely are," he said sarcastically. "Still, I find it strange that some lonely lady like yourself actually got this far past Harlot's Hold without detection by the Wardens. I'm impressed."

"Spare me your keen observations and let me go!" said the Drae'shï as she kept trying to look out of the window by her side.

"Well, and I thought the two of us just might have gotten along. But given your sweet and grateful disposition, I think it's best if I deliver you into their caring hands the minute they arrive and take my leave, along with my reward for doing my civic duties and such."

"You insufferable cretin. Release me now," she roared, pulling once more on the sheets. "Or you'll have more than just one Drae'shï to deal with."

Zain laughed, observing her tantrum purge itself through her deep ruby eyes as she kicked and tugged at her bonds. The din downstairs grew loud again, and the Drae'shï stopped, raising her gaze to the door once more. Silence resumed. Zain stared at the Drae'shï as she looked at the door and then back at him, where their gazes met.

"Anyway, so where were we? Ah yes, introductions—"

The door burst open behind Zain. He turned, and a clenched fist announced itself to his face. A rush of armed men rumbled through. Zain groaned, holding his face as he turned onto his side, looking through his fingers as the room filled with crimson armoured soldiers. All bore the coat of arms of the Wardens: the Black Barbican.

"There's another, Captain. Not Drae'shï though," said the seasoned lieutenant with salt and pepper hair and a beard to match.

"Seen him before, Doran?" asked the captain, entering the room. He was tall with his hair shaved on its sides, and a thick goatee. He bore a stern scowl seemingly fixed permanently on his face.

"Perhaps a contact? There may be more."

"No, no, no," said Zain, now raising his hands to stop the impending catastrophe. "I'm not one of them."

The two paused.

"Idiot! I knew you'd get us caught," spat the Drae'shï at Zain.

Zain raised an eyebrow in confusion.

"Bringing us to a tavern in this city. The Drae'shï will flay you for every coin we paid you!" she continued, eyeing the warden's reaction to her vindictive gambit.

"Oh, no, no, no," said Zain wide-eyed, looking at the judgement taking form on the Warden's face. "No! She's lying!"

"You're coming with me," she mouthed deviously back at him.

"No!"

The Wardens looked at each other and back at Zain. "Fine." said the captain. "Take them away. We'll deal with them once we're back at Harlot's Hold."

"No!" called Zain as the men dragged him out.

Chapter 2

A Harlot's Hold

Another cold droplet tauntingly dangled off the edge of the cell's ceiling before dropping onto the Vampire's neck. "Ah, shit! Every bloody time. Is there any corner of this place that isn't either cold or wet? Harlot's Hold is a real hellhole."

"Shut up," said the Drae'shï flatly from the cell across from him.

"That's all I've heard from you since we met. I must say, you're the worst company in the world. Are all the Drae'shï this talkative these days?" he said as he dragged himself closer to the bars. "Seeing as you've gotten me in here, you could at least tell me your name, so I know who I need to accord the reference to 'worst decision to help anyone ever' when I decide to write my memoirs."

She scowled at him from under her white hair. "Fine. I am Lil'Thra Astemari Sistrah, daughter of the Ussari, Guardian of the White Tower of Ussar Varys," she said with conviction. "But you have no idea what that means, do you? So why do you even care, seeing as you're going to get me killed anyway?"

"Well, Lil'Thra of Hall Sistrah, I'm Zain, or rather Zayenisthor Xyrrtheo Llylaphrias Morismensia," he said as her eyes widened. "And if I know you as well as you know me, I can guess that no guardian of the White Tower can take a walk out of Ussar Varys without good cause. So,

I'm sure that whilst you might have these brutes fooled, I'm a fool who's been around long enough to recognise a Drae'shï deserter when I see one." His voice echoed in the keep's empty cell block.

"The Death of the Undeath." She smirked to herself, shaking her head. "Zain is the name you go by now, is it? Well, you're either a liar, or you're the poorest excuse for a legend I have ever seen." She laughed mockingly.

"Yes, I like the ring to it. Legend," he said, looking away, cupping his chin.

She paused, awaiting further noise from him, but he was now fidgeting with his bootstrap, still entranced by his thoughts.

She moved closer to the bars of her cell. "If you are who you say you are, why don't you get us out? I know what your kind can do, Vampire."

"I prefer the term Eldaresh, thank you— 'Vampire' is so crass. And also, it's complicated."

"What's complicated? I've heard the stories. The power that blood bestows on your kind."

"I don't do that anymore," he said, turning his face away.

She scoffed. "Such is the legend then."

Yet Zain did not reply, staring at his feet, as he shuffled them against the cold floor.

"So, how does it feel to be the last of your kind, Death of the Undeath?" she taunted.

"Somewhat like being a Drae'shï deserter. I think you can relate?" He turned back.

"I'm no deserter, Vampire."

"Then I'm of no help to you." He grinned. "Soon, these fine men will take you back to the loving embrace of the Drae'shï, and you know how understanding they are. What was the punishment for leaving Ussar Varys? Impalement, was it? I'm sure they're still in love with their traditions."

"You—"

The cell block's door flung open. Both went silent.

The captain of the Wardens entered, followed by two other men. He carried himself with conviction and a strong and heavy step. His gaze focused first on Lil'Thra and then on Zain. "The commander is ready to see you," he said in his husky voice.

"Oh, lovely." Zain stood face-to-face with the captain, dusting himself down as the guards unlocked the cell.

The captain's dark brown gaze bore down on Zain's. A certain hardness appeared in his stern brow, yet the captain's Eldarï ancestry was unmistakable.

"It's been a while since I've run into any Eldassari," said Zain as he looked upon the captain's brazen and rugged appearance. His hair was fair yet darkened, his ears barely edged, and all guised under the brutish veil of his human descent.

The Eldassari were distant descendants of the long-departed Eldarï yet they were close cousins of the Eldain from Cielith who possessed a seemingly purer Eldarï ancestry. Eldassari were a common sight among the other human citizens of Raem and more so among the wardens of Harlot's Hold. As the ill-begotten offspring of unsanctioned affairs between Eldain and non-Eldain, the Eldassari were treated as nothing more than orphans and foundlings often left by the Eldain at the steps of the Hold.

"Ready to talk more then, Eldain?" said the captain while Zain was roughly escorted out of the cell by the accompanying Wardens.

"I'm not Eldain."

"Well, you look like them. Come on, pretty boy, it's getting late," said another red-maned Eldassari as he shoved him forward through the cell block's corridor.

"Calm down. Calm down. I'll come peacefully," he said as they manhandled him through the cell block's main door and out of the keep overlooking the bailey. The sun had begun to set.

Harlot's Hold was cold and barren, much like the land it was built to guard. The small fortification lay atop a small hill overlooking a large expansion of land set at the foot of Mount Ussar Varys. The enormous mountain emerged at the tail end of the Ussari mountain range that ran for hundreds of kilometres into the north. The mustard steppe of the Rakshir Plateau stood in stark contrast to the black mountain towering behind it as the pink-blue clouds masked an ancient White Tower of gilded alabaster that sat upon its summit.

Zain observed the many Wardens go about their business, some manning the old black cobbled walls watching the mount incessantly whilst others concluded their training and daily toil. Men of the Hold were known to be of various origins, mostly coming from Raem and coveting a new purpose in life or a military occupation to feed their families back home, but the true Wardens as known in history were unmistakable in their appearance and presence.

The Eldassari appeared to have inherited much of the benefit of their mixed parentage. Often living up to a hundred and thirty years, these men were tall, towering, and strong. Each stood as knights within the Hold, as respected and feared combatants with the knowledge of the many battles they'd fought over their long lives. All Wardens wore thick black and red quilted leather armour with long, black fur cloaks, yet they didn't seem to weigh on the Eldassari much.

"I haven't been around these parts in quite a while, Captain," said Zain as they manoeuvred him around the castle's training grounds to the clashing and clanking of the trainees' swords and shields.

"We don't get many visitors. Inside," said the captain, gesturing to a large double door. The mess hall was a large shack, dark and candlelit, with no windows. "Commander Dorreth, the prisoner."

"Here, Adomas," said Dorreth. He sat at the corner of the long dining table at the end of the hall. He was an old Eldassari, a tall and corpulent man, white-haired and bearded, with piercing blue eyes. "Come," he said, waving them in, bread in hand as he ate his supper. "So, this is the Eldain who was harbouring the Drae'shï? Bit pale but definitely got that purebred look if I've ever seen one." He eyed them as he chewed through his food.

Zain raised his finger. "If I may—"

"Yes, he was," interrupted Adomas. "But much of what he has been saying on the ride back here proved to be of no consequence."

"Do you think he's helping her escape?" asked Dorreth.

"Not sure. But he tended to her wounds in Orestill."

"Do you know this Drae'shï, Eldain?" asked Dorreth, now dipping his bread into his stew.

"First of all, I'm not Eldain, I'm El— look, it doesn't matter. I simply ran into her in the back alley of the inn while taking a piss. I was just trying to help her," said Zain.

Dorreth stopped mid-bite. He huffed as he took his napkin and wiped his hands, chewing away before swallowing his last bit. "Captain, wasn't he interrogated on the way here?"

"Yes, Commander."

"And did he reveal anything beyond what he just said?"

"No, Commander."

"Then why did you bring him here as well?"

"Because they are most likely in league. Despite what he said."

"I'd have thought that by now, you would have either got it out of him or realised that he's telling the truth instead of dragging him all the way from Orestill to my table." Irritation built in Dorreth's tone. "You, Eldain. Where are you from? Cielith?"

Zain groaned and rubbed his head. "You wouldn't believe me if I told you."

The red-maned brute shoved him forward.

"I mean, yes, of course. Cielith, where else?" He laughed nervously.

"Do you know this Drae'shï? What has she told you?" Dorreth now appeared visibly bored, cupping his mouth with his hand.

"She's not exactly talkative," said Zain.

"I've heard them talk. We'll get her to talk to us," said Adomas, earning another disparaging look from his commander.

Dorreth snorted then rose from the table and dusted his hands. "Captain, obtain what you wish to find out about this Drae'shï from either of them, and then send him off and escort her back to the mountain by the end of the day. If she attempts to flee, or go anywhere other than through the gates of Black Pass, kill her. You have your orders. Dismissed."

"Sir. We should keep them both here until we find out all we can about the Drae'shï first," said Adomas insistently.

"Adam," said Dorreth, shutting his eyes and pursing his lips.

"Sir," Adam interrupted, unamused, his hands now flat on the table. "The last time a Drae'shï walked out of Ussar Varys was over six hundred years ago. We can't ignore this."

"And for six hundred years since, the Wardens of the Hold have survived without drawing swords on them," barked Dorreth, now standing and towering above all present. "And I don't intend to start now. You have your orders, Captain. Now, get out and get them out of here. Dismissed."

"Yes, sir," muttered Adam as he turned and barged out of the mess hall followed by Zain and his escort. "Take this one back to the cell." Adam signalled.

"Shall we take her there now or in the morning, Captain?" said the red-maned Warden as he escorted Zain up the steps and Adam stayed below.

"Take her? No, Thane, we need to get to the bottom of this," said Adam. "And if he doesn't know anything, we need to go and find out for ourselves."

Zain opened his palms and raised his eyebrows.

Thane stopped and sighed. "Adam, Dorreth is not going to be happy. Just let it go."

"Dorreth only cares about sitting on his arse all day, not getting involved in anything. This is not what the Wardens are, what we stand for."

"Adam, seriously? We're a bunch of nobodies, holed up in this derelict fort," said Thane as he gestured at their surroundings. "The Drae'shï haven't been seen for six hundred years. No one needs us, except to stop the occasional gang of hoodlums. Face it, the glory days of the Wardens are long behind us, mate."

"For all we know, Thane, they've just begun."

Chapter 3

Fractured Dreams

The reflection in the mirror Shard was remarkably crisp, and the more Lil'Thra looked into it, the more its image appeared to deepen within its reflection. Zain and Lil'Thra sat across from each other in their respective cells once more. The night was quiet.

"You do know that's still you inside there, don't you?" asked Zain, as he rested against the cold walls, finally exhausted of all sarcasm.

"Sometimes I wonder if it really is, Zain," she mused, as she continued to gaze at her reflection.

"Seriously, though. If you're planning on using that to get us out of here, good luck," he said, dragging himself towards the bars of his cell. "Guard! Guard!" he called out once again. "This treatment is inhumane. It's dinner time, and I haven't eaten anything in days." He groaned.

"You know they're not going to bring you anything, right?" she asked, smirking at Zain before concealing the Shard in her boot.

"What happened to you anyway? Where did all that urgency to leave go all of a sudden?"

Lil'Thra paused and furrowed her brow. "You think I want to stay here? You have no idea what's after m—"

The door violently flung open, interrupting her. It was Thane, and he was fuming.

"Stop, Thane! Leave her. She's useless!" said a voice from outside as the red-maned Eldassari slammed the door and locked the iron barrels.

"Finally! You brought food," said Zain with a spring in his voice.

"I'll get this bitch to talk," muttered Thane, disregarding Zain completely. "How many were you when you left Ussar Varys? How many remain?" He banged on the Drae'shï's cage.

Lil'Thra gazed back up at him in calm contemptuous silence whilst she reached into her boot to draw the Shard.

"We know you weren't the only one to leave the mountain. Where are the rest of your men?"

"And what makes you think they are my men, Warden?" she asked, confident and cool as she stood to meet his face, concealing the Shard behind her back.

"We found tracks around the pass and an assaulted caravan along the road to Orestill. Corpses were gutted and stuck with black steel arrows. What are the Drae'shï doing outside the mountain?" he barked.

"What did you do, Lil'Th?" asked Zain in suspicion.

"Nothing, Zain. Absolutely nothing." She laughed to herself, just as the sound of the Hold's alarm bells began to ring.

"You led them here, didn't you?" Thane reached straight for her neck, locking her face right between the bars.

"I didn't do anything," she grunted back through the bars.

"Hey! Let her go," said Zain as he got to his feet and banged on the bars. "Lilith! What did you do?"

"Nothing more than the half-breeds already did to themselves." She sneered in contempt before pressing the Shard firmly against the inside of Thane's groin. Their faces were now within inches of each other.

Repeated banging on the cell block door began, and the sound of clashing swords echoed from outside.

"We'll find you. Wherever you run to," he said, smiling back as he gradually released his grasp, only to snap his hold back, banging her head against the iron bars.

She fell unconscious.

"No!" said Zain, banging against the bars in anger.

Suddenly, the cell block's door crashed down. A dark-clad assassin wearing the black, purple, and red colours of the Drae'shï walked in, bearing a long scimitar at his side.

The red-eyed Drae'shï signalled Thane to move aside.

"Back to the glory days, indeed," said Thane with a smirk as he slowly extracted his battle axe from beneath his heavy cloak. He stepped forward, raising his weapon.

The Drae'shï confidently kept a firm hold on his sheathed scimitar. Thane struck and in an instant the Drae'shï drew his black steel blade, diverting the Eldassari's mighty swing into the wall. The Drae'shï followed up with a swift punch straight to the Warden's face.

Thane stepped back, felt his bloodied lip, and smiled. "Not bad."

The two engaged in a visceral display of brute force and swordplay, the skill and discipline of the other met with each move delivered. Yet the Drae'shï was inherently faster. Using an interplay of sharp jabs and counters with the weapon's pommel, the assassin found every opportunity to slice his opponent's arms and legs with ease.

In the meantime, Harlot's Hold was well under attack. Zain watched from his cell window as the Drae'shï quickly and clinically dispatched many human Wardens as they silently emerged from the ramparts under cover of darkness. Amidst the fray, the Eldassari also found themselves hard-pressed by the small yet sudden ambush.

Zain's view darted from one fight to the next, thinking of his next move. Yet his attention fell upon the gates of the hold as a Drae'shï elite — a Dratesh Khan— walked through, along with his men.

"Oh, shit," said Zain. "Not good. Not good."

The tall beastly knight had shoulder and arm plates of black jagged steel. The breastplate was made from metal layers, mimicking dragon scales, and his legs were covered by long thick black chainmail. The violet-black shimmer of the suit, coupled with the crescent atop his dark helm, truly inspired dread. One step at a time, he swung his great mace from one soldier into another, flinging them far across the courtyard, shattering their bones.

"Alright. It's been fun, but I'm leaving," said Zain as he looked around the cell, but he had no way out. He turned his attention to Thane and the assassin in the cell block, still locked in their affray.

Amidst the fracas, the assassin found an opportunity and grabbed a lantern. He smashed it on Thane's head. Thane yelled as he crashed onto the floor, holding his bloodied, burnt face. The Drae'shï swiftly walked past the downed Warden and drew his scimitar to Lilith's unconscious body, silently muttering what seemed to be her last rites. "By order of the Moirai—"

"Hey! What are you doing?" asked Zain.

The Drae'shï continued, dragging Lilith's body closer to the bars as he struggled to retain concentration during his recitation. He shut his eyes tightly as he concluded, slowly slipping his scimitar down to her neck.

"Hey! Hey! Hey!"

"What?" he barked.

"Nothing," said Zain dryly, but the sharp and deadly swing of Adam's long sword had already cut the Drae'shï's head clean off.

"Great timing. Now, get me out. I can help," insisted Zain. "Come on!"

Adam pursed his lips before throwing the large ring of keys to the Vampire. "Fine. Pick up his sword," he said, as he turned to assist Thane up before rushing back into the bailey.

"Wait! Wait," said Zain as he fumbled through the dozens of clanking fat keys, attempting to fit each one into the lock. "Come on," he shouted to himself sensing the impending arrival of further assailants.

The lock clicked. "Finally" said Zain before he sped out of his cell and to the block's main door.

From the entrance he watched the fight ensue below and noticed the free path to the ramparts. "Well, it's been nice knowing you all but, fuck this," he said holding himself over the threshold, but he begrudgingly turned his gaze back inside and towards Lilith lying unconscious.

He took a deep breath looking back and forth, hesitantly rocking himself in and out of the entrance. Zain looked up, closed his eyes, and sighed. "I don't know why I'm doing this, but I'm sure I'm going to regret it," he said, turning back to free her.

"Hey! Get up," He rocked the cell door but the lock proved to be just as uncooperative as his own.

Silence seemed to reign as the fight below withdrew, the sole sound of the keys announcing the final discharge of the fracas.

Zain stopped. Expectant.

The door at the other end of the cell block crashed down from its hinges under the thunderous swing of another Dratesh Khan's mace.

Zain fumbled the keys. He cursed. His gaze frantically darted at all the options. Beads of sweat formed at his brow. The cell would not open.

He panicked as he looked at Lilith's wrist resting through the bars, her veins barely visible under her skin. The sound of her blood coursing through her taunted the back of his mind, hissing in his ears, gnawing at his parched throat.

He winced. "I'm already regretting this," he said before reluctantly pulling her arm through and biting down, drawing her cool, metallic, blue blood into his body. He stared down the dreaded knight's slow approach as he drank.

The blood coursed through like electricity, awakening, inspiring, empowering. Zain rose. His eyes were blackened, possessed, and eager to engage.

Yet as he walked, his vision blurred, and his legs faltered. "Wh—what?" He stumbled. He grabbed the bars and bent them in his tight grip. He gasped. The last thing he saw was the Dratesh Khan looming in the distance.

She stirred within her sleep, lying in a solemn state.

Calm and at peace. Still. In the apnoea of nothingness.

Soon a rush built up, and, as if from a nightmare, she sprang up in her bed. She was sweating and panting for air. She lay there silent in the night, her dark reflection etched in the mirror across the room. She gazed as the tension soon began building up again. A flurry of feelings exploded within her, along with an array of senses. An intense sense of restlessness ran through every bone in her body. She felt hot, cold, and hot again, trying to come to a balance.

She rose in a cold sweat.

The night sky bore a red overcast tint.

She couldn't understand, yet felt she knew everything around her. She kept looking around the room, feeling safe and calm, but still, she could not understand why. She then looked at her arms and felt her body, wiggling her toes. She rested back onto her pillow, soft and calm, as she heard the sound of her hair brushing on the bed linen. She paused, allowing the world to come to her, staring at the dark ceiling.

A brooding sense of discomfort writhed through her, not belonging, unnatural. Suddenly, an intense surge of feelings filled her very essence, twisting and churning within that subtle body. She was turning mad.

She screamed as pain opened her eyes to the incomprehensible. She was lost, scared, and humiliated. A flow of tears rushed down her cheeks as even more feelings and thoughts flooded her being.

The musky reflection of the red sky poured in from her bedside window, pattered gently by the late summer's rain. Lightning struck, and in one instant, she threw herself on the floor in fright. She crawled away, horrified, toward the corner of the room. She lay there curled up against the wall, half-dressed, cold, and frightened. She rocked herself to calm down, attempting to acclimatise to an array of sensations, and soon enough regained some control. Slowly she went through the memories, understanding and searching.

Yet a sudden rush of negativity went through her body as her true nature spread through her senses. Darkness, true oblivion, pervasive, invasive, and absolute. That which preceded all light and that which will devour all light at the end of time. The mortal understanding of her nature and purpose invaded her, consuming her, consuming itself.

She grew angry and blissful at the same time, realising her relevance as well as insignificance.

She screamed frantically, hating herself and everything known to her.

She rubbed her head in her mindless agony. Squealed, kicking on the floor like a spoilt brat, and in a fit, scratched herself in a fury. The hate boiling within gave her no respite. The more insignificant she felt in her mortal body, the angrier she became as she viciously attacked herself.

Drenched in blood and pain, she could not come to terms with herself. She raged at her neck and tore open her throat.

She lay down on the floor, drowning, jerking, like the dying animal she felt she'd become. Slowly, she slipped into death, haloed by a puddle of dark red blood as the lightning illuminated her passing and the thunder mourned her death.

Lilith awoke.

Chapter 4

Pursuits of Power

Morning drew afresh, and the sun kissed the forehead of the forlorn Vampire after the daring escape he'd made the night before.

Zain yawned, squirmed, and smiled. He stretched, his feet reaching over the bedposts, feeling the comfort of hospitality that he had long forgotten. He enjoyed the stillness and peace of his recent abode and wondered, once more, why he had never chosen to settle for a life amongst the Eldain of Cielith. Soon enough, the sound of domestic drama came to remind him of why.

"I will not have this. I've told you before, and I'll say it again. I refuse to marry him! I have never asked anything of you, Father, please," lamented a faint voice below, followed by an inaudible rejoinder. "I am not like the rest, and you know this. I will not be traded like cattle for your political ambitions."

Zain naturally proceeded to indulge in his daily serving of other people's business. He silently exited his room and placed himself comfortably on the stone balustrade overlooking the manor's main courtyard. Below, stood a young woman with chestnut hair and sweet supple facial features hidden behind her stern look. Beside her stood a tall man, distinct-looking, aged, and with long white hair and a short white beard. Both carried the particular allure that only the purest Eldain families boasted.

"How many times must we have this discussion, Adara? I swear, if I hadn't seen you being born, I'd be sure you were your mother coming back to haunt me," cried the man in paternal exasperation.

"Don't you dare speak about her like that!"

"And don't you dare speak to *me* with that tone, Adara! You will do your duty by your family and your people, as your sisters have, as I did, and as your mother did at your age." He paused as his voice echoed across the hall, silencing all.

She sighed at her father's decree.

He mimicked his daughter's weary resignation. "My love. We must all make our sacrifices, whichever path we choose." He approached her with a soft tone, extending a coarse yet gentle hand to cradle her teary cheek. "Since you were a child, I always hoped you would be spared the drama of politics that came with this family name. That you would find actual love, not a cage. You were always too kind, too gentle, too free—a nightingale among hawks. I knew it. So did your mother."

"It's not just that. I don't want to leave here. Leave you. It will be decades 'til I return," said Adara, clasping his hand to her face as her last tears shone down her peach skin.

"I know, my love, but the time has come to take up your ordained role. The time for fleeting romance has ended. You know the importance of this marriage and the good that will come of it. Thus, I ask you, from a loving father to a forgiving daughter, please find in the kindness of your heart the ability to bear this burden for him and your people," he said, naked of all expected parental reverence.

She let out a long breath and turned her sob into a soft smile. "I love you, Father, and I love my people, but I'm afraid my heart is not capable of loving this man, no matter who he may be."

"Then you will learn to love him, if not for his virtues, then for the love you have for all of us back home. For if he is ever to suspect that your heart doesn't belong to him, all will be for nothing. Jealousy is a symptom that nestles easily amongst men. The brevity of life inspires them to cling to things far tighter than those who've experienced the many ebbs and flows that life presents over our lifetimes."

She smiled and nodded. "I'll miss you. You know that," she said, clasping his hand and kissing it softly.

"I'll miss you, too, my love," he said, holding both her hands to his lips. "Well, at least you know that sooner or later, he'll drop dead at some point, and you can come straight home." He sneaked a devilish wink from under his brow.

"Father!" said Adara as she let out a chuckle.

"Run along now. I'll have no more of this discussion," he said. "Also, because some of our guests have made it their pastime to eavesdrop on family matters that do not concern them," he continued, raising his voice as he turned his gaze to the eavesdropping Vampire.

"Then perhaps you should not leave your guests in want of entertainment, Santhi," said Zain as he raised his eyebrows and grinned just as he descended the lavish white marble staircase.

"Zain!" said Adara joyfully before picking up her long light skirt and rushing to greet him. Her hug crushed him with sisterly love, and her previously mystical allure soon turned to a look of admiration in the way that only familiarity can greet. "It's been so long."

"Ha ha! Indeed, Adara, indeed," said Zain as he returned her embrace. "I still hope I'm your number one. I don't want to hear talk of marriage and other nonsense. You're mine." He made his usual attempt to stick his foot into his mouth.

"Well, of course you still are, have, and always will be my night prince," she said as she wrapped her arm around his and escorted him with her distinct aristocratic manner.

The two looked back at Santhi, whose pursed lips struggled to hide a smile. "I was hoping that spending a few decades in the south would have rid you of that cheap wit of yours."

"Well, actually, they're quite fond of my sense of humour. Something that somehow always dwindles with age, it seems."

"Always easier to entertain the young and dim-witted after all. It seems nothing's changed since I've last visited," said Santhi.

Both smiled at their banter.

Adara turned to Zain. "Now, *you* still owe me your courtesy, Zain, and I *will* have the exclusive pleasure of your company before you disappear once again," she said, eyeing her father.

"I'm afraid Zain's endeavours will cause his stay to be short-lived, considering his furtive arrival in the middle of the night. Am I right, Zain?" said Santhi. "But I'm sure he will find time for a brief reunion prior to his departure," he added as he saw Adara's objection about to leave her lips. "Now, my love, let old men talk of old things and young maidens dream of less darker days," he said, taking her arm and kissing her on the cheek.

"Fine, Father. This is not over, Zain," said Adara, raising her finger after removing herself from their embrace. Soon enough, Adara wisped off into the corridors of the manor, accompanied by a host of chambermaids awaiting her beautiful graces to direct them.

"She has sure grown to match her mother's beauty, Santhi," said Zain, as he found himself strangely enamoured by the light of her subtle presence and the silence left by her bare step.

"Speaking of endeavours, how does our friend fare? Has the medicine yielded the desired effect?" asked Santhi as he traced his way up the stairs, hands held behind his back.

"She rests still, though her wound has almost healed. I must say, your medical skills have improved. Not even the best mystics and medicians in Valendria would hope to achieve such skills in a lifetime. I'm sure you could teach them a thing or two," said Zain as he followed Santhi leading him across the halls and into his study.

"Well, they have a lot left to learn about life before discovering more secrets on how to cheat death." Santhi slumped at his scroll-filled desk. The casualness of old friendships required no fine ceremony.

"And is that what you hope to teach them with this nuptial accord?" asked Zain as he stood by the door.

"Come in, Zain. Shut the door," said Santhi. He signalled Zain to take a seat across his desk.

Zain proceeded to close the tall ornate door behind him. The study exuded the inviting and familiar aroma of old books and history. Tomes, maps, and scrolls lay open across different tables at each corner of the room. The room was encased by heavy bookshelves that hugged the four walls. Zain ran his long fingers across the furnishings. His love of all things Eldain-made was not only for their distinctly ornate and exceptional craftsmanship but also for the echo of nostalgia calling him from an age long gone. His attention soon fell upon the beauty of the sunlit terrace behind Santhi, which framed the underlying lush forests of Cielith.

"Cielith reminds me so much of the Eternal City and what it must have been before the Great Dying, before the veil of the Mother's Light had withered away. I guess it's better this way." Zain smiled wistfully.

"I'm sure it must have been a remarkable sight. To think that what you see here is but a shadow of the Age of the Eldarï," said Santhi.

"You *know* that the rest of the world is nothing like Cielith. It is a place of darkness and cruelty and ruled by men who've only known such things." Zain groaned as he clambered into the chaise longue like an old dog. "She will miss Cielith more than you think. She'll be far more disappointed with the southern air than with the arrangement you seem to have put in place," he said, resting his arm on his forehead, staring at the floral frescoed ceiling.

Santhi took a deep breath, exhaling slowly, sounding his disappointment and fatigue. His shoulders sagged as he reached for his pipe. He focused his attention on packing it tightly. "Sometimes a father must be willing to incur the wrath of his children in the hope of putting them to better purpose."

"And what purpose would a young lady with no knowledge of the world be able to achieve?" asked Zain as his gaze wandered over the higher corners of the room. The walls displayed various maps of the domains of Amenti: Cielith and Raem in the north, Iborellan in the north-west, Valdell in the south and Carthosia in the far west across the Carthosian gulf.

"Peace. Or the hope of peace," said Santhi. He paused to gaze at the maps strung upon the walls in contemplation. "These human trifles tire me, Zain. I don't know how you've managed to spend so much time amongst them," He gazed emotionlessly at the map of Valdell and the Grand Harbour of Palin Bay, a vast wellspring for the four great cities of Valdell, including its capital, Valendria.

"Are you concerned that the war is coming your way from Carthosia?"

"Yes. Or, rather, the Elder Council is. If the Carthosian Shirral is as shrewd a commander as they say he is, then he will not risk another crossing of the gulf by sea as they did fifteen years ago. The battle of the Grand Harbour stopped the war before it even had a chance to start. But this time they will walk the long but sure path until they're right at the steps of the Grand Temple in Valendria," said Santhi as he moved the tail of his pipe through the air, tracing the maps on the wall.

"And that path leads them straight through Cielith."

"The consequence of their past hubris has taught them well, and the borders of Cielith are far too wide for us to contain the onslaught of their 'holy' war. The Shirra, they call it. So now we need Valendria's protection."

"Such follies men do to sit at the foot of a 'holy' tree."

"The Eldarï should have burnt the bloody Enoch trees before they left," grumbled Santhi as he proceeded to light his pipe and expel a long-held breath of exasperation.

"Needless to say, Adara must be thrilled to be the bargaining chip behind this alliance," said Zain as his restlessness sprang him back to his feet.

"She must do what she must. I am no more thrilled than she is to marry outside her own kind, even if it is the most powerful family in Valendria. But we need fighting men to fill the garrisons along the Siensell River, and I will not have war spawned of human frailty claim the lives of any Eldain," said Santhi.

"And you really think that will stop them, in those numbers?" asked Zain as he flipped through the pages of a book set beside him.

"Of course not, Zain," Santhi scoffed, getting up from his seat and picking up a long cane to point at an enlarged map of Cielith's northern border with Iborellan. "It takes a dam to stop a river, but only half to change its course."

Cielith and Valdell both enjoyed many natural borders, including the Siensell River and the Tovash Mountains, which made a northern invasion difficult. Nevertheless, nature had it that the river favoured a crossing via the northern banks in Cielith rather than the southern tributaries of Valdell, which could be easily defended by Valdell's formidable navy.

"More like blowing fire onto your neighbour's house, Santhi."

"I can see how your time with mankind has bought your sympathies, Zain, but I have a lineage to preserve and a family to protect," said Santhi as he leaned over his desk, resting his elbows on his tomes and parchments.

The two looked at each other as the sweet, smoky scent of tobacco slowly filled the room. Their mutual fondness made for good conversation but less for the concealment of their true affairs.

"Do you know what my role as chronicler is, Zain?" asked Santhi.

"A tragic departure from your winemaking days?" asked Zain as he began looking at the open tome upon Santhi's desk, which detailed long lists of names, dates, and corresponding family trees across the vast pages.

"I sit in this room, day by day, reading tome after tome, looking at those lists of families, parentages, and the origins of the Eldain bloodlines. I do this so that I can arrange and approve marriages between people I have never met, nor have an interest in, whether my decision offends them or otherwise. I have done this for the last forty years. And do you know why, Zain? So that the little longevity left in our blood from our Eldarï forefathers will allow my successor to do it for just as long, and so can his children and his children's children."

"Forty years, Santhi? You really need to get out more. How long has it been since our little adventure— thirty, thirty-five?" asked Zain, holding his chin with a silly smirk on his face.

"Indeed. You jest, but your immortality does not afford you the perspective of those you mock," he replied. "And mind you, I'm still a hundred and eleven years old and more than capable of flooring your hide like I was sixty," he added with a slight grin. "I care little for the trivialities of men, their politics, and their pursuit of religious belief, superstition and the veneration of 'holy' trees. However, I cannot ignore the impact of the mind of the many and the consequences it brings."

The two sighed in recognition of the inevitability of the situation that engulfed the world and its weight upon the Eldain. The Eldain always strove to keep outsiders from entering Cielith, yet the Shirral was one guest they would find it close to impossible to refuse.

"I understand, old friend. We all do what we must to safeguard those we love. I'll be sure to check on Adara when I'm around," said

Zain frankly as he patted his comrade on his shoulder before walking towards the balcony once more.

Santhi smiled back in recognition of a friendship long missed but never forgotten.

<hr>

It was a long and hard pursuit along the hills of West Raem and down into the thicket of the Fernstram forests, yet the Wardens stood strong, silent, and undetected by the Drae'shï. The borders of Cielith were just a stone's throw away.

"Adam. We should get closer," whispered Thane through the undergrowth. "If they attempt to cross into Cielith, the Eldain Sentinels will fill them with arrows before we even get a chance to question them." The red-haired giant rustled oafishly around the leaves.

"Shut it, Thane!" hissed a short and nimble-looking scout as he picked the dried leaves and moss from his few tufts of hair.

"Better make sure you counted well before we run into any surprises, Samos," said Thane as he lightly touched his scalded and scratched face.

"Eleven infantry, eight ranged auxiliaries, five heavy infantry, a serviceman, and that beast of a man; the Dratesh Khun. Think we can take 'em, Captain?" asked Samos from their concealed outpost.

Adam sat silent. His stern gaze was focused on the enemy.

"It's Dratesh Khan, Samos," intervened Brandt, a less burly Eldassari with more pronounced features, flowing hair, and a general confident finesse that the others could hardly muster. "Between us seven, what do you think? Make it five, considering Doran's bad back and Willam still bitching about his knee."

"Hey, Brandt. Fuck yourself," said Willam, another short man with beady eyes, long brown hair, and a short perfectly-trimmed beard.

"Silence," said Doran.

The rest quieted.

"Captain?"

Adam remained silent, observant.

"Can we at least agree that this is crazy?" intervened Samos. "What's this obsession you have with the Drae'shï we caught anyway?" He stuck his head forward to look at Adam.

"In case you don't remember, Samos, the bitch blasted a hole out of the cell block and flew out of the Hold, like some sort of hellish black cloud," said Thane, pressing Samos back into concealment.

Adam grunted.

"Captain?" said Thane.

Adam narrowed his eyes as he watched the Drae'shï encampment. "That's abnormal, probably even for the Drae'shï. Something's off about her, and she has something that meant the rest of her kind saw fit to send an entire cohort straight after her and right into the Hold."

"Well, I hope for our sakes' it's worthwhile, cause if these folks don't kill us, Dorreth certainly will," said Willam.

"If Dorreth wants to turn a blind eye to what's happened, he's forgetting what it means to be a Warden. Quiet," said Adam without hesitation.

The rest looked at each other, unsure how to respond. Adam remained silent as he held his crossed hands to his mouth, narrowing his gaze and observing the Drae'shï encampment by the riverbank from their lofty overlook.

The Drae'shï demonstrated a very orderly and disciplined demeanour, with the heavily armoured soldiers being squired by the subordinate and less equipped infantry. The Dratesh Khan, seemingly the prefect of the group, sat awaiting his nourishment and bathing.

The Drae'shï's appearance also seemed to vary according to their role. While their unmistakable white hair did not vary between ranks, their complexions varied in degree of darkness, the Dratesh Khan revealing pale, misty blue-grey skin and the rest carrying darker and greyer tones to their likeness. As the night drew nearer, they pulled their hoods over their white hair as the creeping moonlight sought to reveal them to the night. Their overt movements slowed into a light shuffle, and soon, their dark silhouettes disappeared, leaving nothing but the sound of the rushing Illyum river and the wind brushing the treetops.

"What's the situation, Arren?" asked Adam.

A tall, pale, bald man had emerged from the darkness. He had a reserved air about him. A longbow was strung around his back. "Looks like they're deciding whether to pursue her across the bridge." His face was long and gaunt with deep, dark eyes, and his stern expression didn't invite many sympathies from those he met.

"It's time to move," said Adam to the group still resting on the slope. "We have to wait for them to cross the bridge 'til they provoke the Eldain Sentinels. They probably have no idea that the Eldain are ever watchful of their borders. Once they cross, we'll stake an ambush on the last few that lag behind, capture a few prisoners, and pull them over to our side of the river; ideally the Dratesh Khan," said Adam to the bemusement of the rest. "Hopefully, the noise we'll make will be enough to draw the Eldain's attention quickly enough for a response, but not quick enough to have them kill us along with the Drae'shï in the meantime."

The Wardens quickly found their way to the bridge. Arren and Brandt placed themselves within range of the bridge, up in the higher branches of a nearby tree. Adam, Thane, Willam, Samos, and Doran worked their way slowly behind the Drae'shï's march, sneaking down under the bridge and across the shallows until they placed themselves right beneath the landing on the other side.

The Wardens all stood, waiting with bated breath, their swords slowly and silently unsheathing as the Drae'shï marched over. Adam closed his eyes to listen more intently, silencing all other noise, drawing long breaths, and releasing even lengthier sighs. At last, Adam and his vanguard quickly rose and found themselves a few yards behind the rear of the Drae'shï column.

The couple of Drae'shï at the rear of the column immediately noticed the Wardens and reached for their weapons. Arrows whistled through the air, from the treeline and out of the night, flooring the Drae'shï before their swords were fully drawn. The entire Drae'shï outfit turned as their two comrades collapsed, instinctively drawing their weapons. Though severely outnumbered, the Wardens darted at their foe, maintaining the bridge as cover for their flanks. The five Wardens fought with might and order, maintaining their stand, whilst Arren and Brandt fired away from a distance in support.

The Dratesh Khan roared out his orders, quelling his men's surprise with his military resolve. The Drae'shï immediately turned their previous disoriented column into the war machine everyone knew and feared.

The Wardens slowly backed onto the bridge.

"Where are the fucking Eldain?" shouted Thane.

Their assault had turned into a slow retreat.

"They're coming. Hold on," said Adam, waiting until a soldier lunged with his war hammer. Adam curved its direction right into the jaw of the Drae'shï's neighbouring comrade before elbowing his assailant in the face.

"Well, they better— 'cause—the more—they head this way—the more—we're going to—have to kill everyone by ourselves," grunted Doran with every hit of his sword to the matching clash of his duellist.

Meanwhile, in the treetops, Brandt asked, "What the hell are they doing? Where are the Eldain?" He kept drawing his bow and releasing shots in rapid succession to Arren's.

"Forget the Eldain. We need to go help them," said Arren, becoming visibly impatient.

"We're helping them from here. Stay here. Keep firing," said Brandt as he kept his focus on the enemy.

The rest made their retreat from the bridge as slowly as possible. The Drae'shï's numbers had thinned slightly, yet it hardly quelled their resolve. The Wardens soon found themselves halfway across the bridge and about to lose their cover and tactical advantage.

The Dratesh Khan roared at his auxiliaries as another of Brandt's arrows found its way into the side of one of his men. The auxiliaries directed their entire effort in the direction of the trees, focusing into the distance, waiting to spot their marksmen.

"I think they spotted us," said Arren as he stopped drawing his bow and peered through the thick branches of the tree they were perched upon.

"Nonsense, how can they see this far at night?" asked Brandt just as an arrow darted sharply into the branch above his head.

"Shit!"

Both launched themselves off the tree, tumbling down into the brush as a volley of arrows filled their perch. Bruised and battered, Arren and Brandt regained their feet and, drawing their swords, sprinted down to the riverbank.

Upon the bridge, the rest of the Wardens found themselves at the centre of the entire Drae'shï cohort's attention. The Wardens' attacks found no corresponding invitation as the heavy infantry sought only to parry their advance and push them back over the bridge's landing and out into the open. Adam kept looking back, thinking and parrying. He attempted to slip in another kill, searching desperately for their next move.

"Adam!" shouted Willam.

Adam immediately turned his attention to the opening in the Drae'shï's ranks. An arrow flew past Adam's face, so close the breeze of the passage cooled the sweat dripping down his face. Instinctively, he drew his hatchet and launched it straight at his counterpart's head.

The Dratesh Khan soon barged through the ranks of the Drae'shï, shoving his troops into an aggressive advance. Taunting the Wardens from afar, he picked up one of the lighter maces of his servicemen and hurled it towards Thane, hitting him clean in the chest and flinging him flat onto the ground.

"Thane!" gasped Adam.

Thane groaned as he struggled to rise.

Doran, Willam, and Samos nodded to Adam and intervened to fend off the Drae'shï closing in for the kill.

Adam pulled the winded Thane back to his feet. "Come on, Thane! Get up! Get up!"

"I always knew you'd get me killed, Adam," he gasped and groaned as he held his chest.

"Not today, Thane, I still have use for you,"

Adam grinned as Thane found his footing. Arren and Brandt charged out of the bushes and into the fray.

All the Wardens fought hardily but soon found no protection from the stone bridge. The Drae'shï had backed them onto the open landing, slowly encircling them as the troops poured from the bridge. As the Drae'shï encircled them, the Dratesh Khan signalled the auxiliaries to move to the fore, drawing their crossbows for a conclusion.

"Lower your weapons," said Adam.

"Are you insane?" exclaimed Samos as they all stood back-to-back.

"I must agree, Captain, this is not going to afford us any favour from them," said Brandt.

"No, but it will buy us time," said Adam as he lowered his weapon to the ground and then raised his hands slightly.

"Adam, are you insane?" hissed Willam.

The Dratesh Khan paused and raised his hand. His troops withheld the execution.

The rest of the Wardens reluctantly followed Adam's example.

The Dratesh Khan turned towards them. The imposing Drae'shï spoke Luminar, an ancient Drae'shï dialect of the old Eldarï, vaguely sounding like Eldain yet not completely intelligible. After a short while, the Drae'shï found his words were falling on unfamiliar ears and turned to his men, prompting a light, humorous reaction. He soon returned to Adam and, in broken Eldain, stated, "Do you not fight now, half-breed?"

The Warden slowly lowered his arms. "Who is she, the one you pursue? Why are you after her?" he asked in Eldain.

The Dratesh Khan approached. "So, you understand then? She's not your concern, Eldassari. And even if I told you, what matter would it have to a bunch of dead men?" he asked as he stared Adam down through his black steel helm.

Adam swiftly drew a short blade from his sleeve and stabbed at his foe's side, only to have the blade splinter against the hardened black steel of the cuirass. The Dratesh Khan punched him in the gut and back-handed him across the face, sending Adam staggering back into his friends. The two looked at each other as the Dratesh Khan turned back to his auxiliaries, signalling them to fire. Beads of sweat formed at the top of the Wardens' heads, gleaming in the moonlight as the shifting clouds revealed the moon in the sky.

In the distance, down along the road by their side of the riverbank, the tip of a spear flickered in the night catching Adam's attention. A large horseman draped in shadow held the pole, a red ribbon fluttering from the tip of his helm.

"Drae'shï!" shouted Adam across the field, catching the Dratesh Khan's attention.

Suddenly, a single javelin flew, just missing the Dratesh Khan and landing straight in the chest of one of his soldiers.

A loud horn blew long and clear out of the night, soon followed by the rumbling charge of a cohort of armoured horsemen. As the stunned Drae'shï prepared their defence, the Wardens dashed out of their sights and into the roadside brush as the arrows flew and missed them.

Meanwhile, the Dratesh Khan roared his retreat as his lieutenant immediately tossed him his great mace. The Dratesh Khan promptly smashed the nearest charging horse in its head, flooring the rider and breaking his neck under his heel. The Drae'shï retreated onto the bridge towards the clear Cielith borders.

Horsemen bearing torches and white banners with a red tree kept pouring in from the road to the dismay of the Drae'shï leader and the confusion of the Wardens.

"Who the hell are these people? They're not Eldain," said Samos as they watched from the side-lines.

"Don't care who they are, I'm just happy they're here," said Brandt.

"Come! Let's go!" said Adam as they rose from the side of the road and joined the fray. Adam soon rushed into the scuffle between horses and Drae'shï, fighting his way through to reach the Dratesh Khan.

The Drae'shï soon found themselves outnumbered. Their remaining forces rushed into Cielith across the bridge whilst the Dratesh Khan single-handedly held off two horsemen in the middle of the crossing. Blocked by the flurry of men rushing in to quell the fury of the Dratesh Khan, Adam could not help but watch the dread knight's potency as he unleashed the sheer might of his stature on the onslaught of his assailants, felling horses and their riders, throwing men over into the river, and receiving several blows at the same time. However, the Drae'shï's strength was not limitless.

Adam pushed and pulled men out of the way, forcing his way in as the Dratesh Khan staggered by the side of the bridge. An arrow soon found its way through the gaps in his armour as the rest of the newly arrived soldiers encircled him with caution. Soon a second, and a third.

"Stop!" cried Adam as he saw the enemy slowly conceding. "Stop!"

The Dratesh Khan, now bloodied and beaten, lay against the edge of the bridge. Releasing the hold of his weapon first, he then removed his helm and glanced contemplatively to Adam and then to the clear sky, wincing slightly in pain. The Dratesh Khan's last grin was interrupted by the clean strike of a javelin straight into his chest, pushing him over the edge and into the black waters of the Illyum river.

Adam rushed to the edge, but the river and the night had taken its offering and any answers it may have had with it. Looking at the rest of the Drae'shï across the bridge, there were no further prisoners, only Drae'shï corpses laden with fresh Eldain arrows.

A mass of Eldain archers emerged out of the tree line ready to fire a second volley at any further trespassers.

Immediately, one of the mounted knights and slayer of the Dratesh Khan rushed past his troops atop his armoured black stallion. He picked up a large red and white banner and stopped at the edge of the bridge. "Sentinels of Cielith, lay down your weapons! We are the Saints of the Holy Order of Enoch, and I am Elias Jurani of the Seat of Jurani of Valendria!" The knight was cloaked in white and covered from head to toe in chainmail. The red ribbon on top of his helm fluttered in the wind.

"We have been awaiting your arrival, Elias of the Jurani of Valendria. I am Lieutenant Vorlaisse," said one of the Eldain coming to the fore. "But we were not expecting your Eldassari companions. Do you claim the rest of these trespassers?" His armour shone silver and jade, polished and ornate and bearing the metal craftsmanship of the high-born Eldain.

"I do," claimed Adam as he stepped forward.

"Very well," said Vorlaisse. "Then you will answer the questions your fellow Drae'shï could not."

CHAPTER 5

To Court A Nightingale

The scent of the last days of summer pervaded the wide and open halls of Threlis Manor. The rustling trees and birdsong softly lingered through the afternoon as the echoing voices and footsteps of the household gave it further life. Servants swept through every room and corridor, carrying large vases with flower arrangements whilst seamstresses adorned the columns and balustrades with beautifully woven silks and fabrics, all in anticipation of a long-anticipated guest.

Away from the din of the housemaids' toil, Lilith sat on the large terrace, minded to escape the frustrating noise and chatter of the manor's busy halls. She grimaced in the face of the glaring sun, its distant glow almost too blinding to bear even after having left the darkness of the mountain over a week ago. She sat in peace for the first time in a while, watching the great vale that stretched out beneath the manor.

"I suspect you are still getting used to the fresh air," said Adara as she swayed around the chairs and joined Lilith.

Lilith looked back quizzically as servants soon followed to bring fruit and drinks for the two ladies.

"I often like to spend my afternoons painting out here. Somehow, the air always brings me inspiration." She smiled as she drew across the nearby leafy canopy to shade Lilith's face from the bright light. "Thank you," nodded Adara to her chambermaids as they withdrew from their lady. Adara carried herself with a sweet, friendly allure that made it hard to resist returning a smile.

"Where are we exactly?" asked Lilith in a soft tone struggling not to slouch.

"Easy there," said Adara as she fixed Lilith's pillow, her soft touch lightly brushing over the Drae'shï's shoulders.

Lilith watched silently as the beautiful and peaceful Eldain returned to her seat.

"You look good in that dress. It's more comfortable than that leather armour you arrived in, I take it," said Adara.

Lilith looked down at her light white gown, trailing to the ground. The grass felt good under her bare feet.

Adara wriggled her toes in the grass, smiling back at Lilith just as Lilith stretched hers out from her own seat.

"Oh, sorry! My manners. We're just north of the city of Vinesse, in the southern province of Cielith. This is the Threlis Valley, and that large palace in the middle of the city is the seat of the summer residence of the Court of Agnates, otherwise known as the Council of Elders," said Adara, eagerly venturing into casual conversation.

Lilith took a deep breath, looking deeply past the vale and the acres of vineyards as if trying to spot the peak of Ussar Varys in the distance.

"And this is Threlis Manor, my home and that of my father, of course. My name is Adara Crysanthani, and my father is Santhi. That is, Petrach Crysanthani, the one who healed you, with my assistance, of course." Adara smiled as they both looked down at the bandaged side of Lilith's hip.

Lilith was slightly taken aback by the unexpected welcome and the warmth of her host. She let out a soft sigh of relief. "Then I guess I owe you and your father thanks."

"Think nothing of it. It is hardly a feat for us to treat wounds of that nature. Yet I will hold you indebted to me for the pleasure of your company and conversation," said Adara briskly.

Lilith stared rather blank-faced at her proposition.

"In simple terms, you owe me a little chit-chat, my silver-haired friend," said Adara, her blissful charm rolling off her rose-petal lips with ease.

"I guess I owe you that much," said Lilith when it appeared she would have little choice in the matter.

"So Zain tells me your name is Lilith?"

"Lilith? My name is Lil'Thra Astemari Sistrah," said Lilith with her distinct Drae'shï accent. "Although the Vampire is also right."

"Well, I like both. A beautiful name to match your own. I'm sure you must have had many suitors asking for your hand back home," teased Adara as she reached across Lilith to grab a bunch of grapes, leaving her sweet peach scent under her guest's nose.

"None that pique my interest or that of most high born Drae'shï," said Lilith curtly.

"If interests in men do not drive you, then I would venture jewellery, wealth, power?" asked Adara light-heartedly.

"Charms," said Lilith. "Is this what living in the light does to you? Desire metals and minerals found in the dark?"

Adara laughed. "No, of course not. Well, that's what most people who live anywhere seem to want, I guess. But *you* are clearly not most people."

"I would hate to disappoint your expectations," said Lilith semi-sarcastically.

"I merely ask because I know for a fact that the Drae'shï are master smiths in gold and silver. Not to mention their mining abilities. Father tells me that it is because of your occupation of Cielith during the Immortal Wars that we discovered the silver in the Il'var ravines. Your legacy has bestowed many fruits upon us over the years making Cielith the envy of the world." Adara held out a beautiful silver necklace lined with a series of rose quartz gemstones.

Lilith observed the necklace, intent on understanding the provenance of the distinct Eldain designs. "Hmmm. I see, your metalworkers do carry some Drae'shï influence in their work. Although of all skills, you seem to have picked up the most useless," she said dryly.

"Is that so? Then what is the skill your people *do* prize most above all others?" asked Adara, hiding her slight disappointment in not finding common ground with her guest as easily as with her more usual yet relentlessly boring company.

"The moulding of hard metals. Particularly black steel mined from the darker reaches of the Ussari Mountains. You will not find finer, stronger weapons and armour in the world," she claimed, almost proud of her heritage.

"You are after all, the 'Dra'-'Elishï', right?" interrupted Zain as he walked out onto the terrace with a spring in his step, seemingly intrigued by the prospects of good company and conversation. "The 'Iron Children' or 'Metal Children' is it? Apologies, my Luminar is a little rusty. And that pun, my ladies, was absolutely intended."

"A vulgar translation at best," said Lilith, unamused at Zain's intervention.

"Iron Kindred is the correct term," corrected Adara with her effortless charm.

"Always a pleasure, Lilith. Thank you for your contribution, Adara." Zain sat across from the women with his back to the sun whilst grabbing a fresh red apple and digging his white teeth into it. His appearance seemed less foreign in contrast to the Eldain, although his size and demeanour still made him a man apart. His long black hair shimmered shades of blue and violet when set in contrast with the sun's bright light, and his pale yet handsome complexion. On the other hand, Adara was so laden with the natural, modest beauty of a young woman it was almost impossible not to find oneself staring at her soft and subtle, perfectly imperfect features.

"Finally, Zain. Nice of you to join us. Has my father given you the rundown of the last two decades by any chance?" chirped Adara, her tone indicative of a past youthful infatuation with the mysterious and handsome Eldaresh.

Zain laughed. "If he would spend as much time enjoying the present as he does with the past, he'd probably still have a shade of colour in his hair. Although I do like his beard. Quite distinct, I must say."

Adara chuckled. "Ugh! I can't stand it on him. It probably makes him want to grow it even more when I tell him to shave. But, yes, he has been rather preoccupied lately. I do urge him to get out of that study more, although his tolerance for people and politics seems to diminish with every passing year."

"I'm sure that his books keep him sufficient company."

"That's what worries me!" she said jovially.

"So, what were you two talking about?" asked Zain as he tossed the apple core onto a side plate, dusted his hands, and stretched himself in his armchair, hands behind his head, feet crossed "Any juicy gossip? I heard this dark handsome man rescued a mysterious alluring woman recently; he's yet to be thanked though,"

Adara chuckled and Lilith rolled her eyes forcing herself not to smile.

"No?"

Adara laughed as Zain winked at Lilith jokingly.

"Well actually, I was enquiring as to Lilith's tastes in jewellery," said Adara, grabbing hold of her guest's hand and clasping it with the other. "Although, I'm afraid our Drae'shï friend might be a little hard to impress, but I'm sure I'll be able to find something for her for the ceremony, won't we, Lilith?" She smiled.

"Ceremony?" both Lilith and Zain asked, the former more concerned than the latter.

"The betrothal, of course. Father must have explained. Your timing could not have been better. And Lilith, I'm sure the dark handsome rescuer would be delighted if the mysterious alluring woman accompanied him to the ball, wouldn't he, Zain?"

"Oh, most definitely." Zain smiled.

Lilith sat up slowly. "I doubt it is our place to be there, Adara." Lilith's wide eyes fixed themselves on Zain as the looming fear of pursuit crept back into her heart. "We've *really* overstayed our welcome. We need to be on our way."

"Do we now, Lilith?" Zain smiled devilishly.

"Lilith, I will not take no for an answer," said Adara, furrowing her brow momentarily. "There will be song, dance, food, and wine. Father is sparing no expense, as you can see. You are my guests, and I would love to have you, at least until tomorrow night, after the ceremony." She smiled as her warm hands took hold of Lilith's. "Promise me."

Lilith hesitated before finally giving in to this one concession to frivolity. Her wound still ached, and the comfort of the Eldain's household was not one she could easily refuse.

A horn rang in the distance, rustling the leaves of the quiet forest as the birds flew in announcing the new arrivals.

"So, is that your intended?" asked Zain intrigued.

"I'm afraid so," said Adara, sounding a little less bright as they each stood from their armchairs.

An oncoming column of knights appeared from the ferns of the vale, making their way up to the manor. The long stream of horsemen emerged bearing the red and white banners of the Order of Saints followed by a contingency of squires, caravans, and other foot soldiers numbering around seven scores of men. The company was divided equally between bannermen of the Order and bannermen bearing the sigil of the Seat of the Jurani family, a white charging bull on purple.

"They must have told some tales about you in Valendria for them to have sent half their army to come pick you up," jested Zain as he looked at Adara's astonished face.

"This *is* rather overwhelming, I must admit," said Adara, somewhat flustered as she absorbed the reality of her situation. "I need to go change, prepare myself." She was wide-eyed and uneasy, pacing around haphazardly. "I shall see you both later, my apologies." She picked up her skirt and trotted off into the house.

"Adara! There you are! Come," boomed Santhi as he descended the marble staircase into the main courtyard.

"But Father, I am not presentable!"

"Nonsense. That will do. Get her some shoes." He waved to a chambermaid. "You will stand at our door with everyone else ready to welcome our guests."

The maid immediately brought a pair of sandals and slipped them onto Adara's feet as she struggled to keep her balance.

"Father!"

He ignored her. "You two, also come!" he ordered as he noted Zain and Lilith entering the room.

Santhi led the way to the front of the manor, bearing an ornate double staircase leading down to the front garden. The vast open lawn was walled by tall conifer trees, all pruned to perfection. All the house servants stood along the stairs awaiting their master as the first knights emerged at the cusp of the road through the white metal gate, all dressed in mail and white cloaks, flanked by a small escort of Eldain horsemen.

"Their horses," said Lilith astonished. "They're armoured."

"Perceptive, aren't we?" asked Zain.

Lilith did not bother to acknowledge his comment.

"Cataphracts, they're called. They're quite a force to be reckoned with, but only the best armies can afford to armour their horses, and the Saints are quite possibly the best army."

"Saints?"

"Yes. The Order of the Saints of Enoch. They are all knights anointed under branches of the holy tree, loyal to no one except the Massass. That is the leader of all those whose faith in this world revolves around that tree you see painted on their breasts and banners."

"The Enoch tree? Are you serious?" she asked, now more incredulous than before.

"Yes. Some four hundred years ago, Massassi Itheru, the man from whom the title 'Massass' comes, used the sap from the tree to cure the Vespial Plague that decimated the south. Many believed him to be Eldaï, which I suspect he was. Anyway, from there, he taught others the medicinal arts and Eldaï theology, and four hundred years later all that's left are these trees and the belief in the idol that brought them."

As Adara and Santhi reached the bottom of the stairs, a large, braced carriage made its final halt in front of the Saints. Three knights dismounted, approaching the carriage door, all covered in mail from head to toe and cloaked in white. Each bore a pointed ridged helm with a length of red-dyed horsehair trailing from the tip, their faces masked by a thin veil of mail. Two of the knights proceeded to stand guard as the third opened the doors, revealing a corpulent man with a large rusty beard and thinning hair to match.

"Oh, Mother's mercy, this flaming gout," the man whispered to himself as he struggled to find his footing in the carriage.

The knight aided him to grab hold of his white cane, a stick that looked more like a freshly cut tree branch than a traditional walking aid.

"It's fine, it's fine, thank you, Elias," he murmured to the knight.

Adara looked at her father, visibly perplexed, yet Santhi only displayed a wide smile at the lumbering oaf.

The knight proceeded to direct his attention to the manor's entire retinue, unveiled his face, and with a resounding tone announced, "By decree of his Holy Luminance our Lord Massass, keeper of the Tree of Light, I, Elias Jurani of the Seat of Jurani, Commander of the First Legion of the Order of the Saints of the Grand Temple of Enoch, present to you His Excellency, Alistair Jurani of the Seat of Jurani, envoy and voice of His Holy Luminance and High Prelate of the Grand Temple of Enoch."

The Eldain attempted to mask their unfamiliarity with such pomp and circumstance as a resounding silence fell right after the commander's introduction.

"Alright, alright," said Alistair dismissively as he helped himself down the creaking steps of his carriage and walked towards Santhi and Adara. He stood in wait before him at the bottom of the staircase. The man was large and round at the belly, draped in purple velvet with a silver lining of intricate embroidery, which at a distance resembled a beautiful rendition of their holy tree.

"Do I get to have a similar announcement when I come down for the wedding, Your Excellency?" asked Santhi with a slight grin of familiarity.

"Only if you bring me something that can finally cure my haemorrhoids!" said Alastair, smiling. "Come here, ya bastard!" he boomed with his larger than life voice as he proceeded to hug Santhi tightly and exchange pleasantries.

"I already like him," said Zain to Lilith who was not quite as impressed.

"And you, my dear!" said Alistair as he proceeded to embrace Adara with the same fatherly love. "You are as magnificent as the tales of your beauty do profess."

"Your words flatter more than I deserve, my lord," she said sweetly.

"Your Excellency," corrected Santhi.

"Alistair, please," interjected Alistair softly to Adara, the words rolling off his tongue with the exquisite eloquence that only royalty could carry. "I am overjoyed to have finally arrived in the bliss of the

Eldain vale. There is no cause for such formalities. I face enough of it in the capital."

"Then we shall celebrate as friends, Alistair," said Adara with her unmistakable smile, Santhi still somewhat bemused by their joint disregard for protocol.

"Ah, yes, one last thing. Before I forget. Commander," called out Alistair devilishly.

"Your Excellency," he replied from afar.

"Come forth and bear your liking to our guests, Elias."

Elias marched towards Santhi and Adara and stopped before them, removing his helmet. He bore the face of a man in the prime of his life. He had the distinct short dark hair of southerners, yet his eyes were blue and elongated, his jawline and cheekbones sharp and striking. The man carried a certain confidence in his modest grin, seemingly borne from a lack of acquaintance with defeat.

"My lord, my lady, you have my thanks and that of my men for welcoming us into your home. We are forever at your service." He proceeded to bow slightly, hand on heart, before rising again to meet the eyes of Adara, which remained struck by her intended. "I am Elias."

CHAPTER 6

THE FETTERS OF BLOOD

"I have to interrupt you there, Zain. I find your story absolutely fascinating, but I just wonder if you're making this all up as you go along," said Krea. She sat cross-legged upon a stool by the window of the cell, wearing long black and purple robes that covered every part of her body up to her neck. Her white hair was cut to a tee, and her delicate hands were wrapped in a pair of dainty black gloves, covered in a gold, clawed gauntlet with long sharp nails. Around her head, she wore a black circlet with a multitude of jewels sparkling in the darkness.

A soft buzz rang overhead.

"When you've lived as long as I have, nothing will surprise you anymore." Zain chuckled briefly. "Hey, are you hearing that?"

"And how long has that been then, Zain?" she continued, ignoring him as she tapped away with her golden nails, the sound almost about to start irritating him.

Zain winced for a moment. "Uh, I was born on the seventh day after the summer solstice in the year 4674 of the Age of the Eldarï."

"Meaning?" She paused her tapping.

"Meaning that since the Age of the Eldarï ended some six hundred years ago, when I was at the tender age of ninety-three, I should be 693 years old, give or take."

"Fascinating," said Krea as she observed Zain.

He began blowing little puffs of condensation in the cold empty cell. Zain appeared particularly thin, malnourished, and espoused to death. Apart from the chains that held him, his body and limbs were wrapped in tight bands of cloth and leather that bore the glyphs and runes aimed at dispelling his true essence.

He sheepishly pulled on the chains yet was suddenly stuck with a slight shock. "Ouch! Is all this really necessary? How are you even doing that?" He squirmed uncomfortably in the tight get-up.

"You have your secrets, and we have ours. And after all, for one such as yourself? Such precautions seem appropriate, don't they? Given your predilection for blood and all. Unless, of course, you are human after all," said Krea as she got up and ran her finger along the windowsill checking for dust.

The room gradually brightened.

"Well, unless you believe humans enjoy drinking rat blood for sustenance, then I guess I really am." Zain became tetchy at the pace of this interrogation and Krea's incessant finger play.

The background buzz returned.

"I've seen stranger things done by humans," said Krea.

"I find that hardly possible."

"How so?" she asked.

"None but a true Eldaresh can practice sanguimancy and do the things *we* do. Many have tried: Eldassari, humans, Eldain, even the highest born Eldain with the purest bloodlines, but they all eventually succumb to the hunger. They all become aberrations sooner or later, shadows of their former selves or anything alive for that matter," Zain ruminated as he looked at his thin skeletal hands, squeezing them. "The more time passes, the less they can quench their thirst. Not even if all the rivers of the world ran red would they find peace in the end. And then, after they lose every sense of who they once were, they eventually find themselves scouring the dark places of the world in search of a single drop of blood. 'Til they are hunted like beasts, or the light gets them, whichever's first." A sense of pity lingered with his last words.

"And what if *you* don't drink? What then?"

"I become less talkative and more like a shrivelled-up corpse, waiting for anything or anyone to revive me, 'til the end of time. Frankly, I don't know what's worse, becoming an eternal piece of conscious leather or succumbing to bestial monstrosity."

"Do you have any idea what meaning lies behind all of this? Your condition?" she added in contemplation.

"Meaning? There is no meaning," he scoffed.

"The way you view yourself and your kind as a blight on the world."

He paused. "Well, I guess it was not always so. Some would even say it was the kindness of the Eldaresh that led to their downfall."

Krea raised her eyebrow.

"Some three thousand years ago, in the golden ages of the Eldaresh and before the Great Dying, the Eldaresh lived in the Eternal City of Dos Narak, deep between the Ethirahar Mountains. They still called themselves 'Eldari' back then, before they succumbed to the hunger and were reborn in death as the 'Eldaresh'. At the time the Eternal City was the jewel of the Eldari of the East, a city of such illustrious beauty that it rivalled the very plains of Ciedien. Yet they were always reserved. They never allowed humans into the city. However, with time the Eldaresh felt sorry for the frailty and brevity of human life and eventually began to invite the sickly and unfortunate for aid. The human tribes that lived in the northern regions of Raem and Lothumos were very backward. They could barely survive the winters at the time. Although the Eldaresh still didn't allow them to migrate into their home, they provided them with medicine, knowledge, and healing."

"Yet it seems history does not remember you as the most charitable of patrons."

"Indeed. Over the years, some Eldaresh medicians took a particular interest in the human body. They would analyse and experiment with the blood of their patients to extend the life of humans and also prolong ours even further since the Light of the Mother had disappeared."

"And that's where it happened," interrupted Krea, eager to guess again.

"It wasn't long until they discovered that human blood was indeed very beneficial to those who drank it. To some, it had the effect of rejuvenating life whilst others achieved immense strength and other-worldly abilities such as flying or influencing the minds of others."

"And is that what you did to save yourself from the Dratesh Khan at the Hold? Drink Lil'Thra's blood?" She leaned forward, clanking her claws together, eager to hear the details.

"Indeed."

"And?" she asked eagerly.

"We escaped."

"You didn't fight him? Oh my, Zain. You're so tragically boring for a Vampire." She backed up, scoffing.

"It's complicated. I felt sickly. I hadn't drank human blood in years, let alone that of a Drae'shï." Zain looked at her, hiding his gaze with his long black hair, somewhat embarrassed.

"Yet you managed to escape such a tight spot despite such *complications*?" she asked as she grazed her cheek.

"Yes. So?" he said, recoiling.

"So why don't you escape now, Vampire? What's holding you back?" she taunted him as she rose to her feet and waved her hand towards the door.

Zain raised his chained wrists in a half-baked attempt to obtain his freedom.

"Oh, I'm sure your chains are not bonds that can constrain you. Or do you need my blood as you did hers?" she asked as she walked back towards him.

"Believe me, the blood of your kind is what brought me here in the first place," he said with contempt. "If I'm ever to leave this place, it is certainly not with your help."

"Is that what you believe?" She knelt on one knee, face-to-face with her captive, her red eyes looking into his icy blues, first one then the other. She paused.

"Am I free? Have you left me a key that I am not seeing?" he asked awkwardly, breaking her gaze.

"From what I see, there are no keys that can unlock *your* kind of shackles, Zain." She stood and walked to the exit as the door opened by itself. "One like you has been a prisoner in his own skin for as long as you can remember. You may try to leave here if you even bothered to, and I may even leave this very door open, but your condition will bring you right back here before me. And you can do it again and again until there is far less than what I see before me—a broken man with a broken body and a broken mind."

The door shut, the cell darkened, and the gnawing buzz ceased.

CHAPTER 7

A DANCE OF DEVIANTS

The drums rolled until a blast of trumpets filled the ballroom of Threlis Manor, followed by a loud cheer from the men and the applause of the women. The round hall was immense and regal in its adornment, filled with the faces of those inebriated with happiness and frivolity. Sashes of lilac cloth intertwined with vines and silver hugged the travertine columns all the way to the high ceiling. The white marble floor shone like a mirror, and cherry blossoms littered the floor as the fair Eldain ladies childishly tossed the blooms at knights too dutiful to enter into the floral fray. Slim brass braziers hung off the columns, lighting up every part of the hall and radiating warmth across the room whilst the tall windows made the night witness to the ongoing celebrations. Outside, the stars shone brightly in the sky whilst rows of white lanterns lit the many pathways of the surrounding terraces and gardens.

Santhi and the other Elders of the Eldain noble families ran their deliberations over the upcoming nuptial and diplomatic accords with the foreigners whilst the younger crowd enjoyed dances and other distractions. Adara and Elias were at the centre of the party, initiating dances and leading by example as the knights and maidens of their respective houses met to perform their rituals.

Lilith watched the party unfold beneath her as she rested upon the balustrade of the mezzanine floor, sheltered by the thick purple velvet curtains. She stood there in contrast, with a dark blue and grey dress that hugged the contours of her svelte body, her neck adorned with the reddest of rubies.

"Come on, Lilith, you need to enjoy this," said Zain, once again pleading with her to join him. "Here is a cup of wine. Santhi's seventy-eight vintage. You've got to try it." He pushed the silver goblet almost in her face.

She looked at him unamused.

"Not one for revelries, I take it?" He laughed. "Why am I not surprised?"

"You stink of wine, Zain." She cringed as he stepped over to rest beside her.

"And *you* stink of pure unadulterated boredom," he confided jokingly, only to realise he was yet again the only one laughing at his jibe. "Seriously, you've got to lighten up, woman. Otherwise, people will think you're strange, and the grey skin and red eyes don't exactly help. Although, I do find them intensely alluring." He smirked through his haze.

Her eyebrows rose at his intoxicated sermon. "You're rambling on again, Vampire." She paused bemused, yet Zain's optimistic charm was pervasive. She sighed. "Well, I guess if I'm going to have to tolerate your droning, I might as well numb my senses," she said with a smirk before grasping the cup and taking a sip.

"Atta girl!" He smiled, showing some colour on his face for the first time in a while.

"Speaking of strange, how is it that I haven't seen you drink a drop of blood since we met? Eldain maidens aren't to your liking? Or maybe it's the men who you don't fancy?" she asked, a subtle hint of sarcasm lingering in her voice.

"Well, first of all, I'm quite fond of Eldain maidens and maidens of any kind, quite frankly." He rested himself against the column crossing his arms and looking relaxed. She stared right through his theatrics. "But, until recently, I haven't drunk the blood of people for a very long time."

"A Vampire that drinks no blood? I wonder if anything at all you tell me is true." She drank and crossed her arms as she faced him, resting her hip against the balustrade.

"Not human blood, at least not when I can help it. Usually, it's the blood of young animals, but I'll spare you the gory details," he said as her face slowly twisted in mild disgust. "Given that the last true Eldaresh were seen over six hundred years ago, I doubt most people would be appreciative of any practices of sanguimancy. Not that they really appreciated it back then, mind you."

"Sanguimancy? Blood magic?"

"In literal terms. Your memory serves you well. Have you known any other Vampires, or am I your first?"

"I did not fight in the Immortal Wars if that's what you meant—I have not been around that long. But we were instructed in the lessons those battles taught. Including those lessons relating to your kind and how to kill them." She peered at him as she raised her gaze from the redness of the wine swirling in her cup.

"My *kind*?" Zain stepped back, feigning offence. "You and I, my dear, are but the descendants of our Eldarï kin; exiles in our own right, suffering the *gift* of immortality. The Drae'shï remain bound to their mountain, bearing the shame of their original betrayal, which you now wear in your very skin, whilst the Eldaresh fought their fear of death behind a never-ending stream of blood, to the point where life itself has lost all meaning," he said before downing his goblet of wine. "*We* are the only people here who know the true burdens of immortality."

"Tragic," she remarked sarcastically.

"Then again, you've been in the company of your own kind. Do you have any idea what it means to outlive generations of all people? To lose all friends and lovers over and over to the fetters of time?" he said as he looked down, with a sad grin at the spinning couple in the ballroom.

Lilith pursed her lips. "Is that why you indulge in the Eldain's wine? Because you don't drink blood or because, as the last of your kind, even the taste of blood has lost all meaning?"

"Sharp words, Daughter of Iron." He paused. "Curse of the Eldaresh, whatever you do, you find yourself alone. But, well, you never know what life might throw at you." He smiled under his haze.

Lilith raised an eyebrow. "The Death of the Undeath: a romantic, abstinent Vampire. Who would have thought?" She chuckled briefly into her cup.

Zain smiled. "Well, at least you seem to have regained your strength," he said as he tilted his cup towards a passing maiden, prompting her for a refill. "Thank you, my dear."

"So it seems." Lilith felt her side, the pain still tingling but infinitely better than before.

"Well, you will soon be fit to embark on your long-awaited adventure, with the whole world to discover, away from your old life. It seems like only yesterday when I left the Eternal City to journey the world—good times."

She remained silent, contemplative, looking at Adara and Elias dancing at the centre of the ballroom. It was now filled with more and more guests all dressed beautifully, carrying the colours of their various houses and cultures. She sighed. "And what about you? Where will you be heading?"

"I haven't decided yet. I thought my journeying days were over, but perhaps there are still some places left to explore. Maybe show you around?" he mused hazily, looking down below.

"Eldain life not quite exciting enough for you?"

"Far from it, but unfortunately, war is coming, and I've had my fair share of politics and politicians—and this," he said, pointing dismissively at the ballroom beneath him. He proceeded to drink once more.

"Fortunately, you have everyone fooled, thinking you hate drinking and partaking in their *revelries*." She smirked.

"The revelries I sure don't mind. It's the charades masking the true intentions that annoy me."

"Being?"

"Their desire for wealth and power. These men, the humans, covet these things the most. Everything they do is geared towards amassing or retaining power. Whether it is controlling the masses through the Enoch Tree and their faith or by gaining an Eldain heir to secure a longer bloodline."

"So, all of this? Is about power, influence?"

Zain nodded. "Santhi and the other Eldain Elders use it to their advantage, of course, to protect themselves and the Eldain lineage, which, as you can see, is dwindling. So, they form their alliances with the richest and most powerful. A beautiful pure-blood maiden for an army of men," he said almost with disdain, drinking once again as he looked at the Saints clapping to the tune of the dance. "This and much more awaits you in the south if you choose to head there."

"Well, who said I wanted to go south?"

"Well, you can't go back where we came from, and if you travel further west towards Iborellan, you will eventually run head-on into an advancing army of fanatics. And don't get me started about Lothumos. So south is my best guess, but then again, you've surprised me before."

"Still, if the war is heading to the south, aren't these invaders—"

"Carthosians," interjected Zain.

"Eventually going to invade there, too?"

"Well. There's a long road for them to get there, which includes fighting and conquering their way through Iborellan and Cielith before they get to the capital, Valendria. And those walls, my dear Lilith, not even your kin have managed to penetrate."

Lilith paused to contemplate the situation as Zain leaned over the balcony, teetering on the edge tauntingly as the wine got him in a thrill-seeking mood.

"Don't fret. You'll be safer there than here. Trust me," said Zain as he kept eyeing her half-filled cup.

"Here, have it," she said as she noticed his persistent stare. "I'm returning to my chambers."

"Heading away so soon?" He took her hand, raising it to his lips.

"I want to be out of here as early as possible tomorrow. I'd ask you to join me, but between the lack of blood and copious alcohol, it might be best to leave it for another time," she said in her raspy voice as she slowly slipped her fingers out of his hand.

She turned and began walking, her slender body pacing confidently down the corridor whilst the Vampire watched on as he rested on the balustrade. "For once, you've proven to be more than just a never-ending source of chatter, Zain."

"Good night, Lil'Thra," he murmured, smiling to himself as he raised his goblet to her disappearing figure.

Lilith proceeded down the empty hallways, accompanied only by the occasional whisper of Eldain maidens sharing their interests in the foreign knights that paraded the ballroom. The moonlight shone in the clear night on the main courtyard of the manor. The white marble floor widely reflected the silver shimmer through the loggias, turning night into a lesser day. Lilith ran her hands upon the rim of the silent fountain on the landing. The water was cold and fresh, flowing delicately from its centre without a rush. She climbed up on the base and drew from the cool waters, her eyes closing without her notice as the crisp freshness flowed through her. The sound of the music from the hall had long been drowned by the soft jingle of the lanterns and the fluttering curtains of the courtyard.

She reached into her pocket and extracted the Shard, still mildly stained with dirt and her blood. Lilith proceeded to rinse the mirror in the clear waters, removing the black and blue speckles with her thumb. She raised the shimmering piece into the cool air. The Shard gleamed as droplets slowly ran down its surface, and once again, Lilith brought it before her, yet it showed no more than part of her reflection. She peered in, attempting to see something, anything. "Show me who I am, truly. Help me remember, help me understand," she whispered. "Lilith... Lilith," she uttered slowly as if attempting to perceive something hidden beyond her mere reflection. Yet nothing came.

She sighed, frustrated, looking away from the mirror but as her gaze turned back to the Shard, the corner of her eye caught the glimmer of movement in its reflection. A scathing look that disappeared with the sharp turn of her head.

"Have you lost your way, m'lady?" enquired the man behind her.

Startled, she clutched the Shard to her chest. She stepped down from the fountain ledge, slowly concealing it in her gown.

"Not at all," she said as she observed the knight dressed in the colours of the Order of the Saints. His face was long, tanned, and bearded, and so full of creases that any scars he had were masked by most of his facial expressions.

"Should you not be at the ball, m'lady?" he insisted, smiling falsely through his pursed lips.

Lilith drew an irritated breath, anticipating another courting session.

"I was. Now I am headed to my chambers. Good night," she said, moving past him.

"But, I do not recall seeing you dancing amongst the other maidens," said the Saint as he astutely placed himself in her way. "I'm sure I would recall seeing a woman with such distinct exotic beauty."

"I did not partake. I have not been well, sir knight. Now, if you would move out of my way..." Her scowl began to form.

"How so? You are not hurt, I hope? I trust your journey here was not troublesome," he continued, ignoring her.

Lilith decisively pushed past him only to be stopped as he grabbed her shoulder.

"I hear the roads are treacherous these days," he said as his hand squeezed, prompting Lilith to instinctively slap his hand off, but her wrist got caught firmly in his grip. "You're one of them, aren't you?" He smirked.

"Let go of me," she growled as her red scowling eyes glared right back at his.

"Oh yes, those are the eyes I was looking for, the eyes of a killer. Redder than fresh blood." He raised her arm, almost stretching her to tiptoes. "Your friends from Harlot's Hold, remember them? We met them along the way here, along with the rest of your party. All of whom are now floating down the river."

She spat in his face.

"That's it. There's the Drae'shï cutthroat hidden in plain sight." He slowly wiped his face with his other hand, smiling. "I guess there's no point in prolonging this any further," he said as he proceeded to twist her arm and forced her out onto the front terrace under the night sky. He slammed her body face down into a concealed corner between the fluttering velvet drapes and the long vines that covered the façade of the courtyard.

She struggled but did not scream, her arms held under his tight grip.

"Don't struggle, Drae'shï. Don't struggle, and I might let you live," he whispered in her ear.

Lilith slowly relaxed as she submitted to the insurmountable strength he carried in his hands. He pressed his arm against her back, forcing her into the damp vines even further.

The knight soon found his way along her thigh and buttock, unveiling her silver skin to the night breeze. "Don't struggle, and I might even let you run back to your mountain once I'm done with you."

He pushed her against the wall with one hand as he proceeded to release his belt with the other.

She closed her eyes and drew her breath deeply as her freed hand slowly reached into her gown feeling for the Shard. Soon she felt his bare skin brush against her and, in a moment, let out a yelp.

"Shut up! Or I'll kill you right here and now!" he grunted angrily as he quickly slapped his hand upon her mouth, pulling her head back towards him and meeting her wide eyes. "Don't struggle," Her gleaming eyes pierced his.

In an instant, she lifted her free arm and struck down like lightning into his bare thigh, sending a shocking surge of pain through the man's entire body. The man flung himself onto the grass, whimpering as the blood-shimmering Shard stuck right out of his leg. Lilith walked towards him, completely dishevelled, crouching beside him as blood gushed out of his wound. She stared at her trembling, bloodied hand for a moment. As if from a distance she observed him on the ground and calmly knelt by him, laying her hands on his leg. The man was still in shock.

"Shh. Don't struggle," she said as she slowly extracted the Shard from his leg, amplifying his agony. She looked at her hand as the blood dripped and wiped her palm on his face as she proceeded to cover his mouth, drawing the point closer to his tearing eyes. "Don't struggle," she repeated as she slowly began to raise her hand.

"Lilith! What the bloody—? Fuck!" cried Zain. He ran, dropping to his knees over the body. "He cannot die, Lilith!"

She knelt staring at her assailant, who was now grasping his leg.

"Lilith!" Zain proceeded to reach over to Lilith's skirt, ripping off a length of cloth along the vertical seam and binding the man's wound tightly to dispel the bloody river.

"I'm going to kill you, you fucking bitch!" said the man as he came to his senses, struggling to pull up his pants.

Lilith stood still and content, watching the man's writhing face.

"Look at you, silly man, with a silly face. About to die at the hands of a woman he thought he could have his way with. I'm sure all the little peasant girls you raped never struggled, but I'm no milkmaid of yours," she scoffed as she mockingly grabbed his chin and shook his face from side to side.

"Stop it! Back off!" Zain shoved her back upon the grass. "Go there before they see you! Lay there! Now!" He pointed to the vines. "Fuck, Lilith, he's a captain of the Saints!"

Lilith quickly crept into position as the sound of armed guards came rushing through the entrance to the yard.

"What happened here? Speak!" said the Eldain steward.

"Get Santhi. Now! He's not going to last long. Go!" shouted Zain as he put pressure on the man's leg.

The steward signalled one of his men to return inside for further assistance. As the steward crept forward, he noticed Lilith on one side, bloodied and dirty against the vine, her dress ripped up to the seam and on the other, the Saint covering himself up.

He looked back at Zain, who signalled the steward back. The steward nodded and calmly approached the Drae'shï, gently wiping her bloodied hands with his cloak.

Santhi soon rushed in with his medicine chest.

"Move away. Move, Zain," he snapped, calmly yet sternly, as Zain reluctantly released the man's leg. Santhi's focus was complete. He rummaged through his many tiny drawers, extracting various powders and liquids, mixing them in a small mortar with his silver instruments, and handing the concoction to Zain. "Hold," said Santhi as he proceeded to unravel the bandages and rip open the clothing to expose the gushing wound. His eyes closed as he whispered unintelligible mantras and waved his hands in the air above the man's leg as the wound continued to flow. With every refrain, the air calmed further, the winds seemed to subside, and the blood flow slowed almost to a trickle. "Zain. The well." He eyed the concoction still in Zain's hands.

Zain poured the thick silvery substance over the wound as Santhi brought out fresh bandages and sprigs of birdsage and proceeded to rebind the wound. The man had passed out by this time and lay at peace.

Santhi turned to his guards. "Close the curtains. Do not let anyone in here. Call the Jurani boy, now."

Soon more guards began to pour in whilst the crowds exiting the ball were discreetly directed out of the main entrance as the festivities drew to a close. Lilith was slowly pulled up by the steward, now covered in his cloak to conceal her sullied dress. "My lord, it appears that he was about to rape this woman."

"Thank you, Eluin. I'll seek to clarify the matter with the Order immediately," said Santhi.

Elias Jurani entered the yard accompanied by three of his fellow knights, the latter all armed and armoured. Tensions began to rise as the Eldain stewards moved in to block the bodyguards after letting Elias through.

"What is this? What happened here?" asked Elias.

"A guest in my house shall not be in want of protection, Elias Jurani. Your escort's presence is unwarranted," Santhi stated confidently.

"One of my men, *your* guest, has been stabbed. It leaves me with little confidence that I would not also suffer the same fate as him, Lord Crysanthani," said Elias with indignation.

"Well, this man enjoys no such protection of mine as he is neither my guest nor your knight. It seems my lady here suffered an attack on her person by this man, in the cover of darkness, for certain indignities. I find that the Order would surely not hold such treacherous individuals in its ranks," said Santhi sternly.

Elias furrowed his brow and looked over to see the man regain consciousness and struggle to raise himself with the aid of the Eldain guards. "Lyons..." Elias gritted his teeth in disdain.

Santhi approached Elias in confidence as he looked upon the scene. "He will survive, Elias. I've made sure of that, but I want him off this estate where he won't be of any further concern."

"Lord Crysanthani, I—"

"She's an assassin, Elias!" shouted Lyons as he caught a glimpse of his commander. "She's one of the Drae'shï who we fought at the bridge."

"She's not one of them!" barked Zain.

"I found her wandering these halls alone. I questioned her, and the bitch attacked me."

"She attacked you 'cause you tried to have your way with her, and you got what you deserved, or almost what you deserved," said Zain as he turned towards him, prompting the Order's guards to reach for their weapons, instinctively causing the Eldain stewards to draw theirs.

"Enough!" shouted Santhi, his voice booming in the dead of night.

"Stand down!" yelled Elias.

Santhi drew closer to Elias. "I do not appreciate the filth you bring with you here, Jurani." Santhi's voice was subtle yet deadly serious.

"These are dangerous times, Lord Crysanthani. My swords are not drawn against you but the company you keep. I've only ever heard of her kind from legends and history books. Yet in less than a day, I've already found myself at arms with them twice. I'll have you know that on our way here last night, we ran into a party of Drae'shï attacking some travellers. Your Sentinels will confirm this. When I first saw the Drae'shï woman in your company, I tried to think nothing of it, perhaps a coincidence, despite the fact that the Drae'shï haven't been seen in hundreds of years. Yet I now find myself trading words over a wounded high-ranking officer of mine, a silver-skinned deviant, and her host seemingly going to some lengths to protect her."

"She was running away from them!" intervened Zain.

"Silence, Zain!" barked Santhi, his patience beginning to wear thin.

"I find it very convenient that a foreigner is in your midst, despite the tales of how the Eldain are so protective of their borders," said Elias, now brasher in his words.

"They are both guests of mine. Zain has long been a trusted friend of this house and the Eldain," said Santhi confidently.

"I will not discredit the trust you bestow on others, but you know well enough how my position and family name has attracted more than a few attempts on my life. Not to mention the lives of those who were dearest to me," said Elias as he held his family's brooch on his chest.

"The Drae'shï couldn't care less about you, human," muttered Lilith.

"Perhaps the Drae'shï may not, but the Carthosian Shirral does," he said flatly to Lilith as he began to turn to her, holding onto the hilt of his sword. "The Carthosians have never had any scruples and will employ anything and anyone to harm the Massass, the Order, and my family."

"Then you're lucky he didn't call on the Drae'shï to do such work, or you would be dead already," she sneered at Elias.

"That's enough!" stated Santhi once again. "We will get to the bottom of this tomorrow. I'll not have this blow up into a diplomatic incident at the eleventh hour!"

"And allow this woman to find her way out of here, just like that? That's not good enough," said Elias.

Silence ensued.

"No, it's not," said Santhi, regaining his composure. "In fact, Lilith shall stay here under the watch of my guards. And she shall also be Zain's ward. He will be responsible for her if she goes missing. You have my word." He looked Zain straight in the eyes.

"What about his?" asked Elias as he too directed himself to Zain.

"As sure as the fact that I'll slay anyone else who lays but a finger on her."

Chapter 8

Of Fanfare And Fugitives

The Elders of Cielith gradually turned up again at Threlis Manor throughout the following morning. Santhi greeted them in accordance with Eldain protocol whilst Adara courteously followed along, offering her grace towards the heads of the twelve families of Cielith. All rose as each Elder came through the very hall which, until the night before, had held cause for celebration instead of inquiry. The hall was filled with various members of the Eldain nobility and government as well as the retinue of House Jurani and the Saints. All murmured at each other as the Elders passed by. Each Elder was of appreciable age, carrying themselves with not only the pride of the purest Eldain blood but also that of their own distinct houses. All were sharp-featured and well-groomed, carrying an aura of authority and respect. Everyone in the hall knew where to place themselves in their regard.

Zain stood perched above the hall, peering from between the curtains. "Arden, Costansiel, Reerem, Erintein, nine, ten. Yeah, they're all here," he said as he drew back from the curtains.

"Shouldn't you be down there with them?" asked Lilith before taking his cup out of his hand. "Zain, you're disgusting. Stop it!"

"I'm not disgusting. I'm thirsty, and I'd much rather stand here comfortably and watch this unfold without my involvement." He took the cup back, necking the rest of the booze. "The favourite pastime of the undead is eavesdropping after all."

Lilith remained unamused. "So, have these wise men come all this way to pass their judgement on me?" she mocked.

"As highly as you may think of yourself, to expect the entire college of the Elder Council to come here expressly because of you, I'm sorry to have to break it to you, they're not." He paused. "Your little scuffle is hardly going to stop their diplomatic affairs, although I'm sure the humans will find a way to leverage it to their advantage."

Lilith huffed. "So why are we still here? It won't be long until the Drae'shï send another party to find me. We need to leave. Now!" Lilith turned and paced, frustrated.

"We'll be leaving soon enough. And you're safer with me for the moment, than out there alone. Trust me."

"I find it ridiculous that it's taken you longer to get us out of an ally's home than to get us out of that hellhole in Raem," she said, flaring up as she confronted him face to face.

"It's complicated, alright? Now, quiet, they're about to start," said Zain as he turned his back on her and peered down at the council.

"Order!" announced Santhi from below, and the hall quieted as the audience began. Santhi proceeded first to introduce his esteemed guests.

Elias and Alistair entered one by one as their names and titles were called out in full ceremony. Each Elder greeted them before they took honorary seats beside them. As the heads sat down, the remaining crowd of knights and nobles followed.

"We are glad to all be here today, Lord Crysanthani, Lord Jurani," began the eldest of the group, a tall skinny, wrinkly Eldain, with long white hair, narrow blue eyes and an air of confidence that bordered on arrogance. "Through the union between your great houses, the Eldain and the Valendrians shall finally form the bonds that will last centuries. It is by our blood that we choose to be joined to you, and in so doing, merge one of our twelve houses with yours, Elias Jurani." He directed his pompous, deep voice to Elias. "The council has long waited for this auspicious day and has come to give its blessing in accordance with the law."

"It is truly an honour, Lord Ephystille. May I extend the warmest of greetings of the Massass who is unable to travel but who would have been delighted to meet the council in person." Elias nodded respectfully.

"Of course, Lord Commander, we appreciate the ails that come with age." Ephystille smiled as some other members of the council snuck a couple of cheeky grins beneath their hands.

"They're taking the piss," said Zain, scoffing as the banter continued below.

"What?" asked Lilith.

"They look down on humans and other *half-breeds* like Eldassari. They don't mean any of the crap about joining houses and blood and all that nonsense—this would never happen in normal circumstances," he continued as he quickly took a sip from his empty cup only to be left with visible disappointment. "Ugh. Anyway. The Eldain, always kind of intermarry, across families, like twelfth cousins and such, to preserve the purity of their ancient Eldari blood. It's the only thing that has granted them their life's longevity. They don't look kindly upon marriages between different castes of Eldain, let alone with outsiders. Santhi and his wife suffered tremendously because of that, for instance. She was Ephystille's granddaughter, and Santhi was a couple of castes below them. Ephystille's family never forgave them or let them forget—even made him part of the council to raise him to a higher caste to hide the shame. It was probably all the grief they gave them that sent her to an early grave. Poor woman. So, the last thing the council would want is to have a bunch of bastards from these people," stated Zain as he slowly turned a sullen gaze to Adara, seated quietly and obediently aside. "Adara. Poor girl."

"Why all of this? What's the meaning of it?" enquired Lilith.

"They're desperate. That's why. Not just Santhi, the Eldain," sighed Zain. "Santhi said the Eldain needed fighting men, allies to defend themselves from the Carthosian onslaught, and Adara is going to have to secure those allies for them as the only mature unwedded daughter of Eldain aristocracy."

"But what's in it for the Valendrians then?"

"More influence, more power. The Jurani family secure an Eldain heir, to live a hundred and fifty years, not to mention being tied to the ruling class of the ultra-exclusive Eldain aristocracy, in exchange for some military presence. I think the Valendrians got the better deal on this one," said Zain, crossing his arms as he turned his gaze to the discussion below.

"So, Commander, what news do you bring of the war?" enquired the council member who was seated beside Ephystille. He appeared slightly younger with short thinning fair hair, a finely trimmed beard, and a perennial scowl strewn across his face.

"Unfortunately, the Shirra, as the Carthosians call it, is advancing quite steadily, Lord Erintein," responded Elias.

"The Shirra?"

"Yes, they call it the Holy War of Sequestration. They're merely using this as a call to arms for people who are opposed to Massass' divine authority. The Carthosian leader, the M'yar, went as far as to declare himself to be the *rightful* Massass," continued Elias as other Saints within the crowd could be heard reacting with disdain to this blasphemous claim.

"How is His Holiness' health these days, Commander?" enquired Santhi, sounding genuinely concerned.

"He's in good health for a man of eighty. The medicians have been very careful to ensure his wellbeing. We also thank you for the many manuscripts and herbs you sent us last year. He is most fond of your peppermint sweets, Lord Crysanthani." He smiled as Santhi graciously responded with a nod.

"Commander, the war. You were saying," said Ephystille, resetting the tone of the affairs.

"Right," responded Elias, backing up into his military demeanour. "The Shirra has reached far into Ithiria. This land does not offer much strategic advantage, and the locals there are mostly sparse nomadic groups. They trade with the Carthosians but simply don't care about the war enough to oppose the Carthosians' passage through their lands. We do, however, expect that they will pick up a contingency of mercenaries from those mountains."

"Have you yet engaged them in battle? Are you aware of their numbers and capabilities?" wondered Erintein, seeming concerned with this news.

"Only through our scouts and spies. We haven't fought on the open field since the Battle of Palin Bay fifteen years ago in the Grand Harbour. They won't try another naval assault. They know better," responded Elias confidently. "They learnt never to test our navy again."

"Ah, yes. I forgot. You were the boy prodigy who killed the M'yar himself. Barely still a teenager. How old were you?" asked Erintein as he peeled him with his eyes.

"Eighteen, and I was lucky enough to discover him washed ashore, with my own life intact," stated Elias breaking the Eldain's gaze and searching for other less judgemental faces.

"Then let's pray you are equally lucky with this M'yar too."

"And numbers? What about numbers?" interjected Ephystille.

"At present, we have estimated around a 100,000." Elias hesitated. The room broke out in a din of commotion. "Yet—"

"Silence!" cried Santhi once again. "Continue, Commander."

"Yet, we believe that their numbers are going to continue growing as they invade more land and find more sympathisers to the Shirra." The silence was disconcerting. "By our estimation, by the time they reach the Iborean border, they will be around a 120,000. Should they take the northern region of Iborellan such as the port of Morren's Gate, their supply lines will likely boost their troops up to two hundred thousand." The murmuring increased as each of the Elders began to look concerned. Santhi cupped his chin with one hand.

"And by the time they reach our borders? Should they manage?" asked Santhi, unafraid of the truth he almost certainly knew.

"Unopposed, we could see up to 250,000, between troops and other military staff," said Elias without hesitation as he stood firm whilst the rest of the Eldain in the room reacted in a far less composed manner.

"It's worse than I thought," said Zain to himself.

"I'm leaving. I have no time for this. I'm going to get as far from this place as possible," Lilith stated firmly as she turned, but Zain caught her by the arm.

"Hold on. They're months away from here, not around the corner."

"I don't care, Zain," she said, snatching her arm out of his grip. "If there was a time to leave, it was yesterday. If *you* want to stay here that's your business. But I'm done waiting. I'm leaving whilst they're still caught up in their own mess. Before the Drae'shï make their way here, or one of your human or Eldain friends decide to find some use for me like they've done with Adara." Lilith strutted down the hall and around the corner, the echoes of her heels announcing her departure.

"You can't just leave. There are guards and Saints everywhere," called Zain casually, feigning a lack of concern about Lilith. He was quickly reminded how annoying it was to fall victim to his infatuations the moment he drank a little. "Why should you care anyway?" he asked himself as he fetched himself another drink.

Zain directed his attention to the crowd below.

"It is obvious that we need each other's help more than ever. Cielith will not become some annexed province of Carthosia, and we will not have our lands and blood plundered by these savages," continued Ephystille. "The council shall adjourn until tomorrow whilst we continue to deliberate with our allies in private on more delicate matters."

The Elders slowly walked out of the hall and into the gardens where the household's retinue was attending to the lunch. The rest of the attendees slowly made their way to their respective camps in the grounds of the manor, where small gatherings for food and feast began to form in between the pit fires and the late summer's starry night.

Zain descended to see Santhi exchanging pleasantries with his parting guests.

Santhi approached Zain, shaking his hand and pulling him close. "Where is she?" he whispered.

"I don't know, in her room. She just went there."

"Keep an eye on her. The Sentinels know about her. And when were you going to tell me that you also had a group of Wardens from Harlot's Hold on your back?"

"What? Really? They followed us here?"

"Zain!" exclaimed Santhi as he squeezed Zain's hands.

"Father!" greeted Adara.

"Dear!" Santhi smiled as he half-pushed Zain aside to hug his favourite daughter.

Adara's face gleamed as her cheerful eyes brought new light to his face.

"Lord Zain," she mocked. "Are you ready for more meetings and ceremonies this fine afternoon?"

"Has she been drinking? Have you been drinking?" Zain's gaze darted from one to the other.

"No, but clearly you have. You smell like a wine presser's feet. Venerine Vintage, if I detect correctly," Adara commented.

"The seventy-eight, no doubt," said Santhi sternly and unimpressed.

"Listen, go and get yourself cleaned up, and then you and Lilith should join me. I'll introduce you to my friends in the grounds. There's going to be Sandrell, too," she nudged him mischievously.

Santhi still looked cross.

"Yes. Yes. I'd better go and get hold of her." Zain watched Santhi's eyes order him to hurry off and find Lilith immediately. The Vampire promptly returned up the stairs, smelling himself in semi-self-deprecation as the rest of the party moved along.

Zain marched up to Lilith's bedroom door and knocked. Much like her disposition, it was closed, unwavering, unavailable. He sighed at the predicament he seemed to be in once again, the pleasant haze of the wine now turning to drudgery.

"Lilith?" No answer came. "Hey, listen, we need to head down and meet the Elders. Santhi's orders," he explained. "He already chewed my ear off after last night—so can we not knife anyone this time, please?" he rambled sarcastically. "Lilith?"

"Listen here, Eldassari. When we arrive at the manor, be sure to address the council Elders first, then the humans. I'm allowing this meeting in light of what you told me, but I won't have you disgracing us before these foreigners. One step out of line, and you and your friends will rot in the dungeons for the rest of your days," said Lieutenant Vorlaisse, as he and Adam dismounted their horses.

Adam could not remember the last time he'd enjoyed the benefit of a mount. The life of the Wardens rarely provided such luxuries. Their feet were their supports, keeping them close to the ground, close to the earth. He did not envy the Eldain even if he knew they expected him to.

"Did you hear what I told you?" barked Vorlaisse.

"Yes, sir," said Adam, unmoved by the reprisal. The two remained silent.

"So, which of your parents betrayed their legacy?" mocked the Eldain as the two made their way through the manor's grounds and the Saint's temporary encampment.

"My mother was Eldain," said Adam curtly, hoping to shut the Eldain's pompous trap.

"Another foundling of the Hold, I presume, abandoned on their steps," said Vorlaisse. "At least your Eldain blood should have earned you some privileges among your ranks."

"Such rules on pure-birth don't exist in the real world, sir."

"Ah, yes, the real world! The one your mother chose to run after 'cause this one wasn't good enough, not real enough. Is it?" asked Vorlaisse as he raised his arms, gesturing towards the illustrious natural beauty of the manor and the surrounding areas. "Don't lecture me about the damn world, Eldassari. Not when yours is a rotten mess."

"I'm not here to preach. I'm here to do my duty, sir, as my Order commands." Adam's response was ever so blunt, emotionless, and utterly infuriating.

"Lieutenant Vorlaisse," stated the officer as he reached the manor's entrance. "I have a special meeting with the council. You should have received the message with my envoy earlier."

"Yes, Lieutenant. You are expected. Please make your way to the back gardens through the side entrance; the guests are having dinner presently. Access through the manor is presently restricted to the houseguests and staff only," said the guard, directing them away from the lavish entrance and to a dimly lit passageway. Vorlaisse, now visibly offended by the denial of a more esteemed entrance, turned to Adam.

"Well, you heard them. Let's head on, Eldassari. Let's do our duty."

"Lieutenant," called the guard reluctantly. "You must leave your weapons here."

"Of course," snapped Vorlaisse as he removed his belt, sword, and scabbard and shoved them into the arms of the other guard. Both guards appeared intimidated by the irate officer.

"I guess in some places not all pureblood is as pure as in others," said Adam, plain-faced.

Vorlaisse punched him in the face. Adam staggered back but did not fall.

"Listen here, you ill-begotten cur. You and your bastard friends live and die by my say so. The only reason you are alive for now is because the council asked for you. No more. Had it not been for the Saints riding you in, you would have been pelted with arrows along with the rest of that Drae'shï filth."

Feeling his lip, Adam calmly spat blood onto the grass. Adam was used to his tongue earning him the occasional beating. This hardly hurt as much as the fists of some of his old superiors at the Hold.

Vorlaisse walked ahead of him, towards the light of the feast at the end of the garden, leaving Adam to contemplate his sharp retort. The sound of chatter grew louder, along with the sounds of music and servants scurrying back and forth from the side entrances of the manor. Passing through the sea of servants, Vorlaisse bumped into a white-veiled maid, sending her tray of cutlery straight onto the ground.

Adam stopped watching curiously as Vorlaisse scoffed at the maiden's clumsiness and immediately skirted around her, taking little notice of the maiden's rush to pick up the scattered silverware. Amidst the mess, the maid returned to her feet without a sound and steadied her pace towards Adam with her head held down. Concealed by intermittent darkness, Adam could not trace her features, yet he looked closely, instinctively knowing. The maid quickly took a turn back into one of the side entrances of the manor.

Adam hurried forward to see her through the windows of the kitchens as she hurried further through the rooms like a fish out of water, swimming against the rest of the current amidst the clatter of plates and cutlery. Adam looked back at Vorlaisse, but the Eldain simply strode on without care, focused exclusively on his grand entrance.

Adam quickly turned heel and began to follow the girl from outside, waiting for her to emerge once more, but she failed to reappear. The rustling of the nearby bushes soon revealed her getaway.

The maid doubled her pace, repeatedly checking her surrounding, seemingly concerned about being followed. She shifted around corners and trellises as she made her way through the din of the manor's grounds, avoiding contact and dodging people whilst heading towards the outer gates. The maid soon stopped at the entrance of the makeshift stables of the Saints, peered through the canvas, and snuck into the horses' marquee.

Adam crept up to observe.

As he looked in, he could see her remove her white dress, revealing her unmistakable quicksilver skin and white hair. Lilith's body was shapely and seductive. Her long straight hair draped to her breasts. As she drew her hair together, her back revealed the signs of scarring and her most recent bruising etched upon the smoothest of skin. For a moment, Adam failed to recognise her, mesmerised by the female form he hadn't gazed upon in so long. She quickly put on some garb and a small squire's armour set lying on the side. Fetching herself a helmet, she set out to look through the only other slit in the tent. The entrance was barred by the stable boys and guards seated just outside. She retraced her steps, but now she was barred from the other side by a familiar face.

"Greetings, Drae'shï," said Adam.

Lilith stopped, her face pale. She looked upon Adam for a second before narrowing her eyes the next, observing him intently. Adam's gaze intensified and was now focused on the hunt.

She scowled. "You..."

"I've come to take you back," stated Adam as he stood between her and the only exit.

Lilith looked behind her and then back at him. "Didn't think you would go to such lengths to do so yourself."

"My duty binds me to."

"Don't get in my way. I've had enough of your kind and your *duties*." Lilith began looking her surroundings, searching for another exit.

"I'm afraid you have no choice, Drae'shï. All I need to do is call out, and you'll be in chains in a minute. I do not wish to harm you, but I will if necessary."

Lilith hesitated, gritting her teeth as she stepped back whilst Adam cautiously approached.

"Why did you escape the mountain? And how did you burst

through the wall of your cell?" he asked as he slowly stepped towards her, hands held up, feigning defencelessness.

"Stay back!" she hissed as she looked at each horse, hoping to find a saddled steed.

"Why did the Drae'shï come for you?" He stepped closer.

"I said, stay back!" she barked as she frantically looked for a weapon, panic rising just as the outside chatter suddenly stopped. Her eyes grew wide. "You will not have me, Eldassari. Not you or anyone!"

Lilith instantly skipped up onto the stable's fences and flung herself on a saddleless mare. The horse neighed in fright as Lilith quickly grabbed its mane and snapped her heels. Horse and all, Lilith dashed out of the marquee, throwing the oncoming sentries off guard and thrashing through their campfire in one big ruckus.

Adam instantly followed suit, jumping on a stallion and finding himself once again in hot pursuit. Lilith galloped on through the Saint's camp, hooves churning up the lawn, yet Adam soon caught up, his stallion being a far speedier steed.

Lilith looked back on her pursuer as he gained on her and quickly took a sharp turn into another camp enclosure. Yet again, she dashed under the stream of festive banners and lights, through a host of disoriented knights and sentries whose evening revelries abruptly turned into a rumbling rampage of overturned tables, flying tankards, and swearing drunks.

Adam followed but did not falter.

Lilith turned yet again onto the path, now dashing towards the main gate. The exit was barred. The sentries by the guard post drew their halberds, ready to repel any charge.

A nearby guard proceeded to nock an arrow. Adam raised his hand, signalling him to stop. "Stop! Hold your fire!" he shouted.

Lilith darted her gaze at the approaching guards, spotting the archer and turning the steed once more.

"Damn it!" grunted Adam as he snapped back onto her trail. "Don't shoot!" he yelled across the field once again as the defiant archer drew his bow, taking a long-arched aim at his fleeing target.

The bow cracked. The arrow soared and screamed down, missing Lilith by a hair.

Adam sped after her as she galloped further down the open field to the edge of the estate, nothing ahead but the dark forest of Cielith and the distant city lights of Vinesse.

Another arrow soared over Adam's head, and he screamed as the shaft sailed over Lilith prompting her to swerve the mare sharply. The arrow landed square into the path she'd dodged.

She looked back. Adam almost caught up.

She looked back again and so did Adam, waiting to see another shot fired but as their gazes straightened, the darkness revealed the oncoming precipice overlooking the deep valley. Lilith immediately heaved the mare sharply and violently. The beast cried in anguish and fright, barely escaping the dark maw below and flinging Lilith onto the grass in a swift release as it ran away. The Drae'shï lay there motionless.

Adam steadily stopped his steed a few feet ahead and dismounted. Lilith lay on her side, her white silken hair draped across her face and onto the grass.

"Are you hurt?" asked Adam as he stepped forward, approaching her with caution. "I'm not going to hurt you."

Lilith lay still and silent. Adam bent on one knee. He looked across her length and at her face, and gently brushed her hair aside. She possessed an allure of dark beauty that was difficult to understand. It struck him and sucked him in. He looked upon her for a moment, which felt like an eternity.

In a flash, her ruby eyes opened, locking onto his. Suddenly her hand that was tucked under her waist flew out, cutting forward with a swing of her razor-sharp Shard. Adam instinctively recoiled, throwing himself onto the ground and feeling his face in semi-shock. His chin was wet. The cut was not deep, but a few inches higher would have left him blind. Lilith stood, groaning, almost drunk with fatigue. All she could see was the stallion and her way out of there.

Adam also slowly recovered from his initial shock, realising Lilith had made a break for his steed. He stumbled back onto his feet, half slipping in his rush to claim her. Lilith rushed to the saddleless horse and tried to mount. Once, twice, three times unsuccessfully. She groaned in pain with every attempt. She heaved once more and flung herself belly-first upon its back as her side stung once again.

Meanwhile, the archers by the gate were startled by her sudden recovery. "Blazes! She's up," stated the archer as the guards were still making their way across the fields to reach them. They hastened their pace.

The archer nocked another arrow. "I'm not letting this one go." The archer drew, ready to release. "Easy there," he said to himself when suddenly, a long pale hand snatched the arrowhead and snapped it. "What?" He turned, startled.

"What?" asked Zain, tilting his head tauntingly before he immediately head-butted the archer to the ground. "Stand your ground, sergeant. I'll take care of this." He smiled as he darted forward in a phantom-like mist, leaving a trail of black wisps in the air behind him to their complete bewilderment.

At the other end of the field, Lilith stirred and squirmed upon the horse's back, struggling to find a seated position whilst Adam broke his sprint right into the horse's side just as Lilith finally got upright. Lilith kicked. Adam caught her foot.

"Let me go!" she roared and booted him in the face. The two continued to struggle, with Adam attempting to take hold of the horse, trying to reach around to grab her.

"Don't make me hurt you!" Adam cried as the horse reared nervously on the spot.

Lilith tried to slash with the Shard but letting go of the mane would mean falling off.

"No one's going to claim me. No one!" she sneered and kicked the horse once again, ready to trample Adam with her ride. The horse reared again as Adam snatched a tighter grip of Lilith's leg, and with one swift movement, the stallion slipped clean from under Lilith's thighs. Both Adam and Lilith crashed down, hearts thumping.

Lilith rose immediately, raising her Shard. "I told you to leave me alone!" she barked, staggering in her step.

"Not quite ready to, Drae'shï," said Adam "Yield. You've got nowhere to run to."

She roared and darted at him with the Shard crassly cutting through the air. He dodged her, unarmed, careful, clean. Her movements cut through the night like lightning. All Adam could see was the glimmer of the shining mirror and the enraged gleam in her eyes. Rationality fled the scene as Adam cornered the angered Drae'shï, restlessly panting, yet fearless under her scowl.

She threw herself at him again. He caught her stabbing arm, then the other. She roared furiously as Adam attempted to squeeze the Shard out of her hand, the two locked in a face-to-face stalemate. For a second, he watched the depth of her eyes and the void they harboured save for one thought—him. Blood once again trickled from her hand and onto his as she squeezed the Shard.

"Let go! Let go!" Adam roared, but as they struggled, he caught a glimpse of the Shard's reflection. Time slowed, and for a moment, the Shard's depth lengthened, and all seemed to fall silent around him as he became mesmerised by its beauty.

Lilith struggled relentlessly until she let out one deafening roar. The ground flattened and sank around her as Adam flew in a blast onto his back, tumbling down a few feet away, landing face down in the dirt. Lilith sprinted towards him as Adam struggled to get up on his knees.

She pounced to strike.

The air shifted, and Zain's figure materialised out of his dark mist, charging directly into Lilith, flinging her violently onto the grass. The Shard flew out of her hand, and she landed on the ground, unconscious.

Adam looked up, wide-eyed, at the tall Vampire, his final form taking concrete shape out of the dark mist that followed him. Zain's persona shone into the night sky as the clouds slowly parted to reveal the mystical crescent moon that ushered that evening to an end.

"Are you alright?" asked Zain. "I have to give it to you—you must really take your oath to heart to make it all the way here, Warden, but she's under my protection from here on out. Do we have an understanding?" He reached out his hand.

Adam hesitated, blinking at the mysterious being before him.

Reluctantly, Adam's sense of gratitude could not deny the Vampire. He nodded, then grabbed Zain's arm and hoisted himself up. "Adomas. My name's Adomas, but my friends call me Adam."

"Well, Adam. Welcome to the party."

Chapter 9

Dark Reflections

"Three guards concussed, a stable boy with a broken arm, two trashed camps, and a second fight in oh-so-many days. Really, Zain, if you wanted to fuck me, you should have at least gotten me drunk first!" shouted Santhi as he paced up and down in his study fuming.

"Was it that bad? I really thought it—"

"Thought it was what? Entertaining? Funny? An endearing expression of her exotic eccentricity?" he cried throwing his arms up in anger.

"No. I didn't realise it caused such a ruckus," said Zain timidly, trying to diffuse the irate Eldain.

"Zain, do you realise that this marriage, this alliance with the Jurani, is imperative for us?" asked Santhi, exhausted and exasperated. He rested his elbows on his desk which was now filled with maps of Cielith and the northern regions. "Their army is what stands between us and these incoming fanatics. Do you think Cielith has people left to fight? All that's left are pompous rich fops. Even the lower castes are wealthy enough to afford not to send people to the army anymore. There's no honour left here, Zain, just money, status, and blood." The Eldain slumped in his chair as Zain stood silent, observing him caught between a rock and a hard place.

"Is this why you're marrying Adara off to that man?" asked Zain calmly.

"Man? More of a boy," Santhi scoffed. "Of course, I am. I know it. She knows it, too. How could I give up my beloved nightingale if it was not absolutely necessary? If it was not expressly asked of me by those hawks on the council?" Santhi, pensively raised his clasped hands to his mouth and dipped his guilty gaze.

"Why her, though? I'm sure any Eldain beauty would be willing to form part of the Jurani family." Zain approached the desk.

"Don't be so daft, Zain. Have you learnt nothing of politics in all your years of travelling?" Santhi replied. "They want a seat on the council, not a fairy princess."

"And the Elders are comfortable with this?"

"Certainly not with their own blood. But we don't have a choice, do we? They'd sooner see Cielith burn than give up their family names to some 'filthy' human, but for now, it seems they're still willing to share power. And if they're trading it for *my* kin, so much the better. I'm sure Ephystille is loving this. Still punishing me for marrying Larissa to this day! The folly of their pride makes me wonder if I should even bother trying to save the wretched lot."

Zain frowned. "I'm sorry. Though now I'm assuming this marriage is there to seal the deal and procure the Juranis an heir to sit in your stead one day, right? Wouldn't they reject an Eldassari child?"

"Ha! Eldassari, of course not. But surely the child of Elias Jurani and Adara Crysanthani would be considered Eldain, approved by the council if it remains convenient to them. Bunch of hypocrites," said Santhi with disdain. "Anyway, to answer your previous question, yes, but until then, they get to place a regent council member. And I still don't get to retire. How about that?"

"Do you even want to?" asked Zain, looking around at the books and maps strewn all over the room.

"Who else is going to take care of all this mess?" Santhi threw his hand towards all his things.

"The world wasn't built on your shoulders, old friend. You've given your life to these people. Now even your daughter?"

"Not everyone can afford to live like a vagabond, Zain. I have family here, friends. My people live here."

Zain pursed his lips slightly and the Eldain realised his mistake.

"I'm sorry. I didn't mean to imply anything. You know me," Santhi added sincerely, shaking his head as he placed his palm on his forehead.

"Think nothing of it, Santhi. I understand. I would do the same. Hell, I even tried." Zain smiled. "So, a maiden for an army? Seems like a fair trade," he joked with his devilish smile.

Santhi raised his eyebrow, aware of Zain's jibes.

"What about a Vampire for a maid? I did kill an army before," teased the Vampire.

"Not a chance," said Santhi dryly, half-smiling.

"Think about it. You can proudly say you've brought the Death of the Undeath into the fold. I don't think Adara would mind."

"Most of these buffoons wouldn't have a clue what you're talking about."

"Oh, I'm sure they've heard the tales," said Zain musingly. "Handsome—"

Santhi coughed.

"Young—"

Santhi coughed again.

"Blessings, Santhi," he continued. "Young prince single-handedly defeats the entire Vampire army in one fell swoop in the Battle of Bos Novia, finally annihilating the scourge of Amenti, the bloodthirsty Eldaresh, and thus ending the Immortal Wars."

Santhi coughed again.

"Seriously, Santhi, you should suck on some lozenges before you choke to death," said Zain as he started fiddling with Santhi's portable medicine cabinet, picking up vials and opening its small drawers.

Santhi stood as he furrowed his brow and pursed his lips. "First of all, *you* are not young."

"I was back then. A strapping eighty-seven-year-old," said Zain as he peered at the odd pearlescent liquid contents of one of the vials.

"Second," said Santhi as he snatched the vial out of his hand. "*You* did not single-handedly defeat the Undead Army."

"I may have had the help of a magical artefact. True."

"Which artefact is, in fact, the *actual* Death of the Undeath and not your self-proclaimed personal title," added Santhi. "And third: the Battle of Bos Novia was fought by thousands of men who lost their lives, the value of which you of all people should know by now." Santhi closed his argument by slamming the medical drawer shut, almost catching Zain's finger before returning to his seat.

"Touchy when it comes to history, are we?" asked Zain, sheepishly sucking on his index finger. "But ah! You'd have loved it. It was one bloody battle, I'll tell you that. With the first Wardens leading the charge. Don't you miss our adventuring days? Remember when we had the whole conspiracy with Elder Sylmeran and the rebellion of Telaine after we spent all that time looking for her?"

"Ha! Boy, oh boy! I do miss it. Come to think of it, that time we were also treading on the edge of a knife with the Valendrians. How it is that you're always around when trouble strikes, huh, Zain?" He laughed.

"I was merely attempting to rescue a damsel in distress," suggested Zain, half in jest. "Almost single-handedly ended up preventing a war in the process, too, if I recall."

"Almost being the operative term, Zain."

"Of course, Santhi, your sharp wit and charisma were instrumental in not getting everybody killed in the end," he mused. "And speaking of Wardens, ever heard from the boy? Telaine and Greyson's? Since you left him at Harlot's Hold? How old do you think he is? He must be around thirty-four, thirty-five by now. I totally forgot about him, until I ended up at the Hold recently."

"He was born the same year as Adara, so that's about right. I never checked on him though. I don't even know his name, for that matter. I didn't want to draw any more attention to Telaine after that ordeal. We were lucky enough to hide her involvement in the rebellion. All she needed was an Eldassari child at her feet to blow it all up."

"No rest for the wicked, right, Santhi?"

"Poor woman isn't even all there anymore. Hidden in obscurity and shame. Her father passed away recently, too."

"The former chronicler of the council. Some shoes you're filling."

"More like replacing the whipping boy from the looks of it."

Both paused as Santhi's gaze wandered away.

"Zain?" he enquired once more. "What were you doing in Raem when you met Lilith?"

"Erm, not much. I was at a tavern. I went out to piss and found her," said Zain with his effortless ability to sound charmingly vulgar.

"No, no, no. Please. Spare me. I meant, why were you there in the first place? Raem, Orestill of all places? You weren't coming here. Otherwise, you'd have sent word." Santhi narrowed his eyes.

"Well, if you must know, I was heading to Dos Narak." Zain sighed.

Santhi's eyes grew sad. "There's nothing for you there, Zain. Nothing but pain and death."

Zain sighed. "Can we not talk about this?"

"Zain?" insisted Santhi, suspicious of Zain's impending reply.

"Yes, Santhi."

"Zain!" exclaimed the Eldain, frustrated. "This obsession you have with returning to Sarail has to end. Get over it."

"I know. It was a stupid thought, but I can't help it."

"Even after all this time?"

"What else do I have, Santhi? For the last five hundred years, I've seen every single friend or lover wither and die before my helpless sight. Best of all, I have no one else to thank but myself for annihilating every last Eldaresh in the world. The Death of the Undeath."

"You did what you had to."

"It doesn't matter, Santhi. Now at the end, all I wanted was to return to her and rest beside her, once and for all."

"Oh, Zain." Santhi smiled. "The world can be a lonely place for one such as you, good friend. But still, it seems that something or rather *someone* still lit a flicker of hope in you."

Zain looked away, ignoring him, bashful.

"She does inspire you. I see it in your eyes, how you look at her," said Santhi mischievously.

"Nonsense. The Drae'shï and I are only intertwined by sheer coincidence," scoffed Zain. "Maladapted fate, might I even add," he emphasised, crossing his arms, somewhat embarrassed.

"Well, she is as Eldarï as you are, same life span, same origins, same tendency for trouble, I guess. I'd have thought..."

"Yeah, right. I've slept in iron maidens which were more welcoming than her," he retorted as he nervously began fidgeting with the tassels of the armrest.

"I didn't tell you to marry her! Calm down. Touchy aren't we, when it comes to romance?" Santhi smiled devilishly.

"I swear, Santhi—"

Zain stopped, interrupted by a knock on the door. "Enter," called Santhi. The tall ornate door opened to reveal a steward standing in the entrance.

"Lord Petrach," he stated.

"Yes, Eluin. Come on, come in. What is it?"

"Lady Lil'Thra is awake. She is rather irate because she's locked in the guest room. Perhaps it would be best to calm her before she does any further damage."

"There's your call, Zain," said Santhi as he pushed himself out of his chair. "And please, if you do need to, you know, do her. Please do. Anything to get her to behave. Please?"

"This isn't over," muttered Zain, wagging his finger.

"Oh yes, it is. Tomorrow, we're all going to have one merry time discussing our exotic visitor, and she'd better have some answers," said Santhi, pacing towards Zain and inviting him to move towards the exit.

"What answers?" He stopped Santhi.

"Well, the kind of answers you want when someone knifes a knight a few inches from the groin on a diplomatic mission, and then attempts to escape the following day. All sorts of ideas come to mind: assassination, espionage. This human paranoia tires me, Zain, but their suspicion is somewhat justified."

"Do you really think I'd bring an assassin into your home? Don't you trust me?"

"Of course, I do. But I can't keep making excuses in these delicate circumstances. There's only so many times that you can let a rabid dog snap at you before you have to put it down," concluded Santhi with one of his resounding epigrams.

The two exited the room. Along the corridor, the night's calm drew in, but the echoes of muffled banging and yelling resounded faintly through the halls. "Fine. I'll fix this. I promise."

Zain soon approached Lilith's room, and the guards both stepped aside. Zain took the key from one of the guards and placed it in the lock. The crashing racket and shouting deadened, and only the clanking of the door unlocking could be heard echoing in the manor's halls. Zain stepped in and shut the door, locking it behind him.

The room was turned upside down. The curtains had been torn down, the shelves cleared, the table turned over, and clothes were strewn all over the floor. Lilith stood in the middle of the room, completely dishevelled and still wearing the squire's leather armour stained with blood, dirt, and grass. Zain grimaced.

"Where is it?" She spoke menacingly through her hair, trying to contain her anger.

"Where is what?" said Zain.

"The Shard! Where is it?" She walked up to him, desperation seeping into her eyes. "Where is it?" She grabbed onto his shirt with her sullied hands.

"Do you think we would leave you with a weapon after the shit you just pulled?" said Zain seriously. "You need to calm down. You're going to get killed or worse."

"Do you have it? Is it here?" she continued, patting his body, blatantly ignoring his pleas as sweat formed around her dirt-crusted brow.

"Why's it so important to you?"

"It's mine. I need it. Where is it?" she insisted again.

Zain grabbed her by the shoulders and forcefully sat her down. "You will get your mirror when you calm the fuck down and you tell me why it's so important to you." Lilith sat for a moment, panting and breathless, as if held down by an unbearable weight on her chest.

"Where is it?" she screamed again, standing up and frantically trying to feel her way around Zain's chest, inadvertently scratching him with her broken fingernails.

"Enough!" roared Zain, catching her by the throat, lifting her off her feet, and slamming her back against the wardrobe. Lilith kicked and tried to scream, holding onto his arm with both hands until she met his eyes. His pupils dilated, turning his eyes completely black. His skin almost seemed to smoulder. His strength far outmatched that of any man of such stature and size.

Her fear of Zain was set in her eyes far more than her desire for the Shard. She held onto Zain's arm but ceased to struggle. As her senses started to dwindle, Zain released his hold, and Lilith fell to the ground, holding her neck, looking back at him as he towered over her.

Zain crouched beside her, pulling the veil off his usual oafish behaviour. His eyes were still black as night and menacing with the horrors that might lurk there. "I'm going to ask you nicely, one more time. Why do you need the Shard?" he asked as he drew the Shard of shimmering mirror from his breast pocket, his eyes fixed on Lilith's. Lilith's senses were keener than ever, but she froze in place. Zain held the mirror tightly in his grip.

"I...I don't know," she hesitated. His hand tightened and the sound of the distressed piece of glass pierced her ears. "Stop!" she said begging, trying to reach out, trembling, fearful of approaching him too much. "I...I don't know. I just had it with me when it all started, when I left the tower."

"Go on," said Zain.

"It's the only thing that's kept me alive until now. I don't know how or why, but that's all I know." She winced. "I just can't be without it!"

"What about its power?"

"What power?" She looked back, confused.

"The power! The power you used when you blew the Warden off the ground." His patience was waning once again.

"I don't know," she replied.

"Don't lie to me!" he spat. "Don't!"

"I don't know! I don't know what I did or how. I... I... I can't." Her voice suddenly turned resolute and sullen. "It's like I can't breathe. Without it... It's all black. It's just black. I don't... I...can't. I'm losing. I'm losing... myself." She heaved, staring into nothing.

Zain's eyes narrowed. He stood back, noticing true fear settling in her teary eyes.

"Help me, Zain," she pleaded as her eyes truly revealed the person trapped behind them. "I don't know what's happening to me. My memories are fading. I'm not sure who I am anymore, who I was." Her voice softened in a way he'd never heard. "I thought I died and came back to life. I don't know if I was dreaming or not. It felt so real, but it can't be. It's, it's like I came from the darkest place in the universe and found myself surrounded by pain and suffering and I can't make it stop. I can't take it anymore. I have to get away. I don't belong here. Please help me."

Zain relented and relaxed his gaze, his eyes slowly receding to their former hue. A slight grin formed on his face. He set the mirror back in his breast pocket. Her gaze didn't follow but remained fixed on his.

"I will help you. Come," he said as he leaned forward, hoisting her up in his arms.

She held on safely as he carried her across the room and then laid her on the bed. Lilith seemed at ease for a moment, exhausted from the interminable tension she'd carried with her from the moment they met. She rested her eyes as her clammy forehead slowly dried in the cool breeze wafting through the shutters. She gave a half-smile in gratitude.

Zain looked at her and wondered how the Shard could have such an effect on her, calming or otherwise. He stood, pacing slowly towards the last standing candelabra, reaching into his breast pocket to extract the mirror. The Shard was cold to the touch and extremely sharp in certain angles, with gleaming purple and green hues through its edges.

"Hmmm. What could this possibly do?" He shrugged. "I'm dead already after all." As he proceeded to raise the Shard to his face, the mirror showed his cool dimly lit brow, blue eyes, and black hair. The same face he had seen for centuries. Nothing was different.

Soon the corner of the room quickly grew dim and cold as a gust of wind swept from behind him. Zain instinctively turned but found himself facing a dark cobbled wall. He turned back to find the other side of that cobbled wall with a small narrow window and a thick metal door, his name etched onto it in chalk.

A soft chill ran through Zain as he looked around, stunned by his new surroundings. He approached the door and looked through the peephole, only to witness the distant howling wind flowing through a narrow corridor. The window, on the other hand, led to a white-clouded view, though nothing could be discerned in the distance. The room felt increasingly cold, lonely, and empty. "Hmmm," he mumbled to himself, attempting to keep calm before turning back to the door peephole. "Hey!" he called out briefly. "Heeeeeeey!" he called out again, yet only the distant echoes came back to haunt him. "Hellooooo?" he called yet again, hoping he'd get an answer, but only the wind recited its verse back.

He stood silent for a moment. His ears twitched, sensing distant, almost imperceptible whispers. "What?" he replied instinctively. Zain looked behind him then back through the hole. The whispers grew fainter as if bleeding through the cracks in the walls. Zain touched the cold cobbles, nearing his ear to the walls. The voices stopped.

Zain's discomfort grew palpable. A soft buzz rang in the distance. The room seemingly brightened and then dimmed rapidly, irking his eyes. The whispers resumed, and his breath quickened as the feeling of entrapment grew with the incomprehensible nature of the room. Zain remembered the Shard then fumbled through his pocket and raised it close once again, eyes closed. "Deep breaths. Deep breaths, Zain. It's just an illusion. You're in Threlis Manor with Lilith, Santhi, Adara and the rest," he recited, hoping his mantra would reverse the spell that had befallen him. As his breath stilled, the whispers receded, and so did the wind. A sense of peace slowly drew in as silence surrounded him, and on his last breath, Zain opened his eyes.

The cell was still there in the background, but as Zain's eyes cleared and focused, the face in the mirror revealed a figure behind him. Zain immediately turned to the figure, only to find the cobbled stones behind him were now replaced by a dark mirror instead of the wall. He approached the black mirror but found nothing but his own reflection and the emptiness of night behind him.

His ears began to ring. Zain winced.

He opened his eyes once, yet now there stood a man instead of him, eyes distressed with a burnt face and pain seared in his sight. Zain's fright matched that reflected in the mirror, and he immediately staggered back, tripping on the cobblestones and dropping the Shard on the floor. The Shard smashed into dust, and so did the realm he was trapped in.

All faded into darkness.

Lilith awoke.

Lying naked on the cold ground, she opened her eyes. Blurry eyed, she stared into the crimson sky far above her as tiny shimmering objects slowly fell as though entranced in time. As her senses sharpened, she began to hear the rain of shattering glass crashing all around her. She was cold, but not in discomfort. She continued to observe as she witnessed the contours of her surroundings.

She lay in the middle of an enormous conical structure, a tower of great height. It was hollow in the middle up to the top, where the overcast sky lay dark and red. A wide marbled staircase spiralled around the tower as far as the eye could see. The stairs were all encased in a tall stream of arches made of alabaster, each housing the remnants of a mirror frame. Shards continued to crack and break off, shattering into the courtyard in the tower's centre.

A clap of thunder rocked the halls, the sound amplified tenfold. She gasped as if taking her first breath. She slowly crawled up as the last shards crashed down. She felt the cold, grainy glass floor under her hands and knees. The halls were dark, empty, and cold. Lightning struck again, and the mirror floor beneath filled the tower with light. Recovering from the flash, she looked down only to see the floor reveal her reflection.

She stood up and took a step back, looking around her. The floor comprised a giant round mirror, fractured at a dozen different seams. She knelt on one knee to observe her beauty, brushing her long white hair behind her ears. She studied the softness of her silver skin, the contours of her face and the depth of her ruby eyes against the backdrop of the crimson clouds above.

She raised her neck. She had no scars, even as she trailed her nails along her throat in wonderment.

Out of the floor, a small bladelike Shard was wedged out of the mirror. She removed it, slowly standing up and gazing into it. Her terrifying beauty looked back at her, her wide pupils, dark like the depths of nothingness. For a moment she remembered.

Another clap of thunder roared, and the silhouettes of five armed men appeared in the dark entrance of the tower. As they walked into the shattered courtyard, their silver-skinned faces appeared broken.

"What in the blazes is going on here?" exclaimed the first.

"Lil'Thra, why did you go in? We told you to wait," hissed the second.

"What have you done? We shouldn't be here," whispered the third.

She turned around, her hand wrapped tightly around the Shard, the power of the room slowly coursing through her. Her heart was thumping in sheer anticipation. "Lil'Thra," she whispered to herself, looking at her reflection.

"Lay down the Shard. Now!" one intervened. However, she held on. All bore the colours and armours of the Dratesh Khans, and all towered above her.

"No," she said calmly as she turned her gaze to them.

"You don't have a choice."

One nodded, and another headed over to her, laying his hand on her shoulder. However, she was solid, firm, and utterly immovable. In his shock, the guard turned to his comrades. As his gaze shifted, she grabbed his arm in a bone-crushing clench, bringing him to his knees and warping his plate armour. The guard screamed in agony as the rest of the unit stood incredulous. The guards unsheathed their weapons.

The two guards in front rushed in. The first blow landed on her arm, shattering the blade. The second landed in her grip, the moaning hum of the blade reverberating throughout the hall, and with a twist of her wrist, the steel snapped like a twig, and she plunged both blade and shard into each assailant. Lightning struck once again, and the tremor of the tower rattled the millions of shards spread across the floor.

All the guards raised their arms in fear and stepped back.

"Warn the others that the seal of the White Tower has been broken! Tell the Moirai! Go!" ordered one.

"But... Aramis?" hesitated the other.

"Go!" he barked as he readied himself to confront her.

Lilith looked up into the sky calmly, reaching out, sensing. The sky rumbled once more, and lightning struck down on her in a blinding explosion of power. The arcs of electricity ran wild in the concave shape of the tower, shattering what remained of the mirrors, whipping the walls violently. The guards' fear turned to awe and terror, freezing them in their place.

"Go!" yelled Aramis, shaking his companion, who staggered to retreat, yet her eyes narrowed, and the arc of lightning tore through them until there was nothing left but dust. The rumble subsided, and Lilith slowly stepped out of the courtyard.

As she passed from the mirror's threshold and onto solid ground, Lilith's breath soon waned, and with every step forward, she found herself gasping for air. The power she possessed had slipped from her fingers. She fell to her knees once more, clamouring for help, echoes of memories and voices searing her soul. The mirror called to her, and she crawled to the edge of it and looked over. Another Shard edged out of the frame, broken and sharp. She picked it up. Her breath ran deep once again, and her hand steadied. Her wrist was soon gleaming dark blue as blood trickled from her thumb. She had not felt the pain, but the cut was there to bear witness.

Stepping into the mirror once again, her wound disappeared as if it were but an illusion. She looked into the Shard, feeling the cold brush of the wind go through her. She did not wish to be cold anymore, and as she looked away, she was suddenly clothed. She gazed at herself once more, teetering between familiarity and foreignness. "Lil'Thra," she said as she tried to recall, yet soon in the distance, a new band of voices drew closer.

It was time to leave.

Chapter 10

Dust To Dust

"Krea, can we take a break from the storytelling? I need to rest," said Zain as he hung his head, staring at the cell floor. Zain was tired and hungry, but most of all, he was beat.

"Tell me about the girl of your dream," said Krea ignoring his pleas as she paced from one side of the cell to the other, arms crossed, with a hand on her chin. "Krea, I need to rest. I can't," he said, each word feeling like a mouthful of glass being chewed. The bonds laden with runes and inscriptions stripped him more of spirit than of strength, and the incessant buzz that followed Krea's presence clawed at his mind. "Why is it so bright in here whenever you come in?" He winced.

Someone knocked on the door. Krea approached, exchanged words, and soon returned bearing a jug of clear water and a tiny cup of deep blue blood.

Zain's senses tingled.

"I have blood here for you. Drink, and let's continue."

"Doesn't work that way. Blood must flow from the living, not from a cup."

"It will have to do for now," she said sternly, proceeding to push the cup further to his face.

"No," he reiterated. "I won't drink it."

"You will drink this voluntarily, or I will make you swallow it," she said as Zain turned his face away. She grabbed the back of his head, her talons digging at his skull. "Drink!" she hissed, shoving the cup in his face as he struggled to turn his sight from her gleaming red eyes.

The chains shocked him, and he released his tense jaw. Zain forcefully swallowed a gulp, to his displeasure.

"More!" she said as he filled his mouth again before he shook his head free and spat it back at Krea, covering both of them in the thick cold liquid. Krea instinctively stepped back and slapped him hard with the back of her gauntlet, crushing the cup in her hand.

Zain writhed and groaned on the cold floor as he felt the sting of her backhand and the churn of cold sludge moving through his body.

Krea wiped her hand, revealing a small yet deep cut. The blood glistened and rolled down her palm, gathering into thick droplets that slowly dripped off her wrist. "Is this what you *really* want?" she said as each drop fell to the floor.

Each bead sounded a torrent of rushing blood to the ears of the Vampire. A deep visceral yearning and hunger called from within his chest. His breaths deepened as the sound of her blood coursing under her skin scratched at his throat.

Zain watched intensely as Krea took a step closer, raising her hand high above him, letting her blood drip on his cheek. With each drop, his senses came into focus, his body stiffened, and his ails vanished. He slowly turned his face towards the incoming droplets, taking each drop like a scorching desert starved of rain.

The Vampire's focus grew razor sharp as Krea's gaze lingered, his pupils slowly dilating into a maw of darkness. Suddenly he snapped upright, attempting to take a full bite at her wrist, yet his chains held him back, shocking him once more.

Krea staggered in fright with the swiftness of his movements. The chains seared at his wrists as they electrified his body. She stood back wide-eyed, watching aghast until the Vampire was finally pacified, and his wrists burnt. Soon she wiped her hand clean and wrapped it in cloth, stopping the blood flow and concealing it from Zain.

The air stank of blood and metal. The dimmed light slowly returned. The buzz resumed.

"Now I see why you said they call you the Cursed Ones. Whatever happened to you to drive you to such folly?" she asked, furrowing her brow. Zain's breath remained heavy, wanting. "Zain? Answer me!"

Zain didn't react.

Krea soon brought the jug of fresh water and doused him from head to toe.

Surprisingly, like a man whose burning flame has been quelled, Zain slowly appeared to come to his senses. He groaned and reclined against the wall, sitting down on the cold, wet floor again. "Please, don't ever do that again," he said, gasping for air.

"The blood from a cup or my hand?"

"Both. One is a poison that doesn't kill, the other is a poison that makes me want to do the killing." He coughed and sneezed before wiping his soaking face in annoyance. He coughed again and cleared his throat.

"The latter did not look like poison to me," said Krea, arranging her circlet as she kept watching Zain closely.

Zain felt his face as warmth seemed to return to his cheeks and his contours felt less sharp.

"With just a few droplets, you seem to have found life anew," said Krea. "Tell me, is carnage really what drives you? Can't imagine what you would do with a full person's body."

"You wouldn't want to know."

"I've heard." She smiled as she rested by the windowsill, admiring the cold white mountains in the distance. "Now, tell me about the dream."

"I already told you. We shared the dream of the girl who killed herself." He sighed, frustrated.

"After you drank her blood, when you escaped Harlot's Hold?"

"That very night, yes."

"Isn't that odd to you?" she asked.

"Sanguimancy is something that can bring out different effects in different people and Eldaresh. It's all odd," he continued.

"Or perhaps it was something else? Any idea?"

"The mirror? Who knows? I don't know, maybe. I guess," he said, hurrying his words in frustration.

"I'd say most likely. Nonetheless, weren't you curious to find out? Maybe use it for yourself? Discover its use or meaning?" she insisted.

"I took one casual glance at it, and I got trapped in a room very much like this one with no way out. That's arcane knowledge that I can live without, thank you very much," said Zain, now turning visibly frustrated at the probing questions.

"Can you?" she asked genuinely. "I find the way your mind works incredibly interesting, Zain. You claim you are a beast born for blood but never seek to embrace it. You have an instrument that seemingly holds the essence of raw power but are too scared to even look at it. You claim you are immortal, more so than any of the other Eldarï races, yet you still live with the fear of death. Why?"

"There are things worse than death, I can assure you..."

"Were all your kind like you before you killed them? Or perhaps you killed them all because you were indeed the different one? The one who cast aside one beast and replaced it with another one bearing a conscience," she mocked.

"You weren't there. You have no idea what the Eldaresh had become. The hunger they had as a whole. It would have bled the world dry."

"And you put a stop to that, the moralist," she teased.

"Spare me your contempt. I've gotten enough of it throughout my entire existence."

"So, vengeance, was it?"

Zain sat silent.

"It was, wasn't it? They cast you out 'cause you refused to consume like them. To be like them. So, you betrayed your nature and your kind, killing them all at once. Interesting. Interesting indeed. That's why you call yourself the Death of the Undeath." Zain remained silent. "Indeed, there are things worse than death, Zain, you're right."

"You don't know what you're talking about."

"So why then? Why deny everything that you ever were and then turn on them?" she snapped insistently.

"Because at first, we tried to save them!" he barked back. "We tried to fight it—the hunger. My father knew that if the Eldaresh would not learn to abandon the desperate struggle for eternal life, we would eventually come to drain the blood of the whole world, only to be left to wither into dust, alone. But the Eldaresh were too far gone after millennia of living in death. And when I finally convinced my father, and he eventually tried to change things, to give in to his humanity, my stepbrother found his moment to take the throne on this perceived weakness and began what would eventually be known as the Immortal Wars. Not without obviously blaming it all on me, of course. The frivolous, young, human-loving Zain." He spat in contempt as he looked down and away. "They always found me vile, insane, you know? 'How could the prince mingle with those whose lives were as long as that of flies?' they said. 'Let alone marry one. Or worse yet, sire her.'"

"So that's what it's all about," she mused, caressing her bottom lip with the gold tip of her thumbnail.

"They took everything from me, my title, my name, and then my family. And then when I thought they could not take anything else, they took my identity; they turned me... The ultimate vendetta."

"They made you human? How? The mirror?"

"No. It was one of the seers—the Red Witch of Balur Sephit—the Red Tower in the east."

"But you said the Red Tower of the Eldaresh was destroyed."

"Indeed some 2700 years ago. The Lothumans laid siege on the Eldaresh and failed miserably. But more importantly for them, they managed to secretly scale the mountain and destroy the tower in a bid to end us all. No one knows what happened to that mirror—if there ever was one. Nevertheless, in all of this, the Red Witch survived. And she survives still or so does her power, in a manner of speaking."

"So naturally, if one seer turned you. You sought the help of another."

"My brother had struck a bargain with one and I with another. The White Seer, *your* seer; Altra. But such bargains do not come cheap, as you can tell."

"Is this what you call poetic justice, Zain? The genocide of all your own kind to regain your immortality, to avenge your family? Even you're not so stupid as to not see how hollow you sound."

"That's not what I asked for."

"What?"

"I didn't ask for my immortality back."

Krea looked back, perplexed.

"I asked the White Seer to bring my wife and friends back from the dead after my brother killed them... and to make them human again like me. All in exchange for a 'rapid ending to the Immortal Wars'... as she put it."

"The death of all the Eldaresh."

"I had no idea. The White Seer handed me the ultimate weapon, and I found myself on the battlefield the very next instant. It was absolute chaos: Drae'shï, Eldaresh, Eldassari, humans all fighting. At the time I accepted my fate, that I had been cheated again, I knew I'd go along with them. However, at that point, I just wanted to destroy them all and go to hell along with them," he said, gritting his teeth. "In one moment, the Eldaresh had turned to ash in a terrible blinding light. When I came to, I just found myself there again, an Eldaresh once more. Standing in a field of statues crumbling to ash, now crowned the last of the Vampires. The Death of the Undeath."

Silence reigned for a moment as Zain's head sank to his knees, droplets of water still dripping from his hair.

Krea frowned. "In the end, did Altra keep her promise?"

"She kept her word," he scoffed. "Kept it indeed." He sighed as he looked away. "Once I returned, I found them: my wife, my friends. They were human once again indeed. Yet the same humans that I sired into Vampires over a hundred years before." He looked away, teary-eyed. "Ashes to ashes, dust to dust."

CHAPTER 11

TO COURT FOR POWER

The Council of Elders session reopened the following morning.

Adam nervously peered through the curtains at the edge of the halls, flanked by Vorlaisse and the escorting guards.

In the hall itself, Adara sat at the front of the audience, nervously turning her gaze back and forth, anxiously waiting for her father to fill his seat at the council table.

"Adara, dearest, will your father be joining us?" called out one of the younger Elders, a poised and polite man with short salt and pepper hair and long sideburns to match.

"Indeed. Where is Petrach? Something keeping him up at night?" added Ephystille contemptuously as a small chuckle reverberated around the room.

"Adara?" enquired Rhyliss once more as she suddenly snapped out of her trance.

"Apologies, Lord Rhyliss," she responded, slightly flustered. "Lord Crysanthani is on his way. He was indeed indisposed during the night, councillors. His medical assistance was needed. He'll be here shortly."

"I see," said Ephystille, pausing before starting to tap his fingers on the table. A few short seconds of silence and awkward glances was enough to do the trick. "Then I'm sure he won't mind if we get started without him." The rest of the room seemed to agree.

Adara remained silent.

"Lord Rhyliss, if you please," said Erintein, waving his hand to the scribe who was delicately opening the grey tome before him and scrolling through the texts.

"First item is the audience with Lieutenant Dremheim Vorlaisse of the East Sentinels and Adomas of the Order of the Wardens of Harlot's Hold," stated Rhyliss, standing at the edge of the table. Ephystille waved his hand, and the guards by the entrance drew the thick velvet curtains.

Vorlaisse walked in proudly, hand clenched around his blade's pommel, followed by another guard and Adam held in shackles. "Lieutenant," interrupted Rhyliss, stopping Vorlaisse mid-step. "This is not a courthouse. We do not bring individuals in chains before the council."

"Forgive me, my lord. This is for the protection of the council and all members present," said Vorlaisse, visibly embarrassed and uncomfortable as he stated his case to so many people so high above his rank and caste.

"Vorlaisse, is it?" asked Erintein contemptuously. "Take a look around. I believe there are enough Saints and council guards to prevent your captive from trying anything." He continued to wave his hand around. "So, remove those wretched chains immediately!" he roared, clearly infuriated by the perceived insolence of Vorlaisse's contradiction.

The room went silent as many feared a telling-off would soon find its way to their ears. Vorlaisse silently approached Adam and unshackled his wrists. The two approached the middle of the room right before the table.

Adam was still wearing the original garb he'd arrived in, smelling of grass, dirt, and wet leather. All in the room looked at him with interest. Few had ever seen the likes of a first-generation Eldassari, and fewer still had seen one that was a Warden of the Hold. Many of the Eldain maidens looked at him coyly, spying on his rugged Eldain features cast in the muscular build of a human, under the stern gaze of their male counterparts. The Eldain men on the other hand looked unimpressed, scornful, and ambivalent, whilst the Saints looked at each other, wagering who'd best him in a fight.

Adam looked around also, sampling his audience. His gaze bounced from one person to another, cautious not to provoke lest it linger too long on the purebloods. He knew he was not welcome, his kind especially. The unwanted shame of being an Eldain bastard was something he'd never known until now, but he still held his head up with a straight face the way he'd been raised.

"We have been informed of the attack of the Drae'shï along the Illyum River and would like to extend our thanks to our East Sentinels for keeping our borders safe once more," said Rhyliss as the two approached. "We would also like to thank our honoured guests, Commander Jurani and the Order of the Saints, for assisting in repelling this threat."

All the Eldain in the room nodded gracefully whilst some of the Saints bleated small cheers for their tribute.

"However, it seems we also have another to thank. I understand you are a Warden of Harlot's Hold, are you not?" Rhyliss turned to Adam.

"Yes, sir. I mean, my lord. My companions and I are all Wardens," responded Adam firmly, hiding his insecurities with his cold hard stare at Rhyliss.

"And were these men also placed under arrest for crossing into Cielith, Lieutenant?" intervened Ephystille.

"Yes, my lord, immediately," replied Vorlaisse.

"Even though they fought, slew, and repelled the Drae'shï on the crossing?"

"Yes, my lord. As per the law of safe borders." He hesitated.

"Release them, Lieutenant," concluded Ephystille, calmly.

"Immediately," added Erintein.

"What would our allies think of us if we punish the hands that aid us instead of rewarding them?" asked Ephystille as everyone in the room agreed in unison. "Be sure to release them and reward them before sending them back to Raem," he continued as many Eldain clapped softly, looking at each other somewhat perplexed at Ephystille's farcical and unusual demonstration of gratitude.

"If I may, councillors," added Elias, drawing some attention to himself. "I would gladly grant the men a place to stay and fresh clothes at the Saints' encampment during our sojourn in Cielith. For how can we allow those who spill blood alongside us to be treated as anything less than brothers?"

The council graciously clapped at the response, both factions locked in a dance of political courtship.

"Come now, Warden. Tell us your name, that we may thank you personally as well," intervened Rhyliss, eager to lighten the mood further.

"I am Adomas, sir."

"Just Adomas? What of your family name?" added Erintein, evidently knowing the answer to his question.

"I have none. I was a foundling of the Order of the Wardens. They are my family," Adam said dryly.

"Clearly, you are an Eldassari. There's no hiding that. Most likely your mother. Are you not curious to know who bore you into this world?" Erintein prodded further, and even some of the Eldain had to hide their pursed lips.

Adam hesitated a moment, unable to provide an appropriate response. "All foundlings of the Order are taught that the Order is their only family and that the bond we share runs deeper than blood."

"That was not my question, Warden. Rather, it was whether you were curious to find out? We have records, you know. Our dear Santhi is the chronicler, after all. All births, high or low, are kept in his archives," continued Erintein, evidently reflecting his own curiosity rather than Adam's.

"The Order is my home, and my brethren the walls that make it. I fear not that which arises in the deep, for we are one, and none shall break us," quoted Adam, head straight and at attention.

"Spoken like a true Warden then, Adomas of Raem, Warden of the Hold," concluded Erintein, half smiling at the Eldassari's eloquent response to dodge his question. Adam smiled back. "Nevertheless, rather than send you back to where you belong, we brought you here to understand how these Drae'shï managed to arrive so far south of Ussar Varys."

Adam proceeded to give them a detailed account of the story from his end.

While the Eldassari delivered his narrative, Zain secretly watched from the balustrade overlooking the hall as Lilith nervously paced next to him.

"It's time we headed down. Now, remember what Santhi said. Just tell it how you told us this morning, and it will be fine," stated Zain.

Lilith looked increasingly concerned. "I'm not afraid of them. It's the way they look at you. Prying and prodding. I'd like to have my mirror back now."

"It would be best if you did not walk in there with the weapon that you also used to stab one of the Saints, a legion captain, no less. Some might consider it in slightly poor taste at this point," he surmised, half in jest.

"Hm," she muttered, evidently unimpressed.

"Anyway, I have it here," said Zain, tapping his breast pocket. "Don't worry. I won't be fiddling around with that thing again after last night."

"That's what you get for playing with things that don't belong to you, Vampire."

"Well, it doesn't seem to belong to you either, Drae'shï," he retorted. "So, is that true? What you said about how it came to you. You truly don't remember anything before that?"

"All I remember is waking up in the white tower with glass raining all around me. The guards attacked me, and I ran," she said as she averted her eyes from his gaze.

"And the guards didn't stop you? How did you escape?"

"I just ran. They couldn't catch me. It was dark," she continued, scratching her arm.

"And you remember nothing before that, or how you got in there in the first place?"

"Before the mirror, it's mixed up, confusing. I remember, sort of, but at the same time, I don't. My memories feel more and more foreign with every passing day. I know the past, I know things about my kin, the world, history, but they don't feel mine even though they should, and as time goes by, I fear they are becoming more and more elusive, harder to recall." Lilith stared at her hand, almost saddened.

"Is this why you're so attached to the mirror? It helps you recall?"

"It's like looking through a keyhole. You know there's something behind the door that would help you understand everything, but you can't fully grasp it. It's just there, just beyond reach," she said as she reached into the air attempting to grasp it.

"And your name? How sure are you that your name is Lil'Thra?"

"That I know for sure."

"How?"

"Because, I know, Zain!" she said irritably.

"It is not uncommon for amnesia to erase a large portion of one's life. To make one feel alien to what one has always taken for granted," interjected Santhi as he approached from behind them, hands behind his back. "I would say more so in the case of the Drae'shï and Eldaresh, considering you live for so long. Zain, do you even remember what you did a hundred years ago?"

"I must admit it tends to get hazy after a while. Really need to start keeping a diary or something."

"Indeed. In Lilith's case, it is entirely possible that she has trouble recollecting herself, especially if strong, energetic, and magical forces have been at play. And what about you, Zain? How are you feeling after last night? Did my tonic soothe the nerves?"

"I think I'd have been better off with some of your father's twenty-two vintage."

"Now, that's a wine." Santhi wagged his finger at him. "Perhaps you'll earn yourself a bottle if you can convince the council to overlook these blunders and keep the Saints happy."

"Right. And what about this mirror? Have you found anything in your library?" said Zain.

"Sadly, not much. There's a lot to cover. Are you sure you have no further recollection of events before your moment in the tower, Lilith?"

"None. Distant memories, flashes, dreams."

"Dreams? What dreams?"

"I had one dream that seems lodged in my memory. The night sky was red, and there was thunder. I was lost. Scared." She hesitated.

"Go on," said Zain.

"Then I died. Like my neck was slit," she continued, uncomfortably touching her throat.

Both Santhi and Zain looked at each other.

"You were murdered? By whom?" asked Zain.

"No one," she said flatly.

"No one?" insisted Zain.

"No one. I don't know! It doesn't matter," she snapped.

"It's fine. It was just a dream," Santhi added, wrapping up the painful matter. "In any case, I think it's time to head down. The Eldassari Warden will soon be ready, and I'm done having these old hacks deride me behind my back in my own home, damn it."

"But Santhi, you *are* an old hack," said Zain as he placed his arm on Santhi's shoulder, grinning his mischievous smile.

Santhi quickly elbowed him in response. "Still young enough to catch you unawares," he scoffed. "Shall we?" He gestured the couple towards the marble steps. Lilith headed down whilst Zain held Santhi back for a moment.

"There's more to it for sure. If this is *the* mirror, it may explain why they came after her. The Immortal Wars might have taken place six hundred years ago, but I still remember its importance to the Drae'shï. Also, her dream... I think I had the same dream, too."

"Yes? Come on, out with it," added Santhi as they both began heading to the staircase.

"The night we escaped Harlot's Hold."

As they approached the stairs, they noticed Lilith waiting for them at the bottom.

"Let's speak later, Zain. We've got enough on our plates as it is," concluded Santhi as he led the way down and into the hall.

"A Drae'shï, an Eldaresh and an Eldain walk into the Council of Elders. Sounds like the beginning of a bad joke," muttered Erintein to Ephystille behind his hand.

Santhi headed in first, followed by Lilith and Zain as they were each publicly announced. The room rose once again. The clamour of whispers followed as all the guests began to spot Zain, then Lilith.

Zain observed how Lilith took in all the attention, yet she refused to engage any of the eyes that looked upon her. From scowl to awe, each face that looked upon her remained struck by the unusual sight.

"My beloved." Santhi smiled at his daughter, clearly breaking introductory protocol. "Council members." Santhi nodded to the council. "Honoured guests." He turned to the rest of the room.

"Santhi. How good of you to finally join us," said Erintein, sarcastically.

"Apologies for keeping you waiting, my lords. Though that didn't seem to stop you from starting deliberations without me." Santhi smiled deviously, highlighting their ineptitude in following their own ridiculous rules. "Nevertheless, my absence was not without cause. I have been hard at work conducting my investigations into the matters at hand, of which I'm sure the council would be glad to hear."

"By all means, chronicler. Please enlighten us. We have been most eager to make the acquaintance of your guests," said Rhyliss as he placed his quill on the lectern and took a seat behind his open tome.

"You are all familiar with Zain, I'm sure. He's been a guest of mine and of Cielith many times over the years."

"Indeed, we are. The council extends its welcome to His Grace," added Lord Rhyliss, tilting his head.

Zain gracefully extended the courtesy to the council. The younger women in the room coyly giggled at each other as they observed the handsome pale-faced prince.

"His Grace?" enquired Lilith.

"Technically. I am, or was, the heir to the throne of the Eldaresh," answered Zain quietly.

"What?" she responded dumbfounded as Zain proceeded to sit beside Adara, cupping her hands and affectionately kissing her on the cheek.

"And," interjected Santhi, "this is Lady Lil'Thra Astemari Sistrah. Daughter of the Drae'shï."

"Lilith," she intervened, stepping forward, head straight. "My name is Lilith."

"I'm sure you have all heard many things over the last few days and would like some clarity," added Santhi.

"Indeed we do, Santhi," said Erintein. "The world had not seen any

Drae'shï in its territories since the Immortal Wars over six hundred years ago, and the first that emerges finds her way into Cielith no less, attacks a captain of the Saints, and shortly after attempts to flee, putting the lives of many on the camp at risk, including the Wardens, with displays of sorcery." His voice was stern and devoid of emotion. "Not to mention the havoc wreaked at Harlot's Hold by her followers who sought to liberate her." The room was silent.

"Liberate?" interjected Zain, laughing. "They came to kill her and would have succeeded had I not intervened."

"Nonsense!" barked Captain Lyons from the end of the room, struggling to get up on his feet. He rested his arm on a nearby balustrade, concealing his pain. "Why would they bother attacking the Wardens' fortress then? The Warden said they came to the Hold and slaughtered a dozen of their men. This is no ordinary Drae'shï."

"She was escaping the Drae'shï, not helping them!" called out Zain.

"Not helping them?" spat Lyons. "Perhaps she was already softening the forces of Raem ahead of the Carthosian invasion. Harlot's Hold is an important military target that guards the plains leading into eastern Amenti. Carthosian spies are everywhere. I wouldn't be surprised if the Carthosians already struck a deal even with the Drae'shï at this point!"

Everyone in the room chattered between themselves, some acknowledging the possibility and others laughing at the ridiculousness of the suggestion. Elias watched, cross-armed with pursed lips whilst Lyons looked around, content to see his point was being considered amongst the crowd.

"Silence!" called out Rhyliss, irate with the brazen discussion between the two.

"This is ridiculous!" called out Zain from across the room as he stood up. "How could anyone, let alone the Carthosians who live across the continent, even manage to get to the Drae'shï? How would they even communicate? The Drae'shï can't speak common—they haven't left Ussar Varys in 650 years!"

"Well, she does!" barked Lyons. "When I confronted her the night of the ball! I caught her lurking around the manor, alone. That's when she attacked me! She stabbed me in my leg and told me I'd die. In common!"

Lilith smiled.

"Look! Look at her smiling!" Lyons pointed. "The smile of guilt, if I've ever seen it!"

Zain turned a shaken look to Lilith. He had never heard her speak anything but old Eldarï. A cold sweat caught him by surprise.

Lilith stood. "The only thing I find ridiculous is how one can be so easily bested by someone whom he thought he could have his way with just a moment earlier. And spy or not, if it weren't for Zain, I would have stuck you like the pig that you are. But don't worry, I'll bide my time until I deliver onto you the judgement you truly deserve."

A clamouring roar broke out in the hall. Discord was in full bloom as the accusations flew.

Zain turned to Lilith, fearful of what she would say next. "Are you really a spy?"

"I'm not."

"But how do you know common?"

"I don't!" she said in common without flinching.

Zain took a step back.

"Enough!" Santhi's voice overrode the buzz of exclamations and the din quickly subsided. "I believe I have an answer. Commander Jurani, if you please? What tongue did you hear just now?"

"Common, Lord Crysanthani," said Elias, resting his chin in his hand, curiously waiting for the scene to unfold.

"Lords of the Council?" asked Santhi, and some responded, saying old Eldarï, and others Eldain. "Adara? Everyone else?"

The room broke again into chatter as each person spoke of a different language, a language they perceived the Drae'shï to speak in.

"And Lilith? What are *you* speaking?"

"Drae'shï, Luminar," she said flatly.

"How is she speaking different languages at the same time? I've never heard of such sorcery," intervened Ephystille.

Santhi turned to Zain and then Lilith. "If I may."

Lilith nodded, and Zain extracted the Shard and handed it to Santhi.

Santhi raised the Shard. "This is how."

"A broken mirror? Speak sense, Petrach," said Erintein impatiently.

"Not just any mirror. This is a mirror fragment from the White Seer's Tower of Ussar Varys." The room grew silent. "And this is why the Drae'shï were after our friends. And why now I'm starting to believe they still are. They weren't after *her* when they attacked the Hold. What they were really after is this. Am I correct, Adomas?"

Adam stood up and thought about it for a second. "He isn't wrong, my lords. The Drae'shï were looking for someone. They didn't just attack us for nothing. But once Zain and Lilith escaped, it wasn't long 'til the Drae'shï retreated."

"That still does not explain how this Shard grants her the ability to speak all our languages at the same time. How is it not just coming from her?" said Erintein, for once not feigning his interest.

"She's a witch!" exclaimed Lyons, trying to smother his previous embarrassment.

"I think we've heard enough from you, Captain," Erintein replied dryly, cementing Lyons' embarrassment further.

"How it works, that I cannot explain. I will need to conduct more research. We do not have as much information on Eldarï or Drae'shï arcane knowledge as you would imagine. Though it is clear that the item is valuable to the Drae'shï. Almost indispensable might I add," concluded Santhi, whilst glancing at Lilith as she looked at the Shard, anxiously clasping her hands together.

"Hand it over, Santhi. I want to see this thing for myself," continued Erintein, extending his hand forward.

"I would not recommend you gaze at it for long. It has already attempted to bewitch Zain."

"How so?"

"Let's just say, if the Death of the Undeath is apprehensive of it, it's not something any of us should be handling lightly," added Santhi as Zain nodded behind him.

"I see," said Erintein. "Hand it over." He ignored Santhi's plea placing his open palm before him.

Santhi hesitated before reluctantly passing it to the Elder.

Lilith's expression turned grim.

Erintein gazed at the Shard, watching and waiting as nothing more than his face looked back at him. The room quieted, and his sight lengthened. Beyond his reflection lay a darkness in which his image slowly dispersed. Santhi called to get his attention, but Erintein ignored him, mesmerised by the depth of the blackness that slowly emerged. With each passing moment that Erintein held the Shard, Lilith's breath quickened, and her throat tightened.

"Erintein!" Santhi called once more, but the Eldain remained awestruck as those around him stood up in concern. They shook him, yet the Elder was transfixed, clutching onto the Shard as blood slowly trickled from his hand.

"Release it!" yelled Lilith.

Instinctively, Santhi whipped up his cane and struck the Eldain's hand, releasing it from his grip.

The Shard flew and landed on the ground, splitting in two, sending a surging shock through all their minds. All gritted their teeth and held their heads. Their ears rang loudly as the Shard's snap screamed through their cores.

Lilith wailed as she flung herself before the broken artefact, desperately attempting to put it back together whilst everyone was still recovering from the frightful phenomenon. "What have you done?" she roared.

Zain and Santhi both frowned at the sorry situation.

"Come, Lilith," said Zain reaching out to help her up, but Lilith whipped his helping hand away.

"Leave me alone!" She gritted her teeth, teary-eyed upon her knees in the centre of the hall.

"Clearly, it can't be handled by anyone else," said Santhi as he watched Lilith's anger brew almost into tears. "I apologise, my dear."

"And with good reason," groaned Erintein as he slowly recovered from his trance.

"Whatever it is or was, I want it out of here along with her. You understand me, Petrach?" added Ephystille.

"What the hell?" Zain turned, arms spread in dismay.

"Let's not be rash, my lords," intervened Santhi.

"It's fixed," Lilith said quietly.

"What?" asked Zain as all looked at Lilith holding the Shard once more. The two fragments had seemingly merged into a whole before their eyes.

"It's whole again," she said as all stood dumbfounded by the Shard.

"Well, my lords, it seems that we've got a lot to talk about," said Zain.

***

Over the next several hours, Lilith proceeded to give the same account of the events that had transpired and the unknown nature of the mirror. Between debates and agreements, the day was soon spent along with those attending.

"Order! Order!" called out Rhyliss as everyone slowly returned to their seats, seeking to come to a conclusion on the matter.

"Thank you, Lord Rhyliss," said Erintein. "You may proceed, Lord Ephystille."

"The council recognises the present Lil'Thra Astemari Sistrah as a guest of Lord Crysanthani seeking refuge from the persecution of the Drae'shï," began Ephystille, looking straight down at Lilith. "However, the council also recognises the danger Lilith's presence poses to our borders should the Drae'shï continue to pursue her or the artefact further. Furthermore, given that the mirror can't be appropriately disposed of safely, the council feels that while Lil'Thra may stay within Cielith, the artefact cannot." The announcement was met with mixed feelings.

"Order! Order! I've never seen such an unruly mob in my entire hundred years of existence. Now shut up!" intervened Rhyliss. His patience was now at its limits.

"This is ridiculous! It's clear that she cannot stay without it. And who's going to handle it anyway?" Zain pleaded.

"It's fine. I don't want to stay here anyway," added Lilith, scornfully.

Adam rose, too. "As a Warden, I cannot allow her or anything she holds to be the cause of more Drae'shï flowing into Raem or anywhere else. Even if she is the victim she so claims, the mirror does not belong here. It is best we return it and her as well," he said flatly as Lilith sneered back.

"Lilith," said Ephystille, ignoring everyone. "You shall be allowed to remain here for the next week, but after that, you must leave."

"With me," added Adam, looking at her.

"Forget it," replied Zain. "Santhi!"

"Councillors. Please allow us more time to research the mirror. Perhaps there's a favourable solution for all."

Erintein stood. "The decision has been made. Eight to four votes, Santhi. Now let us be rid of this matter. I can't believe we've spent a day discussing this issue when we have to discuss the war with the Carthosian Shirral!" The room went silent. "Have you all forgotten why we're here?" An echo boomed in the hall. "To address an incoming force of three hundred thousand, not the Drae'shï and their magical trinkets! All we need now is the Drae'shï, clobbering us from the east! This is Cielith! The last bastion of ancient civilization and the blood of the Eldarï! You'd do well to remember that your lavish way of life depends on the protection of our borders and our blood!" The silence was as damning as his words true.

"Lord Erintein. Councillors," intervened Elias calmly. "If I may propose a reasonable solution."

The Elders nodded.

Elias stood, flinging his cloak over his shoulder, and descending to the middle of the hall. "As commander and leader of the Holy Order of the Saints, I have at my disposal the entire Order's resources and men, which presently are fifteen thousand strong. I also enjoy the support of my house's personal guard of around another two thousand men. If indeed we need to defend ourselves from another Drae'shï incursion, the Order will send a contingency of fifty knights, and I will send another fifty from my house to make good for the losses suffered by the Wardens. They will also help train and recruit people to replace them." Elias nodded to Adam, who hesitantly nodded back at the surprise offer. "It is our primary duty to act as protectors of the followers of the Holy Enoch, including their lands and wherever people practise our beliefs. That includes the lands of Raem, Lirari, and Triari, apart from Valdell."

All the Saints in the room proudly nodded in agreement.

"As a child, I always read about the Order of the Wardens of Raem and how it was formed out of the joint effort of all free men of Amenti to repel the forces of Ussar Varys and Dos Narak over six hundred years ago. Today, I say we show the Order that the world has not forgotten their sacrifice and that the Saints are their brothers, too, not just in spirit but also in battle." Elias looked directly at Adam, whose gratitude finally crept into a grin.

"It is a very generous offer, Commander Jurani, but shouldn't we focus all our resources on the Carthosian invasion?" interjected Ephystille.

"And what about Lilith?" added Zain.

"Both your concerns are valid, my lords, and that is why my proposal was not finished," said Elias.

Both Zain and the council held back attentively.

"Cielith may not believe in our religious icons, but their values and beliefs have always been shared with us. Both Valdell and Cielith are blessed by the Holy Mother's light. Both have always proven to be good allies to each other. It is for this reason that not only shall the Saints strive to protect Cielith from the onslaught of the Carthosian heretics, but I shall dedicate our numbers to provide an adequate garrison to defend it, Lord Ephystille." Elias smiled, open-armed, expecting a jubilant reaction from the council, but the members of the council widened their eyes as the rest of the room applauded.

"That is a welcome offer, Commander, a very welcome offer indeed!" announced Rhyliss, pleased to see the Jurani so forthcoming.

Adara's eyes widened, almost incredulous.

Erintein, still sceptical, nodded at the whole affair. "I would imagine your demands for our silver would then most likely increase with such numbers."

"Only enough to support your own garrison, my Lord. Consider this as a prospective wedding gift from the Order and my family to the Cielith to honour the union of the Houses of Jurani and Crysanthani. Nay, the union of the Valendrians and the Eldain!" stated Elias as he confidently joined Adara in the centre of the room, grabbing her hand, kissing it, and raising it to everyone's elation as she awkwardly smiled at the sudden display and resounding applause that followed.

Santhi and Erintein looked at each other. Neither needed to speak, but both acknowledged that while Elias Jurani may be dressed as a knight, he excelled far more as a politician. Zain, equally sceptical of the human's intentions, bore a hole through Elias with his eyes, yet Elias' confidence was far stronger than his armour.

As the applause subsided, Elias turned to Lilith. "And Lady Lil'Thra, last but certainly not least," he stated as he reached for her hand from under his white cloak, kissing it gently as he put forward his most chivalric bow. "Lil'Thra may perhaps be our greatest ally in the war to come. With the power she's holding in her hands, we may indeed have been blessed by her arrival."

"What are you saying?" intervened Erintein, eyes sharp.

"Lady Lil'Thra may indeed be the key to save us all from the Carthosian invasion," said Elias as the room cheered his enthusiasm yet Zain and Santhi looked at each other unamused. "And as her allies, we would grant her the full support and protection of the Saints and House of Jurani. She may travel with us to Valdell in the company of my betrothed, and much like my future wife, she will find all the safety and comfort within the walls of the capital in a manner that is befitting of kings and queens. So, what say you, Lilith, will you help us?"

Adam stood up, prepared to object however, Lilith quickly intervened.

"I accept," she said flatly, glaring back at Adam and narrowing her eyes at his attempt.

The room resounded with applause and cheers as Elias beamed and applauded her, yet Lilith soon turned to him amidst the general jubilation.

"The mirror is mine, Jurani. It answers to no one, and neither do I," said Lilith, narrowing her eyes and looking past Elias' good intent.

"So be it, my lady." Elias nodded with an equally astute half-grin, eager to show her that he was similarly far from underestimating her own cunning.

CHAPTER 12

UNFAMILIAR FACES

The cell was dark once more. A black bag concealed Zain's vision. The muffled sounds of voices and metal came from afar.

"Krea?" He said, but no words left his lips. His body was tightly bound and ached all over, yet he also felt sedated and peaceful. *"Krea?"*

The room brightened through the bag, and the gnawing buzz rang anew. *"More voices? Who's there?"*

Suddenly the bag was snatched off his head.

He squinted, but soon a hard metal punch met his head. His ears rang.

"Where is the All?" said the commander as he entered the room.

Zain groaned as he slowly came to his senses, but the light was blinding.

The commander nodded, and another punch flew from a guard.

"I have been patient, but I'm tired of playing games. Who or what is the All? Where are the All's followers? Tell me!"

Zain hardly reacted, still in a daze.

"He's out of it," said a guard. "Shall I?" he continued, grabbing hold of Zain's chains.

The commander nodded.

The guard pulled, and Zain was shocked, spasming as the current ran through his body. Yet he did not call out in pain; his voice deadened, and his mouth sealed. Blood slowly pooled in his mouth and dripped along his cheek.

"What the hell is going on?" barked Krea as she sped in. "Get out! All of you!"

The room went silent. Krea immediately placed the black bag over Zain's head once more.

"The Conclave is tired of waiting, Krea. We need answers. Now!" said the commander.

"How dare you interfere with what I'm doing here?" she barked. "Remember who entrusted him to me."

"And remember who you still answer to in the process. It's taking too long."

"If you want answers, proper answers, you will have to wait."

"Force it out of him. You're wasting time."

"Let me explain something to you, Commander, since brutality and torture are the only tools you have learnt to master in all your years of experience," said Krea, anger brewing in her voice.

"Watch it, Krea."

"Break a man's body, and he will still retain the resolve to spite you. Break a man's mind, and he will forever belong to you."

The commander paused. "Since you are so fond of your witty epigrams, allow me to extend another in return. Pray that you prove to be correct, Krea, because there will be little use left for one's body if their brilliant mind proves to be useless," he said as he strode out, the sound of his footsteps fading out of the cell.

Krea cursed in silence. Her presence moved towards Zain, still frozen in his seat. "Hm. He's unresponsive," she said, her voice edging closer, yet Zain was unable to react.

Another rushed in.

"Teller," said Krea.

"I'm sorry, Krea. I came to you as quickly as I could," he panted. "We were working on him, and they just barged in and then locked us in the office." Anxiety crept into his voice.

"Pompous, pretentious pieces of..." She gritted her teeth.

"Think he'll be fine? I mean, in the Abstract?"

"Of course, he will. They barely scratched him."

"I can't believe he didn't wake up."

"Luckily for them." Krea sighed. "Let's stop for today. It's late, and he's not ready to talk more."

"Yes, Krea."

"Get the new girl to clean him up and the rest of this bloody mess," said Krea as Zain felt the blood trickling down his chin.

"Right away," said Teller. The two slowly left the room, and it turned to darkness once more.

The hum ceased.

Zain breathed slowly through the bag as he struggled to regain his senses. His head throbbed and his mouth tasted of blood. Each passing minute felt like an hour. "Krea," he finally managed to mutter but found no response.

The door soon opened once more. A soft step followed.

A subtle presence stopped beside him, quietly observing him from behind the blackness of the bag. Water sloshed in a bucket, and a sponge was wrung. Soon the cool touch of her wet hand came to his chin as she dragged the black bag off his face. Zain shuddered, and her hands moved away.

"Shh," whispered a young woman in the softest of voices.

The room was dark, and his eyes did not reveal her likeness. She brushed his hair and cleaned his face as he struggled to find his words.

"Who... who are you?" he groaned.

"It's me. Aria," said the girl.

"Aria?"

"I finally found you," she whispered through a smile.

"Who are you?" he struggled to reply.

She paused.

"Then you really don't remember me, do you?" she asked sadly.

Zain did not respond.

She sighed. "It doesn't matter. What matters is I'm here. I'm here for you. I'll get you out, I promise," she said as she took hold of Zain's hand, though he did not react.

Zain stood, startled.

"Who's there? What's going on?" he gasped in a sweat.

Yet the cell was now vacant.

––––––––––

"Damn, my thighs are bloody hurting," Samos groaned as he rubbed his sore legs, and the horse's trot shook him like a child on a rocking chair.

"For fuck's sake, Samos, shut up! It's been three days of non-stop moaning," said Willam from behind him, his irate morning look ever more intense as his weight continually shifted with the movement of his own mare.

"Would you rather have walked back?" asked Brandt smiling, evidently enamoured of his new steed. "Good girl!" he added as he slapped the horse's neck, irking the beast.

"First of all, that is a horse, not a hound, and secondly, keep slapping that animal, and you'll soon find yourself with your hide on the ground," said Doran as he skilfully steered his mount closer to Samos. "Hold onto the reins. Properly!" he exclaimed, waving his fist. "And don't be so stiff. That's why you're hurting."

"What the hell am I supposed to call it? Nancy?" retorted Brandt.

"How 'bout Namilla? Like your sister?" yelled Thane from behind them.

The entire column of riders burst out laughing, including some of the Saints surrounding them.

"Ha. Ha. Ha," yelled Brandt back. "That's one mare who would never give a ride to any of you bastards. Especially you, Thane."

The riders laughed again at the friendly banter.

"Why? She too busy giving rides to the rest of town?" he retorted, sending another wave of laughter around.

"Asshole." Brandt laughed as he turned back to give his comrade the finger.

The column of knights reached the top of the valley, which opened into the soft brush of Raem's sparse green land. The lands of Raem were littered with beeches, oaks, and other tall thin trees in the soft yellow undergrowth caught in a perennial state of wintry dryness. A soft wind constantly whistled through the trees. It was the sound of home.

Adam sneaked a brief smile beneath his goatee as he saw the lands he grew up in once again. He felt the wind waft his hair. It had grown thicker. He missed the feeling of the cold air brushing the sides of his head. It was time to shave again.

"Your men are in good spirits, Captain," said the Saint beside him, clasping the reins in one hand and resting his free hand on his thigh. His white destrier carried a full pack along with its armour strung safely behind it.

"We don't have any horses at the Hold. Some of us have never even ridden a horse. They can enjoy it for now." He smiled slightly. "We are grateful to Commander Jurani and to you, Lord Maxwell, sir."

"You've got quite the knack for court protocol, Adomas." He laughed heartily through his deep, croaky voice. "Let's dispense with all this pomp and decorum. We are soldiers, not politicians. If we are to be sharing bunks, we'll soon get used to the sound and smell of each other's farts."

Lord Maxwell was a man of war and Commander of one of the 12 legions of Saints; the fourth. He was well into his forties, with short black and white hair and a dense, rugged stubble. A long scar was visible along the length of his face from brow to jaw, close enough to his eye to make him appear slightly disfigured.

"Fine, Tilus. Have it your way," said Adam, half-relieved.

"Atta boy!" He laughed. "So, tell me, are all the Wardens Eldassari? We could use big strong men like you in the field."

"Not all of us are. Brandt's and Thane's parents were. Arren's grandparents, too. The rest are humans from Raem. Most of the Order is human, orphans and other folk who've given themselves to the Order to repay some debt owed or to avoid the gallows. Very few true Eldassari remain."

"Ah, debtors and criminals. The best recruits," added Tilus sarcastically. "And is it true you live as long as the Eldain?"

"Well, roughly 150 years, more or less like them. The purer the Eldarï bloodline, the longer you live."

"That's why they don't like foreigners messing with their women," mused Tilus.

"Or Eldassari bastards, for that matter," interjected Brandt as he caught up within earshot of their conversation.

"Thank you, Brandt," added Adam, calmly dismissing the eavesdropper.

"It's ironic, though, how you both share the same life spans, yet the Eldain still deem it necessary to refer to you as being different from them. Of course, it was also evident how much they detest the idea of integrating a human into their precious bloodline, even if it is Elias Jurani," said Tilus, seemingly intrigued by the intricacies of Eldain culture and customs. "It was also evident how the Eldain maidens looked at you, Captain." Tilus laughed.

Adam grunted and looked away, hiding a slightly embarrassed grin.

"Oh, Ellana! How I'll miss those soft loins!" added Brandt again, smile beaming between his perfectly groomed beard and long brown hair.

"Ha! Managed to have a good time, have you?" said Tilus, looking over his shoulder, seemingly eager to live vicariously through the brazen young man.

"Thanks to this bastard!" Brandt smiled, looking at Adam. "Even though we had to walk halfway around the world to Cielith, almost get killed by the Drae'shï, and spend a couple of nights in an Eldain dungeon, it was all worth it."

All the Wardens smiled as they remembered the few days spent at Threlis Manor after being released. The Wardens had shared camp with the Saints and enjoyed the festivities that lasted for a week. Between the free-flowing wines and the furtive encounters between them and the Eldain of the household, the Wardens collected memories to last a lifetime.

"I'm afraid life in the Hold is far less interesting and the villagers far less gracious than in Cielith. Maybe that's why the Eldain feel the need to split hairs," continued Adam as they spotted the keep of Harlot's Hold in the distance.

The march lasted the rest of the morning amidst moments of light drizzle and patchy sunlight. The Rakshir plain stood as a land between two worlds; the sheer sharp rocks and passes leading to the Ussari mountain range and the semi-decrepit keep of Harlot's Hold atop a nearby hill. The plain was a barren steppe landscape punctuated by a few broken trees and a tiny stream that appeared in the middle during the wintery months. A thin veil of mist lay a few feet above the ground, slowly dissipating as the sun appeared from the cloudy sky.

"Harlot's Hold. It looks as eerie as it sounds," said Tilus, amused by the peculiar landscape emerging before him.

"Staying here might not be as grand as charging into the open battlefield, but at least you will be far safer," said Adam.

"Yes, for now, but the war *is* coming. I would hardly consider any place safe if we fail to hold the Carthosians in Iborellan. How strong are the Hold's walls?" enquired Tilus in a more serious tone as they drew closer to the dishevelled castle.

"The walls are strong and have never been breached, though they are in need of repair. Other parts of the keep have fallen into disuse as the garrison dwindled over the years, such as the southern barracks and training grounds."

"We will take up camp there and house our cavalry in the training grounds. If your commander will allow us, that is."

"When we walk in with fifty knights of the Order of the Saints, he might suffer a heart attack."

"Nothing to worry about, Adomas." Tilus smiled. "The Saints take good care of themselves. We will not be too troublesome. We will help you rebuild the fort to its former glory. We have two engineers with us."

"Thank you, Tilus." Adam looked back gratefully. "I'm sure you will be missed on the front. Fifty knights is a large number."

"Yes. For now, we will be. But this cohort of the Order was only destined to reinforce the Fort at Karankal on the border between Cielith and Iborellan. Thankfully, the Shirra is still hundreds of kilometres away, although they'll soon be at the Iborean borders. That's where the main armies of Valendria and the Saints are headed—to reinforce the fortress at Morren's Gate," explained Tilus.

"Morren's Gate?" enquired Adam.

"It's the coastal fortress at the furthest point north of Iborellan at the very nook of the gulf of Carthosia. It's the only stronghold that stands on the border between Ithiria and Iborellan and the only one for hundreds of kilometres. The next strategically relevant one being Karankal."

"I understand. It must be a long voyage to get there."

"It's around 1400 kilometres from the capital in Valdell. Between fifteen to twenty days by sea. A month likely by horse and even longer on foot," he continued as he fiercely scratched his dense stubble through his gloves.

"And will you travel so far just to meet the Carthosians in battle?" returned Adam, instinctively scratching his own, too.

"When you're talking about the sort of numbers they're mustering, our best chance is to defend their onslaught at every fort we have, thinning their numbers at every pass, learning how better to defeat them. However, the Iboreans aren't capable of doing it alone, at least not like they used to. It's impossible to get the different tribes, lords, and clans to agree on anything, let alone form an army."

"But is it true that there are three hundred thousand Carthosians on the way? How can you possibly fight such an army without help?"

"Nonsense! At least, not yet. Our spies inform us that the numbers are far smaller. For now. The problem with the Carthosian Shirra is that it picks up entire villages along the way and drags the people along with them. Some end up slaves, some men-at-arms, and others become foragers and people who provide for the supply lines of the entire column. It takes them weeks to move even a hundred kilometres. Yet their numbers grow at every turn, whilst ours hardly do, even with the blood tributes."

"Tributes?"

"All communities that wish to enter the graces of the Holy Enoch must provide the Order with a male of age for every three families. Many view this as an honour and a means to escape a life of rural poverty. Hell, some even join us willingly, except when the times of war start looming. That's why a blood tribute is always paid. These tributes ensure their communities have access to our medicians and Enoch Sap when needed."

"I see. Then I doubt you'll find many recruits here. People still believe in the old gods around here, and there are certainly no Enoch trees."

"We are aware. The Eldarï didn't leave any in the great migration, and its effects are quite visible," surmised Tilus. "I noticed how throughout our journey the villages in Raem remained generally small and sparse."

"So, once you are done helping us, you will head to Karankal to meet the other units?" continued Adam.

"Indeed. Also, once we have ascertained that there is no threat coming from your silver-skinned friends in the north."

"The Drae'shï," muttered Adam as he pointed to the ominous mountain of Ussar Varys in the distance across the plain. The mount appeared as the last sheer peak at the head of a long mountain range disappearing into the north. The view of its summit and the White Tower was barely ever visible, usually hidden behind thick clouds and poor weather conditions, whilst at the foot of the mount lay a small derelict fort of black stone, set like a maw of black teeth awaiting its next victim.

"What's that?" said Tilus.

"Black Pass Fort. Built by the Drae'shï even before the Immortal Wars. But now it's nothing but a ruin."

As they approached the black-bricked barbican of Harlot's Hold, Adam calmly dismounted from his horse and took a few steps forward.

"Who goes there?" called a guard standing atop the battlements.

"Barrik? It's me, Adomas." The other wardens in the back called out, too. "Quiet!" he ordered, and each of them quickly went silent.

"Captain? You're alive? Who are these men you bring?"

"They're friends. They have come to help us," responded Adam.

Barrik turned to a nearby soldier hidden from sight. The inaudible discourse seemed to lengthen as the two disagreed on a way forward. "Hold on. I need to bring this to the attention of the Commander."

"Oh, for fuck's sake, Barrik!" shouted Thane from afar. "Open the fuckin' gate, or I'll shove this lance so far up your arse you'll be our new fucking banner!"

"Thane!" barked Adam angrily as the rest remained silent.

The portcullis suddenly shifted, and to everyone's astonishment, it too rose as the internal doors behind it followed suit.

"Nothing like asking nicely, huh, Thane?" added Brandt whilst the column of knights began moving into the Hold as the midday sun rose above their heads.

As the knights entered, more Wardens emerged from the halls and barracks surrounding the bailey. Their faces told a series of tales. Some seemed excited, others suspicious, and some still bore the marks of the night of the Drae'shï's assault. The keep also displayed the scars of the fight. A gaping hole was still visible like an open wound where Lilith's cell had formerly stood. The walls, too, showed the scuffs of swords and the bashes of maces whilst the training dummies were now equipped with blood-stained Drae'shï armour.

As Adam and his companions entered, the Saints were directed towards the southern bailey whilst the onlookers stood amazed at the cohort their companions brought in. As the returning Wardens dismounted, their close friends ran to greet them. Thane roughed up his subordinates whilst Brandt hugged his mates. Arren, Doran, Willam, and Samos each shook and hugged their friends. Adam, too, was greeted with a few solid pats on the back, but all he saw was the stern look of Commander Dorreth's piercing blue eyes.

"You disobeyed a direct order, Captain," proclaimed Dorreth.

"I know I did, but—"

"I should have you hanged from the ramparts. You and all your unit." He pointed viciously at each of their faces.

"Commander," intervened Doran, seeking to appeal to the man with his own age and maturity. "We were acting—"

"Silence!" shouted the old Eldassari as the rest of the Wardens stopped their joyous reunion. He looked Adam up and down in contempt. "Just like Greyson! Always acting first, thinking later. Selfishly. Stupidly. Never knowing one's place," he spat before turning to the rest. "First, you disobey me by keeping that Drae'shï woman here. Then you chase after her, after the rest of the Drae'shï came thrashing through the gates. You were all needed here amongst your brothers! Helping us rebuild, tending to the wounded, and burying the dead, not scurrying off after the first Drae'shï you see!" he bellowed, causing everyone in the courtyard to shudder. "The one reason I wasn't going to have you lot hanging from these walls right now was that we've so few left that your sorry useless hides are still better than nothing. But now, seeing as you got us additional mouths to feed, give me one reason why I should not reconsider making an example of you."

"Because by tracking the Drae'shï woman, he managed to discover and eliminate the Drae'shï that felled your good men and to bring us here to aid you against their next wave," intervened Tilus as he emerged from the crowd, removing his riding gloves.

"And I presume you are the leader of these knights?"

"Aye. I am Commander Tilus Maxwell, Knight Disciple of the Order of the Saints, and commander to the fourth Legion of the Order," said Tilus, nodding to Dorreth, yet the Eldassari didn't acknowledge.

"So, then, Commander. What do you do to the men who disobey your orders? Do you reward them? Provide them with horses, trinkets, and gold?"

"No. Death is often the price for insubordination. However, we, too, know the importance of our mission and what we stand for." Tilus paused a moment to look at the barbican once again. The archway framed Ussar Varys in the distance, and upon it were the words, "To guard and protect the world from the darkness within."

"As Commander to my legion, I, too, have faced such a difficult decision. But I also remember that I serve the same cause. What devotion to our values would I inspire in my men if I punished those who risked their lives to uphold them?"

All seemed to nod as Dorreth stared him down, hiding his frustration and impatience.

Dorreth paused and then let out a long, frustrated sigh. "Another bloody idealist." Dorreth rubbed his temples and winced. "Fine, fine! But they still disobeyed orders, and as a commanding officer, you also know this cannot go unpunished, lest it inspires more courageous acts of insubordination from others. Tell me then, what do you recommend I do, Commander Maxwell, in this case? Twenty, thirty lashes?"

"And have them spend the next few days unable to do anything? No, no. Definitely not. I wouldn't let them off that easy," said Maxwell confidently as he looked around, observing the state of the grounds and the gaping hole in the keep. "They can start by fixing that hole and all the other damaged parts of the Hold's battlements. After that, they can help take care of all sixty-four of our horses as we settle into your southern bailey, with your permission, of course. I believe that hauling stones and shovelling shit for a few weeks ought to set the chain of command straight again, wouldn't it?"

Dorreth smiled at the cunning of Maxwell's intent. He mused for a second, turning serious the next. "Six weeks! Including latrine duty!" he barked. All the Wardens, save Adam, blew a soft sigh of relief. Dorreth turned to Adam's serious gaze. "Now, get out my sight."

CHAPTER 13

KINDNESS OF ANGELS

Day broke over the ridge, and the distant din of the port of Yammimer came in carried by the soft saline breeze of the sea. The carriage that had rattled for the last week on a long bumpy dirt road to the coast had now become a comforting cradle for those within, except when the occasional pothole came as a rude awakening.

"God, bloody hell!" cursed Alistair as he almost fell out of his velvet cushioned seat. The corpulent man stirred and shifted as Adara and Lilith, also seated across from him, slowly came to their senses. "Apologies, my ladies," he said, squirming awkwardly in his seat as he saw Adara sneak a chuckle. He soon turned to his metal window and slid it open.

"Good morning, Your Excellency," said a knight escort riding alongside the carriage.

"Is it too much to ask you to keep this rolling hulk of steel out of all these potholes, Sir Martin?"

"Apologies, Your Excellency, but I'm afraid that after last night's showers, the roads will be a bit bumpy from all the runoff and hidden potholes."

"Alright, alright," he grumbled slightly behind his red and white whiskers.

"We will avoid them where we can, Your Excellency."

"And tell the bloody carriage makers that next time I will be travelling in a carriage made out of wood. I've broken my behind sitting in this box. I don't care about protection. Protect my arse first!" he responded jovially as the accompanying men surrounding the carriage cracked a few laughs.

Alistair stuck his head back in to notice Adara smiling at his jibes and Lilith wistfully looking out of her window. Alistair smiled back at Adara. "I'm sorry we couldn't find a more comfortable ride, my dear. Safety dictates that our posteriors must be sacrificed for our protection against bandits and thieves," he said sarcastically as he knocked on the hard metal frame of the carriage.

Lilith did not return a comment. She watch on, transfixed by the lands that lay before her. Compared to the sight of the sheer mountaintops and caverns of Ussar Varys she was used to, the landscape had now softened into the hills and valleys of Valdell. Where the Siensell River up north was merely a stream, down south it was a rumbling waterway separating the lands of Valdell and Iborellan. Where all she once saw was the limits of the dark halls of the Ussari Mountains, she now saw the infinity that lay in the sea and the horizon.

At the end of the Siensell river lay the port city of Yammimer. Yammimer was a greyish looking town. The city was spread over a small archipelago of river deltas partly walled and partly protected by nature's flowing water. A stronghold lay at the eastern side of the city, overlooking the port where hundreds of vessels and barges trailed back and forth across the channels and out towards the ocean through a long winding maze of islands. The city was bustling with travellers, farmers, and merchants coming from all nearby settlements. Some regularly ferried to and from Iborellan.

"Chirpy as always, are we, Uncle?" called Elias. Fresh as a rose, he rode up to the carriage in full armour atop his cataphract.

Adara opened her own window to greet her fiancé.

"Dearest! Day or night, your beauty doesn't ever seem to wane," he added, purposefully jesting in his pomposity as he reached out for her hand and kissed it gently.

Adara chuckled and smiled back. "Nor does your chivalry, my love," she said prolonging the jovial farce herself.

Alistair quickly popped his head back out. "Will it be long until we arrive? I'm getting hungry. And I need to stretch my legs. And..." He hesitated as Elias and Adara waited. "Well, you know. Must I really say so?"

"He needs to take the proverbial morning shit," interjected Zain as he looked over from the carriage's driver's seat.

"Thank you, Zain," responded Alistair, promptly.

"Always a pleasure," said Zain as Alistair's cheeks briefly reddened.

Adara and Elias both sniggered.

"We shall be arriving within the next couple of hours, Uncle. Think you can handle it?" Elias smiled.

"If this box doesn't keep banging me around at every turn!" said Alistair as the carriage took another stone straight under its wheel, causing him to tighten his grip on the windowsill.

"I sent an arrival party to handle everything last night. Lodging and breakfast will be awaiting us in the city. I shall be heading down there ahead of our arrival to ensure everything is set," added Elias.

"And after that?" said Lilith from within the carriage, still staring at the sea on the distant horizon.

"We go home, Lilith," he said confidently, smiling towards the open waters. "The Valen fleet has already arrived. We will head out and board one of our military vessels and sail south." He pointed.

"That's quite a large fleet, Elias. I count, five, six? Do we get to commandeer one each?" added Adara, cheerfully. Adara's formerly coy smile had now bloomed into full radiance after a few weeks in the company of her intended. The taste of adventure and freedom from the constraints of Cielith's tart social climate had seemed to blow fresh wind into her sails.

"Not just yet. Many of the knights will be heading north instead to reinforce Morren's Gate." He laughed.

"And how long will it take us to get to the south?" enquired Lilith as she continued to observe the antlike people busying their way through the city in and out of the gates and the little shanty towns that mushroomed outside the city walls.

"One week if we sail before the equinox. After that, the winds might not favour us," said Zain, promptly.

"Indeed," said Elias, astonished by his correct remark. "Have you been a seafarer, Zain?"

"Seafarer, you say?" Zain glamorously rose to his feet and swung around the edge of the carriage as if hanging off the ratlines of his own imaginary carrack. "Many, many moons ago in the treacherous seas of the Gulf of Dros, I, Zain, nay Captain Zain Thorne was—"

"Oh yes! I love the pirate stories!" Adara jumped with glee, clapping her hands in excitement. "I loved listening to the stories of Captain Zain Thorne as a child."

"Can we leave this until after we have had breakfast?" asked Lilith, anticipating yet another hour-long drama surrounding the infallible Vampire and his grossly exaggerated sense of self.

"Oh, come on, Lilith. Even you have to admit he knows how to tell a good story!" continued Adara. Her warmth was enough to curb even Lilith's biting remarks.

"What he doesn't seem to know is when to shut up," she said dryly.

Alistair burst out laughing. "The tongue on this one! Ha! She'll settle right in back home, Elias, don't you think? Are all the Drae'shï as sharp as you, my dear?"

"Only the nicest ones, Alistair," intervened Zain, sarcastically.

Lilith rolled her eyes and turned back to the view.

"My, my. We'd better get something in our bellies before our moods get any merrier." He laughed.

"Agreed, Uncle," said Elias. "I'll be going ahead of the column to ensure the arrival party has everything in order."

"I think I'll join you, Jurani. Clearly, my epics are not on the menu right now," said Zain as Lilith ignored his gaze, resting her cheek on her hand as she looked out of the window.

"Oh, come on, Zain, please stay! Lilith didn't mean that," pleaded Adara, reaching out to clasp his hand as he still hung from the side of the carriage.

"Another time, Adara." Zain smiled as he caught her warm, delicate hand. "But I, too, need to stretch my legs and have a look around," he said as he briskly let go, landing on the soft ground, and then hopping onto his horse, which had been tethered to the back of the carriage.

"Fine. Then off you go," she said briefly, feigning a frown and shortly after blowing a kiss to Elias and Zain as the two rode past.

Elias and Zain rode straight into Yammimer at the helm of a small unit of knights. The city smelt of brackish water as the fresh sea breeze had dwindled by the time they arrived. The city's outer walls served not only as a defence against the enemies of Valdell but also as a natural border between the rich and the poor. Many rundown houses were built carelessly around it, some half-sunken in the marshy lands and others serving as houses of ill repute or beggars' watering holes. Barges and makeshift loading docks peppered the banks as fishermen stood by, mending their nets and observing weary travellers and beggars entering the city every morning like drooped hags.

As the knights rode through, a path opened amongst the many locals who were startled by the presence of the Saints. Many looked at the white-clad knights entering as if the Massass himself passed by, reaching out in reverence and beseeching absolution in the form of coin or food. The knights rode on, ignoring the peasantry and trotting through the cobbled city. Valendrian guards patrolled the streets and waved carts and passers-by to stop as they went through. As the unit arrived at the heart of the city, the common rabble seemed to disperse only to open into the rowdiness of the mercantile atmosphere that surrounded the main square. The left side of the square held the mayor's hall tower, whilst on the other stood the renowned Marigold Inn. Between the two lay the archway entrance to the local temple of the Holy Enoch. Shops and hawkers were strewn across the market floor, barely leaving a path for a person to go through, let alone a cohort of knights.

"Rubin!" called Elias above the din, sounding somewhat irritated by the chaos enfolding him.

"Commander?" asked the knight astride.

"I thought I made myself clear yesterday. I wanted everything ready for our arrival. Why are these people crowding the path to the temple?"

"It's market day, Commander."

Elias was unmoved, staring at the empty reply. The knight sat on his horse, hesitant to explain further.

Elias immediately stiffened and turned to his unit. "Wren and Casthrem, head back to the column, inform Lyons of the situation. Let's just push through. Rubin, get a group of men and clear the path." He quickly turned to the passing aged Valendrian guards and announced, "You there. Inform the hawkers around the Marigold and the Temple to move, or they will be moved."

"But, sir. 'Tis market day. I cannot ask them to move," pleaded the corpulent guard as Elias signalled the unit.

"Do it," said Elias as he tossed a small purse to the guard, whose face suddenly lit up with a newfound sense of motivation. "If there's a single basket lying on the ground when I return, I'll have you flogged by the fountain," he continued sternly as he pointed to the monument in the centre of the square.

The guard's grin evaporated instantly as a look of dread came over his face. "Yes, sir!" he called loudly, suddenly turning to his comrade, who, without much hesitation, started shoving people out of the way. "Move! Outta the way!"

The unit soon gathered on the steps of the Marigold, a quaint two-storey cottage built in equal parts of stone and wood. The aged woodwork was inlaid with faded red, blue, and pink engravings of floral patterns, figurines and other springtide imagery that had long since seen its summer days. As the riders each dismounted, the many bums, strumpets, hawkers, and howlers shuffled from the terrace, shooed away by a tall gaunt woman brandishing a filthy overused dishcloth. "Oi, shove off! The Saints are 'ere! Clear out, you miserable shites. Oi, Petry, you better pay your ploughin' tab, or I'll tell your wife how you've been screwin' her blind behind her back!"

"Lilith's gonna love this." Zain laughed to himself as he made his way through the crowd.

"Not to worry. They will keep passing through and head directly into the temple grounds. I hope you didn't think I'd be allowing my future wife to lodge in the Marigold?" said Elias comfortably, as he removed his gloves and handed his reins to his steward. "This is lodging for the rest of the knights. And us for breakfast and an early ale, perchance?" he continued, calling out directly to the brazen woman whilst throwing another pouch of money into her hands.

"How many purses do you carry with you?" said Zain, turning a perplexed brow at Elias.

The woman beamed a toothy smile and headed back in, kicking off the last remaining bum sitting by the doorway.

Elias chuckled as he patted Zain on the back, leading him into the inn. The dimly lit inn was abuzz with merchants and travellers having their morning coffees and teas, regaling each other with tales of the previous nights and daily toils. All stood still for a moment as they watched the tall, dark Vampire and his white-caped companion step in from the light. The din resumed shortly, and the two sat at the only table that wasn't still stinking of day-old beer.

"Not as classy as I remember it," said Zain, as he perused the venue only to be shortly interrupted by the house lady's brash serving of ale, cheese, bread, and day-old cold chicken.

"Was always like this as far as I recall," said Elias from across the table as he broke a hunk of bread and took a bite, followed by a long sip of ale. Zain took a sip of his own and proceeded to take a small bite of cheese as Elias observed him. "Doesn't quite do it for you, does it?"

"Oh, don't worry, you wouldn't want to know what I'm used to. Just not sure how it does for you. Aren't you more accustomed to fine dining, given your coin tossing and all?"

"I can assure you there was no fine dining during my early years in the army. Thereafter though, you do tend to appreciate some of the simpler things in life. Plus, I haven't had a good beer in weeks. The Eldain's wine may be what it is, but nothing beats the hops."

"Don't tell Santhi that, or he'll call off the wedding!"

"That sensitive about wine, are they?"

"You have no idea. All the great houses of Cielith have their own, and all viciously compete for 'best vintage' every year." Zain laughed.

"You would think that with all their love of wine, they wouldn't be so incredibly stiff."

"Maybe it's because they don't have any ale around?" said Zain as they both laughed and knocked tankards.

"So, have you heard anything from Lord Crysanthani?"

"He's going to be your father-in-law, not the Massass. Lord Crysanthani! He's called Santhi for a reason." Zain laughed at the forced formality.

"Fine, Zain. Has Santhi sent word about the Shard?" His voice softened slightly. "Did his research yield any results?"

Zain paused, reminded of the knight's prying interest. "It's been two weeks," Zain mumbled as he sipped his ale and averted his gaze.

"Precisely," said Elias as the silence lengthened further.

"I don't know, Elias," said Zain, yet Elias' gaze lingered once more as Zain awkwardly gulped his beverage. "Look. All I know is that there are many myths and legends. One can barely keep track, let alone document it. I've been around for quite a while, and even I'm not sure what's history and what isn't. But believe me, if someone can get to the bottom of this, it's him." He directed his eyes away from the ambitious Saint, lest they might encourage further prodding.

"Fine," whispered Elias as his eyes lingered a few seconds longer. "Once we get back to the capital, we'll consult the Massass' library, too."

"Good idea," whispered Zain, unintentionally. "Also, why are we whispering?"

"Same reason we didn't discuss the matter further during the Elder Council. Spies," replied Elias.

Zain almost choked on his drink.

"You, Zain, may find all of this amusing, but I assure you it is not," said Elias straight-faced.

"I'm sorry," said Zain, wiping his mouth in the back of his hand, slightly embarrassed by his misreading of the situation.

"We are at war. You may be able to take a few arrows in the back and walk away unscathed, but in war, people die, and you know what kills more than arrows, famine, or plague? Espionage. Know when and where to attack, and the battle is half-fought for you. Feed the right misinformation, and you'll send an army right into a trap. But when that information betrays you, you have nothing left but to sleep with one eye open 'cause there's nothing that will protect you." Elias he kept prodding the table with each point he made.

"Fine, I get it. So, what's the issue with the Shard then?"

"We've all heard and seen what she was capable of doing with it. Speaking in tongues, besting an Eldassari man twice her size in a fist-fight... We need to be sure we're not underestimating a threat."

"Or missing an opportunity for that matter," responded Zain as he peeled Elias with his scrutinous gaze.

"It's war, Zain, and Lilith is now part of it. Of her own accord. I recommend you begin training her," said Elias rather flatly, almost as if giving an order.

"Excuse me? Train her to do what?" Zain raised an eyebrow.

"To fight and to make use of the Shard," he replied in all seriousness.

Zain sighed. "Elias, that thing is dangerous. I don't think you realise what you're dealing with. I'd rather we—"

"Zain," interrupted Elias as he looked Zain straight in the eyes, pausing momentarily as Zain showed no reaction whatsoever. "Either you are purposefully omitting something you know, which we will find out in due course, or you fail to see the importance of its use, which makes you a bad strategist. An article of such power, manifest or otherwise, is not something I'm prepared to let fall into the hands of my, or our, enemies or let go to waste in our fight against them."

"So much for your offer of protection. Already planning to use her for her power?"

"Don't play the fool. You, of all people, should know the ways of the world by now. How long have you been alive? Six hundred, seven hundred years? And you want to have me believe you know nothing of this?" said Elias, smiling but not contemptuous. "All our interests are aligned—mine, yours and hers, my friend. So cut the crap. Also, how do I know that it is not you who's playing us all for fools and have your own idea of what to do with the mirror?" He smiled devilishly.

"As you may recall, I told you how it scared the life out of me just by looking at it."

"Or so you said," he teased.

"Elias, is this an interrogation?" asked Zain seriously as he took a long hard sip of his ale and softly but decisively placed his mug upon the table. Annoyance now welled within him.

A long pause lay between the two.

"Ha! Of course not." Elias laughed, seemingly attempting to diffuse the tension that he'd knowingly orchestrated. "Having a good old verbal sparring match with the Death of the Undeath."

"Sizing me up, are you?" asked Zain, still unconvinced.

"Would I rather have the Death of the Undeath on my side or against me?" Elias smiled as he pointed a crust of bread at Zain before biting down on it and drinking a long draught of ale. "I know a good person when I see them. I know you do not covet power, and I also see why you're here by the way you look at her."

"Nonsense," scoffed Zain, half-embarrassed.

"You're an Eldarï. She's an Eldarï. Must get lonely roaming the world without companionship for all eternity."

"Oh, shut up. Hey, madam! Another round here. Gotta' drink myself stupid if I'm to keep having this conversation," called Zain across the room as the ale he'd previously downed slowly crept up on him. "First of all, we're not Eldarï. We are descendants of the Eldarï. Second, I'm Eldaresh, and she's Drae'shï."

"Third, you make a lovely couple." Elias laughed. "Brooding exotic beauty meets—"

"Wouldn't consider myself brooding—"

"Not you, fool."

"Right," said Zain as the barkeep brought another round, and he quickly took another long swig.

"Anyway, it's quaint, appropriate, if I may say so myself. If you're not after the mirror, then why are you here? Why do you even care? Why go to such lengths to protect her? There are so many better places to see, and where are you now?" He sipped again, now visibly more entertained by this conversation than the previous discussion.

"I have nowhere else to be. The world is my home," mused Zain wistfully.

"The world is a big place, Zain. Too big even for an old soul like you. Maybe it's time to go home." Elias smiled.

"Didn't you hear? I have no home."

"You still don't see it, do you? Seven hundred years, and you still don't get it. Then perhaps let me help you, my immortal friend. Perhaps you should stop thinking of home as a place and start thing of it as a person. Clear enough?" Elias smiled as he took the last sip of his first mug before stepping up from his bench as Zain stood pondering his words. "It's too early for me to knock back another pint. You can have mine. Get some rest. I need to make sure everything's in place for their arrival," He gathered his sword and helm and wrapped his white cape around his shoulder.

"Zain, train her." He smiled. "She may speak everyone's language, but hers is that of steel. 'Children of Iron', aren't they, after all, the Drae'shï?" he said just before heading out into the sunlight once again.

"Indeed, they are."

<hr>

The clamour of people resounded throughout the city as the Saints moved through its streets. A short, dishevelled man barged into the Marigold, followed by the din of the street as he shut the door behind him.

"And fuck off. Fuckin' Saints actin' like they own the fuckin' place," yelled the drunk as he cursed the world behind him.

Zain groaned as he slowly awoke from his mid-morning nap.

"Yorin! Shut up! Or you'll wake the poor fella up," said the barkeep as she proceeded to pour out a tankard of ale for the bumbling boar of a patron.

"Been up for a while now." Zain yawned as he curled upright from the corner he was reclined in. "What time is it?"

"'Tis past noon," she replied.

"Well then. Time to head off," said Zain as he slowly stretched his long limbs and proceeded to head over to the bar and take a sip of Yorin's untouched ale.

"Oi!" barked Yorin.

"Settle down, my friend. No need to get all angsty," replied Zain as he tossed a coin onto the counter and walked out, tankard in hand, whilst the rest giggled.

A sea of people stood outside gathered in the market square, Zain, tall as a post, was able to observe the scene, clutching his drink as people rudely brushed up against him, forcing their way through the crowds that gathered. The Saints' column was passing through with majestic presence. Some people begged, some cheered, some scoffed, and others were merely trying to get on with their day, but the Saints, in their white capes and upon their cataphracts, remained a sight to be seen within the squalor of Yammimer.

Zain slowly made his way through the crowd and climbed onto the rim of the fountain crowded with a horde of rascals attempting to glimpse Alistair's carriage coming through. "I'll see you in the temple," he called out to Adara, who was curiously watching through the window of the carriage.

Adara quickly leaned out to wave as she noticed him.

"There you are! This place is amazing!" she shouted as she almost hung out of the carriage.

Zain smiled at her inexorable enthusiasm and ability to see the beauty in everything.

Meanwhile from within the carriage, Lilith watched Adara gaze at the welcoming cheers and excitement of the people, despite their lowly brows, dirty hands, and missing teeth. The Eldain waved at the cheering crowd, who were seemingly enamoured with their foreign visitor more than anything else.

"I've never gotten such a warm welcome anywhere I've been. Is this the treatment you get everywhere you go, Your Excellency?" she asked as she quickly popped back in.

Alistair laughed. "The crowd cheers the Order and the Massass, not me. Though such a large contingency is rarely sent so far from the capital."

"Well, it sure seems like a joyous occasion for them." She popped her head back out to gaze at the crowd.

"Get in, Adara. It's not safe," said Lilith, sitting across from her.

"It's so exotic. I feel like I'm on a real adventure," she replied turning her head in and dashing a quick blissful smile back at them.

Alistair chuckled at her enthusiasm. "However, she's right, my child. Yammimer is no—"

Suddenly, Adara gave a loud yelp as her head knocked back when someone outside tugged on her hair.

"Adara!" yelled Zain from across the square as he thrashed through the crowd.

Lilith and Alistair desperately began pulling Adara as they spotted a short lass clad in rags clamber onto the edge of the carriage with a knife between her teeth unbeknownst to the escorting cavalry.

"My hair!" screamed Adara as the woman pulled herself closer, attempting to look into the cabin.

"Stop! Stop the carriage! Lyons!" yelled Zain at the Saints, who all failed to notice his signals.

Lilith swore, climbed over, and flung the cabin door open. The heel of her boot landed square in the chest of the young woman, who crashed down onto the filthy cobblestones, her satchel spilling a myriad of vials, ointments, and trinkets.

The carriage stopped immediately, and the Saints finally rushed to their aid.

The crowd went silent.

"What's going on here?" roared Lyons as the crowd stood awestruck by the ominous presence of a living Drae'shï perched proudly on the step of the carriage.

All froze for a moment, having never seen a Drae'shï, and even the wheezing culprit found herself in shock. Lilith stood, head held high, upon the top step of the carriage, revelling in the view as she gazed at the crowd under a brewing sea of whispers.

"Get in, you," sneered Lyons. "Before you make matters worse."

Lilith looked down at Lyons with utter contempt, narrowing her eyes before defiantly turning her gaze to the woman who lay stunned, staring with her big smoky green eyes.

Lyons begrudgingly turned his scowl away from Lilith as the rest of the guards came through. The woman, startled by her hesitation, suddenly attempted to scurry off, yet Lyons caught her by her frizzy hair and dragged her back into full view. "What have we got here?" he taunted deviously as he crushed one vial after another, dragging her along with him 'til he picked up her knife.

"Let me go, asshole! Let go!" she cried as she struggled to fit her dirty little tattoo-covered hands between Lyons' massive grip.

"There you go." He let go of her hair only to slap her with the back of his gauntlet. "It's twenty lashes and a bath for you," he said as the crowd and knights laughed. "After that, it's the gallows. May this serve you all as a reminder that no finger shall be laid on any person under the protection of the Saints." He pointed to the crowd.

"No!" cried Adara as she stuck herself through the window. "She didn't hurt me. There is no need."

"I wasn't trying—" said the girl, but Lyons interrupted her with another slap.

"This wretch attempted to take your life, M'lady," said Lyons, signalling a knight to take the ronyon into custody as the crowd slowly returned to its usual chatter. "She will be dealt with accordingly."

"Please, Sir Lyons. She's just a beggar."

"It is the law, Lady Crysanthani. Now please forgive me."

"Let it go, Adara," added Lilith as she turned inside.

"No! I won't have it." Her voice was now drowned by the noise of the crowd returning to its cheers. "Elias will hear of this!"

"Carry on." Lyons signalled to the coachman. "Let's get them inside. Back off!" he roared at the people as he moved back to the front of the column and mounted his horse.

"Make way, damn it!" shouted Zain as he finally broke through the crowd. "Adara! Get inside! Lilith, take her in!"

Lilith nodded and immediately drew Adara into the cabin and shut the door.

"Let me go! How could you?" she yelled.

"She almost had you by the throat. You're lucky to be alive," said Lilith bluntly as she looked straight into Alistair's eyes, seemingly also stricken with fright.

Adara panted, as she held her chest, staring at the floor, attempting to regain her composure. She tucked her hair behind her right ear.

"Come now, my dear. Sit by my side," said Alistair softly as he drew Adara onto his seat by her delicate hands. "Sadly, the world is a much more dangerous place than Threlis Manor and Cielith."

"I know that. Still, there was no need."

"Maybe you are right, but this time we were lucky. These are times of war, my dear. Many are out to harm the Massass and the members of his family. We've had incidents before, sadly. Elias' mother and sisters were victims of such treachery when he was but a boy. This is why the Saints are so protective," he said calmly, his deep voice now soothing as ever. "Do you know how the Saints came to be, Lilith?"

"No, but it looks like I'm about to find out," she replied, understanding Alistair's ploy to placate the distressed Eldain.

"Well, some two hundred years ago, there was a great man known as Erinderiss the Kind. More affectionately known as Eru. He was a man of infinite wisdom and a master medician. During a great plague that struck the city, he took a branch of an Enoch tree and planted it in the middle of the floor of the hall of lords in Valendria. Its construction had been halted for many months. Everyone thought it was for nought, for Enoch trees took at least one hundred years to mature and another hundred to bear any sap that is fit for medicinal use. However, the plant took to the fallow ground and flourished in a single season. One season!"

"And the Saints?" intervened Lilith as she tapped her fingers on her crossed arms.

"They're coming. They're coming. Anyway, just like Massassi Itheru did two hundred years before, Eru began to heal everyone who flocked for assistance to the hall which eventually became the Grand Temple of the Holy Enoch. Soon the Valens began to follow him as he taught them the rituals and techniques to use the Enoch tree for their ailments. He explained the story of the Great Mother and the values of the Eldarï passed down through the ages from Massassi himself. Just before Eru died, he asked his favourite disciple Lotheo to inscribe upon the walls of the temple the sum of his teachings; this became the Canticle of Lotheo. It's really beautiful. You ought to hear it," he continued.

"I have heard about it. Though never in song," said Adara softly.

"And the Saints," insisted Lilith, impatience brewing further.

"Yes, the Saints," said Alistair as he cleared his throat. "Unfortunately, Lotheo was not the only disciple of Eru, and many of the powerful families of Valdell vied to make use of the power that had amassed around him. Lotheo was a strong, disciplined, and incorruptible man—Lotheo the Golden, they called him. But sadly, he was still a *man*. And one day, during his daily healing of the sick that still visited him personally in his old age, he was murdered in cold blood. This sparked a riot that lasted for weeks until Aiden, Lotheo's brother and also a disciple of the Enoch, gathered a group of men-at-arms to quell the mob and bring the conspirators to justice. They were later hailed as the saint protectors of the Enoch. Aiden later took on the role and title of Massass—leader of the temple. Eventually, the Order of the Saints was formally established by Aiden as the sworn protectors of the Massass."

"No wonder they're so protective of their cargo," added Lilith as she knocked on the metal carriage that enclosed them.

"Alistair, are they going to harm that girl?" asked Adara, seemingly saddened by the tale.

Alistair sighed and quickly smiled. "I tell you what. We'll speak to Elias when we arrive. If there's nothing to worry about, I'm sure he'll be happy to grant you your wish. He's very fond of you, after all. As am I of your kindness, my dear." He smiled as he took her hand, kissing it affectionately and spurring back the brightness in her eyes that shortly disappeared. "Perhaps we can take a leaf out of the book of Adara the Magnanimous." Alistair laughed as he looked back at Lilith, content with himself. "Don't you think?"

"Or Adara the Deceased at this rate," she said quietly to herself, looking away.

"Pish-posh! I'll be more careful next time, I promise." Adara beamed at Lilith, throwing a dismissing hand at her comment. "I also know you'll be there to protect me."

"You're too good," said Lilith flatly as Adara switched seats, hooking her arm, and smiling at her.

The carriage slowly came to a final stop and a knock followed shortly. Lilith swiftly slid the viewing shutter open, revealing her scarlet eyes from the darkness.

"We have arrived, M'lady," said the Saint.

Lilith gazed past the guard, observing the calm of the temple garden. She quickly closed the shutter and opened the carriage door. Lilith emerged first, ignoring the helping hand of the knight. Adara and Alistair followed.

The large green enclosure was surrounded by high white walls and tall cedar trees, which deadened the noise of the city. At the centre of the field lay a small artificial islet with a short footbridge. The island supported a magnificent tall Enoch tree enclosed in an ornate stone frame, inspired by the ancient Eldarï and their architecture. Beautiful statues adorned the columns of the frame, all capturing the essence of figures of old, from Erinderiss the Kind to Massassi Itheru and various knights of the Order.

The Enoch tree stood almost forty feet high with a massive white trunk and roots that draped into the waters surrounding it. Each frond was covered in a shimmer of leaves, which shone green on top and white on the bottom. At the centre of the trunk, almost inlaid within its growth, lay a large stone statue. A beautiful Eldarï woman was cast into its form, draped in a veil that ran to its feet. She carried no discerning features but held a large, tilted flagon, from which dripped a slow trickle of silver sap that fell straight into a marble basin at her feet. The basin was fitted within an enclosed shrine, open only to the trickle of Enoch's sap.

"It's beautiful," said Adara as she looked around the temple grounds.

"Yammimer's temple was built fairly recently, but the tree itself was planted over a hundred years ago. It has just reached maturity," said Alistair.

Lilith watched as Adara returned to her element, tossing her shoes aside and walking on the freshly mowed lawn.

"Just wait 'til you see the one in Valendria, Adara! That, my dear, I think you'll find would put even the most stunning Eldain palaces to shame."

"Only humans could end up worshipping an Enoch tree," said Lilith, as she walked closer to the shrine.

"And only a Drae'shï who hasn't seen the world in centuries could come to such a wrong conclusion," intervened Elias as he emerged from behind the tree.

"Elias!" called out Adara, who ran to meet him as he crossed the ornate bridge of the islet. He kissed her hand softly, followed by her cheek.

"Glad to see you made it in one piece," said Elias.

"Almost," added Lilith.

"Almost?"

"Yes, well, Elias, there was a minor altercation," muttered Alistair, seemingly fearful of Elias' potential overreaction.

"What happened?" enquired Elias sternly.

"It was nothing, Elias. Some peasant girl got a little bit too excited. Nothing happened, really. It was my mistake. I wasn't paying attention," placated Adara. "She did no harm."

"Apart from taking a chunk of your hair," said Lilith, arms crossed.

"Oh tosh, Lilith! That was hardly the case. She barely touched me."

Lilith scoffed whilst Elias was visibly confused. "What happened, Adara? Did she hurt you?" he said as he held her by the arms looking all about her.

"No! I promise!" Adara took Elias' hands, stopping his inspection. "She must have tried to steal my necklace. She looked poor and hungry. I'm fine, no really, please."

"She'd have almost had your neck had I not kicked her off," said Lilith.

Elias cursed to himself. "Lyons was meant to be watching you. This is unacceptable," he spat as he threw his arms in the air and stalked around fuming, just as the rest of the column came through the gates.

"Elias, please, there is no need. Please do not punish her," pleaded Adara, reaching out to grab him as the last knights rode in, dragging along with them the dirty young girl, who was tied firmly at the wrists and forced to keep up with the pace of their horses.

"Elias! That's horrible! She can barely stand. Please, release her," Adara pleaded. "I know it is not my place to ask anything of you and your station, but please tell them to let her go before they do any harm."

"Yes. Before Lyons decides to punish her like he tried to punish me," said Lilith bluntly.

All recognised her reference but were too embarrassed to acknowledge it.

Elias took a deep breath, shaking his head as he held his forehead.

"Well, she is rather scrawny to do any real damage. We're all a little riled up after this journey," said Alistair, cutting through the silence.

As the knights and their captive drew closer, a priest scurried ahead of them towards Alistair. "Your Excellency!" he said hurriedly as he bent his knee and kissed Alistair's right hand. "I apologise for the lack of formality, but I must ask you to intercede with the Saints."

"Calm down, brother. What is the matter?" asked Alistair, calmly attempting to soothe the old medician.

"That prisoner they bring. She cannot be brought onto these hallowed grounds."

"I can assure you she will be of no danger to any of the medicians. In fact, we plan on releasing her soon," said Alistair as he looked back at Elias and Adara.

"No, Your Excellency. You cannot do that either. We cannot just release her under the public eye," he insisted.

"Then what would you have me do? You don't want her here, but you don't want her out? This is not the time to be buttering one's bread on both sides." He laughed briefly as he turned to Elias and Adara.

"You don't understand, Your Excellency. She's a soothsayer—"

"Oh brother, you know the Order does not hold diviners in contempt of the law," interrupted Alistair casually as he turned back to the girl.

"But, she's not just that. She's also—"

"A Cleriheu…" said Alistair begrudgingly as the girl came within a closer view.

The girl was short, skinny, and of olive complexion. Not older than twenty-seven. She had dirty sallow skin, which was laden with hundreds of runes, glyphs, and symbols tattooed from head to toe, giving her an eerie guise of mysticism. Her hair was curly and short, parts braided, and others held together with beads and other charms. Her scent and sombre posture gave away a life of poverty. Her sullen eyes shone one of persecution. Despite all the dismay and dirty outer appearance, a uniquely pretty face with big green eyes lay behind the mask and not that of a hag.

"She must not be allowed on the grounds," said the medician once more. "We had been telling the city guard to take care of her, but they couldn't be bothered. I told them it was against the law to allow her to roam about the city. This trickster, this- this charlatan, has been spreading all sorts of nonsense. Selling *magical* trinkets and medical *charms* to the townsfolk and performing all sorts of cunning arts, all in breach of the Edict of Medicians."

"I understand. We will address the matter, brother. Please carry on with your duties. I will see to it myself with the commander. Commander, we must speak, in private," said Alistair, his casual demeanour quickly washed away.

"Yes, Your Excellency," answered Elias with equal formality.

"Alistair? Elias?" asked Adara. "What's happened? What's going on?"

"We will speak soon, dearest, but for now, fear not, the girl will not be harmed until the matter is resolved," he replied as he kissed her hands once again and proceeded to head with Alistair and the medician to the groundkeeper's quarters.

"Resolved?" said Adara, perplexed.

"I wouldn't hold my breath," intervened Lilith.

"You think they're going to hurt her?"

"Clearly, whatever she did or whatever she is goes beyond our little scuffle."

"So? I'm sure they're not going to do anything to her. He wouldn't deny my request so blatantly." Adara was seemingly attempting to reassure herself.

"Even *you* know that these knights don't take orders from their wives," replied Lilith candidly.

"He's not taking orders from his wife-to-be, Lilith! I told him there's nothing to worry about." Her angst grew once more.

"Not in the least," said Lilith, dryly.

Adara fumed. "Why do you always have to be such an insufferable know-it-all?" she rebuffed, annoyed at the Drae'shi's insinuations.

"I know nothing. I just observe. And what I see are liars, schemers, and tyrants."

"Elias was right. How can you possibly understand the world when all you know is life under that mountain?" she spat.

Lilith laughed. "For that matter, Cielith might as well have been buried under one as far as you're concerned."

"You don't know what you're talking about," Adara said, frustrated.

"You're right. What do I know of good and evil?" said Lilith, smiling as she proceeded to walk away.

"He wouldn't lie to me so blatantly. To my face."

"You're right. He wouldn't." She paused and slowly turned. "Just like you wouldn't lie to him so blatantly to his to spare the girl's life."

CHAPTER 14

ALMS TO THE WISE

Night had fallen on Yammimer, and the daytime chatter turned into a subtle murmur. The streets were calm and clear, only disturbed by the occasional drunk returning home after his evening binge. The Marigold was abuzz, and the knights celebrated their last stop before the next journey. The temple grounds were less entertaining but carried their own charm as crickets and fireflies gave the soft shimmer of the islet's water its own magical allure.

The late summer's eve carried a cool breeze of salt and rosemary, and the Saints still on duty set themselves up a brazier in the grounds away from the main quarters. The sentries stood guard until a tall subtle figure emerged out of the darkness.

"I've come to enquire as to the state of the prisoner and to bring her this meal," said Zain, approaching the men and uncovering a bowl of porridge and rye.

"Without any instructions from command, M'lord?" asked one of the knights.

"What? Do you want an edict from the Massass?" asked Zain, frustrated, scratching the back of his neck.

"Fine, fine. No need to get snappy. In that tent right there. She's tied up to the centre pole. Morrain, come here, feeding duty," said the knight to another.

Morrain groaned.

"Don't worry, I'll handle it myself," said Zain.

"Are you sure, M'lord? She's not very compliant, to say the least."

"She spits," intervened one knight.

"Filthy heathen," spat another.

"I'm sure," answered Zain as he proceeded to walk to the dimly lit tent.

Inside were a number of crates, sacks and other supplies. The room was cramped and cold. A small dim lantern hung from the top of the centre pole, barely oozing any light, much like the girl tied firmly beneath it.

"Savages," he said as he picked up a nearby candlestick and proceeded to replace the dwindling flame.

The Cleriheu soon raised her tired gaze.

"I came to bring you food," said Zain as he crouched down to show her what he'd brought.

The young woman squinted slightly, unable to rub her eyes. She squirmed in her seat, sneezed, and coughed.

Zain looked around and managed to find a spare canvas to cover her in. He found a small pail, flipped it, and sat before her. He proceeded to drape the woman with the sheet as best he could. "This is as much as I can do for now. You're lucky Adara is such a softy."

The woman did not respond.

"Fine, we don't need to talk, but I'm sure you're hungry. So, come on, let's go." He grabbed the bowl and dipped the spoon in and proceeded to place it in front of her face yet she offered no opening. Zain insisted, but again the woman was not responsive. "Oh, come on. Listen, I'm hungry, too, you know. So, take my advice. When someone offers it to you, bloody well take it." He huffed as he scratched the back of his ear anxiously before ruffling his hair in frustration. He slowly exhaled, calming himself as the woman looked back with a raised eyebrow.

Once again, he attempted to persuade her. "Look, it's good, mmm," he said with a forced smile. He stirred the porridge around and pretended to eat, bringing the spoon to his wide-open mouth and brandishing his unmistakable canines. "Ahh."

The woman's eyes widened, and her face turned grim. "Vampir! Fiend! Get away!" she exclaimed in her peculiarly foreign accent, turning her face away and struggling to pull herself away. She screamed.

"Goddammit," he huffed.

"Get away! Away! Vampyr! Be gone!" She squirmed violently in her space, kicking at his feet.

"For fuck's sake!"

"Guard! Guard!" she yelped.

"Shh! Calm down!" insisted Zain as he placed his hand on her mouth. "Calm down! Shh! I'm not going to hurt you. Understand?"

She suddenly did the biting herself.

"Fuck me!" yelled Zain as he struggled to get his hand out of her teeth before flying onto the floor, porridge and all.

Morrain quickly dashed in to see the odd spectacle of the two, one covered in filth and the other in porridge. "Are you alright, sir?" Morrain smiled, clearly aware of what had happened.

"Yes, yes. Help me up, will you?" replied Zain as he wiped the slop off his chest.

Morrain helped Zain up. "You're too kind with them. You need to show them who's in charge. Especially these folk."

She scoffed. "Kindness. What would you know about kindness?"

Morrain picked up the half-empty bowl of porridge and walked over to his prisoner. "What do you know about decency? Purity? Piety?" he asked as he poured the remaining contents over her head.

"Hey! Stop that!" Zain reached out to Morrain.

"She can either eat her dinner or wear it." He smirked. "It's about time she learnt some manners."

The girl looked up and spat as far as she could onto the knight but fell short of his face, landing it on his chest. She grinned a dirty grin, still proud of her shot.

"You piece of shit!" Morrain exclaimed as he raised his hand to strike her only to be caught mid-strike by Zain.

"That's enough. Leave," Zain said angrily as he pushed the man back. "And give me that," he added as he snatched the water bottle hanging from Morrain's waist. "Get out," mouthed Zain showing his teeth.

Morrain stood, confused and taken aback, and then turned heel without a word.

"Are you alright?"

"Thanks for that. And sorry," she replied under her breath, seemingly repentant of her previous misgivings.

"It's fine. Quite a bite you've got there. Here, hold on." Zain poured water into his cupped hand and rinsed her face and wiped the porridge off her head. Beneath the grime was a clear, clean face, unlike the one he'd first seen, yet his hand now smelled of fermented fish and algae. He grimaced. "What the hell is this?"

"Ointment, Vampyr. Keeps away the mosquitoes and ticks."

"And the general population, too," he said as he fed her the bottle for a short drink.

"You try to live ten feet away from the river docks and tell me which you would prefer." She paused. "Are you not here for blood?" she queried hesitantly.

"No. No blood, not human blood, at least. Not in a long time," he said. "I'm Zain. Zayen."

"I'm Pïshkah," she said slowly.

"You're far away from home, Pïshkah. Lothumos is a long way from here."

"So is Dos Narak, Vampyr."

She groaned, shifting as she tried to ease the rope's tight grip around her wrists. Zain peeked over and frowned. He reached behind her, fumbling at the ropes, attempting to loosen their grip but failed. "Damn it. I can't loosen them. It seems like this is as comfortable as it's going to get, Pïshkah."

He sighed, and so did she.

"Pïshkah, why did you attack the lady in the carriage?" He mimicked the hair-pulling incident.

"I... I did not," she hesitated. "I did not mean to attack her."

"Seems to me that you did."

"I swear I did not mean it!"

"They why? What could an innocent Eldain girl possibly do to offend you so much as to drive you to mount a guarded carriage and try to drag her out by her hair with a knife no less?" Zain argued.

Pïshkah gave no response.

"Nothing?"

"Alright. I was trying to steal her necklace."

"Mounting a Saint's guarded carriage, in broad daylight? For a necklace? Bullshit," he said flatly, crossing his arms. "Really? Do I look like I was born yesterday? No! 'Cause I'm seven hundred years old. Quite literally."

"I swear!"

"You swear an awful lot for a Cleriheu. Which is also why I know you're lying. I've known my fair share of cunning folk, and even though you're the first one I've seen in these parts, I know that Clerihei are never in want of money."

"Times have been tough."

"Nonsense. Every bleeding sod in the city comes running to one of you the moment they have the coin to spare, whether it's for your fortune telling, well-wishing, or curing the sniffles. Half these people wouldn't go near the temple unless they were actually dying."

"Yes, and why do you think I'm in need of coin? The guards have been clamping down on us now more than ever before. If you're not a medician of the temple, you're nobody, no matter how good you are. Thanks to the war your Massass started with the Carthosians and the severance of all non-medicians from making use of the Enoch's vitaserum. We're denied what is for everyone's use and benefit. The Eldarï did not leave those trees here for the Massass. They left them for mankind!"

Zain started laughing. "You're good. I'll give you that." He sat on the pail, wagging his finger at her. "But whilst I fully agree with your rhetoric—absolute tragedy, I must say, by the way— firstly, as an Eldaresh, I don't partake in these petty squabbles of belief led by men. Secondly, I answer to no one, not even the Massass. And thirdly, we both know the Shirra and the Edict of Medicians has been going on for a few years now, so don't come telling me that this is news to you."

Pïshkah snorted in frustration.

"Pïshkah. Listen here. It's already bad enough that you're a Cleriheu. You know how self-righteous these guys get about non-medicians practising curative arts and other superstitious mumbo-jumbo. Now, they're also getting quite paranoid about Carthosian spies. Needless to say, attacking a guarded convoy of Saints is so deftly idiotic that I doubt you are an assassin, given your... profession." He pointed up and down at her. "That or else you're just wearing an excellent disguise, but you're downright crazy."

"Maybe I am." She humoured him, sneering.

"Maybe you are," he replied immediately, staring at her blankly.

She paused, but Zain gave no response. She huffed. "Fine! The truth is, I was after her, and yes, I did want to steal. Not harm, just steal."

"Go on."

"Well, I wanted some of her hair."

"What? Her hair?"

"Yes. When she stood out of the carriage, at first, I thought nothing of it. But then, the moment I realised she was Eldain, I had to take a lock."

"Rubbish, Pïshkah! I'm done with this. Good luck. Maybe they won't roast you." He rose from his seat.

"No! It's true! Zain! Please. The girl's hair has certain properties! It's very valuable! Just a bit of the hair of an Eldain maiden can make the perfect aphrodisiac or the strongest love charm to bind a lover."

"Bullshit, Pïshkah! Piss off." He began walking out.

"Yes, I know it's bullshit!" She broke.

Zain stopped.

"But that's the point, you ass! What do you think these folk will pay when I sell them some charm or potion laced with Eldain maiden's hair? And a beautiful one at that. Why do you think I did it? So that everyone could see. It's how I survive, charms and bullshit. There, fucking happy? Now, get lost! If you want to burn me alive, so be it. You wouldn't be the first Vampire to have the blood of innocents on your hands, would you?"

Zain sighed and ran his hands through his hair. "The shit she puts me through"

"Who?"

"The girl whose hair you wanted. Do you know that the only reason you're not being hoisted up a pole is because she felt sorry for you? She actually blamed herself to spare you the rod."

"I see. Is she your—"

"Lover? No. But she's like a daughter to me."

"Well, for all its worth tell..."

"Adara."

"Tell Adara, thank you for trying."

"I will."

They paused and stood in silence for a moment.

"What about the other one? The silver-skinned woman? The one who was less forgiving," began Pïshkah once more.

"Oh, yes. She's a treat."

"Drae'shï, right? Lothumans still tell tales of the Immortal Wars. But I have never seen her kind. Those eyes. Is she also your ward?"

"She's a Drae'shï all right. And no, she's not my ward or anyone's for that matter."

"Either way, you should not trust her. Her eyes give her away," she murmured, watching him through her frazzled fringe.

Zain scoffed. "After all the Vampire hunting stories and myths of monsters you've probably been told back in Lothumos, you'd think anything that looks slightly different to be a threat."

"The stories are there for a reason, and even myths are often founded on grains of truth."

"Aren't you quite the philosopher?" He smiled. "But I've gotta go now. I'll see what I can do and send you some more food. This time, try to be nicer to the guards," said Zain as he began heading to the exit.

"Zain. The Drae'shï. She is difficult to see. She's concealed in obscurity beyond a dark veil."

"What did you say?"

"I cannot see beyond the veil."

"What are you trying to see?"

"Beyond the flesh. Beyond the mind, lies the essence, the cause, and it is always naked to true sight. Even in a cursed one like you, there still lies a visible essence."

"And the Drae'shï?"

"It is difficult to see. Bring her to me. I will gaze upon her again."

"Why is she difficult to see?" Zain stopped, furrowing his brow.

"I don't know. It is hidden. Yet I sensed her arrival long before I laid eyes on her," she continued, a subtle grin emerging as her words squirmed their way under his skin.

"Are you trying to pull another hood over me?"

"What do your instincts say, Vampyr?" she reiterated with a devious grin.

"Damn it. I don't have time for this," said Zain frustrated as he realised how she instilled doubt so easily in his mind to save her own hide.

"Bring her, and I shall gaze again," she said with a devious grin on her face.

Zain pointed at her, irritated, but remained silent and walked out.

"Don't trust the dark one," she taunted from inside the tent as she cackled away at the prospect of execution.

CHAPTER 15

KNOWLEDGE OF DARKNESS

"In the beginning, there was nought,
and nought was everything there doth be.
The dawn of first light emerged from the womb of the Mother,
and so did she for the Will doth speaketh so.
The Mother's Light bore the world and above it,
gave life to its lands, seas, and skies.
All were of the Light but also not of it,
one from one and no longer a whole.
Out of her womb emerged the firstborn,
out of her image and out of the light.
The Children knew not themselves from the Mother,
living in harmony as Children of Light.
In time they grew distant, desirous of wonder,
seeking to find not places within.
They ventured the world filled with abundance,
growing distinct from whence they were whole.
As each did depart, so she diminished,
her essence lost through the fetters of time.
But as the ages grew old, soon they discovered
that so did they too feel the passage of time.

They soon sought the Mother in the lands of Caeden.
From all around the world, they came for the Light.
All sought the life of the never-ending radiance,
free from the shadow of the eternal night.
Three were the Children that returned from asunder.
All called the Mother and the Light that she brings.
The First cameth with love and rested beside her,
yet when she hath withered forceth them to live amongst men.
The Second with deceit sought in metal to confine her,
yet evermore bound to their halls they became.
The Third sought through blood and the knowledge of darkness,
yet, their fate, now eternal, would be the worst of all.
For all of those who sought blood to remain with the living,
would always know death so long as they did."

Applause rang around the dining hall as the brotherhood of medicians all in grey tunics concluded the harmonies of the Canticle.

"Bravo, bravo!" called out Alistair, clapping with glee, as Adara stood up equally enthused by the solemn performance. "So? How did you like it?" he whispered excitedly as he leaned over the side of his chair and she sat back down.

"Oh, it was beautiful! Truly, Alistair. Oh, I do hope it doesn't end there though." She placed her hand on his.

"Oh, of course not, my dear." He tapped her hand in reassurance. "This is but the first of many. The brothers wished to honour our presence with a minor snippet to whet our appetites. For dinner and for the rest of the Canticle once we get home." He winked happily. "Ah, Zain, you finally join us for dinner!"

Zain emerged from the gathered crowd as everyone gradually found their seats. "I always loved that last part of the Canticle; it makes me feel all warm and fuzzy inside," said the Vampire as he grabbed the first carafe he found and poured himself a cup of wine. He drank it all in one breath, followed by a crooked smile to Adara and Alistair.

They both returned an awkward smile.

"So, what's for dinner?" He beamed as he looked around the long dinner table, slowly being filled with an array of modest yet hearty dishes. He scratched his jaw tightly, gritting his teeth, groaning under his breath.

"How's the pork belly, Uncle? Any good?" asked Elias as he joined the party and sat beside Zain across from Adara.

"Looks wonderful! I haven't eaten some good old Iborean pork in quite a while! Not that the food in Cielith was anything short of exquisite, but my, my, nothing does it like bacon," claimed the happy corpulent bishop as he waved his hands across the table, almost knocking down every cup and flagon that came in his path.

Elias instinctively stopped a flagon from tipping over. "Careful there, Uncle, you might start suffering from chest pains and shortness of breath once again. I think I can even see you've loosened your belt too recently," he teased.

"Such calumnious accusations!" exclaimed Alistair, fork brandished in hand. "I only loosened it by one measure!" He laughed.

"Where is Lilith?" enquired Zain, dull faced as he picked at his food.

"She wanted dinner to be served in her room, I believe," said Elias.

"Naturally," added Zain. "Is someone keeping an eye on her?"

"Naturally," replied Elias.

"Very well. If you'll excuse me, I'll be back in a moment. I wish to finish this off in some peace and quiet outside," said Zain as he forcibly smiled, picked up a flagon and a bowl of mutton stew and headed back out of the hall. The others quizzically looked at each other as he left.

"Leave him be. No matter how much one forces it, you can only play cheerful for so long at a time," added Alistair. "He'll be back better than before, you'll see."

Zain headed out into the temple grounds. The night sky was clear, and the wind had softened. He headed to the closest steward and pushed the bowl of stew to his face. "Take this to the prisoner. The sentries are waiting for you."

"M'lord!" said the startled man. "I'm meant to take—"

"Go on! Move it!" barked Zain, confident that his dark ominous charisma could still be used for some minor trifles in life, like intimidating people into obedience. The man scurried along to deliver the food, and Zain took another long drink from the flagon. "Aaaarghh!" he groaned as he walked around the entrance, swinging the jug from side to side, rocking nearby barrels and kicking stones into the distance. Zain cringed and rubbed his chest as a deep longing grew within. He gritted his teeth and winced as the visceral hunger beckoned. He drank once more to dull his deep yearning as he roamed, seeking solace in solitude.

The back of the temple grounds was dimly lit and concealed by a small hedgerow. Zain walked into an enclosed orchard guided by his semi-inebriated instinct. The trees therein were young and full of apples hanging easily within reach. Zain meandered through the rows of trees, wandering aimlessly as he thought to himself. The glow of the moon shone brightly on the red fruit. Zain looked closely, inspecting its shimmer in an apple hanging before him. He picked the apple and walked away. He tossed it in the air and caught it. He sank his teeth in and imagined the taste of the sweet juice trickling along his gums and down to his throat. He bit and chewed and filled his mouth with another bite. He chewed and chewed. Yet his mouth ran dry. He bit in again, and his mouth was dryer still. "Arrrrghhhhh!" he yelled as he threw the apple far across the field in frustration, watching it land on the soft grass and coming to an anticlimactic stop. He stood there and drank once more. Suddenly the snap of a twig threw him off his feet, drenching him in wine.

To the best of his ability, Zain quickly stood alert as he heard movement amongst the trees. His sight was true at night, yet the orchard concealed everything behind it. Suddenly a dopey looking donkey walked right across the pathway, stopping only to pick up Zain's half-eaten apple. "Mother's mercy. You scared me." He blew out in relief before bursting into hysterical laughter. "Scared by a donkey! A Vampire!" His laughter echoed into the night, tears beading in his eyes. "Oh my! Can you tell me the difference between a donkey and an ass?" he continued as he slowly stumbled near the slightly intimidated beast. "The donkey was always donkey. The ass was a Vampire! I swear! I'm dying!" He laughed even more as the donkey moved away, irked by the loud arse.

"Hey, come here!" he called out as the donkey slowly zigzagged through the trees. "Donkey!" he called out as he ran towards the beast, who was clearly annoyed by the Vampire. They ran circles around the trees as Zain taunted the animal and attempted to ride it, flagon in hand, wine sloshing around. The sound of the drunken maniac and the distressed donkey echoed into the night.

"Gotcha!" he cried as he jumped from behind the donkey, landing on its back. The donkey brayed loudly and instantly bucked Zain off its back and onto the ground. Zain quickly rose to recapture his companion, only to be kicked straight in the jaw. The donkey was off, and Zain was out.

Shortly after, the donkey returned to sniff around his vanquished jockey as the sweet wine oozed out of his every pore. Zain groaned as he slowly felt the haze of his drink whirl in his head. The donkey sniffed along his arm and neck and up to his face. The animal's scent was far more pungent than any jug of sweet wine, yet it slowly faded away into nothingness. The soft wind and sound of rustling trees grew distant as a faint and almost imperceptible hiss slowly came to the fore. His hunger grew deep, visceral, and insatiable. The sound of blood coursing through its veins was deafening.

The donkey's bray was snuffed before it barely left its mouth.

The beast's blood surged through Zain like electricity. His chest heaved as he drew in the essence that would quench all deserts and suck all ecstasy from all pleasures. His hunger grew monstrous, and he drew until the beast had nothing left. However, the blood soon started to burn. Animal blood was no comparison to that of a higher being, and it soon ran through him like sludge through a grinder. A necessary evil, as much as the act itself.

"Death of the Undeath," said a voice from out of the night. Zain threw himself off the beast in fright, his mouth and chin still covered in blood.

"Who's that? Come out! Now!" He stood quickly and peered into the night.

Lilith revealed herself. "When you told me you drank the blood of animals, I always wondered whether you told the truth. I thought it was your usual lie. Aimed at preventing everyone from driving you away whilst you secretly found your fix in the occasional whore or criminal. Maybe you'd dispense your own warped sense of justice onto those less worthy of your mercy. But I must say the truth is far more disappointing," she said as she ran her nails over a ruby-like apple she held in her hand.

"Go away, Lilith, I don't need this right now," said Zain contemptuously as he wiped his face and dropped a small purse of money on the beast before proceeding to walk away from her, embarrassed and angry at everything.

"And you're going to pay for it, too?" She laughed.

"I have nothing to explain to you."

"Oh, but you do," she said as she followed him out of the orchard and into the open grounds of the Temple.

"Tell me, Zain Nightwing, last of the Eldaresh, what is it that made you end up drinking the blood of beasts of burden and chaperoning princes and princesses around the world?"

He stopped and turned to her. "I don't have to explain anything to anyone, least of all to you. Not after the way you shift from a tormented girl to the cold woman who stands before me. That mirror is not good for you."

"Whoever I am, I am not afraid to discover it and embrace it. I'm not afraid of the truth. It is you who is afraid of what others might think of you after they see past the lies."

"Fine. I'm afraid. Bye." He evaded her and turned only for her to grab him by the arm and turn him back around.

"Stop it! You're pathetic! You're an Eldaresh, the last of your kind. Blood magic runs through you, and instead of embracing who you are, you pay lip service to these people and play into their politics and wars. You are beyond them and beyond filthy animals!" she barked.

"I will not consume the blood of men and women! Is that so hard for you to accept?" Zain retorted.

"Why not? 'Cause of some misguided sense of morality or kinship you feel you owe them? You owe them nothing."

"That is not who I am, Lilith. It's not *my* truth," he shouted, thumping on his chest.

"Not your truth? Not who you are? You do not drink blood? You do not kill? All lies. You have shed more blood than you can ever drink, and you have drunk blood before, and you will do so again."

"I did all these things because I had to!"

"Spare me your excuses. You are not like them. You will never be like them," she said, pointing towards the priory.

"It's not that simple."

"It is."

"Don't pretend to fucking know me! You don't know what I've seen, what I've lost, what I've had to endure."

"I don't need to know you. You're right. All I need to do is hear the legends and read the books. Death of the Undeath you so proudly call yourself, but in truth, you carry that title like a curse. Instead of inspiring fear, you inspire contempt."

"Enough."

"Instead of living to your true nature, you cower in the dark, afraid of what the lambs may say when the wolf amongst them shows his true colours."

"Lilith, enough."

"You say you don't owe me an answer, yet you still answer to everyone. Every day. You ended your kind because *you* were the monster, not them. You brought them death when they just wanted to live. Judged them abominations when you still harbour your own inside you. How you still live with yourself is—"

"Enough!" he roared as he grabbed Lilith by the throat, holding her three feet above the ground. His bloodshot eyes turned blood red, and his face contorted into that of a foul, vicious creature with monstrous sharp teeth and a mouth that ran from ear to ear. He was seemingly becoming larger, his clothes almost about to rip.

Lilith choked but held onto his arm, barely able to speak. "Do it! Take me!" she gasped, her eyes transfixed with his yet Fear was absent in her eyes.

His anger swelled. He wanted to silence her and her truth, but there would be no point to it all—her echo would never cease to resonate within him. His temper softened, and he let her go onto the ground. He resumed his normal aspect and the sullen shame that came with it.

"Just leave me alone, Lilith," he said as he slowly walked away.

Lilith coughed and slowly caught her breath. "It seems something does move you after all."

Zain continued to ignore her.

"It's quite poignant though when you think about it—how immortality, in the end, has robbed you of all desire to live."

Zain shook his head and walked straight to the dinner hall from whence he came, wiping the last traces of the blood off his face with his elbow.

As he made his approach, one of the knights-errant rushed ahead to greet him. "M'lord, three Eldain horsemen are at the gates. They demand to see you and only you."

The two hurried to the gates, and in a matter of seconds, the horsemen dismounted. They were guards from Threlis Manor and Santhi's personal steward.

"Greetings," said Zain.

Eluin nodded. "Santhi sends his regards," said the Eldain as he handed Zain two sealed letters. "Open them alone," he whispered.

Zain nodded, and the three Eldain were quickly off again. The rest of the knights at the gate resumed their conversation as Zain's young knight messenger stood there staring.

"All right, go on then. I can find my way," added Zain as he nudged him forward, waiting for his private moment alone. The knight reluctantly trotted off to the dining hall under Zain's suspicious gaze, and the latter began walking. Zain then looked at each letter. "This one is probably Adara's," he said as he slipped one in his breast pocket.

He turned to his other letter, snapped the wax seal, and pulled out the parchment.

Greetings, old friend,

I trust that you are well and in good spirits as always. The halls of our home have now quieted. I never realised how Adara's voice made up so much of what I call home. I miss her every day and pray that she is safe and well. Thankfully, knowing you are also there gives me some rest in these uncertain times, which brings me to the second part of this letter.

Unfortunately, the situation is as we thought. The Hall of Mirrors has the power you suspected. I managed to find old records from the Immortal Wars that an Eldain resistance group kept at the time. It seems they believed that the queen of the Drae'shï, Sirith, was using the Mirror to allow the armies of the Drae'shï to move outside of the mountain safely. They also said it aided them in battle, helping the Drae'shï fight but never tire or feel hunger. I don't know whether the Shard itself has the capacity to project such force on the scale of an army, but at least it is working on our friend. I'm sure now you see where the problem lies.

It is imperative that neither Lilith, nor the Jurani, nor anyone for that matter, finds out. An artefact such as this would be another source of power any one of these power-hungry factions would desperately wish to get their hands on and there's no telling what might happen if they do, war or not. I have sent a similar missive to inform Adomas the Warden on the matter. I can imagine that this is primarily why the Drae'shï are after her, and more will likely be on their way shortly. I decided I will head down to Valendria ahead of the wedding to conduct research in their archives. We will discuss our next move once you arrive. Until then, discretion is key, and most importantly, keep Lilith close. Anyone who sees her value in her ability to use it will be sure to try and abuse it. As for Adara, she knows the importance of maintaining discretion, but rest assured she's aware of the dangers.

Take care, Zain.

Burn after reading.

Zain sighed as he approached a nearby brazier and tossed the parchment into the flame. "Fuck."

He soon re-joined the party inside the hall. The knights on one side conversed with one another as they enjoyed the occasional soldier's song whilst the medicians on the other side huddled around their table, debating vigorously on matters of religion and politics. Alistair and Adara were seemingly engrossed in a quick game of knucklebones as everyone around them looked on.

"There he is!" cried Adara, bright as ever, as soon as she caught sight of Zain. "How are you? Are you feeling better now?" she said as she opened her arms and hugged him.

"I told you he would be back." Alistair smiled as both he and Elias turned to face him.

"I am, I am." He smiled as he slowly stepped over a stool and sat down. "And I have a surprise for you."

"Oh really?" she teased.

"Of course!" Zain drew out the envelope from his breast pocket. "With his warmest affection." He smiled.

"Oh, Father!" She beamed as she took the letter and placed it to her lips. "So, what did he tell you? Any interesting news? Why am I asking? I have my own!" she rambled on excitedly as she proceeded to open her letter.

"No news for you, Zain?" asked Elias.

"I didn't get anything myself."

"Really?"

"Yes, really," he said. "He must've put everything in Adara's letter."

"So, here we go. Dearest daughter..." Adara proceeded to read and translate Santhi's long epistle and its encouraging words to the surrounding listeners. His praise for the Saints and their noble endeavours elicited a few cheers, and all were uplifted by the Eldain's speech.

"One final note to you, my youngest. Not a day goes by without my thoughts going to you." Adara's tone began to dampen. "I have watched you from your birth and childhood grow into a beautiful person worthy of great things. Now that you have to depart into your new life, the halls of Threlis Manor have lost their nightingale, and yet every corner is still a reminder of all our happy days." Adara's eyes welled up. "I miss you truly, my dear, but a cage is no place for a nightingale, and I remain ever faithful in the knowledge that you will have a better life outside it. In the end, I know that I am forever with you in your heart as you are in mine and your mother's." Adara's tears rolled down her cheeks. "I can't tell you how proud she would have been. I... excuse me!" she said as she stood up and scurried away from the table.

Both Zain and Elias got up.

"It would be best if I go," said Zain.

"As her future husband, I believe I should be able to comfort my wife-to-be," retorted Elias as he stalked off in pursuit.

"Fine," murmured Zain as he reluctantly sat himself down.

"She'll be fine, Zain. Here, another glass of wine," added Alistair as he filled a cup and passed it on. Zain sipped away as he spied on the retreating couple.

Elias chased after her.

"Adara. Adara, wait!" called out Elias as he trailed behind with her sobs echoing through the halls.

She ignored his pleas, heading straight to her chambers. She flung herself on her bed, curling up and clutching the letter to her chest as if trying to embrace its sender. She wept silently.

He knocked on the door softly but she didn't reply. The door creaked open, yet she didn't deign to turn to face it. "Dearest. Adara," he said softly as he walked in and gently closed the door. "I must apologise to you. I'm sorry that you were forced away from home on my account. I know how much you must love Cielith and having all your friends and family around. I must beg your forgiveness." He sat on the bed by her feet. "You're not the only one who is bound by duty in this regard. However, I still believe every word your father said about you. You are in every way the nightingale he so loves, and at every step of the way, I realise that this is no longer a struggle for me but rather a chance at building our own nest."

Adara slowly turned, comforted by Elias' sweet sermon. He smiled as he placed his hand on hers. "Would it be so hard to imagine? That we could be to each other something more than just an arranged marriage?"

Adara slowly rose and kissed him deeply, seemingly inebriated with wine and emotion, hanging onto him and letting herself go in all respects. "Thank you, Elias," she whispered, resting her head on his shoulder.

He smiled. "Better now?"

"I just need time," she said. "Could I just stay here for a while?"

"Of course, my dear."

"Thanks," she said drawing a smile in relief.

"Before I leave, I wanted to ask you. Did your father leave any message for me or Zain in particular? After the part where you stopped reading?"

"No. Nothing, I'm afraid."

"I see."

"Would you mind if I took a look at the letter?"

"Now? I'm rather tired, and also a bit tipsy now that I think of it," she said as she rubbed her head and chuckled to herself.

"Yes, I understand, my dear. How foolish of me." Elias laughed as he picked up on her cue. "Just one more thing before I go. I wanted to tell you that we've looked into the whole debacle with the girl from the market. It seems like there's nothing to worry about. We'll be sending her off on her way in the morrow."

"Really!" Adara jumped up and hugged him. "Oh, I'm so relieved! Thank you, Elias. I knew you would listen. Thank you. Now I know I can sleep soundly. Can I speak with her then?"

"I guess you can, but someone would have to be present to avoid any mishaps."

"That's fantastic. Thank you!" she exclaimed and hugged him once more. "Oh my, I must get ready for bed, so I'm up bright and early."

Elias smiled at how quickly she bounced back.

She immediately sprang up and took a quick look at the mirror. "I'm a mess!" she said noticing all her eye makeup running down her cheeks.

"You look beautiful."

"I may be *beautiful*, but I'm not stupid." She laughed. "Look at me!"

They both sniggered.

"Let me fetch the girls, and I'll see you in the morning," she said and quickly kissed him on the cheek before heading out to find her chambermaids.

Elias stood back, smiling at the sight of his Eldain beauty.

The Saint waited for a moment and then turned towards the bed. The letter lay there half crumpled and smudged with Adara's tears. He furtively picked it up and attempted to read through the text. His knowledge of Eldain was far from refined, but he could recall some of his studies from when he was tutored in Valendria. "Prefect Marianus would enjoy seeing me struggle now," he said to himself as he perused the letter, seeking some form of answer beyond Santhi's ramblings.

"Found what you're looking for among her things?" asked Lilith from the doorway.

Elias stiffened at the interruption. "I was merely..." he said, awkwardly retrieving his knightly composure.

"*Merely* is hardly the word. You've been looking so hard at that letter you should have burnt two holes through it by now."

"Excuse me?" he said, feigning perplexity.

"It's hardly anyone's place to intervene in matters confined to the bedroom of any couple, but neither is it to go through correspondence addressed to anyone but oneself, is it?" she stated flatly

Elias forced a laugh. "Oh, Lilith, my dear. You have the situation confused. Adara passed it onto me herself. She's getting ready for bed," he said as Lilith walked towards him and grabbed the paper out of his hands.

"Hm. Yes, clearly. Your Eldain was always very keen. Especially when they passed their snide remarks right in your face." She smiled with her devilish grin. "Let me see."

"Give that back," he demanded as he contained his frustration.

"Oh, I thought you wanted to know what it said. Here," she said offering it back to him.

Elias stood still, pursing his lips.

She smirked. Lilith slowly turned back to the letter, drew out the Shard, and placed it beside the paper. Its reflection now revealed the text in Common. She began skimming. "I see. Well. Dearest daughter, I trust you are safe. Hm, fine, fine. Get to the point, Santhi, yes, yes, the Saints, I miss you. Touching. Aha. 'One final matter, my dear. Be careful of who to trust, including those closest to you. Trust only the person with whom I place my own. He will ensure no harm can come to you. It is as we suspected.'"

Elias pursed his lips, gritting his teeth behind his straight face, hiding from Lilith's observant gaze.

"Well, it seems that he was right onto you for that matter," she commented candidly as she slowly folded the letter and slipped it into his breast pocket with her cool touch grazing his chest. "Then again, which married couple never kept secrets from one another?" she whispered to him in her raspy voice as she drew her hand out and trailed her finger subtly down his chest.

"Leave," he said sternly, ignoring her sultry advance.

"At least she can still trust you in *some* respects." She smiled as she walked out, calmly parading herself to him. She stopped by the doorway and turned once more. "Though, I wonder what pains you more, Elias? The fact that she's to trust the Vampire more than her beloved or that you've been outfoxed by the nightingale's keeper?"

Chapter 16

Dark Knight Dreams

"Do you know where Lil'Thra came from, before the mirror, before all this?" asked Krea as she waved her hand at their surroundings.

Zain laughed. "I was hoping you'd be the one to shed some light on that mystery."

"Isn't it funny how two people from completely different worlds, yet so inherently similar, seem to have found each other in a back alley in the middle of a town in the middle of nowhere?"

"Fate has a sense of humour from what I've heard."

"Then you believe in fate?"

Zain scoffed. "I've lived long enough to know that you can see coincidence in anything if you look hard enough for it."

"Still, it's a twist of fate that has had wide implications nonetheless. One that bears still. Her influence weighs upon you on one side as you carry your guilt and shame on the other," said Krea as she stood facing the wall, staring into its nooks and crannies.

"Thanks for the analysis. Any more words of wisdom you wish to share regarding Lilith or the ghosts of my past, Krea?" Zain rested his elbows on his wide-open knees, chains dangling between his legs.

"Not for now. I only need to see your gaze and stricken form to know how much she has invaded your heart and mind." She smiled slyly.

Zain looked away. "So, is this the so-called connection to the All you've been so keen on coaxing out of me?"

"Far from it, Zain. Very far from it. Lilith is different in nature, yet similar in degree." She paced, the echo of her heels filling the room.

"Oh yes. I get it," he mused mockingly.

"Do you?" She stopped.

"Not in the least," he said flatly.

"Never mind. Though I wonder, had you not chosen to head into that back alley, or come to her aid, how else would she have manifested herself into your life?" she asked, turning back to Zain, finger to her mouth in contemplation.

"Ah, the what-ifs. Let me just add that one to my list. Why does it even matter, Krea?" He huffed.

"I've lived long enough to know that when you try hard enough, you can make even the most improbable of coincidences manifest," said Krea.

"Then, like fate, you, too, have a twisted sense of humour."

"Like fate, I control all the pieces of a chessboard, and you, my dear Zain, are nothing but another pawn at the mercy of a queen." She stopped, standing tall before him, looking down, hand on hip.

"Could you at least make me a knight?" he mocked. "Also, can you move? You're blocking the tons of light coming through that miserable window," he added, waving his hand in front of her.

Krea chuckled and stepped away. "Fine. A knight it is then."

Zain stared blankly at Krea.

"Rest easy, dark knight. It won't be long until this game is all over," said Krea as she removed her circlet and turned to the door. Her circlet gleamed red, green, and blue in her hands.

Zain sat quietly, watching Krea leave the cell along with the echo of her footsteps.

Darkness claimed the room once more, and it was finally silent, the constant buzz retreating in her wake. He rested his head against the cold wall, taking a deep breath and staring at the ceiling. He sighed. "Pawn," he said to himself before looking down at his chains. He frowned, then scoffed. He closed his eyes and sighed once more, letting the world go by, and soon he drifted into a slumber.

"Pssst," whispered a voice. "Pssst!"

Zain groaned.

"Pssst!"

"Krea, shut up," he groaned, half asleep, curling up further into his corner.

"Zain! Wake up!" whispered a soft voice.

Zain winced and turned his blurry eyes to the empty room in front of him. "Krea? What the—"

"Pssst. Over here, Zain!" said a female voice from behind him.

"What the hell? Who is that?" Zain rose slowly and twisted and turned, searching for the voice in the wall, yet none returned. "Am I? I must really be losing it..." He turned, lifting himself onto his knees and looking intently through the gaps in the stones, yet no one replied. Zain rubbed his head perplexed. He blinked and glared. "I really must be going—"

"Zain!"

The Vampire flew to the ground as an eye came up to the gap right before his eyes. "Holy Mother!" He gasped for air, holding his chest. "Shit!"

"Are you all right? Zain? Sorry I couldn't speak. Need to be careful of who's listening," said the young woman behind the wall.

"Aria? Is that you?"

"Do you remember me now?" she asked.

"Yes. Well, kind of. Who are you again?"

She sighed. "I don't think that matters anymore right now."

"Are you a prisoner?"

"Of sorts."

"Oh, great. Another cryptic companion." Zain slumped back down with the back of his head to the opening in the wall. "Like I didn't get enough from the other bitch. No offence."

"Contrary to Krea, I give answers as opposed to posing more questions."

"Oh really?" mocked Zain. "Or maybe you're just another ruse of these bleeding Drae'shï to prod me into giving them the 'All.'" He mocked with his hands. "Or else the secret to eternal life or some other imagined piece of knowledge, which apparently, I'm not even aware that I have. To you, all I am is some bear you can endlessly poke and prod for no reason," he said, frustrated, arms crossed. "Can't even sleep for five minutes without someone starting this farce once again."

"I'm sorry, Zain. I cannot prove that I'm not one of them or that I'm not trying to deceive you. All I know is that they have you deceived."

"Go on. Enlighten me. I'm in need of a good laugh," he said, waving his hands to an absent audience.

"You're trapped, yes, but everything around you isn't real. Your ideas, memories, the places you've visited. They are artificial. Fabricated in your mind. The very room you're in is different in reality. *You* are different in reality."

Zain laughed heartily. "Is this the best you can come up with, Krea?" he called out to the door. "Oh, come on. At least give me a challenge."

"Zain. Please," said Aria as her voice became meek.

"Oh, sorry, Aria. No, go on, continue. Let's hear it."

"I beg you. I'm trying to help you. I know it's really hard to believe that all you have lived through never happened, but you have to believe me. I don't know what else I can do to show you or convince you, and I'm afraid time is running out," she pleaded.

Zain sat silent, gritting his teeth.

"Zain—"

"Listen to me and listen well," interrupted Zain angrily. "I don't know who you are or who sent you, but one thing I know for sure. I did not see my wife and all my friends die before me to have anyone try to convince me that they weren't real. That their suffering wasn't real. That my pain isn't real. So take your lies and so-called tricks and go peddle them to whoever is willing to listen, 'cause I won't." Aria remained silent. "I'm sorry, but I have to go." Her voice quivered.

"Yeah, it's about time," replied Zain, struggling to remain stern. "And tell Krea the dark knight told her to go fuck herself."

Chapter 17

Empty Vessels

The sea was not kind to Pïshkah.

Another crash of the waves and the spray came rushing through the galley's portholes, splashing her in the face. Puddles of water listed from side to side as the cargo hanging from the deck swung lazily. Pïshkah felt nauseous again. It had been three days since she had left Yammimer and as many days since she regretted her decision to sneak up on the Saint's galley.

"I can't take this anymore," she whispered to herself. "I swear. If I ever get back to Lothumos, I'll never set foot on a boat ever again." She groaned. Another crash, and the spray splashed straight in her face. She cursed once more as she slammed her fist on the side of the hull and kicked an empty barrel, scaring a little mouse that stood there observing the scene. The sound resounded around the hold, full of cargo but devoid of passengers. Footsteps from above remained a constant nuisance. The crew rested on the mid-deck above her, only ever coming down to retrieve supplies to eat.

Pïshkah was hardly in want of food but found little solace in its consumption. "I need some air." She winced as she felt the humidity's choking embrace clutch at every breath she took. She dragged herself to the closest porthole and gasped for air as the boat continued to rock.

Her consciousness was slowly slipping away, only interrupted by the sound of clashing swords and yelling upon the deck. "Not this again."

Meanwhile above, the sun shone brightly, burning away at the galley's deck. Zain's black hair burned under the scorching heat whilst Lilith's forehead dripped with sweat. The two were locked in a tense one-on-one, their eyes focusing on each other, drowning out everything else.

"Ha!" Lilith yelled as she leapt towards him, slashing down her sword with intrepid zeal. She darted again and again, missing the Vampire but almost hacking away half the ship's ropes.

Zain quickly slipped around, parrying her every move, infuriating her with every hit she missed.

"Concentrate on your footwork, Lilith," said Elias. "Focus."

She twisted and turned, mirroring and parrying every attack from Zain and striking back in return. The two danced away to the amusement of those aboard. The sea was relatively calm and the visibility clear, yet the vessel rocked with every wave crest it broke. She stumbled, he struck, and the blade flew out of her hand and into the sea. A brief clap ensued.

"So much for the blade," said Zain as he looked overboard.

Lilith looked back at him, fuming. She quickly turned to a nearby sailor, unsheathing his cutlass and turning back to Zain.

"You never give up, do you?" he said but Lilith offered no reply. "You know that's a cutlass, right? We've been training with long swords." His words fell on deaf ears as she darted at him once again.

"This is where it gets interesting," whispered Elias to Adara, who sat comfortably, sipping away at her watered wine in the shade.

Once again, Zain and Lilith fought tirelessly under the sun. The clash of swords and cawing of gulls echoed across the waves as the four galleys ferrying the Saints back to Valendria sailed along the coastal shores of Valdell. The two continued 'til Zain, fatigued and bored by the monotony of the endeavour, began to forcibly end the encounter. Lilith, on the other hand, had no intention of relenting.

"How 'bout we take a rest now, shall we?"

"Tired already, Vampire?" she replied, panting away herself as she took a deep breath followed by another attack.

"Alright, give it up," he said as he parried her attack but failed to throw back his own.

"Come on! Fight!" she insisted as she kept on striking fruitlessly.

"Enough!" he barked as he continued dodging her hits.

The two continued their squabble as Zain refused to engage yet failed to make her desist of her own accord.

"I'll give it to her. What she lacks in discipline she makes up for in resolve," said Elias to himself.

"Stop!" called out Zain as he allowed her to thrust right under his arm, locking hers tightly in his and deadening her grip on the blade. The two, now face-to-face, could see the rolling beads of sweat trailing down their faces, their panting breaths inches apart. They paused.

All of a sudden, the pointed end of a blade stuck out of Zain's chest.

The crew gasped, but Zain did not. The duelling partners moved apart as Zain looked down. "Didn't we say no shards?" he snapped irritably.

"It's right here, Zain," called Adara as she shone the object into the sunlight.

"That's your dagger, my friend," called out Elias as Zain fumbled around his side pockets, noticing his missing blade. "Bravo, Lilith. Bravo. Somewhat unorthodox in approach but effective nonetheless," he continued as he clapped briefly, followed by the rest of the crew before they slowly returned to their duties, some cursing and some happy as they exchanged the winnings from their bets.

Lilith smirked back at Zain.

"Ha. Ha. Listen, I may be undead, but that doesn't mean this doesn't hurt. Or that I'm some sort of training dummy," said Zain, rather annoyed. "Also, I'd like not to have my wardrobe full of holes, if that's alright with you."

"Oh, Zain, dearest. Here, a cup to the victim, and for the victor, of course," smiled Adara as she brought over two cups of watered wine for the sparring partners.

"I'm no victim. Merely caught off guard. I had her," said Zain as he tried reaching around his back to grab the blade.

"If you *had* me, then how did you end up with this?" retorted Lilith as she swiftly extracted it out of his back, inciting a slight shriek from the irked Vampire.

"That was hardly fair in a sparring match."

"How about fair for a real fight then? Or is that not why we spar?"

Zain groaned. Just as he was about to retort, the sound of the Saints' horn came from across the sea.

The largest galley, the *Vigilance*, was nearing their vessel within earshot.

Alistair could be seen approaching starboard and being handed a brass megaphone. "Good tidings to you all! How fares the journey upon the *Intrepid*, Nephew?"

"Majorly, Uncle!" called out Elias as the deckhand handed him his own megaphone. "Have you been comfortable aboard?"

"Yes! The chambers are a bit cramped but that's alright."

"Cramped? Does he know we're sleeping in a bloody box?" whispered Zain.

Adara chuckled and nudged him in his side.

"That's good to hear, Uncle. We're all nice and cosy right here," continued Elias as he observed the tight detail of Saints walking diligently across the deck of the *Vigilance*.

"I'll hand over to the admiral, Elias. I believe he would like to have an exchange."

"Greetings, Commander."

"Greetings, Admiral."

"We've approached to inform you that we must forgo our plans to stop at Port Tarie tomorrow."

"What's the word from the port?"

"The *Serene* passed by a few fishing vessels earlier today that informed them that pirates have recently attacked the port. I fear that stopping there would make us a sitting target. We do have the supplies and men to hold off an attack, but frankly, I wouldn't want to risk the lives of His Excellency and the other passengers aboard the ships."

"I concur."

"I'm sorry, sir. It would have been nice to get our feet on the ground, but safety takes priority."

"Agreed, Admiral. We shall then stop further south once we've cleared the area by a hundred kilometres."

"Yes, sir. I shall inform the *Serene* and the *Terror*."

Elias nodded and raised his megaphone, signalling the end from his side of things. "Well, it seems we've got some more sailing to do."

The rest were hardly amused but did not object. They all reluctantly returned to the stage of their sojourn under a canopy seated around the same table they had been at for the last few days. All lay strewn in their armchairs, fanning themselves from the heat, each dying to return inside for some privacy but none of them willing to stomach the heat.

Soon enough, a couple of crew members came running from below deck. "Commander!"

The four slowly raised their attention, and as if through a dream, their hazy sight revealed a familiar face.

"Pïshkah?" said Zain and Adara in tandem as they saw the sailors hoisting up the girl, now looking severely dehydrated. They immediately rose and ran to her.

"Where did you find her? How did she get on board?" said Elias sternly.

"She was hiding in the cargo hold, Commander. We found her half-dead, climbing up to the mid-deck."

"Let her go," said Adara as she took Pïshkah's arm, observing Pïshkah's lips now dry and cracked.

"She's a stowaway," responded the crew member.

"She's dying!" yelled Adara.

Elias nodded, and the crew let go.

Zain carried Pïshkah to his armchair, seating her in the shade.

"Search the entire ship. Let's make sure there are no other unwanted guests. Get me Sir Pontar, immediately," continued Elias.

"Bring me the water, Lilith," Zain instructed.

Lilith slowly passed the jug to him, observing the Cleriheu intently, suspicion cast in her gaze. "I hope you realise that she's up to something."

"You didn't tell her to come, did you?" said Zain to Adara as he gently helped Pïshkah sip and Adara proceeded to fan her.

"No, of course not. We only spoke for a few minutes before we left the temple. I thought she was ordered to leave Yammimer."

"On pain of death," added Lilith.

"Well, she *did* follow instructions," said Zain as they all looked towards Elias for a verdict.

"Hm." Elias took a deep breath and crossed his arms. "This is going to cause problems."

"How's she going to cause problems? She's half dead," said Zain, resting on one knee.

"Never mind for now. Get her up and take her inside. Keep her away from prying eyes," said Elias, grumbling as he observed the crew discussing the rumour of the passenger.

The day slowly dwindled into the evening, and the scorching heat soon turned to a soft wind. The ship sailed silently into the night as the sea's tide set its rhythm and the sailors below sang their shanties. Zain's cabin was once again shared with another invalid.

"I don't know why you insist on giving up your bed for her," said Lilith as she gazed into the Shard, seated in the corner of her own bed.

"Yeah, you're right. The last time I did that, it brought me right here on this boat," he replied. "Bedding distraught women was always an auspicious sign for the future."

"Idiot," she replied casually as she continued gazing into the Shard.

"You're welcome."

Pïshkah rested easily on the bedding. The warm light of the flickering lantern gave the room a warm glow of safety. Zain sat on the ground beside her, flinging cards into a bucket a few feet away from him.

"Lilith," he said.

"Yes?" she said without turning her sight from the Shard.

"What are you going to do with the Shard?"

She paused. "I don't know," she said genuinely as she continued to explore.

"Haven't you figured that out yet? All you do is look at it. No good can come of it."

"Just because it imprisoned you does not mean that it will do the same to me. To me, it may very well be the opposite."

"So, what does that mean? What do you see?"

"I see many things... but also nothing at the same time. Sometimes it shows the things one desires. Sometimes it's just a reflection of what stands before it."

"I can assure you I did not want to be in that cell, my dear."

"Then again, you are trapped in your own way, your moral shackles, your hunger unsated," she mused.

"Ugh. I hate it when you're right." He groaned. "So can't you just make your desires manifest, if that's what you see?"

"I would not be here if that were so, would I?" she stated curtly.

"Thanks," he added.

"Though there seems to be a certain order to everything I see. About me, about the world and all its deepest secrets. It's all about... observing," she said, more and more transfixed by it.

"And what do you see now?"

"Nothing," she said.

"Observing nothing. Yeah, good. Fine. That's great. You really need to get your head checked." Zain tossed another card half-heartedly. Thunder rumbled in the distance. "Looks like it's raining ahead," muttered Zain.

Lilith ignored him, mystified by the mirror.

Pïshkah stirred in her sleep.

The grip of the mirror had its hold on Lilith's very core. Her eyes grew wider, and her pupils dilated.

Zain observed cautiously and concerned. "Lil?" he asked, but she ignored.

"The darkness," whispered Pïshkah in her sleep. "The darkness!"

"What the?" asked Zain, as the situation grew increasingly bizarre. The wind turned into a howl, and the pelting rain followed.

"The darkness!" panted Pïshkah once again, entranced in her dreams. "The darkness within!"

"Lilith! What are you doing?" yelled Zain as he tried to get up on his feet, only to be thrown down by the sudden crash of the galley into the swell. "Lilith!"

The windows banged, and the lantern flew onto the floor, casting the room into darkness. "It's here!" whispered Pïshkah. A sudden deafening bolt of lightning struck the sea not more than a few hundred yards away from the ships, sending a blinding flash throughout the cabin.

"Zain!" cried Lilith as she found herself on the floor disoriented.

"Where am I?" cried Pïshkah.

"Calm down!" yelled Zain. The door blew open.

Elias held up his lantern with Adara close by, holding her own.

"Did you hear that?" asked Adara holding her chest, still somewhat startled by the blast.

"Are you all alright?" Elias peered into the room, finding Zain and Lilith on the floor amongst a dozen other things that had fallen in the ruckus.

"Do I look alright?" asked Zain as he picked himself up whilst Elias helped Lilith.

"Looks like there's a heavy storm along the coast. We're going to have to head further out at sea lest we end up on the rocks," said Elias.

"Fantastic," added Zain as Lilith dusted herself down and picked up the mirror once more as if nothing had happened.

The main door to the deck banged loudly. "Commander. Apologies for the disturbance, but the captain needs your presence," called a voice from outside, followed by a rumble of voices from behind him. "Now, sir."

The Saints' guards by the door looked at Elias, who nodded back. They carefully opened the door and let the chief officer through.

The man was dripping from head to toe. "Commander. We have an issue with the crew. We need to placate certain rumours," he said as he looked straight at Pïshkah.

Elias took a deep breath, furrowing his brow.

"They found certain... how can I explain? Symbols? Engravings? Now I'm not one for superstition or such, but the crew are thinking that they are curses aimed at sinking the ship. Also, the storm—"

"They're sigils, you goon! And they're aimed at protecting this tub of driftwood!" yelled Pïshkah from the bed.

"Be that as it may."

Elias sighed. "I understand, officer. I'll be out in a minute. Fine. You all stay in here. The last thing I need is to protect you from a mutinous rabble at this point." He immediately put on his sword belt and cloak in the main cabin and nodded to his comrades, who in turn opened the door onto the windy deck. Light showers drizzled on the crew that clamoured for the captain's attention. The door slammed shut, and the rambling soon ceased as Elias could be heard barking orders to the Saints aboard to calm the rest of the crew. A long silence fell in the cabin.

"How are you feeling, Pïshkah?" asked Adara as she slipped into the room.

"I'm fine, Lady Adara, thank you. I'm indebted for your generosity once more." The Cleriheu flattered Adara as she took hold of both Adara's hands in gratitude. Zain and Lilith looked at one another unamused. "And also to your friends," she continued looking at Zain but failed to look directly at Lilith.

"Why did you sneak onto the ship?" interjected Lilith, cold as ice. They all paused.

Pïshkah sighed. "I'm sorry. I didn't want to cause you any trouble, but I had no place to go outside Yammimer since I was banned from the city. And when I heard that you were all heading to Valendria, I thought I'd head south. I hear Valendria is full of mystics and healers."

"Yes. Just not your type. I wouldn't count on a warm welcome once we get there," said Zain.

"*If* she gets there," continued Lilith, arms crossed as the din outside intensified.

"Hush! Let's not jump to conclusions," said Adara.

"And no other village or slum in the area would have you? I find that very hard to believe," insisted Lilith, tapping her fingers on her arms.

"Yammimer *was* the slum. What else do you think there was out there?" said Pïshkah, turning an innocent smile to Lilith's narrowing eyes.

"I don't believe you. Why this ship then? Out of the hundreds that come and go from the ports? Why now? Why not walk? I don't recall them breaking your legs, did they?" insisted Lilith.

Zain slowly moved to reach out to her as she grew more agitated.

"Are you afraid of me?" said Pïshkah.

"No," said Lilith, gritting her teeth.

"I don't believe you," said the Cleriheu with a confident grin.

Lilith fumed. "You—"

"Alright, alright. That's enough," said Zain as he slowly walked Lilith out of the room as she and Pïshkah kept locked eyes.

"Leave me alone!" she barked as she shoved Zain off. "Clearly, you're too stupid to realise what she's up to, and I'm not going to wait 'til she slits my throat in my sleep. You spared her once, and she's back for more. Only fools such as yourselves would give shelter to their own assassins."

Lilith turned to the dining quarters and slammed the door behind her.

Zain ignored the ramblings and returned to his cabin. "Though the execution is hardly tactful, Lilith's words aren't far from unjustified. Adara's safety remains paramount, and I've got my eye on you."

"She is right, you know," said Pïshkah as Zain and Adara widened their eyes. "About you two being fools, that is," she said smiling. "It's not me you should be watching but her." She pointed.

"You said this to me before. And now again. Why?"

"About Lilith?" intervened Adara.

"Yes, the dark one," continued Pïshkah. "She's not of this world."

"She's a Drae'shï. They are a race of Eldarï. There are many like her."

"The vessel is not its contents."

"Are you saying she's possessed?" asked Zain narrowing his gaze.

"I've seen many who claimed to be possessed. Some by spirits and demons, whilst others merely by their own delusions and insanity," said Pïshkah.

"And where would she fall then?" asked Adara.

"She is not possessed by anything. There is a void beyond which I cannot see."

"Come on, Pïshkah, enough with this crap!" Zain exclaimed.

"Let her be," Adara insisted, raising her hand to his.

"Really? You, too?" Zain asked incredulously.

"It is as if she is completely vacant, deprived of any essence. I told you this!" Pïshkah reiterated.

"You know what? I think Lilith is right, and you're nothing more than an articulate liar that is very good at what she does," he said, frustrated.

"Zain!" said Adara.

"She's gotten to you, hasn't she?" observed Pïshkah, narrowing her eyes, smirking.

"What?"

"You know what I mean," said Pïshkah.

"I don't know what you're talking about," said Zain, holding a straight face and placing his hands on his hips.

"Who's the liar now, Vampire?" The Cleriheu smirked.

"Perhaps it's the mirror?" interceded Adara.

"What mirror?" asked Pïshkah.

"Yes, Adara. *What* mirror?" repeated Zain, widening his eyes and raising his brow.

"Oh, come on, Zain. It's not like she wouldn't see it anyway. All Lilith does is look at it. Pïshkah might know something."

"Not now, Adara. Not here."

The commotion outside seemed to have subsided, and soon enough, Elias emerged once again, followed by his guards.

"Is everything alright, dear?" asked Adara as she got up to greet her drenched intended.

"For now. It seems that the Cleriheu caused quite a stir amongst the crew, some even saying she cursed the skies to cause the storm. I had to do some convincing. However, the Valendrian navy knows they ought to be more afraid of the Saints than superstition."

"Cursed the sky?" interceded Pïshkah, offended. "Half of those filthy seafarers come to me looking for a cure from scurvy or syphilis when your own folk won't bother opening the gates to the temple! And I'm the cause of their bad luck?"

"Watch your tone, heathen. It's twice that I've spared you. I might not be so inclined to a third."

"Elias!" placated Adara.

"Enough. We'll deal with this tomorrow," stated Elias sternly. "And as for you." He scowled down at Pïshkah. "Pray that your sigils bring better weather tomorrow, or there will be hell to pay."

"Because if not, your solution to bad weather will be to throw me overboard? What do you think there would be to pay if you threw an innocent witch to her death then?"

CHAPTER 18

NOT OF THIS WORLD

The sky above Black Pass was grey as always, framed in the jagged black rocks that formed the path into Mount Ussar Varys. The days grew shorter and the nights colder, but the vigilance of the Wardens and the Saints had never lessened in the past few weeks.

The pass was shut. A large black steel gate held back the scourge of the Drae'shï and the echoes of old wars. The knights and wardens had rekindled the flames of the broken black ramparts of Black Pass, mirroring those across the Rakshir Plains inside Harlot's Hold. Knights were stationed on the old Drae'shï battlements, awaiting any movement, expecting the next wave of Drae'shï to come flooding out, but none deigned to show themselves. The wait was long.

The Wardens sat around a fire, preparing themselves for another night of fruitless sentry duty.

"So, tell me again what the old man said," said Thane as he picked his dirty fingernails with his dagger.

"Lord Crysanthani said the Shard was part of a larger mirror. He said they used it to shelter the army of the Drae'shï as they marched outside the mountain," said Adam.

"Like a large shield?" asked Thane.

"Of course not, you idiot," said Willam. "He meant metaphorically."

"I doubt you can win wars with metaphors, Willam," stated Brandt, rubbing his hands over the flames.

"Must have been some kind of magic. He said the mirror's powers helped keep them free from hunger and heal their wounds faster." said Adam, combing his goatee as he felt the mystic glow of the flames on his brow.

"And where did he get this from?" asked Doran huddled under his fur cloak.

"Old records from the Immortal Wars," answered Adam.

"And the Drae'shï woman? She has that power, too?" said Arren under his breath.

"No. But when she attacked me, she managed to use it in some way. It's not an artefact to be trifled with, and I suspect that the Saints want to use it for that very reason. Whether through her or otherwise."

"The war," said Thane. "Do they even know what it can do?"

"They..." Adam slowed himself as two Saints passed by, chatting to each other. "...don't know as far as I know. At least for now."

"Why not tell them then? We could use the Shard to do good," added Thane.

"We don't know what it can do yet, whether it can even do a fraction of what Lord Crysanthani said. Once we find out, we'll decide," said Adam.

"We certainly can't have all Amenti rushing to take control of a magical artefact that everyone thinks grants their wishes," said Brandt as he picked up a log and tossed it into the fire.

"Or worse, enter the mountain to take control of the Hall of Mirrors itself," added Adam bluntly.

"That would be mad! Do you think that's why they're here?" Thane nudged his head in the direction of the patrolling Saints.

"Undoubtedly," added Samos. "What could cement the Massass' hold over the continent more than the magical mirror that watches over armies? Power-hungry bastard."

"It certainly would give them an advantage against the Carthosians," said Willam as the rest nodded.

"Perhaps," said Adam. "We must be cautious. We must be silent. And most importantly, we must remember our oath."

"To guard and protect the world from the darkness within," they recited in unison.

They paused, all staring at the crackling fire and the popping embers.

"Still does not explain why they attacked us," continued Thane. "For just a shard?"

"Perhaps it only works if it is whole?" added Doran as the rest nodded their heads in agreement. All quickly went quiet as the Saints approached.

"What's the story here, Wardens?" greeted Tilus from behind.

It had been a week since his last visit from across the plain, and it was time for a change of guard. Tilus and Adam greeted each other with a strong handshake as a certain professional fondness had developed over time.

"Deciding who is going out on patrol before sundown," responded Adam.

"A man of your ranking should hardly be forced to run cross-country, Captain," said Tilus as he patted him on the shoulders. "Come, you and I can have a drink or two."

"I'd hate to say no Tilus—"

"Then don't! Come!" He wrapped his arm around Adam's back and leaded the way, as Doran nudged his head forward to acquiesce.

"Fine, then. One drink. Thane, Arren, Brandt. Off you go." Adam nodded as the three grumbled, throwing their poking sticks into the fire in protest and slowly rising like a herd of oxen.

Tilus signalled to his men, who quickly brought them two bottles of ale. The two sat down at a rickety table. Tilus took a long drink and gave a sigh of relief. "The plain is larger than it seems. You would think one would have a merry time crossing it on foot."

"During training, the commander would have us run back and forth twenty times a day."

"Good exercise," said the Saint.

"Good punishment, too," said the Warden.

"Cheers." Tilus raised his bottle as he waited for Adam to pick up his own drink and oblige.

"Cheers," Adam replied and drank a sip.

"I am told that there's been no sign of the Drae'shï."

"Not a sound."

"Don't you find that rather odd?"

"Odd?"

"How the Drae'shï have abandoned their quest to capture the woman and the artefact."

"I don't think they did. And I'm not very comfortable sitting outside their gates as we speak," said Adam as he looked up into the mountain's many nooks and crannies.

"They know you're here,"

"I'm expecting an ambush at any time now," said Adam.

"Good," said Tilus causally.

"What?" Adam furrowed his brow.

"That will spare us having to go in."

"You want to go in?"

"We need prisoners and answers. Can I count on you to get them?" said Tilus confidently, despite Adam's pursed lips.

"Is this why you're here? For answers, or for something else?" asked Adam as he stood from his seat.

"I am here to protect the Temple of the Holy Enoch and the Massass. It means understanding the threats we face." Tilus remained seated calmly drinking his ale.

"And that means risking our men by entering into Ussar Varys or waiting here like sitting ducks?"

"Unless, of course, you're privy to some information that we are not, thereby sparing us the unsavoury task ahead of us." Tilus took another sip whilst Adam stood silent, yet unable to mask his growing distaste for the man. "Do you know the reason why the temple has endured for the last two hundred years, Adomas? It has endured because it has brought order where there was chaos. It brought peace where there was barbarity. And how was it able to do so? How did Erinderiss the Kind manage? One man? He was the only person who knew how to control and use the sap of the Enoch tree. A powerful mystical, medicinal substance capable of curing even the most acute of ailments. Powerful indeed, even beyond its apparent capabilities."

Adam stood silent as Tilus continued, "The temple grew because people believed Eru was entitled to lead them. His followers made him his temple, not him. But was he so entitled solely by the Mother's grace? Or was he the only one able to control and make use of the lifeblood of Amenti where everyone else failed?"

"Wouldn't this kind of talk be considered heresy among your ranks, Commander?" asked Adam.

"I'm a soldier and an old dog. The only thing I believe in is blood owed and blood repaid. I see beyond the dogma. I see the tactics of war and the plays of politicians. You would do well to do the same." Tilus took a long drink. "Ahhhh. Needless to say, Adam, the temple's control of the Enoch trees is what gave it its power. If the rumours about this mirror are true, there is a far greater cause behind us standing right outside these gates than just keeping the Drae'shï inside."

"Entering the mountain is a suicide mission. I will not risk my men that way," stated the Eldassari sternly.

"Agreed. However, one thing has been bothering me since we got here. If the Drae'shï are so intent on retrieving their precious Shard, why haven't they tried again?"

"We're here to prevent them from leaving, not encourage them to come out." Adam pointed at the ominous gates.

"A deterrent," said Tilus.

"Yes." Adam nodded.

"Precisely."

"Precisely?" said Adam, quizzically.

"Yes. It's time to turn it into a trap. We must retreat from Black Pass," stated Tilus, resolute.

"What? I'm not sure I can agree with you on this, Tilus."

"I don't need your agreement. I need your obedience, Captain."

"The Wardens don't claim authority over any of the Saints. I'd expect the Saints to do the same." Adam's scowl intensified.

"You are right, Captain," stated Tilus as he slowly got up from his seat and dusted his hands. "But I do retain command over the knights that are here, and they will follow my orders even if you do not agree with them. At that point, it's up to you whether you want to take on the risk of staying here."

"You can't just leave! If the Drae'shï send out another search party like they did last time, they will overrun us in no time." Adam slammed his hands on the table.

Tilus didn't flinch. "By leaving, we will encourage them to come out and commence their search again. When they do, we'll see if they can outrun the Order's cavalry. Then we will get our answers," he continued as the Saints had been slowly gathering their things and began mounting their horses.

"Is this it then? Your pledge to help us? What about your oaths?" Adam threw his hand dismissively to the departing knights.

Tilus took a deep breath. "Unlike the oath of the Wardens' to protect the world, my oath is far more modest. It is to protect the temple and the Massass. Everything else is inconsequential. I would ask you to heed my words, but I know you more to be a man of honour than one of pragmatism."

Adam stood rigidly with his fists clenched at his sides.

"I would recommend you return to Harlot's Hold by tonight. I would not wish to see you dead in the morn Adomas," said Tilus as he mounted his horse.

"I have men out patrolling and getting supplies," said Adam as the rest of the Wardens started gathering around having clearly eaves-dropped on the last bit of the conversation.

"I will send a couple of scouts to search for them. Best you make your way back before sundown," said Tilus as he directed the horse out of the broken archway of the old fort.

"Fuckin' pissant!" yelled Samos when a couple of Saints looked back to admonish him. "The fuck you want? Go on then! Piss off!"

The two knights promptly obliged after the group of Wardens was quickly gathering around Samos.

"Shut up, Samos!" yelled Adam. The Wardens all seemed dumb-founded at the abrupt change of plans and soon turned to Adam.

"What are we going to do, Captain?" intervened Doran.

"Brandt, Thane, and Arren just left along the north-western slopes," said Willam.

"We can't risk staying here at night, Captain," whispered Doran. "We know little of what goes on behind those gates and far less of what's hidden between the mountain's ravines."

"He's right. For all we know, they could be watching us as we speak," said Samos as he looked up at the jagged slopes around them. "Which, come to think of it, is making the situation more unsettling."

Adam mounted a horse. "We have no choice. We need to move out, inform the rest,"

"Where are you going now?" said Willam.

"I'm going to catch up with the others."

"Alone? No. We're coming with you," said Willam.

"No! Stay here. I'll be much faster on my own, and I need you here in case we do not cross paths. Just wait 'til sundown. No more. I'll meet you at the Hold." Adam whipped his horse into a steady gallop and straight out of Black Pass.

The Eldassari rode out, speeding along the narrow winding roads that led to the sloping edges of the mountain. Each path was a rocky labyrinth that led to even tighter trails along the mountainside. Adam called out to his comrades, but no answer came except for the rumble of the mount and the tumbling of the odd rocks. His search continued to no avail, and dusk slowly crept in along with the evening fog.

The Rakshir plains slowly sank beneath a sea of white haze. Even the orange lights of Harlot's Hold had all but blurred out of sight by now, and Adam soon found himself more alone than ever before. His search pushed him down the mountain's west side and along the slopes that met the rushing Illyum River.

The mountains met the river at a sheer gorge that cut straight along the western side of the Ussari mountain chain. The shores rarely hosted any traveller, for the rapids were treacherous. A single path led down to the waters seemingly cut out of the rock. Hidden pathways and shallow pools afforded him a crossing, and he soon found himself passing through the sparse woodland that characterised Raem's wildlands.

Adam called out, but hardly a sound ran through the fog-laden forest. Night started creeping in, and a deep sense of dread pervaded the air. The fog was replaced by darkness, and the setting sun offered little light to the Eldassari. A rustle of leaves came from behind a nearby tree, and both he and the horse tensed up. "Calm down, boy. It's just a rat," he said as he slowly drew his sword, but as he passed by the source of the sound, a trail of dark blue blood emerged.

He quickly looked around, but there was no one in sight. Suddenly, an arrow shot right past Adam's face, missing his nose by a whisper and throwing him off balance as his steed reared at the fright. He quickly regained control and urged his horse into a gallop, but suddenly, the slash of a black steel sword sliced the horse's hind legs, forcing the beast to collapse along with its rider. Adam found himself with his face to the sky as he heard the clank of armour and shimmer of chainmail approach.

A tall, dark figure with red eyes encased within a black helm emerged, resting his foot on the ailing beast's head. His sword swiftly pacified its cries.

Adam scurried to pick up his sword and rose to meet his opponent.

The Drae'shï was tall and slender, wearing an ornate black and purple breastplate and draping chainmail. His spaulders were sharp and lined with gold engravings. He gripped his long falchion with both hands, tightening his claw-like gauntlets and assuming form. "You tread on the steps of the dead, Eldassari. Your friends have already met their demise, but I will not deprive them of your presence for long."

Adam unhooked his cloak and readied himself.

The Drae'shï dashed at Adam with speed and force. Adam countered and parried, finding his footing difficult to maintain. The two engaged in a dance of blades, but neither managed to land a strike.

Another arrow flew by, startling Adam but not fazing the Drae'shï.

The Drae'shï sliced away at Adam's chest, slashing through the thick leather armour and only missing Adam's skin by a hair. Adam circled the Drae'shï to face the darkness from whence the arrows flew. The Drae'shï and his archer were in complete synchrony.

Adam backed up into the forest, yet few trees allowed any space to turn or hide. The Drae'shï slashed and struck with incredible strength, putting Adam on the defensive.

Another arrow flew past.

Adam backed up further and slowly drew his throwing axe. He flung it swiftly at the Drae'shï, who parried it with incredible dexterity yet allowed Adam to find his opportunity to strike for the kill. The Drae'shï dodged and thumped the Eldassari with the pommel of his sword.

Adam fell flat onto the ground.

The Drae'shï stabbed and missed and stabbed again as Adam rolled away.

Adam soon found himself in the middle of a large opening in the forest as the Drae'shï slowed his pace and walked slowly towards Adam.

Another arrow flew past him.

"Go on. Run. My archers will finish you," said the Drae'shï, mildly fatigued.

Adam paused for a moment, attempting to gauge the location of the archers. Silence ensued.

Then an arrow struck the Warden.

Adam cried out in anguish. The arrow had stuck out of the top of his left arm. He staggered back but didn't fall.

The two watched each other as the Drae'shï drew closer. Droplets of dark blue blood trailed down the Drae'shï's arm. "It seems like you don't fear death, Warden. You hold true to your title. Defiant 'til the end."

Adam dashed once more and slashed at the Drae'shï, who twisted on his heels and struck him in the back with the sword's pommel, sending him to the ground once more.

The Drae'shï quickly kicked away the Warden's blade.

Adam lay on the ground, turning slowly to face the night sky.

The Drae'shï stood above Adam with his blade to Adam's neck.

He removed his helmet with fatigue, letting it fall to the ground. His pale silver-skinned face revealed a battle fought not long ago. Blood trickled down his chin. "Your friends put up a fight. I'll give them that," he said as he touched his armpit and drew blood.

A hooded female Drae'shï soon emerged from the shadows, dressed in light, blue and black leather armour bearing an intricate short bow inlaid with black and silver engravings. "Olpher, let's go. Finish and be done with it. You're bleeding."

Adam panted on the ground, struggling to move as the sharp blade grazed his neck, and Olpher placed his right foot on Adam's left shoulder, pressing onto the shaft in his arm. Adam cried in agony, grabbing the arrow lodged into his arm to ease his pain.

"I know where she is. The one you seek," Adam groaned. "I have met her, and she still holds the Shard. You'll never reach her."

Olpher laughed. "The dead oft like to taunt, but you tell me nothing that I don't already know Eldassari. Each fragment reveals where the other is. We know where the Ilvaresh is, and we will find her."

"Don't call her that," said the archer.

"Matters not what she's called, Sirra."

"You'll never make it," Adam groaned again, then followed with a wheezing cough. "If you want your mirror back, you're going to have to head all the way to Valendria. Not even your ancestors managed to breach the city."

Olpher knelt beside Adam, the dim light of the clear sky now shining onto his scarred old face and blind white eye. His hand grabbed onto Adam's, which still clutched the arrow, squeezing it with glee. "I know, Eldassari. I was there."

"The mirror is broken. You'll never be able to move under its protection. They'll be waiting for you," Adam grunted, wincing in pain.

Olpher laughed. "I admire your spirit, Warden. I really do. But we don't need the mirror to move outside the mountains. If we ever chose to invade, not a corner of this world would remain unclaimed. Your Hold upon the hill would be swept away like silt under the torrent of our armies."

"Then why? Why do you want it back?" cried Adam.

Olpher slowly got up. "I could take the time to explain, but why tell tales to dead men?" asked the Drae'shï as he firmed his foot on Adam's shoulder and raised his sword.

"Drae'shï!" called out Thane as he emerged from the tree line, blood trickling from his brow with two arrows sticking out of his back.

"Seems like dead men still talk after all," said Olpher as he looked at Sirra and nodded.

She quickly drew an arrow and aimed.

Suddenly a throwing axe flew right out of the darkness, striking at the executioner's spaulders, throwing both him and Sirra off guard. The arrow flew into the sky, and Thane charged the field.

Adam instinctively plucked the arrowhead out of his arm and sank it straight into Olpher's thigh. Sirra drew another arrow, but Thane's timing was faster, and the arrow missed. Olpher cursed in agony and slashed at Adam, cutting a clean line across Adam's cheek as the Eldassari staggered away.

The Warden immediately turned and dove onto him disarming the Drae'shï.

Sirra immediately kicked Adam in the side, flinging him over.

"Run!" yelled Olpher as Sirra hoisted him up and he retrieved his sword. She hesitated. "Sirra! Go! Now!" he yelled as she noticed another Eldassari emerging. "Go!" he yelled once more as Sirra began sprinting whilst Brandt began running towards the scuffle.

"You're going to pay for what you did to Arren," growled Thane.

"I have killed more men in one of your lifetimes than you ever could in one of mine," he spat as he drew the arrowhead from his thigh. "What's three more?"

Brandt and Thane each charged the Drae'shï as he masterfully parried all their hits and knocked each of them back with his rebuffs. Adam quickly fetched his sword, but another arrow stopped his reach as Sirra fired from afar.

"Watch out!" yelled Adam as Sirra fired another arrow at the scuffle.

The arrow barely missed Brandt but allowed Olpher to land a clean punch to his face, knocking him down. Thane struck back but soon found his arm locked by the Drae'shï's grip, who then quickly raised his elbow in a bone-crunching move, followed by a smashing head-butt to the red-maned beast. The Drae'shï stood tall behind the felled Wardens. He signalled to Adam to come forth.

Another arrow flew past the Drae'shï and slipped clean past Adam's head.

Adam drew his sword once more and went to meet the Drae'shï in combat. The two began their dance once more.

"Your resolve is commendable. You might even have iron blood in your veins after all," said Olpher, panting.

Adam offered no reply, only focus.

The two circled each other patiently as the Drae'shï baited Adam into giving Sirra his back.

Adam watched Olpher's eyes intently as they focused back on his. He waited, anticipating the sound of Sirra's arrow leaving its bow. The silence lasted for centuries as beads of sweat ran down his face. His eyes burned as he struggled not to blink.

In a split second, Olpher's eyes darted away and back again, but Adam had already dodged.

An arrow that was meant for the Eldassari's back flew straight into the Drae'shï's throat.

They each paused for a moment.

Olpher staggered back and fell.

"Father!" cried Sirra. Immediately, she dashed towards the Wardens with fury, drawing her twin sabres, but she slowed to a stop as she saw Olpher's lifeless gaze. Desperation loosened her grip, and she fell to her knees. The final gurgling sounds of blood muffled his last words. She crawled towards Olpher and rested on his chest, tears rolling from her eyes.

"Are you happy now?" she raged, her scarlet eyes reddened even further with her tears. "Have you done your duty?"

The Wardens stood astonished as they clambered to their feet. In all their years, they'd never thought of the Drae'shï as anything but the vicious invaders of the tales of old.

"We had no choice," said Adam sternly. "The Drae'shï must remain confined to Ussar Varys."

"What choice do you think we have?" she yelled. "You think we want to leave the mountain? Leave our home?"

"Then tell us! Why is the Shard so important to you?" yelled Adam, but Sirra ignored him.

"What have I done?" she wept. "I'm sorry. I'm so sorry."

"Speak up!" he barked reaching for her shoulder.

"Leave me alone!" Sirra instantly swatted his hand.

"Adam," said Brandt as he attempted to hold him back.

"Speak!"

She gritted her teeth, looking back at him hatefully. "The Shard is part of a whole. We live by the light of its reflection. The light of the Mother. We know no sickness or death. Without the mirror, we age, we die, we suffer," she said as she slowly wiped her tears. "We need it to survive."

"Can't you fix it? Why go to such lengths?" asked Brandt calmly.

"You think we wouldn't have already!" she barked, tears still rolling off her cheeks. "Only with all its pieces."

"So why did Lilith take it? The Drae'shï that stole the Shard from you."

"She is no Drae'shï. Her form may have been once, but her essence is no longer. It is not of this world."

"You lie."

"Believe what you wish! I don't care!" She paused, pressing her face against Olpher's chest, rocking herself.

"Then where is she from? Tell me!" insisted Adam once more, grabbing her by her collar before the others could stop him.

"I don't know!" she yelled back, shoving his hands off. "She entered the Hall of Mirrors when she should have been guarding the entrance, and we found it shattered. No one had been in there for ages. The tower had been sealed for hundreds of years. Whatever went in is not what came out."

Adam paused.

"Ever since she left, the Moirai have been sending us to retrieve her and the Shard," said Sirra as she stood up and wiped her tears.

"The Moirai?" said Adam.

Sirra huffed.

"Speak!"

"Fuck!" she cried exasperated. "It's my unit. We're the sentinels and protectors of the White Tower and Ussar Varys."

In the distance, dim lights began to appear, and the incoming cohorts' echoing chatter alerted those present.

"It must be the Saints," stated Adam as the Wardens peered into the distance to trace the silhouettes of the incoming horsemen. In the meantime, Sirra had started to sprint.

"Damn it!" yelled Brandt as he realised the Drae'shï had taken off.

All three bolted after her, but both Thane and Brandt failed to take more than a few steps after their earlier encounter. Adam pursued relentlessly as Sirra skipped off like a cat towards the sound of the rushing river. Adam raced behind her as she sped further into the thicket, disappearing from sight. He sped after her, following her trail of broken branches and footsteps in the messy getaway she left in her wake. The sounds of the rushing waters of the river were soon upon him, along with the cavalry that was not far behind.

Adam emerged from the bushes overlooking the sheer drop to the rapids where Sirra stood hesitant. Adam immediately caught her, pulling her from the impending drop. Yet the ground beneath them faltered and the two slipped down a short precipice lying just above the ultimate fall.

"Stop! Stop! I'm not going to hurt you," he whispered as he held Sirra back from the raging rapids below.

"There's ten kilometres of rapids from there. You won't survive."

"I'll take my chances," she said as she struggled to squirm free.

"I can help you get the mirror back!" he grunted as he forced her still. "But I need your help. I need you to tell me all you know."

"Why would I help you? So you can kill me once you've got what you want?" she asked as Adam slowly let her slide out of his grasp.

"Because I'm your only chance of leaving here alive. If the Saints catch you, they will torture and kill you. I can't guarantee your safety with them, but I can give you my word that I won't harm you unless you try to yourself. So, what will it be, Drae'shi?" he asked as she stared down into the raging waters below and the trotting horses drew closer.

Out of the bushes above, two knights emerged with torches.

Adam held Sirra down, close to the rock face, his hand over her mouth.

"They said he took off after her in this direction. Think they tumbled down?" asked one.

"If they did, they'll be fished out in Orestill. If there's anything left of them by then." The other chuckled.

Adam relaxed his grip. They paused, and soon the knights were off.

The night above was silent once more.

CHAPTER 19

IMMORAL SACRIFICES

Zain barged into the cabin. The women all sat watching the soaked Vampire panting with exhaustion. "We have a problem."

"Is the ship sinking?" asked Adara.

Zain paused, catching his breath. "We have two problems."

"Wonderful," added Lilith.

"Those ships which are following us, the ones we thought were ours. They're not ours."

"They're pirates," continued Pïshkah as she lay down in her pretend grave, closing her eyes and cursing to herself.

"They're still far off, but they're catching up."

"What are we going to do?" asked Adara anxiously.

"We're dumping the cargo into the sea to reduce the weight and catch some speed, but we're not going to outrun them forever."

"That's it. It's time to see whether all that footwork paid off," said Lilith as she rose from her corner.

"No way!" Zain forcibly stuck his arm between Lilith and the doorway.

"Yes way!" she said as she tried to pass under, only to find Zain's hand on her shoulder.

"I need you to protect them."

"If they can't—"

"Not now!" he yelled, pushing her back inside. "Stay inside!" His anger started to creep in. "And Pïshkah. If you've got any tricks up your sleeve to appease whatever unleashed this calamity upon us, now's time to use it."

"I'm a Cleriheu, not a wishing well," said Pïshkah bluntly as Zain's face soured. "But. Hold on." She took off one of her many pendants. "Come here. Get down."

Zain obliged and leaned his head down as Pïshkah crept to the edge of the bed and slipped on the hoop over and around his neck. He picked up the pendant, which consisted of a dark purple crystal cast in a molten silver casing.

"Pretty stone."

"It's an amethyst. Get down." She lowered his head down, closed her eyes, and began whispering a mantra whilst tracing a symbol on his crown with her fingers. She then let go and sat back.

"That's it?" asked Zain as he looked back up at the overly tattooed witch.

"Yes."

"Will it make me fight better?"

"No."

"Will it make me fight faster?"

"No."

He paused scratching his cheek, expecting a better answer.

She sighed. "It's there to help guide you to the right path—and hopefully the rest of us out of this storm," she explained begrudgingly.

"Practical. Right. Stay in here," Zain turned and quickly picked up a sword and belt from a corner.

"Wait!" said Lilith as she approached him from the side. "What are you doing?"

"Picking a sword. I know I'm immortal, but I'd like not to give them too much of an advantage, you know."

"Stop!" She stayed his hand, causing him to drop the sword.

"What?" he barked.

"You *know* what! You don't need a sword. You need these," she said as she held up his hands. "And all the fresh blood that you need is on its way."

"It won't come to that. *This* will be enough," he said as he picked up the sword.

"Not even the blood of your enemies?" she exclaimed.

"Not if I can help it. No."

"You could kill them all single-handedly."

"Not now, Lilith."

"Why do you insist on holding on to your stupid delusions of humanity? You're a Vampire!"

"Not now!" he yelled back as the door flung open once again and a gust of wind and rain poured in. Zain looked Lilith in the eye once more and departed.

Out on the deck, the crew was labouring their way through the heavy cargo whilst others struggled to close the sails fluttering in the wind. The sea rocked the vessel as the men stumbled upon each other.

"Zain!" cried Elias as he, along with a dozen other men, struggled to pull in the mainsail.

"Elias!" Zain immediately took hold of the flailing rope. "We're already moving too fast with the secondary sails. The mainsail won't hold with these winds. It'll either snap the mast or else we might smash into an oncoming wave at full speed. We'll worry about the pirates once we're through this. I'll secure it from up top."

"Fine," said Elias. "Go, hurry!"

Zain confidently dashed to the shrouds and climbed up fearlessly as he took the pelting rain to his face with a devious smile. It was a long time since he had stalked the seas and experienced the thrill of a storm. The thunder called out to him in the distance, and the lightning lit the night sky anew. Their pursuers were not far behind.

The brigands' ships carried the distinct features of Carthosian triremes. The three vessels were long, sturdy, and nimble, equipped with sails and oars, but most importantly, they were known for sinking other vessels by using their bow's metal rams.

Zain proceeded to secure the sail as he watched the storm deepen in the distance. He was familiar with this situation all too well. His excitement soon turned to concern for his companions below. The dawn of first light was a long way ahead. Within a few minutes, Zain had crept his way along the spar, securing the sail properly. However, one small victory came at the cost of another.

Beneath him, the tensions between the crew and the Saints had reached boiling point. His descent was rapid, almost costing him his grip. Elias and a dozen other knights were standing between the crew and the entrance to the main cabin.

"Back off, or we'll have you all hanged once we arrive at port!" barked Lyons as the crew clamoured around the knights.

"You got to make it to port first, ya posh bastard!" yelled a sailor.

"Captain!" yelled Elias, furious at this insubordination. "Get these men in order now!"

"It is out of my hands, Commander. If I stand my ground, they will throw me overboard along with you. You must listen," pleaded the ship's captain as he stood as a mediator between the two.

"Back to your stations now!" barked Elias. "If you do not follow my orders, it will not be superstition that kills you. It will be our swords."

Some of the other less influenced crew members remained at their stations, more fearful of brandished steel than old wives' tales.

"And if you kill us all, who's going to sail this ship?" intervened the second officer.

"Off with the witches!" yelled a sailor as the thunder clapped once more, the rest joining in.

"What the bloody hell is going on?" shouted Zain. "There are three triremes upon us, and you're fighting over the Cleriheu?"

"What about this one? He's cursed us, too! He's another one they've cursed. Y'all saw him get stabbed in the back, and it didn't do 'im a thing," said one sailor as the rest agreed, keeping well away from Zain as he walked towards the Saints.

"They've convinced themselves that the girls are sea crones. Some folk legend of the Gulf Sea," said Lyons.

"Some folk legend indeed, Commander," said the second officer as he looked at Elias. "But it was nay short of an hour after we discovered the third girl that this storm came upon us! All crones are said to be of immense beauty to deceive onlookers but cause untold misery on anyone who dares offer them safe passage."

"Off with the witches!" they yelled again.

"You'll have to kill me twice before you even try." Zain ominously stepped forward and they all took a step back.

"There she is!" yelled a sailor as Lilith peered through one of the windows of the captain's quarters.

A bottle soared across, smashing against the glass.

A brawl immediately broke out between the Saints and the sailors. The rest of the crew either remained looking on or joined in breaking up the fight. Zain threw in a few punches and quickly rose to the quarter-deck to take stock of the situation at sea. On the stern side, the pirates' pursuit did not yield, and their position had drawn close enough to catch a glimpse of the men aboard.

"Help!" called out the helmsman of the *Intrepid*, a large black muscular fellow from Drellanon. "The storm is moving east. We need to get as far west as possible!" he yelled in his heavy Darelese accent as they struggled to hold the wheel.

Zain immediately joined him, holding onto the steering wheel as the enormous waves turned more treacherous. "West? We're already far out from the coast. The pirates are right behind us!"

"It's either the pirates or the storm. You tell me."

"Fuck," said Zain. "How can I help?"

"Get those still water scumbags under control! I'll handle the wheel," said the helmsman as he began turning the ship westward.

The brawl below continued as the Saints refused to draw swords against the unarmed thugs until one sailor drew a pocketknife and stabbed one of the Saints in the back of his shoulder. Lyons quickly drew his sword and sliced the mutineer, spilling his guts out in a splash before the rest of the crew. All the Saints drew their swords. The fight was over.

"If any of you bastards dare disobey a single order from here on out, we'll stick you all and have you dangling from the topmast by your fuckin' innards!" Lyons barked.

Suddenly they were blinded.

A white flash tore at their eyes, and the shrieking boom of thunder deafened them. All fell to the ground, and as Zain slowly caught hold of his senses, his blurry eyes caught glimpse of the main mast crashing down in a fiery blaze.

"Get up!" yelled Elias, fire blazing in his gaze, as he forcibly picked up and pushed each individual one by one. "Back to your stations! Secure the rest of the ship! Throw off the debris!"

Lilith quickly flung the door open. "They're grappling the ship!"

"Shit! I'll handle it," said Zain, his ears still ringing from the blast. "Ready your men," he continued as Elias nodded.

Zain quickly returned inside to see Adara and Pïshkah sawing away at a grapple rope hooked to their cabin window. The rope soon snapped, but more grapples flew.

"There are more stuck outside! We can't reach them," said Adara.

"They're climbing up!" yelled Pïshkah from the other cabin.

Zain peeked out of the window. A string of men were hauling themselves across the treacherous waters onto a grapple hooked within the stern's fixtures. The rope was far beyond the women's reach.

"There's more!" said Pïshkah as an arrow hit the window frame where Zain stood.

"Keep away from the windows!" he yelled back. "The wind is holding them back, but they're not far off. I need to cut these ropes."

"I'm coming with you!" said Lilith.

"No! Stay here. The crew will try to kill you. Protect Adara!" shouted Zain as he dashed outside, banging the door behind him.

Lilith cursed him.

Zain returned to the quarterdeck and looked behind the ship. The pirates had gained more ground.

"They're gaining on us," called Adara from the porthole below.

"Stay inside!" yelled Zain before climbing on the quarterdeck's railing.

In an instant, he jumped down on the side of the ship, sinking his vampiric claws into the wood. He swung around the back and hung on one of the ropes as he latched onto the stern's fixtures. He cut the tensile rope in one swift movement, releasing its grip, but soon an arrow found his back. He cursed, but the bolt did not stop him. As he proceeded slowly across the face of the stern to the next rope, the climbers were almost within reach of the deck.

"Zain! I can't reach it," cried Pïshkah from below.

Zain hesitated and soon found himself flailing from side to side as the ship rocked once more. His grip slipped. He fell.

"Zain!" shrieked Adara.

Yet Zain had caught another rope and was holding on for dear life. He promptly swung around and caught a glimpse of the other two pirate ships overtaking the *Intrepid* at a distance on either side. He looked back up at Pïshkah, who was now fidgeting with a lantern by the window. Lilith appeared on the quarterdeck with her swords, hacking away at another fresh grapple. Meanwhile, Pïshkah doused the pirates with lamp oil and tossed the flaming lantern onto the horde, turning the men into a blazing trail of brigands. Zain climbed up as the men fell, but more grapples shot overhead, hooking on. Arrows flew again and struck Zain once more.

As he reached the window, Adara pointed back. The pirates were almost just beneath them, winching their way closer to the vessel.

"Two other ships are coming up on our sides," yelled Pïshkah from the other room.

"They're trying to flank us," he said as he climbed back inside.

"Zain, you're hurt." Adara looked stunned at his pierced back.

"I'm fine. Just try to pull them... Ouch!" he yelled. "Gently..." He glared back at Pïshkah now holding both arrows in her hand.

"You complain a lot for someone who's undead," she said bluntly as Zain attempted to feel his back.

"What are we going to do, Zain?" asked Adara, concerned and appearing slightly dishevelled from the ordeal.

"I have a plan. Wait here. I'll get us out of this. I promise you," he said as he held Adara's hands to his mouth. "Pïshkah, listen to me." He turned to the Cleriheu and held her by the shoulders. "No matter what, stay with Adara. She protected you. You owe her your life. Don't fail me. Don't fail her."

Pïshkah nodded solemnly.

"Keep the door locked!" he said and then took off once more.

The deck was once again under control as the men struggled to maintain the vessel on course, smashing through the surf in front of them. Lyons held the deck with the Saints whilst the quarterdeck was manned by Elias, Lilith, and the other crewmen struggling to cut the grapples. Zain climbed up top next to the helmsman.

"We can't reach the ropes! You have to climb down again!" yelled Lilith through the pelting rain.

"Look out! Starboard!" called out Elias as a volley of arrows flew from the pirate ship to their right. All ducked, but the helmsman could not.

Zain cursed as the man collapsed, and he swooped in taking hold of the unruly steering wheel.

"They're too close!" yelled Elias as he reached out for the helmsman, but the light had already left his eyes.

"What are we going to do?" yelled Lilith as the vessel edged closer to the *Intrepid*. "Zain?"

Zain stood still for a moment, wind and rain battering his face. He recalled his younger days when he, too, stalked the Gulf of Dros as a pirate himself hundreds of years before. The thrill of championing a storm and the gall to go beyond anything any living being would. He looked to his sides and at the bow. His focus was clear, and everything fell silent all around him. The pirate vessel crept closer to the starboard side, and the first grapple flew and hooked on, as the pirates readied another volley. Zain looked to the bow as the ship was about to tear into the enormous wave before it and called out with a smirk on his face. "Everyone, hold on!"

Zain immediately let the steering wheel fly, and the ship took a sharp turn to starboard, crashing into the port side of the pirates' vessel. All aboard on both ships tumbled as the ships clashed. As they rose, the massive wave followed, smashing into the port side of the *Intrepid*. The vessels creaked and warped as the wave forced one vessel onto the other, holding down the pirate ship under the pressure of the weight of both the wave and the *Intrepid*.

In a matter of seconds, it had tipped over along with its entire wailing crew.

The *Intrepid* sailed on, yet the other ship still hooked to the stern failed to sink under the first wave, its weight now holding the ropes as tight as lute strings. "Get away!" yelled Zain as he once more swung the ship to face the waves at the last second, forcing the trailing pirate ship to suffer one last crushing wave to its side. The tensile force tore the grapples along with part of the stern. Adara's and Pïshkah's screams came from below as their cabins were now ripped open to the wind, desks, bunks, and trunks sliding into the water.

The second pirate ship fell back behind the high seas, but the last remaining ship was still undeterred and found itself ahead of the *Intrepid*. Zain desperately swung the vessel one more time, but the pirates' ram had already grazed part of the hull, and the *Intrepid* soon slowed down as more grapple hooks caught on and drew the vessels side by side.

All aboard drew their swords as the pirates clambered and swung across. The fight ensued, but the crew was quickly overwhelmed. The Saints fought valiantly, smashing more than one bandit at a time as their training was unmatched. Zain and Lilith dove in, cutting through dozens at a time. Her ferocity once more emerged as she picked up a second broadsword and proceeded to dive into the fray without care or caution. Zain soon noticed how Pïshkah and Adara were banging on their windows to catch his attention. "Shit!" he yelled as he noticed they'd also caught the attention of the pirates.

"Zain!" yelled Lilith. "It's time," she called out as she finished off one more.

"Stay here!" he yelled back and dashed towards the group of pirates, quickly dispatching them in a few moves.

The women inside struggled with the door.

"It's jammed!" yelled Adara from behind the glass.

"Never mind that! They're behind us!" said Pïshkah as Zain looked through, realising half the stern was missing but far worse than that was the semi-submerged pirate ship trailing right behind.

"Hold onto anything!" he yelled once more as Adara and Pïshkah held on. A wave soon crashed in, followed by the bowsprit spearing through the cabin along with the ram through the hull. All aboard tumbled to the ground as the cheers of the pirates rang through. The girls hung on as the water from the crashing waves drained from the cabin along with half of their things.

The deck was again filled with more pirates as they skewered each

Saint and crew member too slow to rise. Zain found himself surrounded.

The women inside started smashing the windows in a bid to get out. As he looked once more, Zain caught a glimpse of the captain of the pirate vessel. His eyes were fixed on the Vampire. His long black coat fluttered. Zain could tell he knew what Zain was. Elias also found himself upon the quarterdeck, fending off the horde. Soon there were none but a few left to defend the vessel.

The captain of the pirate ship landed aboard, signalling more crew members to stop Zain. A dozen more people surrounded Zain. He fought and slashed but failed to quell the onslaught. "Elias! Adara!" he yelled as he saw Pïshkah and Adara attempting to fend off the pirates from inside the cabin.

Elias looked over the quarterdeck and leapt, bowling through a group of pirates.

Zain skewered the brigands by the door but was soon stabbed himself.

"Zain!" cried Adara.

"Adara! They're climbing down the stern!" said Pïshkah.

Lilith was also slowly being overwhelmed. "Zain! Drink their blood! Now!" she roared, just before being punched to the ground.

Zain gazed as he watched the tragedy unfold. He turned to find himself surrounded whilst Elias was being hauled away from his weapon by the other pirates. Zain's fear turned to rage as he smashed a man's head against the wall. His eyes reddened, and his claws grew. He tore through the pirates, but his rage didn't afford him any finesse as they, too, cut and sliced through him. The pirate captain watched the beast from afar.

"Drink!" Lilith called once more, her ruby eyes searing his own.

The smell of blood spilt over the deck was intoxicating, and he could no longer hold back. The throbbing feeling of hunger rushed through him as he picked up a pirate by the crown of his head, and his maw widened, revealing his fearsome teeth.

The captain signalled.

Suddenly a massive bolt from a mounted scorpion shot right

through, tearing through the pirate and impaling Zain on the cabin wall.

The Vampire roared in agony.

The fight was over, and so was the storm.

The pirate captain walked up to him. "I've read many books about the Eldaresh but never thought I would ever encounter one. But one thing they always said. If you ever see one, don't let them drink your blood. And most importantly, make sure you drain theirs." He drew out a sharp dagger and immediately slit Zain's throat. The blood poured out of his neck, soaking his body, gushing out far more than any normal man would ever imagine.

Zain attempted to mouth his final curse, but his body failed him.

Lilith cursed as she lay on the deck, observing the scene. She crawled towards her swords, but the pirates kicked each one away. She turned over and reached for the Shard in her pocket and stumbled up to face them. The men laughed at the puny piece of glass held at them, trembling in her bloody hands but they approached cautiously, circling her like a wild animal. She cut and cut again, viciously clawing at her predators until she slashed a pirate's arm.

"Drop it, and we won't kill you," said the captain calmly.

"Fuck you," she roared.

He nodded, and a pirate took a swing at her.

She dodged and stabbed him in the calf, sending him to the ground.

The captain nodded again, and two more entered the fray. She quickly dispatched one, but the other proved to be more than just a simple adversary. She dodged and turned but soon tumbled in the debris. She lay on the ground and the pirate swung. She raised her arm and closed her eyes.

The sword struck. It wobbled, warped, and hummed, and suddenly burst into a hail of splinters, hitting both Lilith and her assailant. The Shard flew across the deck and landed right under the foot of the captain.

"Interesting," he said, as he approached and recovered it. He looked for a moment at the haunting artefact, narrowing his eyes as he gazed at it.

"Captain? Captain?"

His attention was broken.

"The ship is sinking," said another. "We need to unhook. We also found two other female passengers. The rest are all crew."

"Take them aboard. Take the other one, too," said the captain as two other men grabbed hold of the vicious Drae'shï, now peppered with cuts.

"Help! Let me go!" screamed Adara as she and Pïshkah were being hauled across the deck.

"Stop!" yelled Elias, attempting to buck his way out of constriction as he was held down on his knees. "Do you know who we are? The Massass will have the entire Valendrian fleet searching for us! You will be flayed alive for this."

"And how will he know where to find us, sir knight?"

"There's nowhere you can hide! They'll scour every port from Valendria to Morren's Gate," spat Elias as the captain calmly approached him.

"Oh really? Then maybe you should let them know where to start looking," he said sarcastically before booting Elias in the chest, throwing him overboard.

Adara yelped.

The pirates laughed as they gradually returned aboard their ship whilst the *Intrepid* was slowly being claimed by the sea.

"I wonder if they still float with all that armour." He laughed as the rest of his crew laughed along before booting the rest of the Saints into the billowing waters.

Chapter 20

As Above So Below

"He's fading out," said a male voice.

"Get him up," said a female.

"He's not going to make it," said the man, concerned.

"He will! Make sure he's properly reconnected and strapped in," repeated the woman sternly.

"What happened?" asked another man as he entered the room.

"The trauma has been substantial, but he's still alive," said the woman.

"How did this happen? Is he compromised?"

"I don't know."

"Krea?"

"I'm not sure. I don't know yet! He must have moved, ripped everything off." Krea huffed, flustered.

"On his own?"

"Yes, of course on his own! How else? Commander, I need to work."

The room went silent.

The buzz hissed around the room.

Zain's ears rang as he opened his eyes, the bright white light obfuscated by the black bag over his head. He coughed.

"Seems like he's still with us." Krea sighed in relief.

"Good. Keep up with the interrogation," said the Commander.

"Can't you see he's barely breathing?" barked Krea.

"Get him able to speak and continue. Quickly."

"We're pushing him too far. His body might not take it. What if he dies? What then, huh?" she responded.

"If he dies, we'll find someone else to tell us where to find the All," said the Commander.

"You realise that he's our only known connection to the actual All. Just give me more time. He needs more time."

"Then find out. And fast! The Conclave is getting impatient, Krea."

"Yes, Commander," said Krea with dread.

"Hurry up."

The door slammed shut, and the room ran cold again.

All Zain could sense was the ringing in his ears and the light fading before him. His breath quickened, and he roared loudly as he felt his arms and legs bound once more, surging with agony. He struggled and stirred as his breath began to fail him. He gasped with every breath through the black bag. Soon his senses dulled, and his eyes felt heavy. His breath softened, and his pain subsided just as he slipped into a comfortable slumber.

Hours later the lock of the cell clicked open and Krea opened the door once again.

The room was dark. Even the light of the moon had stopped shining through the window. She drew her circlet and placed it on her head. She paced slowly towards Zain as he slept quietly in his corner, bound and chained. Krea approached, kneeling within inches of his face, quietly observing him. The jewels sparkled on her circlet, shining into their eyes.

"You really can't die, can you?" she mused as Zain barely let out a whiff of air in his sleep. "You are a wonderful thing. A thing of terrible beauty." She reached out slowly, aiming to brush his hair away from his face. She hesitated, fearful. Yet she persisted, and with her long gold nails, she moved a lock of hair out of his face.

Zain did not react.

Krea remained there, entranced by Zain, still locked in his sleep, the pallor of his skin, the silk-like hair. "Is she really inside you?"

She reached out once more.

Zain instantly grabbed her wrist.

Krea yelped.

Zain remained immobile save for his hand clamped around her wrist. His eyes were shut.

She yelled in pain as his grasp kept tightening like a vice. She pulled and shrieked, but he would not relent. "Teller! Help!" she cried, pulling away with all her strength.

The cell door burst open, and another came in.

The room brightened, and the buzz returned.

"Get him off me!" she yelled.

Another two guards flew in and forcibly attempted to drag Zain's fingers apart as Teller pulled Krea, yet Zain's grasp only tightened further. They pulled on him with all their strength, and soon his chains sparked and shocked him into release.

All flew down onto the ground but Zain remain immobile, unawares.

Krea held her wrist in pain as Teller and the guards helped her to her feet. "Arghh. I think he broke it." She cursed and winced deeply, holding her wrist.

"Shut it down," said Teller to the guards.

"Stop," yelled Krea. "Leave it going. It's working."

"It's dangerous. I told you, he's getting more unstable."

"I know what I'm doing. Just do what I say!" said Krea, gritting her teeth. "Leave!"

"Krea, please."

"Out! Now!"

All left the room as Krea lay by the door, holding her wrist, pushing through the pain. She observed as Zain sat silently in his corner, oblivious to the world and her pain. She cursed to herself before exiting the cell and slamming the door. It darkened once more, and the buzz ceased.

Krea rested against the cold metal door as she gathered herself. She removed the metal circlet that sat around her temple as it continued to flash minuscule lights into her eyes. She paused and took a deep breath, and the dark cobbled halls soon turned into a smooth white corridor. She looked down staring at the clean white tiles, observing in its reflection how her Drae'shï skin turned back to her white and fair complexion and her red eyes turned blue. She sighed, touching her true face, rubbing her eyes.

The door beside her slid open.

"Krea?"

Krea dropped the circlet and her notepad in fright. She cursed.

A tall, scruffy, blond-haired man with a short day-old stubble emerged dressed in a long white coat. "Are you all right? Let me look at it," said Teller as he crouched beside her whilst she gathered her things.

"Not now. I'm fine," she hissed and cursed once more, sweat forming on her brow.

"Fine, but at least take some pain killers."

A group of guards dressed in black and accompanying the commander emerged at the end of the hall. The Commander was tall, black-haired and perfectly groomed, dressed in a black, white and gold uniform.

Krea cursed under her breath as Teller helped her to her feet.

The guards entered the room beside Zain's cell as the Commander stopped before Krea. "The Conclave is waiting."

"We're not ready yet. How many times must I tell you?" she snapped.

"After you, Krea," said the Commander, ignoring her pleas and gesturing her towards the door.

Krea entered the next room, followed by the rest.

It was small, dark, dimly lit and filled with dozens of screens, consoles, and storage devices, paper and files stacked in every corner. Each screen showed various monitoring and observation scans as well as camera feeds that reflected what was happening in the next room.

Zain lay on the other side of the monitoring room separated only by a two-way mirror. He was bound tightly to a reclined metal chair, his eyes wide open yet completely devoid of the vision of his true surroundings. His body was part metal and part human. A series of tubes and wires were draped from his body and through his spine, running to the floor, where a large blood-stained grate sat under the chair. Above him stood a large machine with multiple arms, all fitted with a multitude of surgical and mechanical tools. The machine was constantly working upon metal limbs and body parts.

"The Conclave is on the line, Commander," said a guard.

Krea sighed as she placed her things on the table.

The Commander signalled, and the guard pressed a button. All the screens turned into one consistent picture. A council of men sat around a large triangular table under bright white light, yet their faces remained shrouded in darkness.

Krea and the rest of the people in the room stood silent.

"Krea," intervened one.

"Your Excellencies," she said as she held her wrist.

"Tell us. Has he revealed the identity and location of the All?"

"Not yet."

The room went silent.

"And how much longer will this process take?" asked another.

"You told us you would get him to talk," said a third.

"I already told you that using the Abstract would allow me to extract information that would otherwise never be accessible to you. It's not my fault if he was built to withstand any form of intrusion or coercion. He'd sooner erase the memory of the All or die than give it up voluntarily."

"Watch your tone, Krea."

"These things take time," said Krea, frustrated.

"The one thing you are increasingly finding yourself lacking."

Krea gritted her teeth, her wrist's pain flaring up into the sweat of her brow. "The only chance we have of him divulging the identity of the All is by tricking him into doing so through the Amenti Abstract and me."

"Yet all he has been saying is nonsense. How is any of this helping? He's talking rubbish, and *you* seem to be enjoying his ramblings a little too much from what we have been told."

Krea struggled to maintain her composure as she sneered at the

Commander behind her. "We both know that the Abstract was not designed as a torture device. If we're going to get the All's identity out of him, it will be my way. Not yours. And my way needs time. I need to analyse, understand, and interpret."

"You'd better watch it, Krea. The Conclave has its eyes fixed on you and your subject, and our patience is running thin."

"That's why I'm here to do what others could not. No one. Not even those built like him," she said, pointing towards Zain.

"And how do you expect him to reveal everything? If all of what he's saying is fantastical, imagined?" resumed the Conclave.

"It's complicated."

"Then *un-complicate* it for us."

Krea sighed. "The Abstract is a simulation populated with his memories and subconscious, in a sort of feedback loop. We enable him to enter his own mind's reality and live it tangibly—or that is what he believes he is experiencing. Though imagined, there is a logic and solution to the symbols and ideas he's experiencing. But ultimately, much like our own dreams, whatever he experiences will always be framed and viewed through the lens of his own imagination and his own world view. If he sees himself as a Vampire, in his mind, it is only because he has already had a lot of blood on his hands in the real world. And much like he's a prisoner in the real world, he's a prisoner in his own," said Krea as she pushed a button. Zain's room flashed briefly in the darkness and a hologram slowly appeared over everything, giving the room the appearance of a cobble-walled cell and turning his wires into chains.

"Meaning?"

"Names, places, and events are parallels on some level, even though his world is fictional. There's hardly ever genuine inspiration in what one experiences in the Abstract. If he truly is connected deeply to the All, he or she will manifest at some point in some form, in a name, place or event. As above so below."

"And what about scrubbing his mind through all these memories, ideas? Isn't that possible?"

"If it were, we'd have done it already. Even if we could crack his psychic I.C.E. (Intrusion Countermeasure Enforcement) walls, which is again impossible, these are not exactly factual, concrete memories—

much like our dreams aren't one-to-one replicas of our waking life. The Amenti Abstract only allows us to experience his world second hand. The circlet allows me to see what he's seeing as he's recounting his story, his dream—the cell, his surroundings. But much like we cannot actually see our imagination, dreams or memories as we later recount them, nor can he. In simple terms, we cannot just invade his mind ourselves. We just need to listen carefully. I need to listen in detail and record it," she said as she displayed her notepad on the screen.

The Conclave paused for a moment, looking at each other and silently deliberating before passing their final verdict.

All in the observation room stood in awkward silence.

"Noted, Krea. We only pray that he gets to the All fast. The Conclave cannot afford to allow this current situation to continue lest more drastic action would need to be taken against the All, and there's no telling who'll get caught in the crossfire this time."

"I can't perform miracles!" insisted Krea.

"Yet you've built worlds for our prisoners to inhabit. Do not disappoint us."

The stream cut off.

"Get it done, Krea. Quickly," said the Commander as he left the room, followed by the guards.

The door slid shut.

Krea slammed her fists on the console. The pain surged once more. She yelled, winced, and cursed. The screens resumed monitoring Zain's vitals and bioware. Krea stared at Zain in frustration, eyeing the semi-lifeless machine before her.

"Krea?" said Teller.

"What?" barked Krea.

"Do you think they'll send the Burning Ones if we don't succeed?" said Teller with dread.

"We *will* succeed," she stated.

"And what about him?" He nodded towards Zain. "How long 'til it won't contain him? How long 'til he'll break out of it? Then what?"

"He won't. He can't."

"But what if? Yesterday, he got disconnected from the tethers. Today it's your wrist, tomorrow what will it be?"

"I said he won't!" she barked. "Not unless *someone* has something to do with it. How do you know it wasn't the new girl? Or one of the other serfs they just got in?"

"Of course not. He weighs triple her weight. We're lucky she was here when it happened."

"Yet I find it incredibly convenient there's no camera feed recordings for the last twenty-four hours."

"Krea, you're getting paranoid. The system has been acting up from day one. This equipment is antiquated. You're keeping notes on paper, for crying out loud," said Teller frustrated as he waved his hand across the room and pointed to her notes.

"Be that as it may, keep her out of that room. I don't want anyone other than us in there. Got it?" asked Krea as she snatched her pad from the console and slapped it on his chest.

Teller sighed.

"And keep your fucking pants on. I know where you found her."

"Krea." Teller sighed. "Fine, whatever. I'll leave you to it then," said Teller as he headed to the door.

He stopped.

"Krea?"

"What?"

"Does the Conclave know? 'Bout the Sentient Intelligence?"

"It's not their concern. I have specific instructions that go beyond their authority."

Teller sighed. "I'm scared, Krea. We're playing with fire here. What if they find out? And we've never done this before. And what's going to happen once it takes over? It's dangerous."

"I don't want to hear any more talk of it. Not where we can be heard. And as for the Abstract, I built it. I know what it can and cannot do."

"I'm just not sure whether you know what *you're* doing with it."

Krea said nothing.

"Let's hope the reconditioning will take hold then," said Teller

"It'll take time 'til it takes hold, but he'll break. Everyone does, in the end."

Chapter 21

Shear Truth

The air smelt of sweat and salt. The lower deck was wet, sometimes with water, sometimes with urine. At least it was quiet. The last two days had been calm, and everyone, even the prisoners who had been chained to the floor, were relieved of the terror of the storm. The occasional whisper followed the lonely groan, and Pïshkah woke from her slumber.

The situation had not changed, despite how much she dreamed of being back on land. Adara sat awake beside her, both filthy as ever. Lilith sat across from them also in chains and flanked by another score of crewmen and prisoners picked up along the way. All were exhausted and battered. Lilith looked livid.

"Did you sleep?" whispered Adara.

"Do I look like I can sleep?" asked Lilith through her filthy curtain of hair. Her red eyes gleamed as her cheeks ran black with crusty eye makeup. Her right arm was sunburnt, and the rest of her limbs were peppered with scratches and bruises. She huffed and puffed as she struggled to pull her hands to her face to move her hair. The daisy chain held her arms tied to everyone else through a series of loops linked to the floor. Her frustration flared into a fit, and she yanked the chain, forcing it to pull onto two slumbering sailors chained to her sides. One man fell on her lap, and the other banged his head on Lilith's. "Get off me!" she shrieked as she swiped one's head from her thigh and pushed off the other.

"Calm down!" whispered Adara. "Keep quiet, or they'll come for you again."

"Good. I want them to," she growled as the sailors straightened themselves grimacing at the belligerent woman.

"Yes, please. Go ahead. Like this could get any worse," said Pïshkah as she also slowly sat upright.

"Just calm down. We'll get out of this. Somehow," whispered Adara.

Lilith sat back in frustration as the men beside her went back to sleep.

"Adara. Is there *any* chance the Saints might actually come for us?" asked Pïshkah.

"Well, yes. I hope so. I mean, I am— was— betrothed to Elias after all."

"What?" asked Pïshkah as she noticed how some of the other prisoners seemed to have overheard.

"Yes, we were going to—"

"Shut up!" hissed Pïshkah attempting to cover Adara's mouth. "Keep it to yourself. Do you know what they would do to you if they found out?"

"Pay a ransom. That's for sure," said a former crew member of the *Intrepid* chained in the corner.

"Hey, fuck face!" barked Pïshkah. "You want to get home alive? Then you better keep your mouth shut."

"Like you're gonna do anything from there." He scoffed. "Cursed witch. Why don't you curse these buggers and bring a storm on their heads like you did us?"

"I can't conjure storms, but I could curse you so that your testicles will drop off by the time we land ashore." She smirked.

"Oi! Shut up! Try'na sleep 'ere!" barked another man as a small choir of grunts nodded in agreement. A ruckus soon broke out, and a tall Darelese pirate from Drellanon lumbered down in a matter of seconds.

"Shut up!" he boomed. The deck went silent. He was black, scarred and shirtless, carrying an apple and a penknife, slicing away slivers into his mouth. "Well. Well. Well. Seems like some people are ready for breakfast," he said as he walked down the middle of the deck. "And I definitely am hungry for some meat," he continued as he stopped in front of the women, eyeing each one. "Do you know how long it's been since I've eaten a nice juicy steak?" he asked, looking over Adara menacingly as she evaded his gaze.

"Since you last took a bath maybe?" said Lilith from behind him as some of the prisoners sniggered.

He slowly turned back and crouched before Lilith, yanking her chain and forcing her forward. He tried to grab hold of her face as she struggled. He then calmly but forcibly grabbed her by the hair.

"I said I'd save the best for last, but I always found it difficult to wait for dessert," he said, brandishing a lecherous grin.

She spat in his face.

He didn't flinch. Slowly he wiped the spit off his face, tasted it with the tip of his tongue, and with a smile, proceeded to rub her spit all over her face slowly. He paused, and in a flash, he slapped her hard with the back of his hand.

"Lilith!" cried Adara.

"She is a feisty one," he said to the crowd, as he rose and rubbed his knuckles. "But they're all the same. Once you break them in, they become as meek as lambs."

Lilith spat a raw goop of blood onto the deck and laughed. Her teeth were blue with blood.

All stood shocked at the resilience of the Drae'shï.

"You have no idea what's coming for you." She laughed.

"We're three hundred kilometres away from the nearest coast. No one is coming."

She laughed again. All were confused. Pïshkah watched closely as the Drae'shï's gaze grew more fearless.

"Pïshkah," whispered Adara, concerned. "I fear she's losing her mind."

"And I fear she isn't," said the Cleriheu in all seriousness.

"Shut your trap!" shouted the pirate as he slapped Lilith once more, silencing her cackle. She fell onto her chained mate, spitting all over him, and slid to the ground. She paused for a moment and slowly started giggling again from beneath her dirty white hair. All stood silent.

"I saw what's coming for you. There will not be a corner of this world where you can run to. You're all going to die," she mumbled from the floor.

The Darelese grew impatient, picked her up by her hair and raised his fist. Her face was covered in blood and tears of laughter. "Shut the fuck—!"

"Enough!" barked the Captain from across the deck as he walked down, followed by two deckhands. The Captain was another Darelese, tall and black with red-dyed dreadlocks. His dark eyes sat sunken within their sockets with a scar stretching from the bottom of the right cheekbone, running towards his upper lip. The man was dressed in the typical intricate Carthosian textiles that ran from shoulder to shin, wrapped around his waist in a vibrant coloured sash. "Throzzad! Let her go."

"Yes, Captain Silvan," said Throzzad begrudgingly, dropping Lilith on the floor.

Captain Silvan casually walked down the deck, trimming his nails with a long pair of sheep shears. He blew over his nails before putting his right glove back on. He signalled to Throzzad.

"Sit her up," said the Captain as he tucked away his shears and then took a bottle from the hand of one of his deckhands. He knelt in front of her. Lilith rested for a moment, peering through her blood-sticky hair. "I know you are thirsty. I know you want to drink, and I will give you a drink. But if even one drop of spit lands on me, you can be as sure as the seas that flow beneath us that you'll be swallowing glass instead of water by day's end. Got it?" he asked before loosening the daisy chain and handing her the bottle.

She drank until the bottle was dry.

Silence reigned.

"That's better. Isn't it?"

"What about us?" yelled a sailor.

"Shut up!" Throzzad kicked the sailor.

"You will get your food and drink, don't worry," the Captain said as he signalled to the other deckhand, who proceed to hand each of the prisoners a day-old boiled potato and a cup of water.

Pishkah immediately swallowed hers whilst Adara gazed at the grey starchy blob in her hands. She was almost certain she saw something move.

"You'd better eat that before someone else takes it," said Pïshkah as she swallowed her last dry bite.

Adara tamped down her fuss and began eating slowly.

"It's not that bad. Hunger is the best spice, they say. You get used to eating anything after a while," said Pïshkah as she forced a smile to cheer the Eldain up.

The Captain took a cloth from his pocket and gently wiped the face of the Drae'shï. She sat silent, scowling at the man, patiently waiting for her face to be cleaned. "Deary me. That look. I have never seen such scorn leave a woman's eyes in my life." He chuckled, pointing at her as he looked towards his men. "Not even from the Darelese viragos," he said turning back at her, but the Drae'shï said nothing. "Nothing? No threats?" He faked a frown.

She remained silent, but her eyes gave her away. The mirror peeked slightly out of his sash.

"Ah yes. This is what you really want," he continued as he slowly drew it out. "We all saw what you did. Pretty impressive, I must say. Including the company you keep. A Cleriheu from the far east, an Eldain, and a Vampire. Or rather used to keep in the latter case. Very interesting indeed."

Lilith breathed deeply through her nose, pursing her lips.

"Then you know you'd best keep away from her," intervened Pïshkah.

"Ah, the Lothuman accent. Unmistakable." He turned to Pïshkah. "Let's see. Ah yes, your glyphs are quite particular," he said as he moved her dirty curls out of her face, scrutinising each tattooed sign on her forehead and cheeks. He then swiped her sleeve up her arm, revealing even more tattoos, yet one sign stuck out in particular. "Ha! There it is." Pïshkah recoiled her arm as he let go. "Is this why you're here? To regain your honour amongst your tribe? By taking the mirror back to them? Or was it to slay the Vampire?"

"What's he talking about?" asked Adara.

The Captain gloated at the surprise of the Eldain and the shame of the Cleriheu.

"Oh, my dear fair maiden from Cielith. You are as beautiful as the rising sun. I would never let these filthy animals lay a finger upon you, but you are as naïve as you are beautiful. Your friend here is more than just a Cleriheu. She's also a Yuen'hii. A fiend huntress, a huntress of the *unnatural*, or rather an exiled one in this case, from the looks of it. What happened? Ran out of fiends to hunt in the far east?" said the Captain as Pïshkah sat silent.

"Well, unfortunately, we did the job of killing the Vampire for you, so there's no point in going home just yet, am I right? In any case, healers like you are in short supply in Carthosia. I'm sure you'll fetch a good price." They all stayed silent. "What? Are you surprised? That the pirate is worldly, literate? How do you think one ends up captain and commander of a fleet? Drinking wine and ransacking ports? Well, obviously!" He laughed as the other pirates joined in. "But also tapping into knowledge. That's where the gold is really hidden."

"What about talking then?" The Drae'shï sniggered. "If you conquered as much as spoke, you'd have the world by now."

He turned back to her with a charming smile, casually wagging his finger. "You mouth off because you know you have something I want, but let me assure you, I will get what I want from you. The question is, how much am I going to hurt you and your friends before I get it?"

"You could slay them all for all I care," she whispered, exhausted.

"So heartless." He mocked a frown. "If it weren't for the fact that I would definitely trust a Drae'shï to slay me in my sleep, I would offer you a lofty position on my ship," he continued as he swaggered around with a smile. "I tell you what. Let's play a game. Who's got the bigger balls?"

Throzzad pulled a blood-stained chopping block up to Lilith and forcibly pulled her hands forward. The prisoners all started to get squeamish as Lilith struggled to pull away.

"You'll all be able to watch. It will be a good lesson. Here are the rules." The Captain calmly drew out his shears and twiddled its points on the block. "Anyone tells me how to use this fine instrument like our Drae'shï here, and you all get to live another day, got it?"

He instantly took hold of Lilith's jaw, forcing her distraught gaze to focus on him and stated, "If you refuse to answer a question. I'll throw one of them overboard. If you refuse to answer a second question, I'll cut off one of your fingers. Simple, right?" Lilith desperately struggled to pull her hands off the block as Throzzad held her down. "And we've got a long list of fingers and men to go through. And *I* have a lot of patience."

Adara and Pïshkah began trying to quell the captain's dark intentions as the rest of the prisoners whimpered away. The two deckhands came down, removed two of the shackled slaves from the chain beside Lilith, and dragged them to an open loading bay.

"How do you use the mirror? What do you need to do?" he asked as the surf splashed outside, spraying those close to the loading bay.

Lilith struggled. "Fuck you! Kill them all!"

The Captain nodded, and one deckhand slit the throat of a slave and booted him overboard to the shock of the others. "Anyone has any answers for me?"

"We don't know anything!" yelled Adara. "You have to believe us!"

"Once more. How do you use the mirror?"

"I don't know," Lilith snarled. "But even if I did, I'd sooner die than leave it to filth like you."

The Captain nodded to Throzzad, who stretched out her right arm through her shackles and pushed her hand flat on the block. Lilith screamed and struggled, but her hand was immobile. The Captain walked each leg of the shears over her fingers. "This little piggy went to market. This little piggy stayed at home. This little piggy had roast beef. This little piggy had none. And what did this last piggy have to say?" He paused, giving her one last chance to respond.

Her eyes widened.

"And this little piggy cried," he said and chopped off Lilith's ring finger.

Lilith screamed in agony as blood gushed over the block.

Adara screamed, and Pïshkah held her close as best she could.

"What does the mirror do?" he roared, rolling up his sleeves and grabbing her by the back of her hair. "How do you use it?" he asked but Lilith wailed in agony, holding her hand to her chest, crying in pain and anger, covered in blood. "Well, at least we know knives still can cut her. How do you use it?"

"I don't know!" she shrieked.

"No one knows!" yelled Adara, tears in her eyes. "Can't you see? Stop it! Stop torturing her!"

The Captain signalled again, and another prisoner was stabbed and thrown overboard. The prisoners cried once more as the tensions grew higher. All began screaming at Lilith, begging her to relent. Throzzad grabbed hold of Lilith's left arm and set her hand upon the blood-soaked block.

"You're good at this. You really are."

"Fuck you!" she roared.

"But I'm better," he said and pulled off his left glove, revealing a hand with all four of his fingers chopped in half. "I'm way better..."

Lilith stared at his hand.

The Captain drew his shears again.

"This little piggy went to market."

Lilith closed her eyes.

"This little piggy stayed at home."

She took a deep breath.

"This little piggy had roast beef, and this little piggy had none." The Captain sighed. "And this little piggy—"

"Stop! Stop!" she yelled. "I'll tell you!"

The Captain had barely broken her skin. He pulled up the shears within an inch of her eye. "If you lie to me. I'll cut out your eye. Understand?"

"Yes. I promise I'll tell you what I know." She gasped.

"Go on."

"I don't know how to control it."

The Captain grabbed the back of her head.

"Wait! Wait! There's more!"

He stopped.

"I may not know how to control it, but it works when I really want something. To fight or to protect myself." She panted.

"And?"

"And that's it! That's all I know!"

"Oh, I believe you, but I think I've overestimated your utility. It seems I'm going to have to figure it out by myself," he said as he slowly pressed his blade against her cheek.

She screamed once more. "Stop! I know! One more thing! Stop!" she pleaded. "It can show you things."

"What things? It shows nothing but my reflection."

"Visions of whatever is your deepest desire. What you truly desire. Wealth, power, freedom!"

"I have all such things. What could it possibly reveal that I do not already possess?"

"If you have everything, then you don't need it." She blew, exhausted.

"Perhaps you are right. Then again, there are things hidden beneath us, begging to be heard." He looked Lilith straight in the eyes. She didn't flinch. He slowly stood and pulled the mirror back out of his sash without breaking eye contact. "Throzzad. Tell me what's your deepest desire," he said as he offered it to the hulking man, now hesitant to pick up the artefact.

Throzzad reluctantly picked up the mirror and gazed at it. He could only see his reflection. He looked around it and it gleamed. As his eyes lingered a while, he looked back and forth, but nothing happened.

"It will not work if you are too afraid to look," said Lilith, wincing in pain.

"Give it to me!" The Captain snatched it back. "I know what my deepest desire is right now, and it is to find out what this thing can do. So, tell me, oh mirror, nay, show me. Show me what is it that you behold," he said mockingly as the rest went quiet.

Captain Silvan gazed at the mirror intently and patiently. The Shard shimmered but showed nothing but his reflection. "Yes, as I thought. Nothing," he said. "Nothing but," his voice quieted. His image slowly faded away. "Interesting," he said as he became more and more transfixed. The mirror revealed a cascade of images, people, places, and millions of other things. "This is incredible."

"Keep looking," she said.

The mirror continued to reveal more and more chaotic images like a kaleidoscope of the universe. The captain was hooked, and the rest of the pirates grew anxious. "I can see it. All of it. It's, it's—"

"Yes," she said as a grin started to form.

Out of the cacophony of the mirror, a deep black spot emerged in the middle at the end of the tunnel of colours. The Captain furrowed his brow but did not break his gaze. "What is that?" he barely muttered.

"It's beautiful." She smirked through her sweaty brow as the mirror revealed the depth of oblivion to the Captain.

The black maw in the Shard was enthralling, calm and captivating. The chaos was swallowed in the depth of darkness, congealed into a pearl of perfection, iridescent with power and terrifyingly seductive.

The crew called to the Captain, but no response came.

For one brief moment, the Captain knew.

His gaze slowly turned to Lilith as her laughter echoed in the distance. The calls of his crew members could not help him. His fingerless hand now smouldered into fluttering ashes, and his person soon followed. Not his clothes, not even his ashes; nothing was left— only the Shard.

The room was silent save for the laughter of the Drae'shï.

All looked at Lilith and the Shard. The pirates were dumbfounded.

"What have you done?" yelled Throzzad. "Witch!" he accused as she laughed in her corner.

As he approached Lilith quickly slid her feet to pull the Shard towards her. "Oh. Not this time, bitch!" he snapped as he drew his club and whacked her hard in her temple.

A crack.

She gasped and fell straight to the ground, her wounded hand twitching as blood pooled beneath it.

"Lilith!" cried Adara.

Pïshkah sat speechless. The rest of the prisoners were also in shock.

"What did she do?" barked Throzzad to Pïshkah.

"I don't know!"

"Cursed wretches! You'll all be dead!"

"She's still alive!" yelled Adara. "Help her."

He spat on Lilith instead.

"You have to help her!" said Adara. "If you have any chance of finding out what happened to your captain. You will help her!"

Throzzad turned around, flustered, running his hand across his face. He cursed and turned to Pïshkah. "If I release you, you can treat her?"

"I'm not sure I can."

"Then you'd better find out, or you're next." He unlocked her shackles and dragged her over to Lilith.

Pïshkah gently moved Lilith's blood-soaked hair to find a large gash running from the tip of her eye to the side of her head. She took a long breath. "I think it's too late," she said hesitantly.

The rest of the crew came down, and an argument broke out on the other side of the deck.

"Please, Pïshkah, help her," said Adara softly but sternly.

Pïshkah hesitated. "Adara, I'm sorry, but I don't think I want to..."

Adara looked back, stunned.

"It's true what he said. I'm a huntress. That day in the market, when I tried to grab your hair, I thought it was Lilith's. I sensed a darkness, thinking it was you, but now we know where it's coming from," said the Cleriheu as she looked at Lilith and the Shard.

"Pïshkah. You listen to me."

"No, you listen! I knew there was a darkness around her. I saw it in my dreams. The darkness that caught him. She carries it with her."

"Pïshkah. You are not a killer, and she is not a fiend. She is a Drae'shï. If there's any chance of surviving, we need to stick together," said Adara sternly, without hesitation.

"I've given up on surviving. You think we stand a chance?" she asked as she pointed to the crew.

"Pïshkah! You owe me your life! I saved you! If I hadn't pleaded for your life, you would have probably been killed. You do not have my permission to die! If you hold any oath sacred, then you know that a life saved entails a life debt. If you were going to kill me that day, then she was the one who saved me. I owe her as much as you owe me. Save her life, and your debt will be repaid. Do not deny me, Cleriheu!"

Pïshkah sighed as she gripped her tattered skirt. "Fine!" she said. "I just hope you don't end up regretting it."

Pïshkah rolled up her sleeves and dipped her finger in Lilith's blood. With it, she began drawing sigils and glyphs upon the floor and on Lilith as she whispered to herself and moved her hands across the Drae'shï's body.

"Thank you," said Adara.

"She's bleeding a lot from her head. Without any essence of Enoch, I can't close the wound fast enough. Hey! You! Throzzad! I need supplies to heal her," she yelled across the deck.

"What's happening down here?" enquired another pirate, as the newly arrived party began approaching the prisoners.

"Why the fuck is she helping her?" said another.

"Because if you let her die, far worse things will happen to you than what happened to your captain," interrupted Pïshkah devilishly to the visible confusion of the pirates. "We are the Crones of the Sea. You must grant us safe passage, or another storm will come upon you like it did to our former captives."

"You see! I told you! They're witches and the sea crones at that!" said a pirate, visibly distressed.

"Shut up, Krota! And you stop your lying! It was that mirror! It's cursed," Throzzad barked back.

"Yes, the mirror. The very mirror that drove you and your captain mad with greed. That which forced your hand upon him in betrayal."

"What?" exclaimed Throzzad.

"He saw the power he could have in the mirror and wanted it for himself," said Pïshkah as the rest of the crew started staring at him. "They fought, and he bested him. Now your captain lies in oblivion."

"She lies! I saw it with my very eyes. She turned him to ash in a second," said Throzzad, pointing to Lilith, still shackled and beaten black and blue.

"By a beaten and shackled maid? I think not," she said as she looked at her fellow prisoners for confirmation.

"Yes. He did it! He threw the captain overboard with the other two!" yelled one prisoner.

"They threw him overboard!" yelled another, and soon all jumped in to hurl accusations. The rest of the crew began moving towards Throzzad as the other two pirates found themselves caught by the scruffs of their necks, pleading their innocence.

Feeling overwhelmed, Throzzad drew his sword. "Get back, you scum-sucking mongrels or I'll have your livers for dinner. She's a liar."

"Protect us from those who harm us, and your ship will find no ills in its path. Fail to do so, and the Crones of the Sea shall never rest 'til you are all buried a hundred leagues beneath the sea. This man has killed your captain and violated a crone, and she now lies here. Should she fall, you will all suffer the same fate," Pïshkah proclaimed with the full charm of her mystique and the eeriness of her appearance to complement her gambit.

Throzzad fumed and turned to strike Pïshkah but was instantly skewered by another pirate. His face dropped as he saw a grin leave Pïshkah's lips. The mob quickly dragged him away and tossed him overboard before sending his alleged accomplices along with him.

"Now. Get me some Enoch essence!" barked Pïshkah.

"We're pirates, not priests! We have none aboard," said one of the pirates.

Pïshkah cursed and looked around, trying to draw inspiration. "We could cauterise the wound. But—" she said to herself, cursing the sea.

"What about the Shard?" asked Adara. "It protected her before. Maybe it can again?"

Pïshkah looked at her bewildered. "You're going to make me do it, are you?"

"Don't stare into it. I've seen others handle it, even look at it—just don't look too long."

Pïshkah reached out slowly. She picked it up and, from the corner of her eye, caught a glimpse of her reflection. A deep feeling of dread came upon her. She was not sure whether it was the mirror begging her to look or if it came of her own volition, but the haunting nature of the tool filled her heart with curious terror. A terror that came ahead of dark discoveries.

"Pïshkah!" called Adara, snapping her out of it. "Stop staring at it!"

"Right. Yes!" she said as she shook her head. Pïshkah observed Lilith's cuts, running along the side of her head and her cheek. "I don't know how to do this, but here goes." She closed her eyes and held the mirror upon the side of Lilith's head. The glass was slippery with blood, and Pïshkah could already feel it cutting her own hands. In her mind, she saw the wounds and saw them sealed shut, and in an instant, a searing sensation was felt in her hands. Pïshkah instantly flew back as the mirror turned red hot, burning her hands as well as Lilith's wounds. She immediately got back up and hit the scalding mirror off Lilith's temple. Her wounds were closed in a burnt mess of blood, hair, and flesh.

Pïshkah fell back once more as she took a moment and then turned back to the pirates. "Now, get me some fucking gauze and elderspice"

CHAPTER 22

BEYOND BELIEF

The cell was dark, yet the night came with its own calmness. Zain sat in the corner, observing the moon shining through the bars. It was cold yet comforting. All seemed to have found rest, and Krea had long since been to visit. Zain hummed to himself as he stretched out his legs and yawned.

Through the wall, he heard the soft sobbing of his cellmate.

"Aria? Is that you?" he asked as he shifted towards the crack in the wall.

The sobbing came to a halt.

"Aria?"

"Can you hear me?" asked Aria through the walls. She sniffed.

"Are you crying?"

"Yes. I was. I'm sorry."

Zain paused, uncertain of what to say. "Sorry for what?"

"You wouldn't understand."

"Well, try me."

"I don't know what to do. I tried to help you, but I can't. I've only managed to make things worse." She sobbed.

"What are you talking about?"

"Would you even listen? Believe me?"

"I can try," said Zain sheepishly, slightly embarrassed by his previous outburst in her regard.

"I doubt it would make a difference. But at least know that I've tried my best, and I won't give up," she said as she wiped her tears, muffling her sobs.

Zain sighed. "Not sure what you did, but I'm quite sure that the beatings would have come either way. Also, I don't know why you'd go to so much trouble to save a wretch like me. But I guess, if you're not one of *them*, then I appreciate it anyway, Aria."

"Thank you." She snorted a chuckle through her sobs. "Are you hurt? Do you remember what happened?"

"Other than the occasional beating, I'm right as rain. Though I've been out of it for a while. Can't even remember how long I've been here."

"Longer than you think, Zain. If only you knew."

"Ah yes. The false reality you mentioned. Really? We're going there again?"

"No, Zain. I understand now. I was wrong to say that it means nothing. That it's not real."

"Right. Thanks, I guess."

"I don't know how to convince you that this isn't one of their tricks, but it would make me happy to hear your tales, to understand you and the world you're from. If you wouldn't mind sharing with another lonely prisoner?"

Zain paused and smiled. "Well, if it is one of their tricks, they should have sent you instead of Krea in the first place. You're a little more, how can I say? Palatable."

Aria sniggered. "So, is that a yes?"

Zain sat back and got comfortable. "Well, Aria, since we've only got eternity ahead of us; once upon a time in the lands of Amenti, there lived a Vampire."

Zain woke, lying there impaled to the galley, observing the sky. Part of what was left of the *Intrepid* was strewn on the shores of Valdell's coast. Nothing but beaches stretched for kilometres in each direction. Zain found some rest in his helplessness. The bolt had impaled him but was far from able to kill him. The pain he was almost used to, yet it was the only thing the Eldaresh could never definitively cure.

He coughed, and seawater flew out of him— but no blood.

"It would be so much easier had I just died," he said as he slowly faced the reality of his failures. "Maybe one day, when this is all over."

He slowly winced around the bolt stuck through his chest, cringing and grunting as the boards creaked and moaned until soon gravity took its course, and the brittle wreck broke, causing Zain to slide off the bar and fall flat on the shores of another day.

He was weak. He felt the waters go through him as the hole in his body slowly started closing. He raised his face from the wet sand and crawled his way onto dry land. He fell asleep once more, secretly hoping he would find his eternal rest, but reality was far more punishing than his nightmares. It was not long after that he found himself gazing at the speckled canopy of a forest as he lay strewn across a bed of hay at the back of a cart.

"Papa. He's awake!" said a little blonde girl, peeking over the driver's seat. The moustached farmhand turned back, a pipe in his mouth and creases all over his tanned face.

"Ah, you're finally awake. I really thought you were a goner."

Zain slowly turned to face him and the pretty girl in pigtails spying on the pale corpse-like Vampire with intense curiosity. Zain smiled. He was fond of the kindness of strangers.

"Where are we?"

"Ah mornin' to ya, my friend," said the man.

"Morning," mumbled Zain as he tried to raise himself. "Where are we heading?"

"We're on the high road, headin' to my village, Maribell."

"Are we close to the capital?"

"Valendria?" He laughed. "Far from it, we're about five days ride from Valendria, and we're headin' north not south."

He sighed. "I'm sorry, friend. I have nothing to offer you but my thanks."

"Think nothin' of it. Seems like you took a good beatin' by the storm."

"We also took a beating from the Carthosian pirates."

"Ah, sorry to hear friend. And they're not 'thosian, Darelese. Nasty bunch. Been harassin' all vessels comin' up and down the gulf. They say the Shirral is payin' 'em to do so. You're lucky you survived."

"Lucky. Yeah." He paused. "Did you see any others on the beach?"

"No. Just you I'm afraid. Anyway, where are my manners? I'm Rebus, and this is Pinarilla," he said as he extended his arm over his shoulder in a handshake.

"I'm Zain. Nice to meet you, Rebus, and nice to meet you too, Pinarilla." He smiled as he shook the man's hand, and Pinarilla popped her head up and shyly smiled at him.

"Rebus, can I ask you something about these pirates?"

"Ask away."

"You said the Shirral is paying these pirates."

"It's a rumour."

"Yes, but do you know, or does anyone know where they berth?"

"Nowhere on this side of the continent, that's for sure. Valendrian fleet always patrollin'. They would not seek refuge here unless they're desperate. They say they make port in Sarthamia. Are you familiar with the island?"

"That's all the way across the gulf! It would take weeks to get there from Valdell!"

"Pirates don't trade with any Valendrians, on pain of death from the Shirral, and anyone on our side caught dealing with 'em..." Rebus drew his thumb across his neck. "Though I did hear that both sides tend to trade on the high seas. At least that's the word from Yammimer. Risky business. Anyone caught breaking the embargo always gets the gallows, and if you're peddlin' any sort of medicinal things or Enoch sap, heavens help you."

"They really value that stuff, don't they?"

"Carthosians got no Enoch trees ay, and I hear the vespial plague is emerging there again. They must be getting pretty desperate."

"That's it. I gotta head for the high seas and get on one of these boats," said Zain as he struggled to get himself up.

"Whoa. Hold your horses! You can barely move."

"I've been through worse." He groaned. "Just tell me where to find the closest Temple of Enoch."

Rebus looked back, perplexed. "Hey, Zain, you're not thinking of stealin' any of that stuff, are you? Listen to me, come to my home, have some rest and somethin' to eat. I'm sure you're famished," he said but Zain did not respond. "Zain?"

Rebus' voice was slowly drowned out as Zain was reminded of his hunger, the real hunger. The hissing sound of the blood of Pinarilla coursing through her veins sang a sweet tune to his ears that grew deafening with each moment. His senses sharpened, and his teeth, too. "Zain? Are you listening to me?"

Zain shook his head. "What? Ah, yes, sorry, Rebus, but I must go," said Zain as he quickly rolled off the back of the cart.

"Whoa!" said Rebus as he stopped the cart. "Where you going? You're in no state to walk, and it's kilometres to the next village."

"Don't worry, Rebus," said Zain as he awkwardly stepped away from the cart, scratching the back of his neck furiously, "Go, go. I'll be fine, and thanks for lending a hand. I appreciate it. I hope I'll be able to repay you one day."

"Fine, suit yourself." He smiled back. "Just remember my home is always open if you want to swing by Maribell."

Zain quickly distanced himself in hurried steps away from the haunting call of their blood. He then remembered and turned. "Rebus! What about the temple?"

"I have *no* idea," said Rebus as he nudged the horse forward once more and felt the watch of his daughter bearing down on him. As the cart drew away, he slowly pointed to a sign that read 'Hillburn'. "See you around, Zain. Hope you find what you're looking for."

The bells tolled all morning. The streets of Valendria flooded with noblemen and peasants as they made their way to the Grand Temple.

Valendria was the capital of Valdell, set around a large natural harbour, home to hundreds of vessels set in all its nooks and crannies.

"The beating heart of Amenti, they call it," said Santhi as he looked out of the balcony in his quarters.

Santhi's guest quarters were situated in the Palace of the Massass on the east bank of Palin Bay. The most affluent part of Valendria was there: the East District. All people of repute, wealth, and piety sat above everyone else, protected by impenetrable bastions set upon unassailable cliffs. On the other side of the bay stood the original town where Valendria was founded, a large city bustling with merchants, peasants, and paupers coming in and out, day and night. The two sides of the great city were connected by the fortress island of Vidian's Citadel, a jewel in the centre of the bay and a remnant of the old Salingan Empire that once ruled Amenti from Iborellan to the Ring Sea. The citadel linked the two sides of Valendrian life with the bridge of Valen's Crossing, an enormous feat of engineering that ramped up from the lower West District to the high ramparts of the East District set on pillars which ran almost a hundred feet high.

With each of Santhi's visits, it appeared as though more buildings mushroomed around the coast, and even more people crawled around like ants in and out of all its streets and alleyways. Santhi's steward emerged. "The Massass is giving his address, my lord. We should start heading to the temple for the audience."

"Impressive isn't it, Eluin?" asked Santhi as he watched the city below him.

"Most, my lord, but I much prefer the modesty of the countryside."

"Men seek to achieve with stone what their modest bodies cannot with time." He paused for a moment, observing the seagulls flying high above the bay, cawing in the distance. "Come, let's go."

They proceeded through the halls of the Massass' palace as the mighty voice of the pontiff echoed from afar. The building was a testament to the great architecture of the old Salingan Empire, built with intricate adornments carved into its white limestone. Its tall steeples flew the flags of all the noble houses of Valdell and the Seal of the Temple itself—the Enoch tree. The palace was another fortification surrounding the Grand Temple, a humble ruinous structure surrounding an enormous Enoch tree.

The palace square was often the scene of celebrations and processions of thousands of people, which were held just outside the temple's gate. People had been gathering for hours as a host of Saints ferried them in. The temple itself was encased in a garden barred by a portcullis of white wrought iron shaped into vines. Above it, upon a balcony, stood the Massass, preaching to the crowd, guarded by the white-clad knights of the Order.

"The cruelty and evil of the Shirral know no end. He has not only taken up arms against you. He has not only pledged to destroy all our sacrifices and hard work. But he has now also taken my nephew. I thank you for coming to grieve with me. Thirty-three years after they took away my beloved sister and nieces, so too they have finally claimed my nephew. A great family, a loving family, has been eradicated by their greed, arrogance, and warmongering. But I know that this is one of many great sacrifices we must endure in the pursuit of our mission, my mission—to preserve the Holy Temple and the Blessings of our Holy Mother," called the Massass from above the crowd.

"We shall not let these heathens take what they could not grow themselves! Steal the fruits of the labour of our ancestors! Squander the lives of our children! Eradicate our families!" he continued as the crowd's outrage grew.

"I ask you to join me in your thoughts and pray that these dark forces that want to seize that very temple that stands behind me face the judgement they deserve!" The Massass went down on his knees with his hands raised to his shoulders, and so did the crowd. The silence was astounding. The Massass silently recited to himself as he repeatedly raised his hands from his heart to the heavens as the rest followed suit. As he returned to his feet, so did the crowd. "My brothers and sisters, before you leave today, take a look at one another and thank each other for your kinship, for your loyalty. For it is this loyalty that has preserved us. You are all branches of the same tree. The light of the Mother runs through you, and with that light comes her protection. May the Mother's Light be upon you."

"Forever may we endure," responded the crowd.

Santhi walked along the upper terraces towards the Grand Temple as the Massass retreated to the crowd's applause.

The Grand Temple was set in a quiet garden surrounded by the walls of the Massass' palace. The beautiful Enoch Tree was as high as the tallest spires of the palace and as dense as any he had ever seen. However, the actual temple surrounding the tree was fairly unimpressive. The structure stood in a delightfully peaceful derelict state. The building originally constructed was unfinished and overgrown, and the tree had grown beyond the limits of any building. The walls were partly built around it, and the chequered marble tiles were the only thing not covered in moss and vines. A humble white marble bench sat as a throne of the Massass at the foot of the tree, a remnant of the days when Erinderiss the Kind delivered his teachings, all of which were now carved in large faces of jade that adorned the few walls still standing. The air was humid yet cool.

The Saints waved Santhi through but not his escort. Santhi nodded and went forth. The temple floor was vacant save for the Massass, his steward, and the guards. Alistair Jurani was also inside, waiting, concerned, and fidgeting nervously. The hall echoed with each step the Eldain made, the chequered floor staging his every move towards the men.

Symperell Fermario Jurani was a tall, balding man with age in his face but strength in his presence. His narrow eyes could peer right through anyone before him, and his voice could make even the highest born stutter. His steward helped him to remove his purple ceremonial tunic under which he bore the colours of the Jurani family and the crest of the Temple of Enoch. He calmly washed his hands in a brass basin held by the steward and then drew a towel off the man's shoulders as the young man withdrew.

"Oh, Santhi! I'm so sorry, I don't know what to say," exclaimed Alistair as the awkward silence lingered. "They were with us until the storm set us apart. We had no idea where they drifted off."

"I want my daughter back!" stated Santhi as he struggled to retain his composure.

"The survivors we picked up said pirates abducted them. They might still be alive," said Alistair.

"Enough, Alistair," interrupted the Massass, his voice echoing through the hall. "Lord Crysanthani hardly needs to be reminded of the facts or showered with fruitless apologies. We know all too well how he feels, the burn of anger, the bile of hatred. We are just shy of a few days from the thirty-third anniversary of Bellona's wedding day."

"Elenia. Poor Elenia and the children. Now, Elias, too. How sad." Alistair sighed, shaking his head.

"How ironic it must be that I, too, would be here demanding that my own blood be returned to me when I should have been celebrating her marriage instead," said Santhi, but neither replied.

The Massass stared down the Eldain patiently as Santhi tightened his fists at this silence.

"Send out the fleet. I want her returned," stated the Eldain.

"You know I can't do that," the Massass replied flatly.

"Excuse me?"

"We are at war, Petrach. The fleet is out already, ensuring this city is safe and the coasts of Valdell are protected," said the Massass.

"That's it? That's all you have to tell a grieving father?"

"We don't have the vessels to patrol all the coast *and* protect the city."

"What about your nephew? Your own blood. You'd just abandoned him to his fate?"

"Elias was a Saint, a knight belonging to the Holy Order. He perished in the fulfilment of his duty towards this seat and the temple," said the Massass as he sat upon his throne.

"To you, that is? Is that all he meant to you? Just another pawn?"

"Santhi!" exclaimed Alistair. "Apologies, Massass. I—"

"Save it, Alistair," said Santhi. "You may go out there and pontificate to your heart's content about the ills of the Carthosians and the justice they deserve, but we both know that this war is *your* doing." He pointed.

"Santhi!" exclaimed Alistair horrified as the Saints within the temple slowly turned their gaze at the insolence of the Eldain.

"Leave us," said the Massass, silencing everyone. "We shall talk as men, Petrach, old men." He waved everyone away and got up to his feet.

All others bowed and left silently.

"Your insistence on severing the Carthosians from the Temple is why they are coming for you, and you know that. First you insisted they pay twice as many tributes and taxes than anyone else in Amenti, and when they refused you cut them off completely. All in a bid to make them recognise your hegemony even though they're on the other side of the ocean," said Santhi as the Massass patiently listened. "They want vengeance as much as you. But most of all, they want to survive. They need the Enoch trees. Will you see all your former brethren overseas die of disease just because they won't acknowledge the supremacy of the Massass? Both your ancestors built this very city, this temple. The Carthosians and Valendrians are still branches of the same family tree. It's been thirty years!"

The Massass took a deep breath and rose to his feet, cradling his arms. "It's been thirty years indeed, Santhi, since I passed the Severance Edict, and yet now you've decided to care for the lives of Carthosians? Need I remind you that they chose war when they murdered Elenia and her family, and now even Elias."

"But it is you who chose to punish an entire continent, over and above the guilty few."

"And now you wish me to establish peace with them? To embrace those who attacked and killed us, betrayed their Massass, the Temple and its teachings? And then what? Wait 'til the rest of these people turn on us and each other? Over the sap of some miracle tree left to us by your distant cousins? Or due to our perceived weakness as we compromise with our enemies? You presume much, Petrach. You presume my decisions have made me a tyrant. You think I do not know that the title of 'Symperell the Patient' is but a mockery of my ways, my judgement? As the esteemed chronicler that you're known to be, you would know that I, too, am a servant to circumstance. A servant to this seat. You can either be a good person or a good ruler, not both."

"When I came here just over a year ago, I promised you a seat on the Council of Elders, an Eldain bloodline and my youngest daughter in exchange for your protection. Protection from enemies in a war you have created, and now all you offer me are your sermons on right and wrong, on how your hand was twisted by ill-fate."

"Sending the fleet will not retrieve your daughter, or my nephew, assuming either of them is still alive. They will only expose us to a naval invasion as they tried fifteen years ago."

"So, you expect me to sit here and do nothing?"

"I expect you, Petrach Crysanthani, a person with your reputation for wisdom and cunning, to show it in times when it's needed!" he barked. Both went silent. The Massass turned to face the great tree in contemplation.

Santhi spoke. "Every day that passes, the Shirra grows and slowly creeps along the coast of the Carthosian Gulf. What will you do when the Shirral himself is knocking on your door with half a million people behind him? Reconcile with them, release the embargo on Enoch vitaserum, and let your medicians travel across the gulf. Now, before more people commit to his cause. Show them your clemency before it's too late."

"Oh, Petrach. Have you learnt nothing of human frailty? The Shirral is no more a free man, distinct from his position than I am of mine. The Shirra is a serpent with many vicious heads. Cut off one, and a dozen will spawn. Peace is not a language spoken by monsters. I hear even now that the Shirral is beset by as many pretenders as am I. I can only hope that the plague drives them against each other by the time they arrive." He paused, pacing. "The only difference between us is that those who follow me follow this tree; they follow belief. While those who follow him follow a man, and all men must die. That is why we are at war."

Suddenly the steward barged through the hall.

"Massass! Lord Elias! He's alive!"

Later that evening, the Massass, Santhi and Alistair entered Elias' chambers. Elias was wrapped in fresh, clean linen, yet his face and body were both beaten down by the sun and the sea.

"Your Grace." He tried to rise as the Massass stayed his struggle. "My lord," he muttered shamefully beneath his breath as he saw Santhi.

"Tell us what happened," said the Massass.

Elias obliged and, to his visible shame, recounted his failure to protect Adara and the rest of the crew.

"So Adara, Lilith, and this Cleriheu have been taken aboard one of the ships."

"I'm certain, but there's another thing," added Elias begrudgingly. "The mirror. They have it."

Santhi cursed beneath his breath.

"Is this the infamous mirror you spoke of, Alistair?" enquired the Massass.

Alistair nodded.

Santhi sighed. He proceeded to explain the full nature of his discoveries, which he so desperately wanted to remain a secret.

The Massass was not amused. "What were you planning to do with this information, Petrach? Perhaps advising your allies of the dangers of such an artefact and the importance of its safe custody may have been warranted in times of war? And you dare preach to me about my decisions?" The Massass rose, visibly angry.

"Massass, please."

"Shut up, Alistair. Get out," he fumed as Alistair slowly disappeared. "I have underestimated you, Petrach. Your stupidity, for starters!"

"And I your desire for power. Do you hear yourself? I am trying to protect us all from things we know so little about! Things that men like you crave."

"You have handed a tool that bolsters armies to the enemy!"

"We don't know that for sure. It is but a fragment of a whole, and the Drae'shï knows nothing of it," said Santhi.

"And Adara knows about this, too?" asked the Massass.

"If Adara is alive, she will make sure she keeps the secret. She wouldn't tell me. She won't tell Lilith," added Elias.

"I'm sorry, my lad, but love has blinded you. What if she is tortured? Or they threaten her," said the Massass.

"Enough. I will not have this talk of torture about my daughter!" barked Santhi.

The room fell silent. The Massass sighed.

"It seems like you will have it your way, after all, Santhi, if only by the grace of your own stupidity. We'll be sending the fleet. We must advance the resupply of Morren's Gate. If the Mirror falls into the hands of the Shirral, we must double our efforts."

"I will be the first to head there," groaned Elias as he struggled to rise in his bed. "Whatever it takes, I'll bring her back."

"The time for chivalry is over, Elias," said the Massass. "Now, it's time for war."

CHAPTER 23

THE IRONY OF SWORN ENEMIES

"Are you ever going to untie me? It's been three days, Adomas," said Sirra as she kicked an acorn into the fire.

It was night time, and the two were well into Cielith territory within the Liververn Wood. The thick woodland ran along the northern borders of Cielith beset by the Ciedien mountain range that once separated the territories of the Eldarï from the rest of the world. It was a cold and empty place at all times of the year. The eternal winter had never subsided this far north, and hardly anyone ever ventured in these lands, not even the Eldain Sentinels.

"Only when I can trust you not to kill me in my sleep. Now eat up," said Adam as he handed her grilled fish on a skewer.

Sirra stared back at him unimpressed.

"Trout isn't your favourite?" he asked as he dug into his own.

"No."

"Salmon?"

"No."

"Perch?"

"No."

"Carp?"

"No."

"Eel?"

Sirra went silent. Adam's ability to confound humour with annoyance was a joke not well received. "Not the way you burn your food anyway," she mumbled as she hesitantly nibbled at the crispy fish.

"Then maybe next time *you* can cook instead whilst I do the fishing? Now, tell me about the mirror and Lilith." He munched loudly.

She rolled her eyes. "It reflects the Mother's Light."

Adam looked at her, mouth full of fish, awaiting further elaboration.

She sighed, frustrated.

Adam gestured to continue as he forcibly swallowed the dried-out fish.

"Don't you people know anything? The Mother? The Age of Light? The Great Schism of the Eldarï?" she insisted but Adam kept chewing. She cursed. "Fine." She took a deep breath. "But untie me first."

Adam ignored her as he bit into another fish and nudged her on.

"Don't point your stupid fish at me!" she spat, turning her head away, awaiting a reaction, but none came. "Fine! Alright, fine. You're so bleeding obtuse!" She took a deep breath and let out a longer calming sigh. "So... Where to begin. Yes, so, the Age of Light was a time before the Eldarï split into three races: the Eldarï of Ciedien, the Eldaresh of Dos Narak and the Drae'shï. They all lived in Ciedien, close to the Mother," she said as she pointed towards the Ciedien mountains in the distant north. "It was a time where time itself did not exist. The Eldarï were *truly* immortal because they were part of the Mother. They never died, ever. However, in time they sought to venture into the world. But this came at a cost. Mortality. The further away they moved from the Mother, the shorter their lives became. At first, they didn't notice, but soon they realised how much they were part of her light when they began to die. Yet some were not deterred and never returned to her. They still lived on for tens of thousands of years. Some even relished the idea of death. Some even say that humans are their descendants, the husks of what once held the Mother's pure light within. Living a lifespan in what would be considered the blink of an eye of a true Eldarï. "

The fire crackled and popped as Adam listened attentively.

"Anyway, in the beginning, it is said that the Eldarï were all images begotten of the Mother, they would not have their offspring, they would not need or desire anything but her light. But as the separation grew, they learned what it means to desire things— wealth, power, love, freedom.”

“And there is no record of this anywhere? Just the legend?” asked Adam as he picked his teeth with his pinkie and sucked his teeth.

Sirra cringed. “Well, no one really knows why no records were kept. Then again, who needs to keep track if you’ve actually lived through everything. Timelessness eradicates history, I guess.”

“And meaning,” said Adam as he eyed the meal she had barely touched.

Sirra paused as she took a reluctant bite into the trout and stared into the flames. “Anyway. As the Eldarï ventured into the world, they established the city of Dos Narak in the Ethirahar Mountains and the many cities in Cielith like Myalthas and Vinesse. The Eldarï that populated these cities were the offspring of ancient Eldarï but hardly anything like their forefathers. The younger Eldarï were much more mundane in their whims, more base. In time, however, many of the true Eldarï returned to the Mother as they sensed the Mother’s influence diminishing. Nobody knows why her light faltered, but in the diminishing light, all Eldarï came to know the meaning of fear. For the first time in their existence, they felt lost. And as I said, many returned to her, but others remained. But those who remained, well, they weren’t happy to part ways with her light and their longevity. It’s said that as her light withdrew, their lives shortened further, and they knew death more intimately than before. Many tried to replicate her light but failed. The Eldarï had tried to build the three great towers to expand her influence, but even then, it was already too late.”

“And one of those towers is the one of Ussar Varys, right?”

“Along with the one on mount Balur Sephit, next to Dos Narak and the one on mount Calantis Juna in Rhyn, a few hundred kilometres northwest from here. One for each of the three races.”

“Rhyn? Never heard of a tower in Rhyn.”

“That’s because the tower was never completed. Only the ruins at the base remain. Anyway, as time went by, the Eldarï of Ciedien became protective of the Mother’s light. They coveted it above all else. However, the rest wanted her to yield it to them. Many of the Eldarï considered the attempt of replicating the Mother's light as impossible. Until the Eldarï of Cielith thought they could capture her light into the Hall of Mirrors to preserve it."

"The hall from which the Shard came?"

"Exactly. Soon the Great Schism of the Eldarï began. The Eldarï of Cielith marched into Ciedien unopposed. They were the only Eldarï ever to forge weapons from iron, and they would forever be known as the Children of Iron, the Iron Kindred—the Drae'shï. Many Eldarï pleaded with them, but they did not relent. The Mother willingly turned over her light to the White Tower to prevent the conflict but in doing so she faded away much faster to everyone's horror. Ciedien froze almost overnight, and all Eldarï left their former homeland as the eternal winter crept south. The Drae'shï had won, but it came at a terrible cost. The light of the Mother the was captured by the Mirror was so dim that it would only shine within the mountain. Thus, we've been forever since bound to its halls, the darkness of which became cast in our very flesh. We did come to benefit from her light, however dim it might have been, the longevity, the ability to not know the clutches of disease, the brevity of life outside the mountain, but we were—we *are* forever, buried alive. Doesn't get more ironic than that. The others did not fare too well either. The ancient Eldarï, meek and powerless, began their pilgrimage south in search of a new home, as eternal nomads of the world, only leaving their mark in the Enoch trees they planted along the way for sustenance. Some say they found their end across the southern seas, others in the bloodlines of men or melded into the Eldain and Eldassari. But the Eldarï of Dos Narak— the Eldaresh— well they brought upon themselves a curse worse than death."

"Is this why you want the Shard back? The Light is diminishing? You are diminishing? Why not just fix it?"

Sirra laughed. "Come on, Adomas. Even you can't be that dense. The mirror is ancient. There are no ancient Eldarï anymore, haven't been for thousands of years. No one has the knowledge. These things have become the stuff of legend, even to us. We had no idea it could be broken, let alone how to fix it. All we know is that its effects have since diminished, and we suspect that the Mirror will only reform if all pieces are there."

"What about the Mirror itself? Can't it reveal such knowledge? How to fix it without the Shard? It has brought you this far."

"For now, the Moirai only figured out how to use fragments to find the missing part. But the true abilities of the Mirror aren't clear even to us. Some say you can do anything you desire. Some say nothing. Others say it just reflects the *truth*, whatever that means. But even such simple things can be dangerous. Before Lilith, no one had stepped in the Hall of Mirrors for six hundred years, and that was during the Immortal Wars. The Drae'shï have been forbidden from entering the tower ever since. The Moirai, are responsible for preventing such things from happening. That's why we're here."

"Is it true that during the war, the Drae'shï used it to protect their armies and guide them in distant lands?"

"It is. Or at least it was at the time. The last seer, who managed to control its power for longer than a day, was also the one who used it to end the Immortal Wars. She was known as Altra. Before her, Sirith had spent years locked in that tower, using it to push our armies across the land. It consumed her 'til she withered to dust the moment she let go. After that Altra restored its natural balance and the Drae'shï have been forbidden to enter ever since. The entrance was then sealed shut by decree of Altra, lest its power would end up dragging us through another gruesome ordeal. That's when the Moirai first formed, in order to enforce Altra's decree and maintain order."

"And using these fragments hasn't killed anyone?"

"It seems the power is diminishing, one would say—"

"Fragmented," said the two together as they met each other's gaze.

"Anyway, let's put it this way. Would you want to be the one to stare long enough to find out if you'll turn to dust?"

He groaned as he shifted uncomfortably in his seat. His arrow wound was stinging once more.

"Still burns?"

"Uh-hum," he said shifting his shoulders and neck uncomfortably.

"You should have sealed it. Without any medical supplies, you probably have an infection by now."

"Where we're headed, we'll find all the supplies I need."

"Ah yes. Your Eldain friend. I'm sure they'll be waiting with open arms as you turn up with another Drae'shï by your side. If you even make it that far," she said, trying to taunt him, but Adam took no offence. "Why go all the way there anyway? Just let me go, and you can return to Raem. I've told you all you need to know."

"I'll be the judge of that." He groaned as he looked at his festering wound, now looking sore and irritated. He took a deep breath.

"Your stubbornness will get you killed, Eldassari," she said as she pointed to his wound. "I give you what you want, and then you don't release me." She raised her bound hands once more. "Did you ever trust anyone but yourself?"

"I trust my brothers and the Order."

"That's it? The brothers you wanted to hide me from?"

"Those were Saints. They are not my brothers, and I don't trust them any more than I trust a Drae'shï and her stories," said the gruff irate Warden.

Sirra paused, lips parted and brow furrowed.

"You, sad, sad, lonely man. Look at you, out here alone, lapping your wounds like a lone wolf, growling at anyone who tries to help. You are so blinded by your beliefs that you won't acknowledge the truth, even if it's in front of you. What's hard to believe? The truth or the fact that a Drae'shï is the one delivering it?" She sneered as the flames intensified, but Adam gave no response. "I know what it is. You don't want to believe me because believing me means accepting that you and your brothers have dedicated your lives to a pointless endeavour. That it's the Drae'shï that is protecting the world from you, and not you protecting the world from us. You think that your band of merry men held up in your Hold would stand a chance against an invasion? We are millions," she said seething, watching him through the flames.

Adam said nothing as he stared into the fire in contemplation as her words seared his heart. "I'm sorry," he said softly.

Sirra recoiled astonished.

"I wanted to tell you I'm sorry for your father. I know it's not much, but if I do perish of my stubbornness, at least I'd like you to know. He was a skilled warrior, and he would have killed me had I been alone." He gazed straight into her gleaming red eyes.

"Stop," she said, tears springing to her eyes. "Just stop." She turned her head away.

"And I believe you. You are right, but my mission still stands. 'To protect the world from the darkness within.' Now I realise that not all darkness emerges from beneath a mountain," he said as she slowly turned her gaze back to meet his. "I must protect the world from those who wish to use the Shard to conquer it. I want to help you retrieve the Shard, Sirra. But I must inform Santhi of this before it's too late. Before the Saints get their hands on it. I'm... I'm..." Adam suddenly felt faint. He attempted to rest his arm on the nearby stump but missed it completely, falling to the ground and thrashing his feet through the flames.

"Adomas!" cried Sirra as she struggled to her feet and knocked his own out of the fire. She knelt beside him and felt his head. "Fever. Stubborn bastard." She cursed as she tried to lay him on his back.

She soon freed her hands from bondage carefully using the hot embers of a charred stick. She looked around squinting into the pitch darkness of the surrounding forest. She picked up her bow, arrows, and dagger, took up a torch and wrapped herself in her black and blue cloak.

Adam groaned.

She hesitated then sighed and left.

The next morning, the fire was out, but Adam was not. His wound was still burning, yet from the scald of hot coals. His head, on the other hand, was no longer ablaze. The smell of elderflower and berries wafted from a wooden cup steaming beside him. He picked it up and drank the medicinal concoction in one long gulp as he slowly rose upright. The drink filled him with a spicy warmth that his senses had long been waiting for.

As he set it down, his fast was broken by the presence of a horde of Drae'shï that emerged from nowhere. He turned to reach his sword, but his wounded arm betrayed him first and the boot of a Drae'shï second.

The Drae'shï pressed his foot on Adam's shoulder forcing his arm against the tree trunk. Adam yelled in agony. The rest laughed. They were tall, dark, white-haired, and armed to the teeth.

Their leader came forth, brandishing a distinct Drae'shï scimitar of black steel clearly denoting his rank. "Tell us where the girl is, and I will make this quick," he said. His face showed signs of an earlier scuffle, and so did those of the others.

"Vuriel. I think he's the one who killed Olpher," intervene another. "He's wearing the same armour as those Eldassari we encountered."

"Other ginger bastard nearly broke my jaw," added a Dratesh Khan through his helmet.

"Come to think of it, this one's an Eldassari, too," said their leader as he turned Adam's cheek with the tip of his boot and looked at Adam's slightly pointed ear. "Which must mean he's one of those Wardens." The rest laughed. "It's your lucky day then, Warden. You get to die for your cause, but before you do, Sirra, the girl, where is she? Is she alive?"

"She's alive," Adam grunted, pain searing through his arm.

"How do we know you didn't kill her already? said Vuriel, trailing the tip of his blade along the side of Adam's cheek.

"I didn't. After her father died, she ran. I caught her. She's the one who healed my wound."

The Drae'shï looked at each other frowning.

"And why would she decide to heal you instead of slit your throat in your sleep?" He held his foot on Adam's shoulder and pressed harder.

"Why don't you ask her?" Adam grunted, but the Drae'shï immediately nicked his cheek with the blade in response. A trickle of blood flowed from the tiny incision.

"Funny, are we? Who's laughing now? Now, answer, why were you tracking us three days ago?"

"I wasn't."

The Drae'shï punched him in response.

"Liar. We all know what you do. Your patrols. Your outposts. We both know you haven't moved out of that pile of rubble you call home in decades. We have seen your horsemen. Speak Eldassari or die." Vuriel placed the tip of his blade at Adam's throat.

"I'm not afraid to die," grunted Adam.

Vuriel pressed and the blade began to draw blood at its edge, yet the Eldassari did not flinch. "Ugh!" grunted the Drae'shï as he dug the blade into the ground and proceeded to punch and kick Adam.

"Stop!" yelled Sirra from afar. She dropped her bow and a brace of pheasants, speeding to reach them. "Stop! Vuriel! Stop!"

Vuriel stepped back panting as Adam rolled on his back and coughed blood onto the ground.

"I'm glad to see you're alive, Sirra, but you have me confused. You treated this man? You brought him food? What's going on?" asked Vuriel sarcastically as the other soldiers stood between Sirra and Adam.

"Oh, shut up! I have more cause to kill him than any of you. Olpher was my mentor, not yours."

"Is it true you called him father?" another sniggered to her embarrassment.

"Go fuck yourself, Lurith," she spat.

"Enough. So? Why haven't you?" asked Vuriel flatly.

"Because they know about the mirror and the Shard."

The Drae'shï all looked at each other concerned. Vuriel cursed.

"And he's the only one who we can trust to convince them not to pursue it."

"That's it then. We will have to kill all the Wardens before the word spreads," concluded Vuriel as he rubbed his forehead.

"Vuriel, it's more complicated than that. Those white knights, Saints they're called. They're powerful people. They saw the Ilvaresh use it. For now, they know very little, but it's only a matter of time. He said they're taking her to Valendria. It's going to be impossible to retrieve. We need him to convince them to give it to us."

They all paused as Sirra walked past them and helped Adam up.

"She told me about the mirror, what it means to you. I want to help you," said Adam, wincing in his speech.

"Why would we need your help? We will send assassins and kill her even if it takes a thousand."

"Because where she's headed, you will need a hundred thousand to reach her, and I'm the only one still in a position to convince them to give her up. I have powerful friends. Friends who fear the power of such things. Who know where they belong, to whom they belong. Those knights covet power above all else. If they believe they have the tool to have it, they will try to obtain it in whatever way they can, but we must act now before they know more, before they can control it."

"Did he say they're headed to Valendria?" intervened another short-haired and skinny Drae'shï, as he looked intently at a tiny fragment of the mirror suspended within an armillary sphere; a small instrument made of three golden rings all inlaid with markings and notches. The shard within the armillary sphere twisted and turned and eventually settled.

"Yes. Valendria," said Adam as he peered at the curious device.

"Isn't Valendria in the south?"

"Yes, Tenet. South," said Vuriel.

"Well, it's quite the opposite. From where we are, it's actually northwest. What lies to the northwest? Iborellan?" asked Tenet as he looked to the group.

"They were meant to travel south. There's no way they'd have gone north. I'm sure of it."

"Wherever your friends may be, the Shard is not with them. It's somewhere very far away in that direction. Possibly at sea, too, by my calculations," said Tenet.

Adam looked to the ground perplexed. "Unless they took it to the front?" he whispered to himself. "If there is any chance they know how to use it, they'll try to use it in their war against Carthosia, and it starts at Morren's Gate."

The Drae'shï all looked at each other concerned.

"They wish to employ the Shard in war? Do they even know how?" said the Dratesh Khan.

"Lilith," said Adam.

"The Ilvaresh," intervened Sirra.

"She can stare into it without consequence. She might be able to control it. I've seen her do things with it, but not much. I don't know what they'll be able to do with it by the time they get there, but they *would* try to use it," said Adam.

The Drae'shï all looked at each other concerned as Vuriel stared at Adam, urgency coiling in his clenched fists.

"Well then, Eldassari. It seems we both have a long road ahead of us," said Vuriel.

"I will head to my friend in Cielith. He's well connected. He'll help us stop this before it gets out of hand," said Adam as he edged towards his things.

"Not so fast, Eldassari," said Vuriel as he picked his sword up and placed the blade to Adam's chest. "The road I was referring to is the one north. You didn't think I'd let you troddle on back to your allies after Sirra here gave away all the story," he said, eyeing her with contempt.

"I want to get the Shard back as much as you do. We're on the same side," said Adam hand on heart.

"Well, we'll just need to figure that out as we go along, won't we? It's a long journey to Iborellan, and I *love* a good story."

Chapter 24

The Lies Of Peace

"How's the wound healing?" enquired Adara through her dried, cracked lips.

"She'll survive. It doesn't seem like she has an infection. The Drae'shï, they are very strong," said Pïshkah, holding Lilith's head on her lap, now almost as sore and battered as her patient.

The creaking ship and the groans of the captives aboard punctuated the monotony of their seafaring sojourn. It had been over a week since their abduction, and time seemed to stand still in the endless ocean that surrounded them. Their wrists lay worn within their shackles, and their faces were sullen with hunger and dry with salt. Nobody talked. None had the energy, day or night. Some had died of dehydration. Others were thrown overboard as disease began to claim them.

The left side of Lilith's head, along with her eye, was covered in bandages. She'd been somewhere between life and death for the last three days and had since not returned to consciousness.

Adara looked out into the star-filled night through a small porthole. The moon was out, and its calming aura brought her some respite. "Where do you think we're heading? They should be planning to do something with us, right? Since they haven't killed us yet."

"Shh!" hissed a captive as the rest huffed and puffed in their sleep.

"Probably Carthosia. Somewhere along the coast," whispered Pïshkah.

"And then?"

"I don't know."

"Do you think they'll ask for a ransom?"

"I don't know," lied Pïshkah sheepishly as another prisoner shushed.

"I'm sure they probably already know about us. In Carthosia," whispered Adara.

"Adara... I..." Pïshkah hesitated.

"No one's coming, girl, and if you're smart, you'll take the quick way out," intervened one of the men in chains.

"What?"

"Hey, you, shut up," hissed Pïshkah.

"A pretty girl like you. You're lucky these men think you're cursed. Otherwise, you'd be spinning around their cocks from coast to coast."

"Listen here, you piece of shit. If you want to off yourself 'cause you're too chicken shit about what they'll do to you, that's your problem, but don't take us along with you," snapped the Cleriheu.

"Just telling the truth, girl. Like I see it. I'm sure others will look past the superstition," he said.

"Hey, shut up! Before you earn us all another beating," called out another man from across the deck. The deck rang with shushes.

"But the others, they know we went missing. There were the other boats. They can't just abandon us," said Adara, now seriously concerned. "They should be chasing after us, right?"

Pïshkah took a deep breath. "Adara. Listen, forget what they're saying. I'm sure they're planning something as we speak. Elias." She hesitated. "*Was* a powerful lord. I'm sure they won't let this go."

Adara did not answer as the hope flushed from her now pale face at the realisation of her intended's passing.

Pïshkah frowned. She paused. Then raised her head again with forced excitement. "And Zain! What about him? I'm sure he's coming for us. He's a Vampire. He cannot die, right?" said Pïshkah with a tired grin.

Adara caught her gaze. "You're right. It's true. He did tell me of a story where he was chained to a rock and was thrown into the sea and walked all the way back to shore," she stated, forcing a smile half-heartedly.

"No one is coming," uttered Lilith as she struggled to speak through her bruised lips. "No one's coming."

"Lilith!" exclaimed Adara in a sigh of relief. "You're awake. We were so worried."

"You truly are tough." Pïshkah's eyes aghast by the Drae'shï's resilience as Lilith slowly forced herself up. "Don't move. You're still weak. You've been unconscious for days."

"Where is it?" asked Lilith, gritting her teeth, seemingly more irate than in pain. Being the only one still unchained, she forced herself to stand up. She cringed deeply as the pain surged through her, rubbing her head as the pulsating headache shocked her nerves. She fell to her knees. Her hands, laid flat on the blood-spattered deck, showed nine fingers in the moonlight.

"You shouldn't move, Lil. You're still weak," Adara said, hesitantly reaching out to her.

"Where is it?" she growled beneath her breath.

"It's been with you the whole time. No one else touched it," said Adara.

Pïshkah brought it out from under her legs, wrapped in a blood-stained cloth.

Lilith snatched the Shard and clutched it tightly, still staring at her mutilated hand.

"Zain is coming. He won't give up on us. He's—" said Adara.

"Zain is not coming," Lilith muttered behind gritted teeth.

"Zain is a Vampire. He cannot die. He will not leave us, he's—"

"Zain is not coming!" she barked. "He is not a Vampire! He *is* dead! Stuck to a ship at the bottom of the ocean, along with his convictions."

"What?"

"He couldn't save himself. How can he save anyone else? He lied to himself and others, and *that* got him killed. Just like you did and just like you will," said Lilith pointing the wrapped Shard at her.

Adara went silent.

"You knew what the Shard could do. Yet you didn't utter a word," accused the Drae'shï.

"What?" asked Adara, confused.

"What's she talking about, Adara?" added Pïshkah.

"More lies? I read the letter your father sent you. 'It is as we suspected.' What did you suspect? What was this little bit of knowledge that you were so willing to guard with my life?" Lilith's red eyes gleamed in the darkness. "Do not turn away from me! The dark will not hide your shame from me."

Adara sat in silence as Lilith turned to her, kneeling in the spotlight of the moon.

"It's not that simple."

"Speak!"

"Lilith. Please. It's for your protection," Adara pleaded.

"My protection?" She scoffed. "I never needed your protection or anyone's! *I* was your prisoner." She angrily pointed to herself. "Everything you've done. Everything, you, your father, the Eldain, the Saints, everyone! All you do is for nothing but your *own* protection, your *own* power. All of you," she barked, her voice almost breaking with rage.

The rest sat speechlessly.

"You won't deign to tell me the truth?" she continued. "Then allow me to extend the courtesy to you instead. No one is coming for you." Lilith's eyes locked onto Adara's.

"Lilith. Calm down. We know you're angry," placated Pïshkah, but Lilith ignored her.

"And even if by some miracle the Saints do find you, and somehow you are still alive after you've been beaten and raped for days, you will be nothing more to them than the whore your father chose to peddle off on behalf of your people." Adara's lips quivered, tears almost brewing in her eyes. "Just another instrument of power, to be used and abused. Like me."

"We weren't trying to use you. We're all on the same side in this war! We just can't let anyone in, not even the Saints, not even Elias. We're all trying to survive, Lilith! Like you!" Adara barked back.

Lilith laughed.

"Lilith. I'm sorry that horrible fiend tortured you because of me, but believe me when I tell you that had I spoken, we'd be in a far worse place than we are now."

"It doesn't matter anymore. I finally know the fundamental truth that matters," she continued as she slowly unravelled her bandages. "In the end, no matter how much you will struggle, how much the Saints struggle, how many wars are fought in your name or any others, the one truth is in the depth of this mirror, as ugly as it may seem."

Lilith looked at the reflection the moonlight revealed.

Lilith's face was purple and full of cuts. The side of her head was partly shaved and partly burnt. Three long cuts protruded from her left eye, which was blackened with blood. One ran from the tail of her eye to her temple, another straight down her cheek, and a diagonal one between the other two.

Adara looked back, scared.

"Don't worry, Adara, I won't force it out of you. I won't cut your delicate fingers or rip out your hair, but you will come to see in time."

"Lilith, enough," said Pïshkah.

"I'll just wait and see you carry the weight of your lies on you 'til it breaks you. Like it did Zain."

"Enough!" yelled Pïshkah angrily as Adara slowly began to sob, sinking her face in her hands. "Sit down and shut up, you horrible piece of shit!"

"We're all horrible in our own ways, Pïshkah. She just didn't know it," said Lilith.

"You hypocrite! What about your lies? Your secrets. What about the Shard? How did you kill that man?"

Lilith laughed. "The Shard killed him, not me. I was surprised as much as you were, Cleriheu— or is it Yuen'hii?" Pïshkah sat silent and looked away. "Maybe I should ask you, who *you* were really hunting? The Vampire, the Eldain, or *me*?" asked Lilith as she pointed the Shard at her.

"I hunted you," said Pïshkah, scowling, fearless.

"That's better," said Lilith as she withdrew.

"But I also saved you, even though no part of me wanted to. I saved your fucking life because *she* asked me to. Because she saved my own, and you saved hers that day," said Pïshkah as she pointed to Adara.

"It's true then," said Lilith as she looked at both. "The three horrible harlots. Maybe you were right about the legend."

They all quieted down as none had any energy left to fight. Soon they could hear the shuffling of feet and the shouts of men scrambling across the deck above them. Lilith moved towards a porthole to peer into the night but immediately backed off as the shadow of another galley sailed right before her. The ship suddenly rumbled and followed with a sharp break to its side. Everyone who was not still sleeping awoke as Lilith struggled to keep herself on her feet.

"What was that?" asked Pïshkah.

"It's another ship," said a man.

"More pirates?" asked another.

"Silence!" said Lilith as she tried to see what was happening through the narrow space between the two vessels. "They're not fighting."

"Lilith!" said Pïshkah. "Sit down! Someone's coming!"

Lilith looked back and noticed the dim light of a lantern creeping down the stairs and quickly took her place beside Pïshkah. A band of pirates came in, followed by a separate group of seamen uniformly clad in blue, white, and gold textiles. The two groups discussed quietly amongst each other as they pointed to different captives upon the deck. As they gradually moved closer, the pirates unchained some individuals and cuffed them in separate shackles whilst the other sailors escorted them topside.

"What are they doing?" whispered Adara to Pïshkah.

"They're selling us off," she said with dread.

"I'm no—" interjected Lilith.

"Listen here, shut up!" interrupted Pïshkah, grabbing her by her wrist. "Keep quiet and leave it to me. Unless you want the other side of your face bashed in."

Lilith snatched her hand back and sat silent.

"Well, well. Are these the ones you mentioned, Karrif?" asked one of the sailors in uniform as he used his short whip to point at the three girls, who had now grown to look like the crones they called themselves.

"Look like a bunch of dirty wenches to me," replied Karrif jokingly through his missing front teeth, but the humour was nowhere to be found. "Anyways, yes, these are they."

"Well, she's obviously a Cleriheu, so we'll take her. What about the others? I'm in no need of prostitutes. The men are already riled up as it is, and I don't want to have another outbreak of syphilis aboard."

"Well, you got to take them together, Meshall. It's all or none."

"Excuse me?" said Meshall unamused.

"Well, yes. They come in threes." Karrif fidgeted nervously as he insisted courteously.

"Karrif, I don't care if your merchandise comes in twos, threes, fours, or a dozen," said Meshall sternly. "I'll take the girl and those two men in back there," he said, pointing once again with his whip.

"But Meshall. You misunderstand. We'll give them away for free. A tribute to the Shirral" insisted the slimeball.

Meshall raised an eyebrow at the unusually generous offer.

"He's trying to get rid of us cause he thinks we're the sea crones," said Lilith flatly to the dismay of both the pirates and her sister crones.

"Enough out of you," said Karrif as he went to strike her only to find himself caught by the scruff of his neck.

"Please, explain," Meshall requested as he held the scoundrel back.

"Take no notice of her. She's a Drae'shï. Her kind are lying assassins. She killed the captain with her magic," said Karrif, hurriedly fumbling his words as the other sailors encroached on him.

"Go on…"

"We *are* the Crones of the Sea," intervened Pïshkah. "Should anything happen—"

"I know the stories, Cleriheu. Well enough not to believe them. What interests me, however, is why Karrif here appears like he's desperately trying to shaft me," said Meshall as he put his whip to the chin of the trembling pirate whilst Meshall's sailors grabbed hold of him.

"Please, Meshall, apologies. But the men are scared. You can have them for free. Even the Cleriheu," said Karrif as Meshall continued to hold him. "And those two in the back. The dark one killed the captain, Meshall."

"That will do, Karrif," said Meshall as he nodded to his men to release the squirming pirate, who was instantly pushed forward, almost falling to his knees. The sailors laughed. "See that they are taken aboard. We'll see whether we can turn their magic into good fortune."

"Just ask what happened to their captain after he did this," said Lilith as she showed him her hand close to her face.

"These brigands never knew how to treat women," said Meshall as he signalled his sailors to unchain the ladies and help Lilith up.

"I can walk," said Lilith.

The sailors looked at Meshall, who nodded in acquiescence.

"Where are you taking us?" intervened Pïshkah uneasily as they unchained her and brought her to her feet.

"Who are you? Are you saving us?" added Adara as she, too, finally got up.

"Of course." He smiled as he began walking back to the stairs. "You've just been rescued by the Royal Admiralty of Carthosia."

CHAPTER 25

THE OTHER WAR

It had been almost four weeks since Adara had last bathed back in Yammimer. This time they even had servants tending to them. She stood pale and coy as the serfs in white gowns scrubbed the filth off her almost blackened skin. Lilith stood beside her, upright and unabashed whilst Pïshkah seemed more distracted by her companions than concerned by her own skin. A tall, fair, middle-aged tanned woman, stood there wrapped in beautifully intricate orange, teal, and pink Carthosian robes. She watched cross-armed at the rather crass process, which was undeniably still welcome after weeks at sea.

The warm winds blew into the room from the terrace as the sound of the cicadas buzzed in the distance. It was still summer on this side of the continent. As the women stepped out of their filthy bathwater, they were anointed with soothing oils and fragrances and then tightly wrapped in soft cotton towels as each was eased to a dressing table by their respective group of serfs. All seemed to find themselves at ease, even though still somewhat confused.

"I am Norella Ish'tarii, Seneschal to the Shirral and the Royal Family," said the woman distinctly. "The reason you are here, being bathed and dressed is not for your own amusement—and certainly not mine," she continued as the serfs began applying makeup to the women, each having their own distinct reaction to the powders, brushes, and colours being put to their faces. Adara sat quietly, at ease with the familiarity of the process. Lilith observed with a scowl at every brush that came close to her, and Pïshkah scrunched her face with every new powder they patted onto her nose. She sneezed.

Norella continued. "You are lucky enough that the Shirral has heard of you and has requested your presence at the Royal Riad as it is. You will obey all instructions and maintain proper formality and protocol when addressed. You sit up straight!" she said, and Pïshkah immediately attempted to straighten her slouch as Norella poked her in the back. "You will always address the Shirral as Your Grace. You will only speak if and when spoken to, and you will bow at his presence as he arrives and departs before you."

"I'll bow to no one," said Lilith as the serfs delicately cleaned her head wound and picked off the scabs that stuck out. They patiently proceeded to shave and trim her hair around the wound appropriately.

"Hmmm. I see. Is that why you ended up with those scars?" said Norella, unimpressed as she held Lilith by the chin and looked at her injuries. "We'll have to cover your unsightly injuries. I'm not so sure his taste for *exotic* women includes those that have been bashed and battered," she continued as she looked at the other serfs. "Sintra." She snapped her fingers. "Swap with Lit'jira. Yours hardly needs any help as it is. This one, on the other hand...."

The older serf dealing with Adara's makeup rose immediately and switched places with the younger one that was dealing with Lilith's.

Lilith sat quietly as Sintra sat before her without engaging her eyes. The tanned women were all beautiful in their own right, with long brown and curled chestnut hair and full lips. She dipped her brush in the black eyeliner and proceeded to colour Lilith's eyelids and trace the shape of her eyes perfectly. She continued to paint sharp curved lines along the traces of her three scars, masking the unsightly aberration perfectly.

Norella crossed her arms and tilted her head as she observed. "Ah, much better. Even has a certain Panthesinian charm to it."

Soon enough, Lilith, Adara, and Pïshkah were adorned in similar robes to the Seneschal. The Carthosian fabrics were thick yet incredibly soft and cool, designed in a cacophony of colour and moods. One fabric could differ from the other so much that it would often be considered unique in its creation, from embroidered vines to fig leaves, from paisley to pansy. Lilith wore black, red, and purple, Adara white, teal and pink, and Pïshkah grey, orange and blue. All were escorted to a carriage outside the barracks where the admiralty had kept them.

The road led them through the city and up to a small hill over-looking the port. The city hardly looked like the warmongering state that many professed Carthosia to be. The streets were narrow and dusty, filled with the poor, hungry, and maimed, yet all seemed to go about their day without much hindrance by their conditions. Trade was abuzz, and the measure of one's wealth could often easily be seen by the quality of one's clothing and the shoes on their feet or lack thereof. Yet everyone was apparently content, even in their own misery. The busy city was a host to many people, but squalor was not one of its guests. Men and women dressed in white robes with red and blue sashes ran from corner to corner, spreading a white powder across the street to cleanse it of impurities and deter vermin. As the carriage entered the road to the palace, the number of people in need of food or care only seemed to increase, and so did the graveyards.

"If you're wondering why there are all these lame people, it is because the Royal Riad has been receiving them on its grounds since the Shirral arrived two weeks ago," intervened Norella as she watched all three look upon the Carthosian way of life intently.

"Is this not Sindabath, the capital?" asked Adara.

"We could not be further away. We are in Arthusa," replied Norella, but none found their bearings. "Arthusa is two weeks north by sea from the capital. It is the Shirral's current residence whilst the Shirra's vanguard paves the way forward up north."

"Does the Shirral always have others fight his wars for him? Or does he do so himself at times? Or does he only interest himself in women and dresses?" intervened Lilith.

Norella's eyes narrowed. "The Shirral fights one the most important wars—this one," she said as she waved her hand at the dozens of sickly people they passed by. "I would be very careful with your words. It seems that wherever you're from, respect and propriety are difficult to come by. You would do well to extend some yourself before you claim it so forthrightly from others."

Lilith ignored her and continued to watch.

"What about you? What's your problem?" she asked as she saw Pïshkah visibly uncomfortable, scratching herself.

"She's not used to being clean," answered Lilith dryly as she continued to gaze out of the window.

Adara chuckled.

"Though you did seem to enjoy the view," added Lilith slyly, looking at her from the corner of her eye.

"Oh, shut up!" Pïshkah blushed. "Do you know how long it takes me to make and apply those ointments?" She huffed awkwardly as she proceeded to scratch an itch. "And I'm not used to these clothes and this heat. Is there any chance I can have mine back?"

"Your clothes were the first thing we burnt the moment you took them off."

"And my charms? Jewellery?"

"Everything. However, Arthusa is a den for all sorts of jewels, precious stones, and other charms you will find of interest, Cleriheu," said Norella, as Pïshkah stared back at her. "Oh, yes, we are aware of your types. All medicine and its practitioners are of interest to us. Unlike the Massass, we don't have the luxury of persecuting practices we deem unsavoury or unable to control exclusively. Should you agree to the Shirral's offer, we will give you all the tools you need."

Pïshkah smiled briefly.

The carriage eventually drew up to the Shirral's Riad, a modestly sized estate built at the foot of a hill surrounded by a large olive grove that gave shade to the many pilgrims that came seeking alms and cures from their leader. The building's walls were a complex weave of tiles and carvings depicting historical scenes in a mesh of intricate geometrical shapes. The architecture was fundamentally simple but adorned with the most interesting furnishings, from the mosaic floors to the frescoed ceilings. As the women walked into the Riad, the main parlour appeared in a small open-air courtyard in the middle of the building.

"Wait here," said Norella as she headed into the courtyard.

The yard looked more like a study than a lounge. A large table and a number of shelves had been introduced, which clearly did not belong there. Nevertheless, the space was incredibly soothing as the echoing voices in the yard were set against the subtle flow of a fountain into a pool in the middle of it all. The women watched closely, waiting to see who the infamous Shirral was. In the middle of the room stood a group of men dressed in black tunics save for one in white and gold. All were engaged in debate around the table. The ladies listened intently.

"I'm telling you, Your Grace, the Valendrians are on the move. If we prolong the advance on Morren's Gate, we're going to find it harder to take over. The Vanguard Army is ready. Ithiria is secure. We must push forward now," said a tall, dark man in his fifties with short curly hair and a salt and pepper beard. The man carried himself with dignity and the sign of years of military experience.

"Nephrim, I ask you once more not to push this matter further before I lose my temper," said another man dressed in a white and gold robe with a bright golden sash bound to his waist. He was a slightly younger, handsome, bearded man, with amber eyes and straight brown hair that grew to his cheeks. "Is it true the Saints are also moving troops and calling in more blood tributes?"

"Yes, Your Grace. Our spies have reported an increase in recruitments," answered another fair yet tanned man.

"And are the rumours true? Is the Jurani boy dead?" said the Shirral.

"Apparently not," said the advisor.

"Elias!" whispered Adara to herself.

"Conjecture, it seems. He's been spotted in Valendria several times since the reports," added another.

"Understood. We shall adjourn until the morning after I give this some thought and consideration. Thank you," he continued sternly yet gracefully as he invited them to leave.

The group of men respectfully bowed and took their leave.

Nephrim, on the other hand, lingered.

"With respect, Your Grace, this is no time for hesitation," said Nephrim impatiently. "We cannot wait 'til we move all seven armies to the front. We must take hold of Morren's Gate to establish a solid foothold in Iborellan. With the fortified port, we can open supply lines from there and—"

"Nephrim," he interrupted. "I know that when my father died and the title of Shirral fell on my shoulders instead of yours, you must have loathed the very idea of it."

"Your Grace, I never—"

"Do not interrupt me!" he scolded. "I did not ask for this title. Yet it has fallen onto my shoulders like your role of commander fell on yours. Nevertheless, I possess the wisdom of my father's teachings and mistakes and can look past your ambitions and value your talent instead. You are a great general, Nephrim, but the Shirra is not just about battles won or lost. It is about our people and the world we fight for them, which extends from the shores of Pliny to the tips of the spears on the front. Moving hundreds of thousands across the land has proven to be a near-impossible task. Without water, without proper medical supplies, without timber for ships. If we run too fast, how will we quench our thirst? How will we sew our wounds and cure our fevers? If we invade too soon, too fast, it will cost us more lives than we strive to save through this endeavour."

"We have the numbers, though, Your Grace."

"Indeed, 245,000 by the most recent calculations, and increasing daily. But of these, how many are professional fighters? Half? One third? Many who join come of their own will and with their own supplies. And why? Because this is our journey for survival and because the Shirra is only as strong as the belief in its success. It is more than just an army. The moment we start losing men to famine and disease, the sooner we will see our numbers dwindle as people abandon the cause. We must tread carefully, lest a step forward would push us two steps back."

"Just remember, Your Grace, your father promised us. The Shirral's promise does not die with him. You must fulfil the oath he took," said Nephrim as he bowed, hand on heart.

"I have not forgotten my obligations, nor do I discount them. But I promise you this, should you ever question my devotion to the Shirra again, such a mistake will be your last." The Shirral extended his ring-laden hand, and Nephrim kissed silently before departing.

Norella approached. "Your Grace, the captives of Admiral Meshall. As requested," said the seneschal gracefully.

The Shirral proceeded to wave them over. Meanwhile, he headed to the nearby fountain where a serf attended with a towel as he removed his top and lightly bathed himself. As he dried himself, another serf placed a bronze tea set on the low side table beside a nearby armchair in the room. The room smelled of nettles and mint. After drying himself, he proceeded to change into a lighter tunic and approached the women who now stood in the courtyard under the sun. He quietly observed each of them as they looked back, unaware of what to say or do.

Norella eyed them to bow. Pïshkah awkwardly began to oblige, but as both Adara and Lilith refused, she stood firm.

The Shirral did not react. "I, too, would not bow to my enemies, even if it were the Massass himself. At least you have some resolve, if a lack of proper manners," he said as he casually picked up a cup of hot tea by the rim and took a sip. "I am Altheo Serkario Tarrasque, head of the Tarrasque Dynasty, M'yar of Carthosia and Shirral to the seven armies of the Shirra." He continued to look at each without cracking a smile. "They tell me you are witches or have claimed to be. That you even killed the infamous Silvan in front of his crew whilst chained. My guess is that *you* did it." He turned to Lilith, gazing at her scar and maimed hand.

She looked him straight in the eyes acknowledging his assumption.

"My father always stressed the importance of knowing your history. He said, 'know your enemies first through books before battle.' He was an avid scholar of the Immortal Wars and the Drae'shï. Having studied such battles myself, I could not pass up the chance to see living history before me, and I can't say I'm disappointed. You are indeed a Child of Iron— I am honoured."

Lilith stared him down but chose to remain silent.

"And the Cleriheu, you are most welcome in our midst. You will not find closed doors and persecution in Carthosia."

Pïshkah smiled and looked down, trying to hide her appreciation of the handsome man's charm.

"And finally, the remnant of the Eldarï bloodline. Are you Eldain, true and true?"

"As my father bore witness to my birth," said Adara sternly, unable to hide her scorn at the hands of the enemy.

"A woman of your beauty should not be forced to bear such a scowl. Come, sit," he said as he invited them to sit on the poufs around his side table. He proceeded to sit at his low armchair and pour the tea into three brass cups. He extended his ring-covered hand to Pïshkah first, who gladly obliged. The others stood sceptical yet soon followed. "Let me assure you that so long as you are in Carthosia, no harm will come to you."

The sweet news met them, along with the spicy sweetness of the tea.

"Then are we free to go?" asked Adara.

"You are, but where will you go, and who will take you?"

"Then, why are we here? Is it knowledge of the Shard that you have come to ask of me, like everyone else? It has no master, other than myself," intervened Lilith as the other two looked at her in astonishment.

"Is that so?" he asked as he opened a small chest beside the table, revealing the clean Shard. "Admiral Meshall told me of the impact you've left on Silvan's crew, or rather the impact your Shard left." He paused. "Well, I am a man intrigued by the artefacts of the ancient world and have read many volumes about the Immortal Wars and your Mirror — enough to know that a fragment is hardly a reflection of the whole. And as far as protection for my armies, well, my dear Drae'shï, I ask you one question; can your broken Shard give me food and water for an army? For a nation? Immunity from illness for an entire people? And what about protection from harm? It certainly has not yielded the latter to you," he said as he pointed to her scars. "I have all the soldiers and weapons I need to win the war. And we *will* win, it's only a matter of time. But what I lack, what Carthosia lacks, are far simpler things, yet far greater. Tell me, how do you convince a man to fight and die for you if all you can offer him is all the gold and jewels in the world but no food and no medicine to spend it on?"

"The Severance Edict's embargo," said Pïshkah.

The Shirral nodded. "For thirty long years, Carthosia has been severed from the rest of the world. We went from the richest people in the world to the poorest. A once great empire was reduced to nomads of the desert with barely enough arable land to feed ourselves. There is nothing more humbling than scrounging for bread whilst draped in gold and silver."

"You still haven't answered the question, Your Grace," said Adara contemptuously.

Norella in the back was fuming and embarrassed. The Shirral smiled as he set his cup back onto the tray and leaned forward. He drew the mirror from the chest with a white cloth and casually handed it to Lilith. All stood astonished.

"I will indulge you some leave from the requirements of proper behaviour if your courtesy would grant me your names, even though a king did so ahead of you," he said politely with his undeniably intimidating charm.

"Lilith"

"Pïshkah"

"Eirene," said Adara without flinching, and so did the others.

Altheo smiled and rose to his feet. "Follow me," he said as he led them through the Riad and into a large hall that had been recently converted into a ward. The room was full of bedridden people of all ages and classes tended to by medicians, nurses, and other clerics. All nodded to the Shirral as he entered and continued with their business. "Since we cannot obtain any Enoch sap, recovery from disease is always long and never certain. This is the plight of our nation, the spirit of our cause," he continued as he went from patient to patient, inspecting some and comforting others with a light touch to meet their devotion. "Before I was bestowed this title, I was a medician. Sometimes I wonder which of the two I really am," he said as he continued walking through the ward and out into the olive grove. Small camps were set up for people having less serious ailments. "I understand that you have clerical skills, Pïshkah?"

"I do. I have cured people of sweating sickness, dysentery, typhoid, and cholera. Some even of the plague."

"Vespial?"

"Common," she said sardonically.

"Understood. I didn't imagine they'd allow you into the temple, let alone use the sap. Nevertheless, one still hopes that another cure that doesn't require it can be found," he said as they continued to walk around the grove. "Eirene, how about you? What is it that you did in Cielith?"

"I helped my father. He was also versed in clerical arts. We spent many years taking care of my mother before she passed. All I know is thanks to him," said Adara hesitantly.

"I'm of no use to you. The Drae'shï know nothing of the weakness of humans," added Lilith before he even turned to her.

"Spoken like a true Drae'shï. Then again, we may discover a better use for you and your Shard." He smiled.

"Is this what you want from us? To be your clerics and nurses?" Adara lashed out. "And what if we don't want to be? Will we be tortured as they tortured her?"

"Sadly, the barbarity of pirates is not under my control, but Lilith has had a fitting settling of scores from what I hear. Had we the timber to build our own fleet, we would have been having this conversation on your shores. What I ask of you is that you make yourselves useful whilst you still can. I know far too well that a forced hand does not work as well as a free one. Your Valendrian allies and so-called benefactors only see the barbarity of others but never their own," he continued as he showed them many more ill people, some suffering from leprosy and other terminal diseases otherwise curable with Enoch sap. "As for Lilith, I will see that her loss is replaced in a fitting manner," he said as he looked at her maimed hand. "As for your return home, I assure you that in time you will return if you help these people. And I, along with the people of Carthosia, will be forever indebted for your service," he said as he continued to lead them into the cleric's quarters, where the rest of the staff had their rooms. "You will not find guards or locked doors in this manor depriving you of your liberty. However, should you leave, know that you travel alone at your peril."

He stood in the doorway of the room and signalled the serfs to prepare the rooms for them. They obliged, and the Shirral proceeded to nod to the women before he turned his heel and headed back to the Riad. They all stood there for a moment before Adara took off after him.

"Wait!" she called out as they stopped beneath the shade of an olive tree. "Your Grace, I... I must tell you something."

"Please."

"My name is not Eirene. At least not my first name," she said as he did not react to the revelation. "I am Adara Crysanthani. Daughter to Petrach Crysanthani and betrothed to—"

"Elias Jurani," he said to her astonishment. "You'll be happy to know he's alive." He paused as she continued staring. "Oh, I knew. Perhaps not your actual name, but word travels fast. My spies make sure of that. And a parade of Saints in a port like Yammimer, where an Eldain beauty is accompanied by an equally terrifying Drae'shï is certainly news that is fast travelling."

"But why pretend?"

"To indulge whatever illusions of safety you wished to entertain, my lady. Even if you'd refuse to believe my claims."

"Then I *am* your prisoner."

"You are not. My offer is as it stands."

"So why haven't you asked for a ransom? Why not harm me out of vengeance on your enemies?"

"My dear, you confuse me with the ilk of your betrothed. I am in no need of money or vengeance. What might I gain from harming an Eldain who is as removed from the world she's in now as she was in the hands of a Valendrian prince?" he continued bluntly, much to her disdain. "Or perhaps you wish me to indulge you, to convince you that, somehow, they are on their way to retrieve you? Or that it is you rather than Lilith and her artefact that they are most likely after?"

"I... I'm not sure," she said as her lip quivered at the realisation of her abandonment. "I..." Her eyes welled up. "I'd like to see my father."

Altheo stood still as his gaze fell on her.

Adara went quiet, her calm nature having been broken time and time again. "Send out an emissary. They will respond. Elias will come to terms! If you want Enoch sap, they will make the exchange. I can help end this war," she pleaded.

"There are things that extend far beyond the reaches of any one man, even if it is Elias Jurani. And even if you're willing to find out what value the Massass would put to your name, even ten boatloads of Enoch sap wouldn't end anything. We cannot grow trees here, they simply do not take. And mark my words, the Massass is not a man who values the lives of others highly."

"So, you will not even try to settle or come to terms? It is war then that you want after all," she said angrily, tears in her eyes.

"The Shirra is more than just a war. It is a war of belief between those who believe salvation is offered only to those who deserve it and those who wish to offer it to all. The scope of this war may have started as a feud between factions of the same ruling class, but today it is a movement that far outweighs the power of any leader. The Massass knows this. I know this."

"You're wrong! They will settle. You yourself said they are moving north. My friends are coming to find us. They will not abandon us. Not everyone looks at the world as their battlefield."

"I pray for your sake that it is true," he said bluntly as he began to turn away.

"If I mean nothing to you, then please help me return home," she pleaded once more.

"That I cannot. I would not risk a ship or the lives of others to sail across the gulf."

"Then I *am* your prisoner, whatever you say," she said poignantly.

"What you choose to be is entirely up to you, Adara," he said calmly, but she showed hardly any reaction other than the smudging of her makeup.

She paused, looking away. "I didn't want to marry him, you know. My father didn't want me to either. But we both agreed. To protect my home, my people. I always hoped to marry for love, like Mother did," she said in weary resignation as she wiped her tears. "I never loved him, but I hoped I could, at least to save my people."

"The circumstance of our lives oft puts us at odds with our true desires," said the Shirral as he offered her his handkerchief.

She hesitated, then took it. It smelt of frankincense and sandalwood, the distinct scents that often also came from Santhi's medicine chest.

"I did not choose to bear this crown of swords. It befell me fifteen years ago at the age of twenty-six, when my father died in the Battle of Palin Bay, a battle fought out of desperation. To have the means to save lives, not end them. After having seen friends and family die of fever easily cured by just a drop Enoch sap, yet deadly if you had none," he said as she gazed back at him, saddened and weary. "We all have our sacrifices to bear. It is up to you to decide if its weight will strengthen you or crush you, and perhaps, in your plight, you might find that there's something bigger than you, something you can do for others. That somehow in rescuing others, you also manage to save yourself."

CHAPTER 26

HUNGER OF VAGABONDS

The wind blew hard and strong into the sails. Zain hurried down the sloop's deck, struggling to catch hold of the ropes and tie the sails into place. The boat crashed into another wave, drenching him completely. He cursed as he kept pulling on one rope after another, darting from one side of the boat to the other before rushing back to the helm. "I hate sailing without a bloody crew!"

In the distance, the shrieks and yells of an angry fleet of fishermen and port authorities from Constance could be heard clamouring in hot pursuit.

Zain looked over his shoulder and clenched his teeth. "Oh, come on! All this for some bloody Enoch sap and this tiny little sloop. What the hell?"

Arrows flew, yet they missed.

"Getting serious, are we?" asked Zain as he watched the archers rush to the edge of Constance harbour's breakwater, eager to intercept his escape. Zain stirred the sloop away from the edge of the shores as angry villagers kept waving at him. "Yes, my friends, cheerio, good-bye, and ta-ta—"

The sloop suddenly shook and threw Zain flat onto the deck. The vessel had hit a reef.

Zain cursed as he pulled himself up. "Fucking reefs." He straightened the helm as the ship groaned and scraped over the underwater landscape. His pursuers were upon him, and the arrows were now starting to hit their mark on the vessel. "Come on!" he insisted as he shook the helm as if trying to push the boat forward by himself.

The ship soon freed itself and began its slow creep out of the bay. Zain rushed below deck into knee-high waters. "Ah, shit! Where's the pump?" he cursed as he looked around through the floating cargo and other odds and ends. He tripped, falling into the water. He cursed once more as he stood back up, grabbing the first bucket that floated by, and began violently bailing water out of the stern of the boat.

"Stop, thief!" called out a Valendrian soldier aboard the pursuing brigantine trailing behind him.

"I'm busy!" yelled Zain, exasperated and exhausted, bailing away.

As the diminishing water started to reveal the leaks in the hull, Zain threw the bucket back and reached for a hammer and some old rope lying around. "Always the same story. I always end up fixing the bloody holes. I'm the captain, damn it!" he said and stuffed the oakum into the spraying cracks, hammering it in as the boat rocked him up and down before slamming his head onto the ceiling. "You really don't like me, do you?" he said to his commandeered vessel.

"Get off the boat!" he heard coming from the ship.

"What?" he said, startled by the response. "How could they catch up so quickly?"

Zain immediately rushed to the deck only to discover that the waves had coaxed the vessel back towards the harbour, heading straight into his pursuers. "Oh, for crying out loud!" he said as he grabbed hold of the unruly helm. The rest of the ships were upon him.

Another volley of arrows flew, peppering the deck and almost hitting Zain.

"All right. If it's Captain Zain Thorn you wish to challenge, I fully accept." He smirked. Zain pulled a length of rope and secured the helm in position as it kept sailing straight towards its oncoming pursuers. Zain dashed over the railing and under the deck, rummaging through the mess of water and floating tools. "A-ha!" he exclaimed as he pulled out a grapple and rope.

Zain sped back up on deck and swiftly tied the end of the rope to the lower part of the mast. The pursuers called out and waved Zain to desist as the vessel sped on its collision course. Zain held on as his sloop raced straight towards the brig.

The smaller vessels quickly veered out of the way, some into safety and some onto the reef, much to the crews' dismay. Yet the brig held fast cutting through the surf.

"Come on. You know you're not going to do it," said Zain, smirking as he caught a glimpse of the Valendrian captain atop the brigantine.

The vessels sped on, ready to collide at full speed, and Zain descended onto the deck, picking up the grapple hook as the towering vessel sped towards him. "Come on!" he yelled as he spun the grapple around, watching the captain's weary gaze as his crew panicked abroad. "Come on!" yelled Zain across the crashing waves as the two were about to collide.

The brig suddenly veered to port, dodging the sloop as the two vessels scraped each other's hulls at speed. The captain looked back, and the sloop was gone, but Zain's grapple was tightly latched around the stern of the brig. The brig shook and spun to starboard. Zain cried in awe whilst the sloop swung round the stern of the ship and back towards the high seas. Zain cut the ropes, and the captain cursed as all watched Zain speed out, waving and saluting his pursuers.

"Captain!" called out the first mate. "The reef!"

The brig's crew quickly scrambled to turn the vessel's altered course as the brig crashed into the reef. The captain cursed, throwing his hat on the ground as all watched the Vampire sail into the distance with little care and full sails.

Zain laughed heartily. "Haven't had this much fun since that time we stole all the ale and grass from Orwell's ship. Or was it Rowen's?" mused Zain as he continued emptying water from his ship. "Hell, probably this is the most fun ever," he said as he finally patched up the vessel and popped open a bottle of wine. It wasn't long 'til he was back on deck, happily inebriated and far out at sea.

Days soon turned to weeks as Zain tirelessly scoured the coasts of Carthosia, trading Enoch sap for one rumour after another. Some about sea crones and others of disappearing pirates, yet none seemingly yielded any concrete results as to the whereabouts of Lilith, Adara or Pïshkah. It wasn't long until Zain found himself short on supplies and adrift in the ocean.

"Is he dead?" asked a sailor.

"Looks pretty dead to me," said another as they gazed down from atop the galley onto the deck of the sloop. Both wore filthy white tunic uniforms with blue scarves around their arms. In each case, it was slightly altered to give a semblance of individuality.

"Wouldn't he be stinkin' by now?"

"Is he breathing?"

"How should I know? Go on, check 'im."

Zain felt a pole push against his cheek.

"Did I say poke him? Get on the boat and check 'im," insisted the sailor.

"What if he's dangerous?"

"Then you better go check 'im now, before he becomes more dangerous. Go on," he said, shoving his mate forward.

The sailor mounted the edge of the galley and slowly climbed onto the sloop as the two vessels creaked and moaned under the scorching sun. The top of the deck was bone dry, and below was a filthy mess of seawater, rotten food, and empty bottles of wine. Zain lay immobile, flat on his back under the canopy, his lips cracked, and his skin shrivelled.

"Still looks pretty dead. Only stinks more from here."

"Is there anything worth taking?" called out the captain as he emerged from above. He was a tanned and seasoned seadog with a ragged beard and balding head. His sleeveless coat was tanned and stained, and he wore a short red scarf around his neck and another on each arm. A small monkey crawled upon his shoulder as the captain opened and fed himself a pistachio before handing another to the primate. The monkey fiddled with the nut, cracking the shell apart and tossing it onto the sailor who inched away from the little rascal, trying to conceal his contempt for the animal. "Not like that, Pogo," said the captain softly as he fed him another and the cycle resumed.

"Not much, Cap'n. Looks like everything's been either consumed or sullied by the sea," called the sailor as he peered into the filthy under-deck filled with brackish water and floating garbage.

"Meh. What a waste. Just check him one more time and get back," said the captain as the monkey climbed onto the sloop and hung over to watch. "Pogo! Come here!"

Pogo ignored him.

The sailor sighed and knelt by Zain, placing his head first to Zain's mouth and then his chest.

The hiss of the sailor's blood coursing through his neck slowly entered Zain's ears, echoing in his empty mind, awakening his desire for the depths.

"Still dead. Not breathing, no heartbeat," said the man as he leaned back, hands on his waist.

The rush of the sailor's blood sounded like a torrent in Zain's mind.

The sailor caught a glimpse of Zain's amethyst pendant. "What's this?" he whispered to himself as he looked around before furtively reaching into Zain's open shirt.

The rush was deafening and the yearning absolute.

The sailor took hold of the trinket and tugged on it.

The rush stopped, and Zain's hand immediately grabbed the sailor's. "Don't you dare," croaked Zain.

The sailor wailed in fright and threw himself across the deck. Pogo screeched and sprang back onto the captain's shoulder.

"What the hell's going on down there?" called the captain.

"He's alive, Cap'n." The sailor gasped, holding his chest as Zain clutched the pendant around his neck.

"Great. Another mouth to feed. All right, get him up," said the captain as he returned to the quarterdeck.

Soon Zain felt his body being lifted up and over the sloop and onto his new ship. It wasn't long until he found himself below deck amongst the rest of the crew's bunks, strewn upon the many sacks of grains and spices. Zain eased in and out of conscience over the next few days, with intermittent flashes of the weary looks of concerned sailors and the arguing of their mates.

Zain woke up a few days later. The Vampire found himself in the lower deck, locked in the brig amidst the vessel's cargo. A host of dead rats lay scattered around him amidst the tightly stacked crates and barrels of the cargo hold. He winced as he attempted to get his bearings.

"Where the hell am I?" he asked, rubbing his throbbing head.

"At the Shirral's Riad," said a sailor sarcastically who was stretched out in his hammock across from him, staring at his playing cards.

A fat man sniggered from where he was seated on a creaking box beside him. He drew a card and played it onto another box under the dim light of the swinging lantern above them.

"What? Who? Wait," said Zain, confused.

"Looks like he's still out of it, Rami," said the young sailor as he swung in his hammock. "You're on the *Charon*, mate, by courtesy of Captain Jandos," he called out.

"Come on, Gwen, play," said Rami as he repeatedly snapped his fat fingers in front of him.

"Ouch," said Zain as he touched his head. "My head hurts. How long have I been... Hold on. What the hell is this ship? Who are you?"

The sailors laughed.

"Yeah, especially after that beating they gave you," said Rami.

"Beating?" asked Zain as he attempted to sit up, and all the bruises started to call out to him. "Ah, shit. Are you pirates?"

The sailors laughed once more.

"If we were pirates, you'd be dead by now, especially after what you did," said Gwen whilst Rami grabbed a bunch of nuts and stuffed his face. "Hey, give me some of that!"

"Did what? All I remember was being adrift on my ship. Now I'm here talking to you assholes," mumbled Zain.

"I see why you needed a good thrashing. Add the insults to the monkey, and he'd been thrown overboard. You're lucky you remained mum the whole time," said Rami.

"Monkey?"

The two looked at each other and burst out laughing.

"You really don't remember, do you?" Rami chuckled as he wiped his jiggling cheeks.

"No," said Zain with dread.

"Well, let me paint you a picture," said Gwen as he placed his cards on his chest, resting on his hammock. "You encounter what seems to be some goner on a boat in the middle of nowhere, who by some miracle still seems to be alive. You take pity on the poor sod and haul him onto your ship. You give him food and water, but he seems to want none of it. He looks like he's a walking corpse and yet doesn't die. He mumbles unintelligible nonsense in his sleep and gets the crew all riled up after all the recent talk 'bout sea crones and curses in the gulf. Next thing you know, he's drinking the blood of any rat that comes within his grasp. Soon the crew want him off, and you, as the good old captain that you are, take pity on the bastard, and you tell your crew to back off. Well, that was until your new friend decided to take a bite out of your old friend."

"Oh no. The monkey," said Zain with dread.

The two laughed. Rami almost choked on his nuts.

"I swear I've never seen the captain so furious, and that includes the time when the hull leaked and screwed up the entire sugar shipment," said Gwen as he finally played a card.

"That was also quite bad," said Rami.

"I'm telling you. You got lucky."

"Frankly, between you and I, I'm glad you got rid of that horrible little shit," said Rami, disgust painted on his moist brow.

"Oh, come on, Rami, Pogo was so cute. Remember when he would leave little shits in your boots?" Gwen laughed.

"Good fucking riddance." Rami chuckled as he played another card.

"Yeah. The crew of the *Charon* extends its gratitude to you," said Gwen, saluting Zain.

"Some way of showing it," said Zain as he prodded the gate of the brig.

"Well, you ate the monkey, mate," said Gwen

"You never eat the monkey," said Rami.

They both laughed.

"I guess I deserved that," said Zain as he stood up and stretched his back. "So where are you fine gentlemen heading then?"

"Sarthamia."

"I just bloody came from there," said Zain as he looked up in frustration.

"Why, what's the problem? Ate their monkeys, too?" mumbled Rami before bursting into laughter again.

"Good one." Gwen pointed to Rami just as he played his card.

"Ha. Ha. Very funny." Zain hung along the bars.

"I've seen some weird stuff in my time, but you, you're one of a kind."

"I've seen weirder," added Gwen.

"Who are you anyway?" said the brash sailor.

"Name's Zain, and you wouldn't believe me."

"Try us."

Zain huffed. "I'm a bloody Eldaresh."

"Eldarï? What?" ask Gwen.

"Eldaresh."

"Is he saying he's Eldarï?" asked Rami.

"I said Eldar-esh." Zain huffed as both paused their game to look at him.

"Ah yes. I've heard of them." Gwen snapped his fingers. "They live in... in... in Cielith, right? Live like one or two hundred years?"

"I've heard of them," added Rami. "Didn't know they drank blood though. Aren't you people supposed to be rich?"

Zain began slowly banging his head against the bars as the two rambled on between them.

A bell suddenly rang, and everyone stopped instantly.

"Is that?" asked Rami, alerted.

The shuffle of the crew's feet on the mid-deck followed.

"Shit. Let's go," said Gwen as he quickly descended from the hammock and tossed his cards on the floor.

"What now?" moaned Zain.

Zain sat quietly in the brig as he listened to the above commotion. "How is it that wherever I go, I end up in some form of captivity? If only I had just a little more blood," he said as he eyed the rats across the deck, nibbling away at the sacks of grain stacked in the back. Zain looked around, but there was nothing to bait the rats with except for a few sacks placed behind the brig, which slowly shifted as the vessel began to list as it turned. Zain cursed, then huffed.

The commotion above deck grew louder, and the vessel began to change course and catch the wind. "Whoa. Looks like we might be heading into another storm," said Zain as the boat rocked again, shifting a sack a little more. "All right then." He clapped his hands and pushed himself up. "Let's see if my lock picking skills are still what they were."

Zain bent over and took hold of the padlock of the brig, inspecting it closely, looking through the keyhole and jiggling it to his ear. "Hmmm," he said as he blew through it and looked around it once more. "Aha, yes, I see," said Zain as he calmly stood up, dusted himself off and proceeded to kick the gate repeatedly with his heel. The gate rocked, and the padlock rattled, yet the Vampire failed to achieve much except for the contemptuous looks of the rats whose dinner he had rudely interrupted with his racket.

Zain kept kicking, yet no one came to silence him. The Vampire persisted and raised his leg for one last kick when the vessel veered sharply to the side, sending his leg straight through the bars, forcing him to bang his face onto the cell. "Ow!" he cursed as he fell back and slipped to the ground. "What in the blazes is going on up there?" he called out as he held onto the bars in the corner of the brig.

Zain stopped for a moment, attempting to listen, yet nothing discernable came to his ears. He stood and listened for words above the yelling. "What's going on?" he said to himself as it all went silent.

Suddenly the vessel shook violently as it collided with another, sending Zain face-first into the cell bars once before flying backwards into the other side. He slid down to the floor, holding his face in agony. The cargo tumbled across the deck as the vessel listed to the side and slowly came to a halt.

"Arrrghhh! Mother's mercy. My fucking nose!" He felt the pulsing pain emerging from his broken sniffer. "I hate breaking my fuckin nose, shit!" He cursed once more.

The ship went silent, yet no one descended. Zain stopped attempting to listen. "Pirates? Again?" Soon the sounds of clashing swords and fighting began. "Lovely."

Zain looked around, spotting the sacks of grain, which had now slid within his reach. A handful of barley spilt onto the deck as the rats cautiously emerged to scout their next feed. The Vampire stuck his leg through and reached for the sack, barely touching it with his toe. A rat scurried before Zain. "Come here you!" He snatched, but the rodent dodged his grasp and climbed up on the sack. "You little!" Zain reached further, slowly inching the sack with his feet until he finally got it within his grasp and took it from the disappointed rats. "Ha! Now, you'll have to come to me." Yet the rats had their small stash at a safe distance from the Vampire. "Oh. Come on!"

Soon the fighting stopped, and a host of men began descending onto the lower decks.

Zain cursed and quickly sprinkled the barley onto the floor. "Come on. Look. Barley. Look." Zain proceeded to empty the entire sack into his cell, yet the rats stood at a safe distance, eating away at what they could grab. Zain snatched at one and then another as he heard the voices above him.

A group of Darelese and Carthosian pirates landed on the bottom deck to find Zain stretched out, fists full of barley, desperately attempting to bargain with the rats. "Oh, hello," he said awkwardly. It wasn't long 'til he was dragged kicking and screaming upon the top deck.

"Stand here," barked the Darelese pirate as they shoved Zain at the end of a long line of sailors in chains.

Another man brought up the long chain and shackles to Zain's hands.

"What's that?" asked the Darelese as he pulled out Zain's clenched fists. "Let go," he barked again as he pulled his wrists forward and squeezed.

"Alright, alright, it's nothing," said Zain as he let go of the barley, spilling it all over the deck.

"Shackle him." The pirate sneered as the other man locked the Vampire's wrists into the chains.

"Is this really necessary?" asked Zain as they secured the chains and tugged on them to test.

"Shut up!" yelled the Darelese as he moved back up the deck.

The crew of the *Charon* were either shackled or dead. Zain observed the pirates in the darkness of night, as one face after another began to grow vaguely familiar.

"Just when I thought that pirate scum like you couldn't sink any lower. You attack a vessel bearing the sunburst flag," spat Captain Jandos of the *Charon* as he was brought forward to a group of four pirates.

"Why trouble ourselves with the Valendrians when we have easy pickings on this side of the gulf?" intervened one as the rest laughed.

"The Shirral will have your heads for this treachery," said Captain Jandos.

"What the Shirral doesn't know can't hurt us, but it can hurt you." The grimy old Darelese pirate smiled.

"Which of you is the captain? I demand to speak to your captain!" barked the shackled seadog.

The four hesitated for a moment.

"We are all the captain," said one of the Darelese with some hesitation.

Jandos chuckled. "You mean to tell me you four are all captains?"

Two of the pirates agreed, and two didn't.

Jandos laughed, and his crew sniggered.

The Darelese punched Jandos to the ground.

"Lomar! Leave the man be. If you injure him badly, he won't sell," said one of the pirates as he emerged from behind Zain. He was short, creepy, and hunched in his posture.

"Shut up, Karrif!" barked back the towering Darelese. "Maybe next stop, we sell you along with them and rid ourselves of the curse you brought upon us."

"I told you. There's no curse. We got rid of the women months ago," said the slimeball as he walked forward.

"Wait? What women?" asked Zain, but Karrif ignored him.

"Yet we go from one mishap to another," intervened another. "Ever since Captain Silvan disappeared. Better yet. Ever since *you* convinced him, we should start taking prisoners to sell them as slaves instead of killing everyone as we always had."

"Calm down, friends. Our luck has turned. We've got a host of slaves, a merchant vessel full of wares and not a sea crone in sight," said Karrif as he charmed his way around his four leaders.

"Sea crones?" whispered Zain to his chain mate.

"Yeah. Sea crones," said Gwen as he popped his head forward from where he was shackled a few positions away from Zain. "This is the crew of the *Dead Lady*. Black Tooths they call themselves. They claim their captain died at the hands of three witches; the sea— eeek!" he cried as a rat scurried over his feet, causing him to jump on the spot.

"Shut up!" barked the guard as he slapped Gwen hard, sending him to the ground along with Zain and the group of other prisoners tied to the chain. The rat quickly dodged and jumped over the tumbling crew as Zain reached out to catch it.

"Izzur! What did I just say?" yapped Karrif as he returned down the deck. "Pick them up."

The guards slowly picked up each one of them until Zain was lifted last. His nose was bent, and his face all bloody. His chin was now dripping with fresh blood.

"Look! You broke his nose!" barked Karrif. "Now we'll need to..." Karrif's words slowed as he took a long look at Zain's electric blue eyes gleaming back at him. The Vampire had a slight grin. Karrif furrowed his brow at the Vampire's eerie reaction. "Wait. Who—?" he said as he narrowed his eyes, observing the pallor of Zain's face slowly regain some colour and his nose returning to its place.

Zain smiled devilishly as his nose snapped into place.

Karrif's eyes widened. "Lomar!"

"What?" he yelled back.

"Remember me?" smiled Zain as the shackles fell through his misting wrists and onto the deck.

"You! It... It can't be!"

Zain stepped forward, tossing the rat to the side as everyone stared in disbelief. Zain cracked his neck and his knuckles as the pirates fumbled for their swords.

Karrif immediately turned tail as Zain grabbed him by the scruff of his neck and slammed him to the deck. The guard behind him reached for Zain, but the Vampire quickly dodged his burly arm before twisting it and snapping it as everyone cringed at the sound. Zain drew out a cutlass from his felled aggressor's belt and waved the rest forward

"Get him!" yelled Lomar as a bunch of pirates rushed him.

Zain immediately dispatched one after another, slashing one, punching another and throwing a third overboard until he was just a few feet away from the captains.

"Get away from him! He's the Vampire! The one with the Saints and the crones," yelled Karrif as he hid behind another guard, and they all slowly encircled Zain.

"It can't be," said Lomar with dread, frowning. "It can't be! I saw you die! I saw you sink with the ship! It can't! It can't be! What the hell are you? Who the fuck are you?"

"I'm Zain fucking Nightwing," growled Zain, "and I'm here to *fucking* kill you."

Zain lunged forward in a flash, stabbing the cutlass right through Lomar's heart, shoving him forward and drawing out a Saint's long sword from the pirate's belt. He instantly spun on his heel, painting the deck red as the long sword's tip slashed through the necks of the other three leaders.

All were aghast at the speed and strength of the Vampire as he dodged and attacked with intrepid zeal and finesse.

Captain Jandos soon called out, and the entire chained crew joined the fray, chains and all, choking their enemies with their chains and ganging up on those within their reach. Chaos ensued.

"Kill him!" yelled one pirate, desperately trying to get the crew organised as some engaged the Vampire and others the chained crew. "All of you. Kill the Vampire!"

All dove onto Zain as they began viciously attacking him with anything that could reach him. Arrows, hook poles, swords, and whips backed the Vampire into a corner as twenty men surrounded him. Zain staggered in his step, and a pole struck his side only for him to catch it and pull the man forward, cutting him down in an instant with his sword. Zain panted for breath. The blood splashed upon the deck. It beckoned. His head throbbed, and his thirst deepened. He shook his head as his throat felt parched. "Keep it together, Zain. Just a little longer."

A loud crack came from the *Dead Lady*, and a second later, a scorpion bolt flew over the deck. Zain cursed as they all ducked.

"Move!" yelled the pirates, manning the scorpions.

Zain dashed away to the quarterdeck of the *Charon*, dodging and sprinting as bolt after bolt struck ship and sailors. Sea and blood sprayed on his face. He rose to the edge of the quarterdeck and leapt off the stern, snatching a rope in mid-air and swinging round the vessels before landing upon the *Dead Lady*.

"Not this time," he said before launching himself off the quarter deck as another round of bolts were being loaded by the panicked pirates. He rushed one scorpion after another as fear truly gripped the pirates' hearts, cutting each of them down before they could fire their shot until the last scorpion stood alone and fired.

The bolt soared and struck Zain. He staggered back as the shaft jutted out of his chest, and he fell on one knee.

All stopped.

Zain panted as sweat gathered on his brow. The call of blood beckoned more than ever as it crept on the wooden boards of the deck, the cry of its sweet release seductively begging him to embrace it.

Zain gritted his teeth and shook his head, focusing on the pain. "Fuck, I hate this," he groaned angrily. He slammed the sword into the deck and slowly stood up as all stood shocked at the sight of the Vampire, who managed to stand despite being skewered by the long metal shaft. He took hold of the bolt with both hands as everyone cringed. He took a deep breath, and in one deafening roar, he extracted it under the horrified gaze of all around him before launching it straight into the chest of his shooter, launching him straight off the boat.

The remaining pirates surrendered, tossing their weapons onto the deck.

Zain ripped his blood-soaked shirt off and hopped onto the *Charon* under the watchful eyes of the crew and its captain. All backed off as Zain walked towards Lomar's corpse and casually flipped him on his back. His long black coat was still relatively clean, albeit with a small slit through the back. Zain slipped the coat off the body and dusted it. After giving it a quick inspection, he casually put it on amidst the disbelief of those around him. He rose again and adjusted it on himself, confidently looking around under a hundred watchful eyes. He narrowed his gaze as he searched behind the crew until he spotted Karrif squirming away to safety.

Zain began walking towards him as the lowly pirate scurried away.

He pulled out a scorpion shaft stuck in the mast and steadied his pace. Karrif whimpered and stumbled, trying to get away from him gaze until he found himself at the edge of the deck, sweating, fearful and out of options. As Zain encroached, Karrif looked over the edge, gulped, and in a second, Zain launched the shaft. Karrif yelped, yet the shaft stood firm in the deck between his legs, pinning his coat. A second later, Zain clutched the pirate's face.

Zain held the man's sweaty mug tightly as he reached for Karrif's keys. "Take these. Free your men and shackle the survivors," said Zain as he tossed the ring of keys to the captain, leaving Karrif with his pants half down.

"Wha-What d-do you want?" asked Karrif through Zain's bloodied hand as he watched Zain's chest wound slowly heal before him.

"I spent three months looking for you pieces of mortal excrement, and every day I wondered what I'd do to your captain once I got my hands on him. But it seems justice has found him before me. Now all I have is you and the rest of your soon-to-be-dead friends to go through— but it'll do. Now, tell me, slowly and clearly, where are the women you've abducted?"

"They're—"

"And just remember," interrupted Zain. He smiled deviously as his mouth revealed his teeth slowly sharpening. "If you lie, I will eat you."

Chapter 27

The Cost Of War

"Hmmm. Let's see," said Pïshkah as she slowly unwrapped Lilith's bandaged finger under Adara's watchful gaze.

Lilith sat calmly on a fresh bed, looking down the ward of the Riad. It was clammy and hot. The sun was slowly setting, and the mosaic floor shone like gold under its rays. The many serfs, medicians, and nurses were quietly going about their business as they treated the sick coming in and out of the ward through the gardens. "Looks like he's keeping you busy," said Lilith.

Adara looked back and forth and sighed. Adara was dressed like the rest of the nurses in a long white tunic, her hair tied back, and her oily forehead shining under the heat. The rings around her eyes were slowly darkening with every passing week.

Pïshkah revealed Lilith's maimed finger. Adara and Pïshkah examined it intently as Lilith hesitated to turn her gaze. "Much better. Much, much better. In a week or so, it will be completely healed," said the smiling Cleriheu as she turned to Adara, her new necklaces and bracelets jingling in her wake.

Lilith looked at her hand. Her ring finger was half missing, yet the bruising had already receded. She raised her hand, opening and closing it. She didn't smile. "It almost feels like it's still there. Funny."

"It can happen. Ghost limbs," said Pïshkah as she put away her things. "Right, Adara?"

"Uh-hum, but you'll be fine. I'm sure. She's of the Iron Kindred after all, right?" Adara smiled forcibly. "Here, have some tea." Adara instinctively took hold of a scalding cup of peppermint tea but dropped it.

The ornate metal cup rattled on the floor. Everyone in the room stopped as the cup rolled onto the floor and came to a deafening halt. Everyone returned to their business.

"All right there, Adara?" asked Pïshkah, eyebrows raised.

"I'm sorry. I'm just tired. It never stops," said Adara as she crouched on the floor to clean up.

"Whoa! Stop. Let me get that." Pïshkah put her things on the side of the bed. "Sit here. I'll clean it up." The Cleriheu casually sprang up from her seat and went to fetch a rag.

Adara sat and rubbed her eyes and then her forehead, yet she kept looking back and forth at the entrance where new patients constantly gathered for alms or attention.

"You're starting to bear the same pallor you had when we were still at sea," said Lilith.

Adara sighed once more. "It's just endless. There are so many people."

Pïshkah returned and wiped the floor in a whisk of her wrist. "There we go. All cleaned up."

"Thanks, Pïshkah." Adara smiled.

"You're welcome, M'lady. And here's a tea for you, Lilith." Pïshkah handed over another cup of tepid tea to Lilith.

Lilith took a sip. "Good thing you reserve your best bedside manner for the select few," said Lilith through the cup.

"Would you rather I call you m'lady, too?" joked Pïshkah.

Lilith thought for a second and raised her brow, conceding the Cleriheu her point.

"Precisely."

"And what about you?" asked Lilith as she crossed her legs and pointed to the Cleriheu with her pointy shoe as she casually sipped her tea.

"What about me?" said Pïshkah.

"Aren't you also exhausted?"

"Oh. Me?" She laughed. "Completely. I haven't slept in days, but after a while, I get these strange bursts of energy just before I collapse completely."

"Or maybe you've been inhaling one too many of your ointments when no one was looking," said Lilith, watching her from the corner of her eye as she took a long sip.

"Psh! Nonsense," said Pïshkah red-cheeked.

"Well, you've been at it for four days straight, Pïsh. You need to sleep," said Adara.

"It's a good thing that I'm not versed in medical arts, lest I'd find myself a slave to the Shirral's staff," Lilith added.

"Excuse me? It's not like you're sitting around all day either. Aren't you supposed to be training?" asked Pïshkah.

"Yes. Six hours a day. The rest he has books concerning the Eldarï, the Hall of Mirrors, and other stuff brought to me for studying. Can't say I thoroughly enjoy the latter, but seeing how you are being treated, perhaps I ought to count myself lucky."

"Well, it could be a lot worse," said Pïshkah.

"It could be a lot better," added Adara.

Pïshkah frowned.

"And where is His Grace? Isn't he a medician, too? Or is he too busy carving his way through the map of Amenti?"

"All right, Lilith. Time to go." Pïshkah promptly led Lilith off the bed and took her cup.

"No, she's right," said Adara. "All those we heal from illness are almost doubled by those returning with injury."

"It's war, Adara," said Pïshkah.

"Yesterday, it was the Ludjeck tribe. Today, it's the Muhadras. Tomorrow, it's someone else. It's one war after another. But when will it end?"

Pïshkah and Lilith looked at each other and back at her.

"I'm afraid that's a question not even I have an answer to," said Lilith as she began walking towards the exit, her heel echoing with every step. She stopped and mused for a second, "Or perhaps it ends only when the Shirral has no one left to fight but himself."

Adara and Pïshkah looked at each other and then back at Lilith as she disappeared down the hall.

"I hate it when she's right," said Adara.

"Well, that's one way of looking at it," added Pïshkah. "Anyway, listen, never mind for now. Let's just get this day over with, shall we? How about that?" asked the Cleriheu as she rubbed Adara's arms and smiled. "Come on, Adara. Smile."

Adara stood sulking, attempting to contain a brewing smile. She huffed, then sniggered. "All right, Pïshkah."

"Let's go," said the Cleriheu as she took her under the arm.

"How do you do that?"

"Me? I did nothing. It's just so hard for you to stay angry for so long."

"You're such a pain." She smiled.

Pïshkah winked.

"All right then," she said as she gently pushed Pïshkah towards her patients, and she returned to hers.

Adara and Pïshkah continued with their work throughout the rest of the day, sewing wounds and treating fevers, feeding the bedridden, and coddling the infirm. Their feet ached, and so did their backs, as they walked a thousand times across the floor and for thousands more walked up and down the hall. One by one, they treated the people all patiently gathered on the terrace, awaiting their turn, until the moon rose, and the guards finally closed the outer gates for the day.

They returned to their quarters, where Lilith and the rest of the non-medical serfs were already fast asleep. Adara crashed into her bunk face-first, clutching her pillow like a long-lost lover. The chirp of the crickets set their rhythm to the cool breeze of the night. She slept.

The bells rang. Everyone in the serfs' quarters slowly stirred in the middle of the night.

"Adara," whispered Pïshkah as she gently shook Adara. "Wake up."

Adara winced and turned as she tried to shut out the clamour developing around her.

"Adara. Come on. We have to go."

Adara turned, squinting back at Pïshkah. "What time is it? What happened?"

"It's only been a couple of hours. Shirral is back. There are wounded."

Adara cringed as she covered her face with her pillow.

Pïshkah sighed and slowly helped the Eldain up.

The entire ward was once again abuzz with people rushing in and out. The guards brought men in on stretchers whilst medicians examined and treated others laid across the terrace floor. It wasn't long until Adara's gown was soiled in blood once more, and so were her hands. Tensions rose as the number of injured increased the urgency. Medicians shouted at nurses whilst nurses barked at the guards, all in an attempt to contain the situation.

"Pïshkah, I don't think he's going to be able to take it," said Adara, sweat on her brow as she held down a royal bodyguard, writhing in pain.

"We need to push the arrow through. He's lucky it's a clean shot through the chest. Just missed his liver. Now turn him, Adara. Help me!" snapped Pïshkah. Her hair was frizzier than ever, despite being tied back.

Adara huffed, and together they turned the ailing man on his left side. "Right. Gently," said Adara. "Now, listen to me, Jaru," said Adara as she caressed his face, seemingly pacifying him with her calming beauty. "We need to push the arrow through. It will hurt, but it's the only way we can remove it," she said as Pïshkah nervously waited. Adara placed a cloth in his mouth and held his forehead.

Jaru nodded as the Eldain held his gaze. Then Pïshkah pushed hard.

Jaru screamed, biting through the pain as the arrowhead almost breached his back. Adara comforted him as Pïshkah pushed, and another medician made an incision, finally letting the arrowhead through. The soldier momentarily passed out from the pain, and Pïshkah blew a sigh of relief.

"Well, that was easy," said the Cleriheu as she fell back in her seat, and the medician turned back to another patient.

"We're not done yet. We need to remove the arrowhead and the rest of the shaft. Come on," said Adara as Pïshkah struggled to get back up. They slowly began removing the shaft and prying it through with forceps and pliers.

The Shirral barged into the ward.

All save a few stopped in his presence.

The Shirral's attire was a far cry from his usual regal appearance. His white and gold armour was covered in dust and sand, spattered in blood. His face was now rugged and bearded, his hair matted and dry. He looked around, anxiously perusing the rows of patients strewn all over the ward. "Jaru. Where's Jaru?" he enquired.

Adara and Pïshkah kept their focus, slowly trying to pry out the shaft without breaking it. "Shit, it's not coming out," said Pïshkah as she kept pulling, but the shaft would not move.

Jaru was once again conscious and in pain.

Adara handed a tiny cup containing a milky white substance to the suffering patient. "Drink this. It will dull the pain."

"Jaru!" said the Shirral as he hurried up beside them, ignoring Pïshkah and Adara.

"He's under our care, Your Grace. Please give us space," said Adara irritably, attempting not to get pushed out of the way.

Pïshkah struggled to keep hold of the arrow with the prongs.

"Move, I know how to remove it. I've done this a hundred times," said the Shirral as he removed his dusty breastplate and dusted his hands.

"Your Grace, this is not the time," said Adara as she stood between the Shirral and her patient. "You are in shock. You still carry the weight of battle on your shoulders."

"Step aside, Adara."

"No."

"Step aside."

"No!" said Adara, slamming her hands on the surgeon's tray, sending everything to the ground.

Everyone stopped.

"Get out! You're not fit to treat any of these patients!"

"How dare—"

"Out!" she barked and pointed.

"He'd better not die under your care, or you will both have to answer for it," said the Shirral as he stormed off under everyone's stunned gazes.

Pïshkah and Adara immediately returned to their patient under the watchful eyes of the rest of the room. Soon enough, they successfully removed the shaft and stitched the wounds before returning to the rest of their patients.

Everyone worked tirelessly until, one by one, each patient's fate was determined. Soon the ward quieted down, and by the end of it, the sun had already announced itself into the twilight sky. Gradually, all the staff dragged themselves back to their quarters whilst others prepared themselves for the next day.

Adara approached Pïshkah, who sat on a step in the ward's entrance and sat down beside her. "Pïsh, are you...?" Yet the Cleriheu was fast asleep, leaning against the wall. Adara smiled and then turned to the sun slowly rising in front of her from behind the hills. She buried her head in her knees and sighed as she rested for a moment.

Voices emerged from down the hall beyond the ward. Adara turned, squinting into the distance.

The Shirral was fresh and composed in the Riad's parlour, as various generals and officers appeared to congratulate him.

Adara fumed. She picked herself up and stomped her way through the ward and into the parlour.

"Yet another victory brings us closer to the capital. Praise be the Shirra and the Shirral. May the Mother's light guide him!" said a stout and corpulent man with a white beard and dressed in black as he raised a cup along with the rest of the crowd.

"Forever may he endure," they all said.

"Thank you, General D'var," said the Shirral as he drank last.

The crowd slowly stopped at the sight of the Eldain standing before them, covered in a dirty and bloody tunic. The Shirral turned last.

"You're celebrating?" asked Adara, gritting her teeth.

"Of course, my dear," said D'var. "Have you also—"

"I wasn't talking to you," interrupted Adara to the visible disdain of everyone as she fixed her eyes on the Shirral.

"I assume then that you haven't come to apologise," said the Shirral calmly.

"Apologise?" asked Adara incredulously. "You have people on what will probably be their deathbeds in the very room beside which you are toasting your victory. What victory? Are more dead and wounded people littering your palace's floor a cause for celebration?"

"I don't expect you to know the true cost of war. So, I'll excuse your impertinence, if only for the fact that you're a good medician."

"I don't know the cost of war? Me? Let me remind you, *Your Grace,* that it is I and all the medicians and nurses in there that are paying the cost of your war. Not to mention those who die in our very hands daily. Perhaps it is you who has no idea what the cost of war really is?" panted Adara, red-faced.

"How dare you!" accused one of the generals.

"I dare! I do dare!" barked Adara. "When I arrived, you told me your mission was to liberate the world of a tyrant who starved your people due to his own greed and lust for power. Tell me then, you who call yourselves liberators, have you ever looked at yourselves through the eyes of those you've conquered?"

All looked at each other, half confused and half astonished at the impertinence of the Eldain.

The Shirral did not flinch. "You know little of the Shirra and far less about me," said the Shirral with a stern gaze yet without emotion.

"You call the Massass a tyrant, but you have killed more innocents than he did, and you haven't even set foot in Valdell yet. Is this what the Shirra is all about? Deposing one murderer to install another?"

"Guards!" barked an officer aghast by the Eldain's behaviour.

The Shirral raised his hands and stayed their intervention. He walked up to Adara, hands behind his back.

"I will not be complicit in the butchery of your war," said the Eldain, trembling. "And if you're truly not a tyrant, you'll allow me to leave, and if you don't, then I'll be sure to make a murderer of you. I won't stay here. Over my dead body!"

"Get. Out," mouthed the Shirral containing his anger.

Adara promptly turned heel and headed back through the ward. She slowly came to a stop and collapsed against a column, bursting into tears, and sliding to the floor as she attempted to muffle her cries from the sleeping patients. She wept as she rested her head against the column, staring at the mosaic ceiling above. "Father, where are you?" she wept. "I can't do this," she whispered to herself. She sobbed softly. "I can't."

"You can," croaked a voice.

"Who? Who is it?"

"Lady Adara," whispered Jaru softly from his bed.

Adara wiped her tears and got up, heading over to him as he lay on his side, barely able to move. "Jaru, you must rest. You'll be fine."

"I know I will. Thanks to you and Pïshkah. I'm more worried about you." He struggled to smile.

"I'm fine," she said as she sat on a stool beside him.

"No, you are not. I heard you before. Please do not leave us."

Adara looked away glassy-eyed. "I can't stand to see any more blood on my hands," she said looking down at her red-stained hands.

"And we can't stand to let anyone who cares so much leave." He heaved and coughed. "The Shirral is not a bad man, and our deaths are a sacrifice to a greater cause; that one day, days like these will be a thing of the past."

"What about those he kills? Those who oppose him?"

"War will always exist where two fail to unite. The Shirral does not fight unless forced by those who won't see reason. We were attacked. We always offer the olive branch before the sword."

"Is war truly the only solution that is left? The Shirral must learn that the world is not a place where the only alternative to peace is death," said Adara as she rose, containing her frustration.

Jaru caught her hand. "Then maybe you've arrived here to teach him something he could never learn from any of us."

Adara stopped. "I-I can't."

Jaru closed his eyes in acknowledgement. "Then I thank you. Once more. For saving my life. Peace be with you, Adara Crysanthani."

"And also with you, Jaru Nassuri." She nodded before leaving the ward.

Adara returned to the serfs' quarters, where many of the medicians and Pïshkah had already fallen fast asleep whilst others got ready to start their day. She gazed at Pïshkah as she slept soundly, face down like a sack of potatoes, drooling onto her pillow. Adara smiled. "You'll be happy here, but I'm not a fighter like you," said the Eldain as she gently kissed Pïshkah on the head before gathering her few things, placing them in her satchel and leaving. "I'm sorry, but I won't let even a night's rest soften me," said Adara, teary-eyed as she left.

Adara sped out of the serfs' quarters and across the grounds, between the olive trees and encampment, around the Riad, until she finally arrived at the gates. The gates stood open, yet no guards or people were gathered by it as usual. Adara stood wearily, staring at the empty gate as the sun's rays warmed her skin and the birds began to chirp lightly. She looked back at the Riad one last time before turning back to the gate and heading out.

The Shirral stood a few yards past the entrance, looking towards Arethusa and the hills behind it.

Adara walked up to his side. "Have you come to stop me?"

He stood quietly observing the hill as the guards slowly descended and dispersed the few oncoming people. "If I wanted to stop you, you would have found a barred gate and guards standing here. Instead, I've come to tell the guards to turn away the people for a day. To give you and the others some much-needed rest. To show you that I, too, understand the weight you carry and the cost of the war."

Adara frowned. "You don't get it, do you? You think you can simply wave away the ills of the sick and make everything fine? How is this helping?"

"It is helping you."

"No. It is helping *you*. You will not buy me with false acts of generosity. You turning away those who came to seek your help today only passes the cost of *your* war from our shoulders onto theirs. How many of them are in desperate need of your help? People sick with disease, whose beds are now being occupied by your wounded?" asked Adara angrily as she pointed towards the city below the hill. "I thought you were a medician, too. I thought you were an honourable man. Clearly, I was wrong."

"I wouldn't be here if I wasn't."

"Then show me!" yelled Adara.

"Tell me then! What would you have me do?" barked the Shirral frustrated.

Adara was stunned.

"You think it is my will to see my people, friends, and family die after I've seen the strife that plagued us for the last thirty years? You think I enjoy having to subdue people into accepting the Shirra? This is an unshakable legacy I carry upon my shoulders that I must fulfil. A legacy created after a bitter, vengeful old man met his death because of his anger and hubris, dragging Carthosia along with him. The very man your betrothed slew; the man who raised me, my father."

"Elias killed your father?" asked Adara.

"Fifteen years ago. My father had bankrupted the M'yar's coffers to build a fleet to sail the gulf. We sailed straight to the Grand Harbour to kill the Massass. We fought for our right not to be severed from the temple and the rest of civilisation, not to be left cut off at the fringes of the world. But the truth wasn't just that. It was also a bitter feud between the Juranis and the Tarrasques. We killed each other; my family has Jurani blood on its hands as they have ours. But in the end, it was all about a struggle for power between my father and the Massass, between two angry, greedy old men."

"And Elias?"

"Elias was a boy in the navy, still in his teens, found himself washed ashore along with my father after the bloody battle in the Grand Harbour. I watched him slay my helpless, defeated father before me and claim his *honour* as we sounded the retreat."

"So, is this it? This is what it's all about? Avenging your father?"

"No. I've never felt so relieved yet terrified at the same time."

"What?"

"My father was a tyrant. He forged Carthosia out of blood, sand, and gold. He cared as much for our people as the Massass does for his. That was my father's way. The Shirral's way. Those were rough times, and it was the only way to maintain order in the chaos left by the Severance. And now as his firstborn, that title has fallen onto me. To carry out the mandate, to depose the pretender and lead us out of the chaos left by our forefathers." He sighed. "I hold the integrity of Carthosia by a thread, Adara. Our survival depends on our unity, and our unity is founded in the Shirra. What we've achieved in all these years would have been impossible otherwise. Once a land of broken factions and families is now united under one banner, under one cause."

"So, you need your war to survive? And once you win? Who will you fight then? After the world is finally at your mercy?"

"We will have peace. I'll make sure of it. One way or the other."

Adara paused and walked up to the Shirral.

"Peace? Peace starts here," said Adara, firmly pointing to the ground. "And not after the dust has settled on the battlefield."

The Shirral stopped.

"You are not so different from the demon you paint Elias to be. You are waiting to stand upon a defenceless land and defeated people before finally showing them how *honourable* you are. Extending your olive branch in one hand and holding a sword in another. There is nothing honourable about the peace you offer."

"Don't compare me to that coward! At least I am offering an alternative! Something Elias never did offer my father. If he were so honourable, why did he fail to defend the followers of the Enoch from the corruption of his uncle? Why did he slay my father without offering mercy or surrender? And why would he abandon you to your fate?" he barked.

"He did not abandon me. They think we're dead because you will not let us reach out to them or request a ransom," she barked back.

"Is that so? Then why haven't we encountered a single Valendrian vessel on the horizon? Or heard of spies enquiring as to your whereabouts whilst we've heard of dozens enquiring about Lilith and the Shard?"

"You're lying."

"I have nothing to hide and no closed doors to keep you. But we need you. I—"

"Don't lie to me!" she accused, almost teary-eyed.

"I'd never. All I know is that if you were my betrothed, I wouldn't stop scouring the world 'til I found you. One way or another."

Both stood in silence as Adara looked away under the stern gaze of the Shirral.

"I can't promise that no more blood will be shed on account of my name. I can only promise that I would rather see peace spring from the Carthosian spirit rather than from Valendrian blood, but to do that, I need people who already have peace in their hearts."

Adara looked back silently.

The Shirral walked up to Adara and pulled a scroll out of his breast pocket. "You won't find any closed doors here. I stand by what I told you. You may leave. Though I would much prefer it if you stayed. This will grant you safe passage through the lands and escort you to the northern borders, should you need it."

Adara hesitantly took the scroll. "Thank you."

"No. Thank you, Adara. For everything, and for sometimes reminding a man that the even the noblest of causes can make tyrants out of the most honourable of men," said the Shirral as he bowed his head with his hand on his chest. "I bid you farewell," he said as he slowly walked away under Adara's awkward stare.

She looked at the open road and then back at the Riad. She sighed and squeezed the scroll.

CHAPTER 28

SOUL SACRIFICE

"It wasn't an easy decision for her, but in the end, she stayed," said Zain.

"Interesting," said Krea. "Looks like Adara took up her own cause after all."

"True. After meeting the Shirral, things started to change. They all worked. Hard. They helped many people and sowed more peace than they reaped war. Somehow in all of this, she found something beyond her initial captivity. I never really asked her, but I think she was happy, despite being so far from home." He smiled briefly and looked away.

"What about the Shirra?"

"Oh, it progressed, and the Shirral learnt that not all who oppose his views are necessarily his enemies. Less blood and more compromise, and soon the Shirra moved further in a matter of a couple of months than it did in ten years, with its Vanguard Army being far into Ithiria and just shy of a few kilometres from the fortress at Morren's Gate." Zain rubbed his wrists through the shackles.

Krea signalled to continue.

"Anyway, in the meantime, Elias had gathered his men and sailed up the gulf with five galleys of the Valendrian fleet whilst the Saints' first legion cavalry made it overland. They found the fortress manned by barely a hundred Iboreans."

"And you?" she replied.

"Well, after my fortuitous encounter with the crew of the *Dead Lady*, it didn't take much bashing heads around to get them to spill the beans and hand over the ship. Some of them begged the captain of the *Charon* to take them prisoner, claiming the ship was cursed. Naturally, the captain of the *Charon* was happy to oblige." He laughed briefly.

Krea smiled. "Seems like the sea crones had it their way after all."

"Whatever they told them, it sure worked." He smiled, shaking his head. "In any case, I began sailing north whilst I figured out my next steps. I knew they were captive somewhere within the Shirra, but going through the hundreds of kilometres of coastline would have been like searching for a needle in a haystack. The rumours around Lilith were manifold and muddled between fact and fiction. Some were saying they were slaves, others dead, and others saying they were guests of the Shirral. In the end, I decided I would find the Shirral himself, and that path soon led me to the helm of the Shirra: Morren's Gate."

"And Adam and the Moirai?" asked Krea.

"They were up north, way before everyone else. They hid in the forest just outside Morren's Gate, planning their way to get the Shard back from Lilith."

"And Lilith?"

Zain took a deep breath, eyeing Krea. "Needless to say, her sojourn in Carthosia was not going to last indefinitely. The ails of the weak and sickly were hardly ever of interest to her." He paused. "However, I don't know what it was. Whether it was the blow to her head, the torture, or spending way too much time with the Shard, but something changed in her. Whatever vulnerability she had once displayed had vanished. Where before she tried to get away from Ussar Varys, she became adamant about returning, at all costs. Where the Shard was once enough, it wasn't anymore. At the time, no one could see it. I couldn't. I still wonder if she ever did."

"We often fail to see our dark desires until we choose to yield to them," added Krea. The silence resounded in the room, the buzz humming overhead. Suddenly the metal door banged sharply three times. "Rest easy, Zain. I'm looking forward to tomorrow."

"Yeah, right. Another day in paradise," said Zain as he decided to lie down with his head in the corner. The buzz in his ears ceased once more as Krea left. The door shut, and so did his eyes.

———

It wasn't long 'til his sleep was broken.

"Zain. Is she gone? Zain!" whispered Aria through the tiny hole in the wall just above his head.

"What?" asked Zain irritably. "Aria, some of us are trying to pretend to sleep."

"Oh, please, Zain. Come on."

"I told you already. I'm not going on with the story 'til she's back. You'll have to wait 'til tomorrow to eavesdrop on the next part of the story. I'm fed up with repeating the same bloody things to everyone like I'm some kind of lunatic."

"They have you wrapped up like one pretty tight," she prodded quietly.

"The bandages? They're magical sigils. If it were just the chains, I'd have shattered them to pieces by now."

"I wonder if you would even try," she muttered.

"Yeah, I wonder, too."

Both went silent.

"Zain?"

"Yeah."

"Did you ever love someone?"

Zain paused. "Before her? Well, I loved my wife dearly, but that was hundreds of years ago. In fact, I almost can't remember her face anymore. Time tends to blur things after a while."

"Didn't you have any children?"

"No. Not really, but I did have someone I cared for like she was my own," he said as his voice saddened. Silence ensued once more. "Did *you* ever love someone?" he asked.

"I loved my father very much. As for lovers, I've had many, but hardly those one would care to remember." She scoffed softly to herself.

"Where is he now, your father?"

"He died in the war long ago, but he's still with me, in his own way," she said as her tone echoed Zain's sombre mood.

"I'm sorry, Aria," said Zain.

The room went silent again.

"Aria?"

"Yes?"

"Why did you ask?"

"If you ever loved someone?" said Aria.

"Yeah."

"They say the most powerful memories are those of your loved ones. Perhaps I just wanted to see what your best memories were in your long life."

"Huh. I never thought about it that way. All I know is that love makes you do things you thought you'd never be capable of. For better or for worse, whether you like it or not. You'll give up anything for love, even yourself."

"And is that what you did with Lilith?"

"I-I don't know. Maybe."

"From the moment you met, she seems to have occupied your very heart and mind, and she does so still from what I can tell."

"Yeah." Zain sighed.

"And has she won the battle for your soul, too?"

"It doesn't matter, Aria."

"It's what matters most, Zain."

The two went silent. The room was dark as even the moon set into the night. "Aria?"

"Yes?"

"Can you tell me the story of the city in the sky again?" he asked kindly as he cuddled up in his corner.

She smiled.

"Once upon a time, there was a man who had a dream."

Aria yawned. It was late. She sat quietly in the dark, watching Zain lying in his metal chair, immobile as if frozen in time. She switched off the microphone and turned the already dimmed lights of Zain's cell off. The console glowed in the dark, and so did parts of Zain's body along with the machines in the other room. The control room, on the other hand, was small and cold. Servers and other storage devices cluttered the space, and the console took up half the room on its own. Diodes and fibre optic wires gleamed in the darkness from time to time.

She kept looking, through the darkness, through her reflection in the two-way mirror. She rubbed her eyes and tucked her blonde hair behind her left ear. She took a deep breath and pulled her white hood over her head. She fiddled with her hair again, nervously tucking it in, then wiped her teary light blue eyes once more, now redder than before. She sighed and rose from her high stool.

Aria quietly picked up her shoes and stood by the entrance barefoot, listening into the corridor through the white metal door. The clock on the console marked 03:33. She took a deep breath and pressed open. The door slid open in an instant, barely making a sound. She peered out. The corridors were dark and empty except for the tiny lights by each entrance down the hall.

Aria quietly stepped out and began walking hastily down the corridor, running her hands against the smooth wall at each corner, listening intently. Past the guard room, past the cells, past the labs, Aria walked quietly as fast as she could. Her heart was pounding as she crossed the facility, eager to reach the dormitories.

She stopped. She listened. Steps. She heard steps. She stood at the corner, right before the dormitory block, ready to dash back to her cell. She held her head as close to the edge of the corner as possible, attempting to listen, yet their origin was not discernible. She had to see. She had to look. Gradually, she moved her head as subtly as possible past the wall. She caught a glimpse. She retreated, holding her gasp.

The steps stopped. A click and a bright white light cut through the corridor in search of her.

Aria held her breath as she watched the torch dart along the long corridor. She was waiting, listening, praying that the guard would walk away. The steps began once more. They got closer.

Aria immediately turned tail, walking as quickly as possible down the corridor, muffling her feet and pulling up her skirt, the cone of light getting smaller and smaller as she crept down the long corridor. Aria stopped by the lab, reached for her card, and swiped it. The lock flashed bright red as it sounded its disapproval of her credentials 'Unauthorized access'. Aria gasped and scurried away, down the corridor, begging not to be heard. The light had arrived. It turned right then left, yet the corridors were empty.

Aria gasped as she rested against the wall around the corner. Sweat formed at her brow. She prayed and hoped once more. The lull of silence was unbearable. The light went off. She blew a sigh of relief. Yet, the steps didn't recommence. She waited. And waited. And waited. The steps resumed once more in her direction.

Aria rushed down the hall, past the control room and to the next intersection, before stopping immediately at the edge. Another's footsteps could be heard down the hall. They stopped too. Aria froze. She could not tell where the sound was coming from. She gritted her teeth in panic and prepared to pick a lane as her other pursuer was closing in. She looked left, right, and down the hall, paralysed by choice.

Suddenly a red glow slowly emerged at the very end of the long hall in front of her. A large metal humanoid stood immobile, ominously giving its back to the corridor. Its body and limbs were made of armoured black and red steel, all smoothed and polygonal. The red glow shone from its triangular head which had no face.

Aria gasped and ran back to the control room, fumbling the key card as she hissed at the door to open. The door opened.

A pursuer emerged from one corner, and the other turned on the spot.

She was in.

She rested against the door, panting for air, tears almost brewing in her eyes. Yet the steps did not go away. Aria winced. She flattened herself onto the cold concrete floor and slid under the console. She squeezed herself between the low bottom of the massive console and the floor, her head flattened to the ground, pushing herself in as much as possible, feeling every step getting closer through the floor.

A muffled voice came from outside. It called out. The steps had stopped in front of the control room door.

The door slid open.

Aria froze, shutting her eyes.

The red light flashed in. The sound of metal tapped the floor as the slender, seven-foot drone stepped in, lowering its head through the door. It made no sound, yet Aria soon felt its red gaze inch upon her through her eyelids.

"Hey!" called out a voice from outside. The android turned and stepped back out in an instant.

"I'm Administrator Arcturus Teller. Code 912432. You are not permitted to enter any of the cells or control rooms in this sector. Return to your station, Throne. Immediately!" he barked.

The throne paused as it stared down Teller in the corridor.

"Didn't you hear me? Go on, move!"

The throne stood silent for a moment before turning its head back into the room.

Aria gulped.

"Hey! I said, stand down! Now!" he said once more.

The throne froze and went back out. It watched Teller for another second before it finally sounded its acknowledgement, turned its red light to white and returned from whence it came.

Teller paused before entering the room. He stepped in. The door closed behind him. He stood in the dark, looking around the room in silence. "I know you're here. Come out."

"Arthur?" whispered Aria, hesitantly.

Teller crouched and looked at Aria, squashed under the console. "How the hell did you fit in there?" he asked as he pulled Aria out.

"Thanks, Arthur. I don't know. It was the only place I could hide," she said as she struggled to her feet with his help.

Arthur turned on the buzzing light. It was bright, white and cold.

"Choose better, or there won't be a next time," he said as he pursed his lips at Aria who coyly looked away as she pursed her own.

"I thought you were a guard. I tried to hide, but I couldn't get into the labs. Then I found the throne."

"The card I gave you only gives access to this room. The last thing we need is to have you discovered in another restricted section. They're starting to suspect something, and I can't keep covering for you," said Teller as he drew a long white cigarette from his lab coat.

"I know. I'm sorry," said Aria as she took hold of his wrist and shook her head. His awkward gaze softened, and she returned a modest smile.

He paused and huffed.

"Listen, this is a black site, so it may not have the constant surveillance we're used to at home, but it's the one place where the Conclave doesn't have eyes all the time, though they're trying. Believe me. Security is getting tighter."

"Is that why there's a throne?"

"Thrones, plural. At least none of the airborne ones for now, but you need to be extremely careful, especially after the panic you caused trying to unplug him," he said, nodding towards Zain. "If you get caught, there's no telling what they'll do to you. To me. You don't need much imagination to guess."

"You're right, Arthur. I'm sorry. I just lost track of time," she said with her hand on her forehead, shaking her head.

"Aria," he said, about to grab her shoulders, yet he stopped and awkwardly brushed his nose. "When you asked me to get you here, I thought you were crazy, and I still think you are, but there's only so much I can do. You're lucky I managed to fake your bloodwork so they can't trace you to him. Just don't catch their attention 'cause next time I might not be there, and then it's over."

"I know, and thank you for protecting me," she said as she grabbed his hands and held them together.

"No, Aria, thank you. I just wish I could help you more," he said as they turned towards Zain.

Both went silent.

"I tried to make him remember, but it's impossible," said Aria, a calm acceptance lingering in her voice. "He won't wake up. No matter what I try."

"I know. Even I don't know how. I'm not sure Krea herself does either."

"Is he going to be trapped there forever?"

"No, not forever. At least that isn't the plan."

"What are they going to do with him, Arthur?" she asked in all seriousness.

"It's all new. The Abstract was not originally designed as a means to invade or alter the minds of the living. There was never a return ticket for those who entered. Once you're in, you're gone, 'the Elysium of human consciousness' as Krea once put it," he said as they scanned across the console and screens, watching as heart and mental wave monitors intermingled with those displaying thousands of lines of code and meters and graphs visualising the exabytes of data constantly being processed.

"I know. But what now?"

"I don't know." He looked back at her.

"Arthur!"

"I don't! I swear it," he said, raising his hands. "Krea is becoming distrustful, even of me. Her orders come from beyond the Conclave."

"From *her*?"

Arthur nodded.

Aria took a deep breath as she watched Zain.

"There's another thing."

Aria looked back, concerned.

"The Sentient Intelligence. Well, Krea found a way to insert it in the Amenti Abstract. In Zain's Abstract."

Aria took another deep breath and shut her eyes. "Is this why Lilith is there?"

"Yes," he said. "It's not just his imagination. The S.I. is slowly trying to take over. You'll see it, even in the stories he's experiencing. Yielding to her in one way or another."

"And what happens when it does? What's gonna happen to him?" asked Aria, attempting to remain composed.

"At that point in time, not even I want to know."

"But we have to do something," she hissed.

"Like I told you when you asked me to bring you here, there's nothing we can do. You saw it for yourself. Unplugging him almost killed him," said Teller. "It's just impossible at this point."

"No. It's not," she said, shaking her head and smiling awkwardly in disbelief.

"Aria, I'm sorry, but this is beyond you. It's beyond us. How can you possibly—"

"I don't care!" she said. "Is there nothing you people haven't already taken from us? That you won't even allow us chance or hope?" She pointed angrily at Zain. "And from him? You took *everything* from him! His body, his mind, and now even his soul. I'd sooner see him dead than another instrument of your wretched world!" she said as tears ran down her cheeks.

Arthur frowned. "I'm sorry, I—"

Aria sobbed as she looked at Zain. She wiped her tears with her sleeve.

"I won't give up on him. I'll free him, one way or another. With or without you," she said, placing her hand on the glass, reaching out to Zain.

"I wish I could give you another answer, Aria, but I can't. It's too late. It's only a matter of time."

"Don't tell me what I can and cannot do," she sniffed. "If you're not going to turn me in, then help me."

"Aria, listen to me. Once the S.I. has taken over, all parts of him, all aspects of his conscious and subconscious will cease to exist, and all he ever was will become part of the S.I. That includes his memories, hidden or otherwise. That means he'll know where to find you and everyone else. The only difference is that the S.I. will be behind the wheel. This is why Krea has been ordered to do this."

"Unless we stop it."

"I'm telling you, Aria. You cannot stop it! Fucking hell, man," he barked, rubbing his head in frustration. "If we don't stop it in time, there's no turning back. He'll hunt you and everyone else down 'til there's nothing and no one left. You get it? It's not just you. It's everyone you know, everyone who follows you, who believes in you. You'll be making a nation of martyrs out of them."

"Then what would you have me do?"

Teller frowned.

Aria stood back aghast.

"Is this why you brought me here? To watch him die?"

"I brought you here because you asked me to and to say your good-byes." Teller paused and took a deep breath. "Now I realise it was a mistake. I thought Krea's plan wouldn't work, that the S.I. wouldn't integrate at all, but it did, or rather it is slowly. I'd sooner pull the plug myself than see you dead. Now whilst we still have the chance."

Aria frowned and grabbed him by the coat. "Please, Arthur. I'll save him. I know I can."

Teller frowned. "Aria, if I don't get you out of here soon enough, it may be far too late when the need arises. You're the All. You need to remember that your purpose goes beyond saving the life of one man. Even if it is your father's."

Aria stood back and shook her head, smiling softly as she gazed at the monitor's twinkling lights.

"Aria?"

"Arthur, please listen to me," she said in the softest of voices. "Please understand. I will not abandon him to his fate," she said as she looked him in the eyes with the deepest sense of calm conviction.

Teller could not help but smile slightly. "If you would not leave for him, then please do for those who still need you."

"Right now, it is he who needs me the most," she said, gazing back at Zain.

Teller sighed. "There's no convincing you, is there?"

Aria shook her head and smiled.

Teller smiled back. "You know you have a better chance of moving a mountain than breaking him free of the Abstract and S.I., right?"

"I may not be able to move mountains, but I can move minds, and sometimes, that's all that it takes to move the world."

Chapter 29

The Call Of Truth

Lilith stared at her gauntlet as she opened and closed her left hand. The pain of her missing finger was no longer felt any more than it could be seen. A gift from the Shirral to the Drae'shï. It was black, inlaid with deep purple, gold and silver with reticulated fingers and sharp golden nails. Her grip was as strong as ever before. She sat upon the divan, quietly reading in the courtyard, listening to the fountain flow to the tune of chirps at sundown. Her Shard, now inlaid into her own Drae'shï inspired scimitar, lay beside her after a long day of swordplay.

The echoes of Adara's and Pïshkah's chatter emerging from down the hall soon broke the peace.

"Ahhh. There you are! Enjoying some peace and quiet after a long day's work, are we?" asked Adara as the two confidently walked into the courtyard.

Pïshkah sat in her usual poolside spot whilst Adara checked on the brewed peppermint tea on the side table beside her own divan.

"You're awfully chirpy. What happened? Another man lost his toes to leprosy?" asked Lilith as she laid down her open book and gently grazed her arm with the points of her gold fingers.

"Not at all. We've cured all of them. Thanks to our dear Cleriheu, right here." Adara smiled as she curtseyed to Pïshkah, who bashfully smiled.

"So, what's the cause of your excitement?"

"What excitement?" she said giddily as she took her tea and found her seat.

Lilith raised an eyebrow. "Adara, even you, with all the glee you somehow pull out of your hide every morning, can't possibly be excited after taking care of all these invalids and moribunds all day. So, either tell us or be silent."

"She was invited to a private dinner with the Shirral." Pïshkah smiled at Adara's impish cuteness.

"Oh, great, and I thought I would actually hear something interesting," said Lilith dryly as she proceeded to pick up the book once more.

"Oh you." Adara waved her away in her typical endearing fashion.

"You should start getting ready, Adara," said Pïshkah.

"You're right!" said Adara as she blew swiftly after drinking her tea too quickly.

"We eat with the Shirral every other night. You work with him," said Lilith in a droll tone.

"Do you even know what that means? A private audience?" asked Pïshkah.

"That you somehow forgot about Elias in a couple of months and are entertaining the notion of bedding his sworn enemy? I think I do. Do *you*?" she said dryly.

"Lilith! I swear!" hissed Pïshkah.

"No, she's right. You're right," said Adara as she stood struck but unperturbed. "I've been so caught up thinking about the possibility that I never really thought of what to do if it might happen." She shook her head. "Anyway, it might not be that anyway. He wanted to speak about some new patients and the Shirra's move to Limik. So, it could be just that. It's probably that."

"Let's cross that bridge when we come to it," added Pïshkah gently as she kicked Lilith's divan, forcing her to acknowledge.

The Drae'shï rolled her eyes.

"Yes, you're right. Either way, I need to get ready. It's getting late," said Adara.

"It's teatime," added Lilith.

"Well, teatime is preparation time in Cielith, so I gotta go." Adara sprung up to her feet as she took her tea with her and scurried off down the hall.

Lilith and Pïshkah observed the lass as she made her way down the hall with a certain skip in her step.

"It amazes me how she can bounce back," mused Pïshkah as she watched with a smile telling of a certain sombre fondness.

Lilith watched Pïshkah's longing with interest. "Indeed. It's been two months since our capture. Even my finger grew back," she said sarcastically as she showed off her hand.

"You'll poke an eye out with that if you're not careful," said Pïshkah as her eyes scanned across Lilith's nails and then her sword. "I noticed how you stopped looking at the Shard all day and night. Not liking what you're seeing?"

"There's nothing that I don't already know from it."

"And your fighting? Has it improved with the Shard sword?"

"Are you wondering how hard it would be if you tried to kill me again, Yuen'hii?" asked Lilith as she casually took a sip of her tea.

"If I wanted to kill you, Drae'shï, I'd only need to place two drops of poison in the right cup," she said with a mischievous grin as Lilith was sipping her tea.

The Drae'shï paused for a moment and conceded Pïshkah's victory.

"If you must know, the Shard invites little to the imagination. The blows are harder, the cuts are longer, but it is still just a sword. The Shirral was right. The fragment is no reflection of the whole, but I do invite you to take a look," she said casually as she pointed to the sword.

"No. Thank you. Anyway, what are you reading?"

"Can you even read?"

"I may be Lothuman, but I'll have you know that in my exile, I learnt to read *and* write," she said proudly.

"I see," said Lilith, unimpressed. "'Commentary on the Chronicles of the Age of the Immortals'. The Shirral brought it from the royal library for me."

"And?"

"And? It's a book by an Eldain, commenting on another age-old tome about the Immortal Wars."

"Never thought you to be the scholarly type."

"Not at all, but the Shirral invited me to explore the use of the Shard, and I accepted. Though I suspect that is slowly proving to be a bigger fool's errand than I originally anticipated."

"And?"

"As I said, there isn't much more in books than I already knew. Clearly, the key seems to be in the mirror as a whole. I've read of its ability to see all around the world. Possibly to shape it into one's own image or desire," said Lilith.

"I see. Do you think he will want to use it in the war?" said Pïshkah.

"That remains to be seen. I'm not inclined to trust so easily, and they're not very keen on handling it either. Especially given the stories surrounding our old friend Captain Silvan," she said as she clacked her metal nails on the edge of the divan.

"That son of a bitch got what he deserved," said Pïshkah.

The silence drew out as Lilith calmly picked up her book again and intermittently gazed above it to scan the area. She saw servants and other members of the Shirral's retinue go about their business down the hall. The generals of the seven armies were also in town, planning the next move of the Shirra and behaving with the distinct honour and modesty that the Carthosians carried themselves with. They wore their state of humility with pride, and despite the gruelling circumstances of their history, they maintained the resolve to carry on.

Soon she noticed the Shirral and Adara bump into each other briefly. Their mutual body language spoke more than any of the words they uttered.

"Pïshkah, are we ever going back?" mused Lilith.

"I don't know. Didn't really think about it. Although I can't say I miss being treated like an outcast. Do you?"

Lilith paused then took a deep breath. "I don't belong here either. This isn't my world. None of it is. This world is chaotic, messy, imperfect. But there's a place where everything is silent. Where the trivial wars of men and their beliefs mean nothing."

"Is that what you saw? In the mirror?"

"Yes."

Pïshkah fixated on her for a moment. The Drae'shï carried herself with divine regality as she continued to gaze into the distance. Her golden earring cuff shone against her silver skin. Her distinct eyes and the makeup around her scars painted her fierce nature. She was as beautiful as a brewing storm.

"Lilith, the darkness that you saw, I got a glimpse of it, too, on the ship and before we met. It is not peace that lies beyond it. Only death. Only oblivion. You must cast it aside before it devours you. You *are* part of this world."

"I am not," said Lilith proudly and with contempt. Her eyes pierced through Pïshkah's. "Even this world knows it," she continued as she removed the gauntlet to see her maimed hand. "Even you knew it back in Yammimer."

Pïshkah paused. "As within, so without," said Pïshkah smiling to herself as she looked down in semi-resignation, she pulled one of her many necklaces from under her robes.

"What?" asked Lilith.

"The world only gives more of what you already have within you and vice versa. If you reject it, it rejects you. If you accept it, it accepts you." She handed Lilith a golden eight-pointed star made from two interlocked pyramids.

"What is this?" Lilith held it up to her face.

"It is a stella octangula. A symbol of correspondence. One of the few that still exist. The Shirral gave it to me. Such symbols belong to an ancient world, long forgotten. They don't find their place here anymore. In some places, they would burn you for owning this. Practices and teachings that belong to that symbol have long been abandoned for a more convenient canon. However, it is still part of this world as much as people want to deny it," said Pïshkah. "Lilith, you are from an ancient world, but that does not mean that you are not part of it now—even if you do not recognise it, even if you don't fit in. It is the same world you came from."

Lilith stared at the pendant silently as the words of Pïshkah rang true.

"As within, so without. That is what the mirror showed then. The truth, not one's desire. It was always there right in front of me. The darkness within. The darkness you all fear to look at. I searched desperately to find myself, but in all my dreams before my helpless sight, the mirror has shown me nothing but the void. I have heard my former name become that of a stranger, my distant past become that of someone else. Now, all there's left is nothing. No one. Just me. I have no place in this world." She paused once more.

"What do you mean, no place? You've been around longer than anyone here."

"Whoever I was, whoever Lil'Thra was, is no more; it is irrelevant."

"What are you saying?"

"I am what I am, Pïshkah. Now I know what to do. I must return to the tower to find out the whole truth, about me, about existence, no matter what," she said as she rose to her feet and placed her gauntlet back on. "I'll walk right up to Morren's Gate, if necessary."

"Lilith, it's not a good idea," said Pïshkah as she followed.

"You and Adara can stay here and entertain whatever falsehoods you choose. I must find my place," she said as she turned her back only to be caught by Pïshkah's grasp. Lilith looked her up and down.

"Stop!" said Pïshkah, her brow giving away her fear of the Drae'shï. "You cannot. You must not. Or else."

"Or else what? You will try to kill me again?" asked Lilith calmly as she turned to face her.

Pïshkah stood scared, unable to respond to the haunting gaze of the Drae'shï's ruby eyes.

"It is inevitable," she said as she looked Pïshkah in the eyes with her long hypnotising gaze. "I thank you, sweet Cleriheu. I am finally aware now," she said as she lightly brushed Pïshkah's quivering lips with hers.

Pïshkah's grip loosened, and Lilith slipped away, leaving the necklace in her hands. Pïshkah stood there stunned as the Drae'shï walked deeper into the Riad.

Lilith proceeded down the halls of the Riad as staff and various clerics came and went with the day closing. The ramblings of debate echoed from a library nearby, and soon, she came upon the discussions of the Shirral and the commanders of the Shirra. Diligently, she slipped her way, unnoticed, to where the library met the terrace.

The debate centred around the movement of troops, supplies and people over the massive sub-continent and the point of contention remained one between the prudence of the Shirral versus the hubris of certain generals. The tense air of the discussion could be felt throughout.

"Your Grace, we cannot afford to wait any longer. It is time," intervened one.

"We've waited *fifteen* years since His Grace's passing, thirty if we count since the Severance. We must take action. Now," added another.

"My trusted commanders. Please," said the Shirral confidently as all went silent. "I am the M'yar. The M'yar of Carthosia. In our history, we were nothing but broken factions driven by greed like the Juranis, Merinos, Phinnises and Cretamis. What we have done is something that the Massass in all his years could never achieve without the use of his power, influence, and money. Peace. It has taken us ten years to unite and thirty years of strife, disease, and separation from the rest of the world. Will you not trust me for a few more weeks? Has the lust for war and thirst for vengeance slipped into your dreams?"

"You are also the Shirral, Your Grace," intervened Nephrim.

"I know what I am, Nephrim. I am the trustee of the faith until it is restored to the Grand Temple. This does not make me a butcher."

"Your father would have never waited so long," added D'var.

"And it cost us everything in Palin Bay, D'var. His anger, however justified, was his demise and that of our fleet, setting us further back than when we started."

"With respect, Your Grace. We are concerned that the Shirra is losing momentum," said D'var calmly.

"If we don't act now, the troops we've amassed along the way will slowly return to their homes." Nephrim stepped forward, raising his hand to stop D'var's polite pleading. "We must strike now, whilst the fires in their hearts are roaring and before winter truly sets in."

The Shirral paused and paced around the room with bated breath. The oil lamps flickered in the light breeze as all awaited his response. The Shirral commenced, "Have you considered for one moment whether we do indeed have to complete this journey?"

"Blasphemy!" intervened one as the others broke out in discussion.

"Silence!" he roared, slamming his fist onto his desk and startling the generals into complete silence. Even the staff outside jumped at the scare before quickly scurrying out of sight.

"We have achieved much on our own. We are a united nation that is starting to thrive once more. We have advanced tremendously on the medical front. Where the Enoch trees once constrained us, we have thrived under the pain of our necessity." He paused. "We must offer terms to lift the Severance."

"Blasphemy," some whispered as the room broke out into discussion once more.

As the discussion ensued, Nephrim approached the Shirral. "Your Grace, my armies have been camped a few kilometres from Morren's Gate for a month now. We could have taken the fort in an instant. Please, let me establish a foothold in Iborellan. I will demonstrate to the Massass the power we have amassed. The Massass will have no choice but to surrender ahead of the full invasion."

"Thank you, Nephrim, but I wish to offer terms before we strike. I would rather start the discussion with an open hand than with a clenched fist."

Nephrim sighed, frustrated and unable to contain himself.

"Anything you wish to say? Come on, speak your mind," provoked the Shirral.

"As Shirral, your role is not to make peace but to depose the usurper and his corruption of the faith. Your intent exceeds your mandate."

"And your impertinence exceeds yours!" he stated sharply. "I will not descend upon Valendria as a conqueror. We are liberators, not barbarians. How can we possibly relieve a world of injustice and prejudice when we perpetrate atrocities in its pursuit?"

The room went silent and once again was equally divided.

"It is war, Your Grace. Nothing more," said Nephrim, a scowl seared upon his brow.

"You have my answer," said the Shirral as he looked at all of them ignoring the angered commander.

"Then I shall await your instructions once more, Your Grace." He bowed courteously and turned to leave.

"And one more thing," continued the Shirral as he began going through his desk papers. "I shall be heading to Limik in the coming weeks, along with the household. Once the Jurani boy has arrived at Morren's Gate, we shall reconvene. I shall send a missive in advance for you to deliver to them at their gates. Personally."

"Yes, Your Grace." Nephrim bowed once more and took off into the courtyard.

"Leave me now." He waved his hand and the rest of the generals bowed and followed suit, leaving the Shirral tending to his work.

Lilith entered shortly after as the Shirral sat in his chair, hand to mouth in contemplation.

"You know he's going to betray you, right?" she said as she ran her nails over the wooden bookshelves.

"I wasn't aware you were invited to the Royal War Council meetings. I'd have had them bring you a proper seat," he said, barely lifting his gaze from the desk.

"Open doors and windows are always an invitation."

"Sit," he said as he stood and went to the table across the room to check his brass pot of tea. He returned with two cups, placing one in front of her. She took it and sat calmly. The smell of peppermint filled the room. "Tell me, Lilith. How does one win a war without actually fighting it?" He sat at the edge of the table.

"By killing your enemy's will to fight."

"And what about your own will to fight? What happens when you have not sated the hunger of your own dogs of war?" He sipped.

"They tear each other apart." She smirked.

"Precisely, Lilith. You are quite the politician, I must say," said the Shirral as he smiled and wagged his finger at her. "However, you are still incorrect. That mentality is what breeds the endless cycle of war. I shall break that cycle."

"Isn't that the very cycle that brought you to this throne? The subjugation of the other Carthosian houses? The houses of the men from whom you demand loyalty."

"The Shirra has long been a unifying factor that will not last indefinitely. People follow me out of loyalty but in the depths of their hearts some are also guided by vengeance, faith, or sheer desire for power."

"And you believe that after years of conflict and strife these *loyal* men are capable of understanding anything beyond the language of war and subjugation? Does the Massass?"

"A child must be chastised to mature. I will not spare the rod of war, but neither will I break the child with it."

"Is the Vanguard Army your rod then? You expect the Massass, the Saints and all Amenti to cower before Nephrim's men at Morren's Gate?"

"They are *my* men, and I expect the Massass, at his age, to have the wisdom to avoid the unnecessary bloodshed of his people. The man must relent."

"And what if he who holds *your* rod is the one that can't relent? There's hardly any cure for a rabid dog," said Lilith as the Shirral let out a long breath. She paused. "Allow me to go and make terms with the Saints at Morren's Gate. If Elias Jurani is there, he will come to the table."

"I cannot risk your life or that of Adara or Pïshkah. Your role is to protect them in my absence."

"I was not aware of my duties."

"You protect each other. I thought that was self-evident."

"They have each other."

"No," he replied flatly.

"Altheo—" she intervened.

"No!" he barked as he slammed the table, rattling the cups on top.

"Is that so then? What if all I wanted was to leave? Would your answer be the same?" she replied, equally angered.

He didn't respond, looking away and struggling to contain his anger.

Lilith narrowed her eyes. "I see. It is the Shard then. You want it," she said with contempt.

"The Shirra does not need the Shard, but your friends might think they do. I will not give them cause to believe they can refuse my terms," he said as he rose from his seat, pointing east.

"Ah yes. Their own *rod*," she said sardonically. "Well, so much for the freedom you bestowed upon us. 'You are free to leave,' I was told, but what you meant, what you always mean is, 'you are free to agree with me.' Isn't that so, Your Grace?" she mocked as she rose from her seat and walked around the table.

"Too much hangs in the balance. You and the Shard must stay here 'til this is all over."

"What—"

"This is not up for debate."

"You—"

"You may leave now."

"I—"

"Leave." He turned to face the terrace, hands behind his back.

Lilith stormed out and banged the door behind her. She cursed and headed back to the courtyard. It was filled with various dignitaries as well as the commanders of the Shirra conversing and exchanging pleasantries. She cursed again as her space was invaded once more. She proceeded to walk past unnoticed but soon bumped into Nephrim. His stern look almost matched hers.

"Apologies, my lady," he stated as he bowed his way out of hers. She looked but did not reply. As she stepped away, he continued, "It is a fine blade which you possess."

"Does the Commander envy the Drae'shï?" She turned mockingly.

"It was my steel smith that made your blade and your gauntlet," he said courteously yet without a hint of a smile.

"He did a fine job. He has my thanks. As do you, Commander," she said, tilting her head.

"I hear your skills outmatch that of even the best Sarcheni, yet I have not witnessed a blade of such design in use. May I?"

Lilith drew her blade in a flurry. It rang around the halls as the rest went silent. "I am its master," she said as she handed it to Nephrim.

The man took a quick look at the blade, inspecting its balance, sharpness, and hold. The Shard's allure rippled throughout the blade. He quickly performed a flurry of movements in the open when one of his fellows tossed an orange in the air only to be picked mid-flight by the tip of the blade without a single spatter. The crowd applauded and resumed its chatter.

Nephrim returned the blade. "It is a great sword. Truly."

"It's a pity then that it may never be tested in war," she said as she slid it swiftly back into its scabbard.

"The Drae'shï should not be forced onto the battlefield. The women under the care of the Shirral are his wards, not his soldiers. War is the trade of men."

"Is that why the Vanguard lies in waiting then? Awaiting the real soldiers to arrive?"

"The Drae'shï knows little of the matters of war." He barely flinched at her jibe, looking her straight in the eyes.

"Perhaps, but I do know a lot about men," she said as they watched the Shirral and Adara encounter one another once more under the loggias of the Riad. "Tell me, Commander, how can a man go to war when all he thinks about is love and peace?"

Lilith watched Nephrim as his narrow eyes scrutinised the body language of the two, the awkward steps of the lass and the gentle demeanour of the Shirral.

"The Shirral is well aware of his responsibilities. In no time his name will be hailed throughout Amenti. He would not be distracted by such frivolities," said Nephrim.

"Oh, I'm certain he's not. Who would be? After all, he's building a legacy that will last a hundred generations," she said as they both watched. "Even after history has forgotten these dark days, I wonder how people like us will be remembered. How would you like to be remembered, Commander? Do you have any children?"

The man's anger was palpable. "Excuse me, my lady. I must take leave." He turned heel, called his retinue, and took to the front entrance.

Lilith chased after him. "Take me with you! I want to fight," she said as Nephrim climbed atop his steed and circled on the spot.

"What about you then? What legacy does the Drae'shï want to leave?" he asked.

"Fear."

CHAPTER 30

GREATER IMMORTALS

"In the beginning, there was nothing. And nothing was all there was," said Pïshkah as the cool night's wind fluttered the curtains of the Shirral's library. "There was no place, no time, no light or dark. However, that nothingness was everything there was. It was whole. In its inexistence, it existed. In its non-being, it was. The ancients had no name for it, but it came to be known as the Darkness. Nothingness, the None."

Adara and the Shirral listened attentively.

"Nothingness soon became aware of itself, for such nothingness was everything there was at that same time, and all of a sudden, it manifested itself into existence; into everything that exists. From the tiniest grain of sand to the tallest mountain, in every thought, word, sound. It was everything there ever was and will ever be. In all realities, everywhere and always. The Darkness had willed itself into existence and in so doing became the Will: the Will to exist." Pïshkah paused as the brass lamps flickered in the middle of the table. "The Will is much less than a god, but also much more. For all gods are of the Will for they form part of Everything; the All. The Will to exist is in everything but also in nothing at the same time. It stood for a moment in a state of Nothingness when it was whole and singular but was cast and fragmented into the infinity of existence the next—in the All." Pïshkah explained slowly. "Old Drostharians believed that for existence to be the way it is, there was a certain order that naturally followed. Pillars of existence hold everything together and stop all existence and reality from falling apart and collapsing onto itself. Even things that don't make sense to you follow a certain order. One can't be both dead and alive, here and there. The wind doesn't turn dust to water or trees to feathers," she said as she fluttered her hands into the air.

"These pillars were known as the Children of the Will. Known by many names, they represented time, fate, change, love, wisdom, and justice. In turn, each of the Children had their own offspring. All twins who in unison upheld the order of existence—they were known as the Greater Immortals—for they, too, endured in the eternity of existence. Time had future and past, which together held the present in balance. Fate had freedom and constraint. Change had life and death or rather creation and destruction. Love, war and peace, convergence, and separation. Wisdom; awareness and ignorance and finally and most importantly, justice. Justice had good and evil, or rather everything that is and should be, versus everything that isn't and should not be. Each Greater Immortal was a pole at the opposite end of their counterpart, which together, along with all the other Greater Immortals, held the balance of all things and all things that are not. All that we see and don't see in existence is a descendent of these children, a reflection of their being."

"Pïshkah, where is this going?" enquired the Shirral. "It's a bit late to go over Drostharian legends. I thought you had something to say that was important, considering your insistence that we meet now."

Adara looked towards the pitch darkness outside the open terrace doors and back. "Yes, Pïshkah, and these stories are feeling rather spooky, if you don't mind me saying."

"Just, listen to me carefully, all right? This is important," said the Cleriheu under the dim light of the lamp. "There is a legend in the far east that in the absence of the Will itself, Fate had called upon all the Children of the Will and the Greater Immortals to answer the ultimate question of existence: the Why. Why did the Will choose to be? Why endure this existence? Ultimately, to determine whether existence should continue or not. Fate's solution to this unanswerable question

 JENS C. BÜDINGER

was to send each of the Greater Immortals into the world to fight their counterparts over seven lifetimes to determine the fate of existence." She paused. "Now, you remember I said that the darkness became the Will in order to exist, right?"

They nodded.

"Well, in order for some things to exist, a lot of other things must not."

"But what is this all about, Pïshkah?" asked Adara, now getting rather anxious.

"Justice. Good and evil. Not in the way we know it, but in the way the universe does. Everything that is and should be is good, and everything that isn't and should not be is evil, so to speak." Pïshkah paused. "I believe Lilith is evil manifest; the darkness... the Nothing to the All. I always suspected, but now, I'm sure."

"What? How? Why?" asked Adara, perplexed as the Shirral furrowed his brow.

The Shirral took a long, deep breath. "Are you sitting here in the middle of the night trying to tell me that Lilith is some sort of God?"

"Your Grace, She may not know it yet but—"

"Pïshkah, I know these legends are important to you, but they're just legends. Drostharianism is dead for a reason. Their ideas never made sense," said the Shirral dismissively as he rose to his feet and walked to the windows, watching his reflection in the dark panes.

"She wants to go back to the Hall of Mirrors. She's going to cross the field." The Cleriheu as she rose out of her chair.

"Even if she does, how will any of this matter?" enquired Adara, clasping Pïshkah's arm.

"I saw the Darkness. I saw it when I first ran into her and on the ship when the storm hit us. I always thought there was something unnatural about her. How she was seemingly soulless. Difficult to see. Without concrete memory of her past. At first, I chose to ignore it. Between having saved her on the ship and Lilith being Lilith, I didn't think too much about it. Especially since she seemed to be doing fine here and wasn't doing much with the Shard anyway. But at some point, somehow, maybe after our captivity, something changed in her, and today, she confirmed it. Whatever inhabited her body before is no longer there, and as the Darkness devours Lil'Thra, it will hunger for more 'til there's nothing left."

"Nothing left?" said Adara.

"Nothing, but her. Lilith."

"What about who she was, her person, her soul? Is it possible it is just the mirror that has bewitched her?"

"I cannot tell for certain what role the mirror has to play, yet it seems that when she gazed into the abyss. The abyss spoke back."

Adara looked at the Shirral with concern.

"You need to keep her from crossing to the mainland. She has already expressed the intent to leave," said Pïshkah as she flattened her hands wide over the table. The lamp flickered once more.

"I purposefully put Lilith to the task of training and reading about the Shard to keep both her and her Shard occupied and more importantly under my watch. We'll find something else to distract her, if necessary," said the Shirral, waving his hand casually.

"That's not good enough!" said Pïshkah, seething.

The Shirral took a deep breath as he rubbed his eyes and the bridge of his nose. Silence ensued.

"It is not in the nature of such powerful beings to be patient or merciful. She will come after us, after everyone. Don't ignore me!" Pïshkah insisted.

"Pïshkah, we are at war!" he barked. "I have enough problems with my commanders second-guessing me at every turn. What do you think people would have to say the moment I begin talking about Greater Immortals, doomsday scenarios and other Lothuman mumbo-jumbo with a Cleriheu standing right next to me?"

Adara gasped, and Pïshkah snorted. "May I remind Your Grace that the war is tied to the Drae'shï's fate and that of the Shard she possesses," said Pïshkah contemptuously. "The Jurani knows of the Shard and will seek to use it, and she will, in turn, seek to use him."

The Shirral paused in his step. "She already requested, after my meeting with the commanders, that I allow her to leave," said the Shirral. "She insisted she'd be the one to deliver a message to Elias herself."

"She couldn't care less about the war. She'll use any means to get there, anything, anyone," insisted Pïshkah. "Lilith's resolve is unrelenting."

"Anyone..." murmured the Shirral to himself before he suddenly called to the door. "Reshar! Reshar!" The door slowly opened, and the steward walked in.

"Yes, Your Grace."

"Were you attending the commanders' dinner this evening?"

"Yes, Your Grace, myself and Norella."

"And was Nephrim there?"

"No, he was not. Your—"

"Wake him up. Now!"

"Your Grace, I'm afraid it's impossible," said the steward, rather embarrassed. "Commander Nephrim departed before dinner, his retinue included."

"Curse him!" yelled the Shirral as he threw all the papers from his table, shocking everyone in the room. "Curse his poisoned blood!" he yelled once more. "Wake up the rest of the commanders and call for Captain Serik of the Royal Guard. Now!" he barked.

"Wait!" said Pïshkah, calling to the confused and frightened steward. "Was Lilith with him? The Drae'shï?"

The man looked at the Shirral hesitantly.

"Speak!" barked the Shirral.

"I did not see myself, but I heard she was with him when he departed."

"And it did not occur to you to inform me of this?" asked the Shirral, now fuming.

"I-we th-thought you were aware, Your G-grace." he stammered.

"Get Serik here! Now! We'll see how far they get."

"Adam," whispered Sirra. "Adam! Wake up!" she insisted as Adam slowly opened his eyes. Dawn had not yet broken. "It's time to move. The Carthosian scouts are moving."

"I'm up, I'm up," said Adam as he gradually got up to see the rest of the troop packing up their things. "Morning." He saluted as the Moirai nodded to him.

Vuriel stool bare-chested in the cold northern wind by the river-bank, scrubbing his teeth with his fingers and rinsing his mouth in the crisp waters of the Brunik River.

Adam approached to splash his face alongside the Drae'shï captain. Adam cleared his throat and spat into the river.

"You Eldassari are extremely noisy. Do you know how loudly you breathe? Let alone snore?"

"We never felt the need to hide, Captain," said Adam as he took another sip of water to rinse his mouth and spat.

"Well, you're going to need to. Unless you're willing to go headfirst into the battlefield," said Vuriel as he took a final gulp of water and rinsed his mouth clear. "The Carthosians are making a move, look." He pointed into the distance past the tree line of the Nemrhun Forest.

Their perch upon the hills offered a view of the entire southern bay area around Morren's Gate. The Brunik River ran all the way down the hill to and under the large bastions of the mighty fortress. The fort stood firmly upon the creek that divided Iborellan and Ithiria. Once surrounded by woodland, the area had been cleared for several kilometres in all direc-tions. To the west of the forest stood rows of Carthosian mounds and trenches surrounding the open plains to the sea. Patrols and troops rolled in and out daily, but the mass of their army stood over the western ridge.

The Carthosian camps ran for kilometres. Their sunburst crest flew on every flag and banner as far as the eye could see. Hidden behind the ridge, siege towers and artillery had been constructed over the past weeks. Scouts and lumber teams constantly ventured into the Nemrhun Forest to obtain the much-needed timber which Carthosia itself hardly provided.

"Looks like they're close to launching their attack," said Dreskar, the Dratesh Khan, in his deep yet friendly voice. "Are you excited about your first battle, Eldassari?" he continued as he slowly put on his heavy armour.

"Isn't it also your first battle, Dreskar?" added Sirra with a slight grin as she sharpened her blades.

"It's not a battle if you don't have an army," said Lurith, already dressed in his tight assassin's suit, covered in knives and as black as night. "You're not suggesting we fight, are you, Vuriel?"

"We'll have to see what Ellior and Tenet find out about the location of the Shard. It seems it's getting closer," said Vuriel.

"Thank your lucky stars it turned up after all, Eldassari. I'd have loved to cut your balls off after having made us walk all the way here for nothing." Lurith smirked as he juggled one of his daggers.

"Hey! Back off, Lurith," snapped Sirra. "Don't start again."

"Ooooo!" taunted the rest of the group.

"Quiet down," said Vuriel as he put his shirt on.

"Seems like the Eldassari's girlfriend needs to do the talking for him. Perhaps I might not need to cut off your balls after all since she already took them herself," said Lurith. "Good job Sirra." He winked.

"Asshole," she said as she turned away to continue packing.

"Stop. This is not the time," said Vuriel in a calm tone.

Adam forced a smile and stood. "Give me a sword, and we'll find out who's got the balls and who doesn't, Lurith."

"Yes. Upon the battlefield, you never know," added the Drae'shï as they stood face to face, the Eldassari towering above him.

"You talk a lot, Drae'shï. Be sure not to trip over your tongue when we're down there," said Adam straight-faced.

"Enough both of you!" Vuriel pointed his finger at each of them. "Save it for the fight."

"Captain!" intervened Ellior as he emerged from the brush. "The Shard! It's approaching fast! Looks like it's coming from the western side."

"The Ilvaresh must be with the Carthosians," said Vuriel.

"If she's even alive," added Sirra.

"She is. I'm sure of it," stated Adam.

"And the scouting parties in the woods? Have they moved Ellior?"

"Yes, but I'm sure we'll manage to ambush a group. I've earmarked some spots where we can ambush the next lumber crew. They have horses."

"Can the Drae'shï even ride horses?" asked Adam sceptically. The rest laughed.

"We got horses, too, pretty boy," responded Tenet as the ranger emerged from the brush. "Just not as many."

"All right, everyone. Let's move," said Vuriel as the rest finished packing and followed the Drae'shï along the riverbank.

"And you, stay out of our way," said Lurith as he bumped shoulders with Adam.

The party ventured upwards along the Brunik River and crossed the shallows into Ithiria. As the group made it into the thicker and steeper part of the Nemrhun forest, they found themselves beyond the perimeter of the Carthosian scouts. The view of Morren's Gate and the bay were astounding as the crack of dawn painted the skies pink and blue, and a nutty smell of morning dew pervaded the air.

The group made it slowly and silently down to the first encampment. The sound of casual Carthosian conversation gave away the position of a morning patrol. In a matter of seconds, Lurith emerged from the shadows, slicing through the two guards' necks before they could finish their last syllables. Sirra and Tenet quickly dragged the corpses into the bushes as Vuriel signalled the rest to encircle the camp.

The smell of peppermint tea filled the cold air. A subtle whistle caught the camp's attention, and alert ensued as the Drae'shï all emerged, firing their arrows at point-blank range with barely a yelp leaving their victims.

"Alright, everyone. Time to strip," said Vuriel. All looked back perplexed. "Come on, start undressing. If the armillary sphere is correct, we're going to have to head behind enemy lines."

"Most likely," said Tenet as he dangled the sphere attached to his necklace before his gaze.

"Sir, I'm not sure that's a good idea. We're just six, and there are thousands out there," said Dreskar.

"I don't suppose you want to charge head-on, do you? We'll wait for the right opportunity when the shard reveals itself. Ellior, when do the lumber carts come usually?"

"I'd say every two hours."

"Good. Prepare the ambush." Vuriel picked up one of the sheathed swords of a dead scout and threw it to Adam who caught it in mid-air. "You too, Eldassari. Time to see what the wardens are made really of."

The morning winds swept through the Carthosian headquarters. The tarp on the marquee flapped as it stood open. It was just under the cusp of the western ridge overlooking Morren's Gate. All the officers of the Vanguard Army entered slowly as news of the arrival of their commander arrived. Soon the famed Nephrim entered, followed by Lilith. Both looked stern and eager to proceed.

All bowed to his presence. "Commander," they said.

"Continue, Merral, please." He nodded and waved briefly.

"Yes, sir," said Merral, another general wearing the typical black robes of the Carthosian military elite. "As you can see from the map, the fortress has a massive outer curtain with five prominent bastions, three on the west bank of the Brunik and two on the east. There is one entrance on the west, directly across from where we are, and one on the other side of the fortress. There is a drawbridge crossing over the river right under its northern walls. This is the only way to cross the river without passing through the fortress—it is impossible to pass without heavy losses—this is why we are only attacking on the west bank. The keep inside Morren's Gate is an earlier and more rudimental structure, a remnant of the Salingan Empire, strong but not impregnable. As we've been observing, the Valendrians have been supplying the fortress with their army as well as with some Iborean troops." Merral moved various markers showing the Eagle's Crest of the Iboreans and the Laurel Crest of the Valendrian Army to the battlements.

"The south side of the fortress has an opening to a sheltered harbour just under its walls. The river flows right under the fortress and into the creek where they built the harbour. The port itself is barred by a small breakwater island with two spiked chains which can be lowered from the inside. We now also have our naval blockade, which won't allow anyone in or out."

"I noticed there's a Valendrian ship outside our blockade on my way here," intervened another.

"Correct, General. This ship must be an additional supply vessel that arrived late. However, the four vessels carrying the Valendrian army had arrived long before ours."

"Numbers?" enquired a general.

"Around a thousand, two thousand at the most," said another.

"We're looking at a great victory, Commander. The Shirral will be proud," said Merral, slightly enthused.

Everyone smiled save for Nephrim.

The sound of hooves and commotion came from outside, and soon Captain Serik along with a handful of members of the Royal Guard barged into the tent.

"Captain, have you finally come to announce the arrival of the Shirral?" enquired Nephrim.

"Commander, you are under strict orders to stand down until the Shirral arrives and to hand over the Drae'shï maid and her sword to me," stated Serik with authority, his golden robes shining in stark contrast to the black garb of the generals in the tent.

"And why would the Shirral wish to hold us from advancing to victory? A victory in his name, in the name of the Shirra, in the name of Carthosia?" said Nephrim, calm and composed. "Surely, you must have a missive with you."

Serik nodded and handed over a golden tube from which emerged a rolled-up piece of fine parchment.

Nephrim read it casually and tossed it dismissively onto the table. "Is this the grand message which could not wait? Commanders. See for yourselves. The Shirral wishes to sue for peace. The Shirral of Carthosia wishes to bargain with two thousand rats."

"Watch your tone, Nephrim..."

"No, Captain, you watch yours," said Nephrim, slyly. "How many men have you passed on your gallop through the camp? There are 35,501 men in this encampment, including the ten in here. We have fought and bled and starved to see this day, and now we sue for peace? Like cowering dogs?" His patience boiled as the rest of the room stood silent. "Generals, captains, friends, the Shirral is stricken by a disease." The room filled with astonishment. "Not a disease of the flesh but the mind and heart!"

"How dare you!" Serik drew his sword, followed by everyone else.

"He lusts for love and peace. He's been bewitched by notions not becoming of his great title! I have seen it with my own eyes."

"If you stop this now, the Shirral might show you clemency, Nephrim. Stop this blasphemy now!"

"The Shirral wants to negotiate with the Jurani boy and the Massass when his mission is to remove the usurper and his hegemony over the Holy Enoch! Tell me, Captain, who is the blasphemer?"

"Nephrim, we've known each other for years. Don't make me do this," Serik pleaded as all within the tent watched each other intensely as tensions became palpable and hands laid themselves on the handles of their swords. "I do not wish to fight my brothers, but I must follow the Shirral's word. It is my oath. Our oath."

Nephrim signalled to lower their guard. He smiled, slowly approached Serik, and embraced him, holding him from his arms. "You are an honourable man, Serik, and for this, I will allow you to carry out the orders of the Shirral yourself." Serik froze. "If you are successful in obtaining that which the Shirral so desires from our enemies, as these men are my witness, you have my word that I will submit myself to you and the judgement of the Shirral. However, if you fail to obtain the peace, this will be the last sunrise you will ever see."

"You expect me to walk out on the battlefield alone with nothing but a promise?"

"I expect you to know that if you fail to carry out your duty, you will die right here where you stand. The Shirral may have your unconditional loyalty, but these men know who their commander is," said Nephrim confidently. "So, what will it be, Captain?" Serik hesitated, and Nephrim turned to the rest. "The Shirral is no longer in a place to lead us. I am no seer. I am not the predilect leader, but I shall let fate decide for us. If I am wrong, I shall die. That much I am willing to bet. Even this man, a captain of the Royal Guard, has lost his faith in his leader. Even he will not take on the folly of the mission given. What does it say of the man that commands his loyalty?"

Serik gritted his teeth. "Fine. I shall take the message to the enemy."

Nephrim paused, then smiled. "Prepare yourself then."

In a matter of minutes, the men were all out on the ridge, watching the grey walls of Morren's Gate. Serik and his guards were atop their horses, holding white banners by their sides.

"Remember, we will only come to terms with the Jurani, no one else," said Nephrim.

"And how will I know if the man before me is he?"

Nephrim walked slowly towards Lilith and presented her. "The Drae'shï shall accompany you."

"What?" asked Lilith, aghast. "I will not head out there to be slaughtered!"

Nephrim grabbed her wrist and she tried to pull away.

"You think I don't know what you're planning on doing?" She tugged and he jerked her back into place.

"You can take your chances, or both die here and now," said Nephrim.

"Leave the Drae'shï out of this. The Shirral has strictly forbidden it, Nephrim," said Serik cautiously. "There is no need."

"You're right, Serik, he did." said Nephrim as he quickly slid Lilith's Shard sword from its sheath. "But *this* is what he wants to keep."

Lilith roared and swiped at Nephrim, cutting his jaw with her talons.

He threw out the back of his hand and struck her down. "Indeed, I must congratulate Jenuar on his craftsmanship." He touched his face and then looked at the blood on his fingers. "You didn't think I'd allow you to deliver the secret weapon to the enemy, did you? The Eldain woman may have the Shirral wrapped around her fingers, but I've lived long enough to know better than to be beguiled by whores and sycophants."

"I'll fucking kill you!" she roared as the soldiers picked her up.

"Put her on a horse and tie her hands to the saddle, lest she tries any sudden moves. And bring me a large mirror," said Nephrim as they forcibly mounted her on a horse and bound her hands. Nephrim handed the reins to Serik. "Ask for Elias Jurani. If she confirms the man before her is he, wave your flags. If it is not, drop your flags and return to us immediately unless you wish to die."

"What makes you so sure that the Jurani himself will come out?" asked Serik.

"Ah, here it is," said Nephrim as his guards brought a large mirror out and stood it before him. Nephrim picked up the closest rock and smashed his reflection to pieces, startling the horses and the crowd alike. He slowly knelt and carefully picked a shard. "This will do," he said as he proceeded to slip it in Lilith's waist sash in prominent view. "The Jurani will not resist the temptation to seize it. She alone is of no value to him."

"So, the legacy you leave is one of treachery after all," said Lilith with contempt as Nephrim secured his newly fitted sword belt.

"Then I must ensure that at least one of us should fulfil their legacy, even if you're the only one who is taken by fear," said Nephrim as he unsheathed the Shard sword and signalled the troops forward.

Lilith, along with the five other horsemen of the Royal Guard, made their way through the mounds on the ridge before the open battlefield and Morren's Gate. The men clutched at their poles and reins and began their descent, gritting their teeth and swallowing their fear. The sea breeze brushed their faces as the winds picked up in the bay. The Carthosian blockade held strong whilst the lonely Valendrian vessel struggled to maintain its anchorage.

Lilith looked into the distance as the breeze brought some comfort, yet in the distance, another vessel appeared. Her eyes widened as the echoes of her capture came haunting her with the flutter of its black sails.

"Sir, there's a Carthosian trireme approaching at speed. Pirate ship by the looks of it," said the Valendrian deck officer.

"Dimas! Report on the approaching vessel," yelled the captain to the crow's nest.

"Trireme, Carthosian made. No flag. No one on deck, Captain," said the lookout.

"No one?" asked the deck officer to the captain, somewhat confused.

"I'm sorry. One on deck, sir!" added the lookout.

"Primus, get everyone ready to engage," said the captain. Soon the deck officer began barking orders. The crew scrambled to the deck, readying bows and arrows as the vessel began lifting the anchor, and men climbed to unfurl the ship's sails.

As the trireme approached, its mainsail crept up and its speed slowed, yet only one man appeared, a sole sailor scrambling furiously from one side of the deck.

"What the hell is he doing?" The captain narrowed his eyes, as the vessel slowly approached, turning on its side to avoid a collision.

"Captain, they'll be coming upon starboard shortly."

"Men," called the captain. "Light." The archers proceeded to dip their arrowheads into the nearby braziers. "On my mark, be ready to fire." As the trireme rolled up, the thrashing sound of the anchor chain rolled. The vessel groaned as it jerked to a halt almost instantly, and the lonely sailor tumbled down the stairs before coming to a complete stop. "Nock!"

"Wait! Stop!" cried Zain as he pulled himself up to the edge of the ship, waving frantically. "I'm on your side!" The Vampire stood bare-chested under a long dark pirate's coat, pants, and boots to match. His pale white skin looked stricken by the cold. He panted desperately, hands on his knee. "I hate sailing alone. Arghhhh."

"Are you alone?" yelled the deck officer.

"Yes! Yes!"

"Identify yourself!"

"I'm Zain Nightwing. I knew Elias Jurani. Two months ago, we sailed upon the *Intrepid* together before it sank, along with him, I'm afraid." Zain caught his breath.

"Elias Jurani is alive," said the deck officer.

"Really?" asked Zain surprised. "The bastard can swim then. I'll give him that."

The deck officer looked back at the captain. "Sir?"

"Board the ship. Check for any soldiers."

"There's no one aboard. I swear. It's just me," said Zain as the rest of the crew began to haul the two ships together with grapples. "Permission to board, Captain? I'm unarmed," he said as he climbed on the edge ready to jump off, opening his arms. The captain nodded, and Zain skipped over.

"May I ask how you came in possession of this vessel, Zain?"

"This is the infamous *Dead Lady*," he said, arms held wide. "Formerly owned by a band of buccaneers known as the Black Teeth, or Tooths, not sure." He paused, finger to his mouth in confusion.

"Is this the vessel that sank the *Intrepid*?"

"Correct. I was aboard. They sank it along with me. So, then I decided I'd sink its crew and keep their ship," said Zain with a smirk as the captain looked back unamused.

"No one aboard, sir," called a soldier.

"I asked them nicely for it, though. Once," said Zain.

"Right," said the captain as he looked at his equally confused deck officer. "And why are you here now?"

"Isn't it obvious? I've come to rescue the damsels in distress and save the day."

"I'm afraid you're a bit late then, Zain," said the captain as they walked to portside. Between Morren's Gate and the ship stood a long blockade of Carthosian vessels barring entrance into the Fort's port. The blockade ran from beach to beach, blocking even a landing on the shores of the battlefield. "Even if we did make it through, I suspect we'd still be outnumbered twenty to one."

The view from the sea gave little hope to the soldiers aboard. The thousands of Carthosian soldiers ran through the camps like ants, scurrying around siege towers and artillery, which were slowly being moved under cover of the ridge.

"Seems like they're making a move." Zain pointed to the Carthosian ramparts on the western ridge.

"Looks like it," said the captain as a small party of horsemen emerged bearing white banners and the orange and yellow colours of Carthosia.

"Sir?" enquired a deckhand.

"Bring the man some bread, dry meat, and water. You must be hungry."

"Starving, Actually. You don't happen to have anything fresher, do you?"

The captain's brow furled.

"Never mind. That will do." Zain frowned.

"Captain, it seems like a group of Royal Guards are asking for a parlay," cried the lookout. "Five men and a woman, it seems."

"A woman?" said the deck officer.

Zain's eyes widened, and he dashed upon the ratlines.

"Hey, you, get down!" yapped the deck officer.

Zain looked long and hard. Her look was unmistakable. "I can't believe it." He stood stunned with incredulous excitement. "She's alive!" He watched happily as his search had come to an end. "I don't know how you did it—but of course! The Shard!"

Zain quickly scanned the field, watching the Carthosians ready themselves at their posts, loading their catapults and ballistae hidden from sight. "Captain! How would your men wish to join your friends in combat?"

"Hey! Come down! Immediately!" barked the deck officer as the captain stood perplexed, watching the Vampire's bravado.

"It's time to head to shore. A battle is about to commence." Zain jumped back down.

"What are you saying? There's a parlay going on. We cannot attack now!" snapped the deck officer.

"Yes, Zain. If you know something, say it now," said the captain.

"It's a trap. They wouldn't send her out for any reason other than to lure out Elias. Trust me on this," said Zain as he walked past them, twirled around, and jumped onto the edge of the vessel before skipping over onto the *Dead Lady*.

"Stop! You will disrupt the parlay!" yelled the deck officer. "Captain?"

"Stop him!" ordered the captain but Zain had already pulled out a hatchet from the capstan and chopped off every mooring tied to the *Dead Lady*. "Stop him!" the captain yelled as the confused soldiers ran back and forth, trying to get back on their vessel and others tried stopping the *Dead Lady* from going adrift.

"I'm going to open a road for you, Captain! You're welcome!" Zain smiled as he saluted. Zain unfurled the sails once more, which picked up the wind instantly, and with a rough tug, the anchor chain ripped off its winch. "Well, there go any second thoughts," he said to himself as the vessel began rapidly distancing itself from the scrambling crew of the Valendrian ship.

CHAPTER 31

THE BATTLE OF BLOOD

"Commander."

"Yes, Lyons?" asked Elias, watching his reflection as he proceeded to secure the white bull brooch of his house upon his white cloak.

"The Carthosian Royal Guard is approaching the walls, with white banners," said Lyons. The Saint was in full uniform, white, grey, and mailed from head to toe. "They want to talk."

The two Saints emerged from the keep of Morren's Gate followed by other knights, zigzagging through scores of troops. From knights to men-at-arms, from Iborean spearmen to Valendrian archers. The air inside was tense as the looming omen of their demise taunted them from across the field. As Elias and Lyons reached the western gate walls, the party of Carthosians stood in the middle of the field, waving their white flags.

"We demand to speak to Elias of the House of Jurani," called out Serik as his voice echoed across the field. "We have come to offer terms under the protection of parlay."

"Elias?" asked Lyons as he watched Elias peer intently at the group in the distance.

"Is that?"

"Fucking Lilith," said Lyons with dismay as the two observed her closely, narrowing their eyes.

"She looks well."

"Too well. She must have turned," said Lyons.

Serik continued. "I am accompanied by a friend of the house of Jurani. We offer to allow her safe crossing as a sign of good faith."

"How the hell is she still alive?" whispered Lyons.

"The Shard," said Elias.

"What?"

"The Shard! She has it on her!" Elias pointed at her. "Have the third and fifth cavalry cohorts arrived?"

"Not yet, sir. You're not suggesting that we go out there?"

"The Massass was clear. Retrieve the artefact at all costs."

"What about Lady Crysanthani?"

Elias sighed. "If she's still alive, they wouldn't give her up just yet."

"But they would leave the Shard?"

"Assuming they don't already know what it does? I hate to say this, Elias, but this looks a lot like a trap."

"I'm afraid I don't have a choice, Captain. It's too close a chance to ignore," he said as he put his helmet on and drew the thin chain mail across his face.

***

The Royal Guards stood on the field. Even the horses nervously stamped the ground in the silence of anticipation.

"What if they don't answer?" asked Lilith.

"It's all up to Nephrim," said Serik begrudgingly.

"You know that if you signal that it's Elias, they will kill us all, right?" she said.

"Then you better hope that it's not him."

Soon a white banner flew upon the battlements, and the portcullis began to rise as the wooden gates drew apart. Six Saints emerged on horseback, bearing a single white flag and one of the Holy Order. The two groups met in the middle. Serik moved forward separately to meet their commander in turn.

"Blessings of the Mother upon you." Serik as he placed his hand upon his chest and bowed.

"May her eternal light guide you," said the Saint. His chained veil glimmered under the spot of sunlight peering through the overcast sky.

"You bare the bull crest of the House of Jurani upon your cloak. You are Elias Jurani, are you not?"

"I am him," said the Saint.

Lilith's frowned.

Serik went silent and took a deep breath.

"And you are?" said the Saint.

"I am Captain Serik of the Royal Guard," said Serik, as he watched the Saint's head turn, focusing on Lilith. "You know this woman?"

"Yes, I do," the Saint said dryly. "You offer terms as well as her safe passage?"

"I do." Serik slowly drew out the gold tube from his side. He signalled to the guards who slowly led Lilith's horse to them and returned.

Lilith followed the Saint's eyes as they scanned her and the Shard closely. He then extended his arm to receive the message. Lilith peered, trying to discern the hidden yet familiar expression of the receiver.

Serik began to extend his arm but stopped. "First, Commander, I must confirm your identity. Please be kind enough to remove your veil."

"Of course, Captain Serik," said the Saint as he slowly unveiled his scarred face to the Carthosian. It was Captain Lyons.

Serik observed but gave no reaction. Lyons and Lilith looked at each other without flinching. Lilith gave a nasty grin.

"So you do know each other," said Serik.

"Oh, we do." She laughed. "We really do," she continued as she began laughing almost hysterically.

"What's so funny, Lilith? Are you not happy to see me?" added Lyons, struggling to retain his composure. "Come let's get you home."

"Enough!" said Serik. "What's going on, Lilith?" he insisted as she continued laughing. "Lilith, if this man isn't who he said he is, tell me now! Is he or is he not Elias Jurani?" yelled the captain.

"He is," she said with a smile and immediately kicked the horse into a full gallop towards the fortress, startling all those around.

"Lilith! Stop!" yelled Serik as the horsemen twisted and turned in confusion, hesitant about whether to give chase or not.

Lilith looked back as Serik turned towards the ridge and began desperately waving his hands along with his flag post.

Nephrim observed with glee from the ramparts. "Cunning cur," he said smiling and then signalled his men. A clacking sound soon followed from the distance and the sky was suddenly filled with soaring balls of fire.

Lyons and Serik turned their heels in panic as the rest of the horsemen scurried off in all directions. The sky burned above them, and as they bolted together a ball of flame crushed them in an instant.

Lilith rode hard and fast, twisting and turning as the horse reeled in fear, galloping away from the crashing apocalypse behind it. The reins were impossible to grasp, and Lilith struggled to hold onto the horn of the saddle. "Straight! Damn it!" she roared as from across the field, she witnessed the portcullis slowly opening.

"Open the gate!" yelled Elias from atop the battlements. "Faster!"

A second volley of artillery took flight.

Lilith looked back, watching as the last remaining horsemen that lagged shortly behind her were blown to pieces. "Faster!" she yelled as she turned her gaze forward, seconds before she felt the blazing heat fly right above her head.

Then the crash followed.

The horse reeled back as the fireball exploded a few feet in front of it, throwing Lilith to the ground. Her ears rang, and her vision was blurred. The muffled call of her name came from the distance through the cacophony of terror.

"Lilith, get up!" boomed Elias from the walls as the gates opened high enough to allow a couple of men through. "Get up! Get her now!" He waved frantically as the men hesitated to leave the fortress to get Lilith who was a mere hundred metres away.

Lilith slowly came to her senses as the Carthosian front began its advance in the distance. Siege towers emerged from behind the ramparts, and soldiers followed behind. Once more, she realised how her hands were still bound, and another volley took flight. "Fuck!" she cursed as she looked to her sides in a bid to find the fake mirror shard to free her bonds. Yet the shard fell a couple of yards behind her. "Fuck!" she cursed once more and swiftly crawled back up to her feet in her mud-covered robes, dashing for the shard and tripping right before it as the crash of fireballs flew overhead and into the bastions of Morren's Gate.

"What the blazes is she doing?" yelled Elias as the bastions rumbled at each bombardment.

"I think she's retrieving the Shard, Commander," said the lieutenant taking Elias by the shoulder. "You need to take cover, sir!"

Elias immediately shrugged him off. "Get that Shard! Now!" he roared as they descended into the bailey.

"Sir, the men will get killed. We need to close the gate! Now!" said the lieutenant.

Elias grabbed the lieutenant by the collar. "Do what I fucking say, Dagon! Now!" he growled, shoving him forward.

The men moved out reluctantly and slowly emerged from the gate's narrow opening. "Move!" barked Dagon as three knights emerged on horseback, galloping to retrieve the Drae'shï and her shard.

Lilith's shard soon freed her of her bonds, and her sprint marked the departure of another volley. She ran like she had never run before as the knights galloped towards her. She reached out as the foremost rider tried to catch hold of her, but the only thing he caught was a direct hit. Lilith screamed as she flew back, watching men and horses being torn limb from limb by the blast. She forced herself up once more, bloodied and splintered, stricken and her hair muddy. She ran, teeth clenched and forceful.

"Get in!" called the men as she was a mere stone's throw away from the gate, but another volley took flight. All screamed as they hurried in ahead of her. "Get down!" they called as they pointed to the sky, revealing to Lilith the impending doom of her trajectory.

She immediately threw herself on the ground as the volley struck the western gate, forcing the portcullis shut and bending the wrought iron. As Lilith raised her gaze, she saw her fate sealed shut. A barricade of corpses and rubble lay in front of her. She groaned, gritting her teeth as she forced herself on all fours and then to her feet. She panted and turned back to see the advancing troops. She was cut off. She stood there watching, breathing deeply, as the few survivors outside the walls desperately clambered to their feet, struggling to find a way inside.

She turned with a sombre grin and faced Nephrim's oncoming horde. She gradually walked forward and picked up one sword and then another. Both were heavy, but her grip and resolve made her arms as hard as steel.

"It's jammed!" yelled the gatekeeper as they struggled to raise the portcullis.

"Carthosians have no shame. What tactical advantage do they gain by destroying the only way in?" spat Dagon.

Suddenly, the next volley struck the keep behind them. All dropped to the ground as burning stone and rubble flew in all directions.

"They don't want a way in. They don't want us to have a way out," said Elias with dread. "They want to leave a mark for the rest of the world to see, and they won't stop 'til this fort is nothing but a pile of rubble."

"What are we going to do, Commander?"

"They've extended the range of their artillery to avoid hitting their advancing troops. Ready the horsemen on the east gate! It's the only way," said Elias as he ran up to the bastions overlying the west gate.

"Lilith!" he called out, but the Drae'shï stood still in the face of the advancing havoc.

She slowly turned her dreaded, angry scowl to Elias.

"We're coming for you!" he yelled as the full might of the Shirra presented itself before them.

A never-ending sea of sunburst flags and soldiers advanced ahead of a dozen siege towers.

"Mother of Light protect us. We'll never hold them all," said Elias.

"Must we retreat?" said Dagon.

"We can't outrun them, even with our cavalry, and we're trapped," he said angrily as he looked towards the blockade at sea. "This is going to be a slaughter."

Yet a ship with black sails emerged in the distance, sailing head-on, unperturbed by the numbers ahead of it.

The *Dead Lady*'s ram crashed through the breaks as the gulls flew away. "Few degrees to port," said Zain as he slowly turned the helm of the vessel, pointing the bow towards the slight gap in between one Carthosian ship and another. The winds had filled the sails and stretched the ropes to their limits, and as Zain looked behind him, the Valendrians gave chase. "Get ready, boys." He smiled devilishly. "We're about to crash this party!"

He watched the battlefield from afar as the towers slowly approached mid-field. "Sixty seconds," he said as he looked straight ahead, seeing the crews of the Carthosian blockade scramble to their stations, waving their flags and blowing their horns. Zain smiled once more and took a wooden plank, jamming it in the helm and blocking the rudder. He confidently walked down the steps to the front of the vessel, arranging the swashbuckler's coat he'd stolen, and picking up a long sword and unsheathing it. Tossing away the scabbard, he climbed upon the bowsprit, holding onto the rope and waving in his welcome as arrows flew past him.

The ship crashed with thunderous might through the blockade, dragging a Carthosian ship from its stern and quickly breaking free as the vessel sank behind it. The Valendrian galley rushed through in rapid succession. Arrows flew on both sides, but the breaching party broke through. A few moments later, the vessels crashed through the Carthosian jetties on the west bank's shore, popping each jetty plank by plank as the small outpost of men dove for their lives. The ships soon ran aground, landing on the sandy shores of Ithiria.

Zain skipped off the bowsprit, landing straight onto the wet sand as the Valendrian crew also disembarked in a rush.

Zain sprinted to the battlefield as a cohort of Valendrians emerged from the sally port of Morren's Gate, joining his charge as the sky suddenly filled with volleys of arrows and fireballs fired from the fort's bastions. The Carthosian advance suddenly felt the roar of artillery as balls of fire smashed through siege towers and crushed the densely packed infantry. Soon the Carthosians dashed at the walls as the rain of fire provoked their ire. Siege towers moved faster, and ladders were ferried with haste.

Zain and the Valendrians spearheaded the advance, dashing towards the gate as the Carthosians sprinted towards it in turn. "Lilith!" he exclaimed as he saw the Drae'shï charging head on down the ramp followed by a handful of men.

Zain dashed further, but his bloodlust did not allow him to manifest into his dark mist. "The Vanguard!" he roared as all the men behind him dashed towards the head of the Carthosian column, coming to a bone-breaking and gut-wrenching clash as, Valendrian, Carthosian, Vampire, and Drae'shï landed upon each other in the field.

Sword met polearm, scimitar met axe, spears met shields. The roar of battle screamed into the dark day as arrows rained upon the incoming hordes and the couple of hundred men beneath the walls fought brutally against those who got through. Zain caught a glimpse of Lilith a few yards away as he danced his way through parry, slash, and stab. Lilith viciously tore through her enemies with her two swords and nothing but a muddied and half tattered dress.

"Two-swords. Stubborn bitch." He smiled.

***

Lilith screamed out orders to the men around her who rallied to her might. She stabbed, cut, and maimed any Carthosian who came within her reach. She stuck her sword in the back of one and simultaneously reached around the neck of another, tearing his throat open with her talons before retrieving her sword from the collapsing cur. Her skill was only outmatched by her ferocity in the fight.

Suddenly, two fireballs collided in mid-air, high above their heads, bursting into a meteor shower of splintering flame and rock. Lilith found herself and those surrounding her on the ground once more. She struggled to rise. A Carthosian javelin flew and stuck her dress into the ground. She cursed as she attempted to tear the thick fabric. The next wave of Carthosians trampled upon the corpses and ailing soldiers, whether friend or foe. Lilith reached over; a long gash along her forearm oozed blood that trailed down her blade. Her lip was bloody, and her makeup trailed down her cheeks with blood and dirt. Despite the bruising that limited her every movement, she cut through her dress, and climbed to her feet, readying herself before the final onslaught.

As the horde dove upon the lone Drae'shï, the sun breached the morning sky behind her. Her dark silhouette was shrouded in gold. She stood alone, ready to die as all those around her failed to rise. The soldiers charged and she raised her guard but in one fell swoop, another flew from above her and stomped their advance with a mighty crash.

"Zain!" cried Lilith.

The Vampire spun and slashed with surgical precision, cutting through the enemy as the rest of the Valendrians caught up. Zain was cold, calculating and fast in dispatching his enemies. Each parry led to a kill, each kill to another strike.

Lilith dashed down, picked up her second sword and entered the fray once more. "Where were you?" she yelled as the two came shoulder to shoulder.

"Sorry I'm late, dear." He winked as she sneaked a devilish grin. "Let's show them what the Drae'shï and Eldaresh can do!" The couple transcended their beings and fought seamlessly as they set each other apart from the rest of the soldiers.

In the meantime, the remaining siege towers had reached the walls, and the artillery barrage from the Carthosian ridge had ceased.

"Lord Zain!" called out Dagon from the bastion. "Make your way back to the sally port! We won't be able to cover you much longer." His calls were repeated as he blew the Saint's trumpet over and over, and volley after volley of arrows flew from the bastions onto the hordes. Soon, the siege towers flung open and the soldiers climbing them were now able to turn the top of the walls into a battleground. "Zain!" called out Dagon. "We're losing support on the walls!"

Zain cursed. "Lilith!" he called as she continued to fight viciously, exhausted and bloody. "Lilith!"

"What?" she shouted as she caught her breath.

"To the sally port! Now!" ordered Zain.

She nodded, and the troops slowly fought their way back to the beach, but their paths were blocked by the unrelenting number of Carthosians descending upon them.

"So, this is the might of the Shirra," said Zain as he stopped along with Lilith to catch a glimpse of the entire battlefield being covered in Carthosians. The two looked at each other.

"It's time to embrace it, Zain." She looked back at him and then onto the hell standing before them.

"I..." said Zain hesitantly.

"Don't let the lies you tell yourself drown you again. You're an Eldaresh! You're death!" she said coldly as she watched on.

Zain clenched his sword in his blood-soaked hands.

A horn blew in the distance around the north side of Morren's Gate. Its distinct sound pierced through the air, echoing in the valley. The sound alerted everyone as a group of ten cataphracts emerged from around the northern bastion.

Upon the Carthosian ramparts, the generals all turned their gaze north.

"What's going on, Merral?" asked Nephrim as he sat astride his steed.

"It seems there's a small relief force of Saints approaching. Ten, if I'm counting correctly."

"Even with their armour, they won't make it past the men."

"Commander, there's more," said Merral, astounded as a legion of two hundred cataphracts followed the leading party.

Nephrim narrowed his eyes. "So, that's how the Order chooses to die." Nephrim turned to the Carthosian horsemen behind him. "Cavalry!" he roared, signalling them to start pouring out of the ramparts and onto the ridge side. "Get in formation! Now!"

The Saints slowly came round the side of the fortress as the sparse troops on the north side dispersed at the sight of the hulking metal horses and their armoured knights. Elias halted the advance, awaiting the approach of the rest of the two hundred horsemen of the third and fifth legions.

"Hold strong, my fellow Saints, and may the Light of the Mother guide you and your lances." His voice echoed with might as he began slowly moving forward as their forces converged, their red ribbons atop their helms fluttering in the wind. "Do not let your courage wane under the forces that stand before us. Keep your aim true and your hearts heavy, and by the Mother's will, we shall break the back of this leviathan before it devours us." The golden rays that peered through the clouds he drew his sword. "For the glory of the Holy Enoch!" he yelled as their pace quickened. "For the Glory of the Massass!" he shouted as they broke into a gallop. "For the glory of the Saints!" he roared as the cohorts drove their lances forward and trampled over the ground like an avalanche of muscle and metal.

Wave after wave of arrows flew against their relentless approach, bouncing off their armour and that of their horses. The charge ran forward as the Carthosian flank desperately tried to ready itself for impact. The dugs the spears and raised their shields.

But it wasn't enough.

The roar of the cataphracts echoed throughout the valley as they crashed through the Carthosian lines, splintering shields, spears, and scimitars. Wave after wave, the Saints sliced through the middle of the battlefield like a searing dagger through butter, tearing the Carthosian advance in two as men got crushed by the horses and their hooves.

"Scorpions! Fire!" yelled Nephrim from atop the ridge as the smaller siege engines began firing long bolts of iron towards the impregnable cavalry. A Saint tumbled with each bolt, and another tripped behind, but there were far too few batteries and far too many horsemen. The Saints had almost reached the main gate.

"Cavalry! Charge!" Elias roared as he sped forward unceremoniously, and the rest followed.

The Carthosians descended the ridge in all their might as quickly as possible, trampling on anyone who wasn't quick enough to move out of the way.

Lilith and Zain's retreat to the beach slowed its pace as they witnessed the disarray of the troops and oncoming banners of the Saints. "Yes! Elias, you bastard! Yes!" exclaimed Zain. "This is our chance! Let's go!" he yelled as the Valendrian troops rushed to the sally port, but Lilith slowed her pace and stopped. "Lilith?"

The Drae'shï watched the Carthosian cavalry descend to meet the Saints, Nephrim at the helm, along with the Shard sword. She gritted her teeth. She immediately tore what remained of her tattered skirt with her sword, freeing her stride, and began sprinting back across the open field.

"Lilith!" yelled Zain with incredulity. "What are you doing?" he asked as he noticed the fake mirror shard stuck in the mud right next to the tatters of her skirt.

"I'm getting back what is mine!" she roared as she sped on, dashing between skirmishes and bloodthirsty assailants, watching Nephrim from afar as he coursed through the field.

Meanwhile, the Saints on horseback were beginning to slow their race as the mass of infantry grew thicker by the gate area.

"We can't get held down here. If we stop, we're done. We've bought them enough time." yelled Elias. "Left flank turn!" he bellowed as his lieutenant barked the order down the line. The massive sea of horsemen began a u-turn manoeuvre just as the Carthosian cavalry was descending to their right. The Saints sped around a burning siege tower, trampling over the men around it and sending the rest into disarray.

The Carthosian cavalry rushed in, catching the tail of the Saints. A volley of javelins from the horsemen flew into the knights' flanks before smashing through a score of knights sending them through the air ten feet high as Nephrim emerged with the glowing Shard sword upon his steed. Knights flew and crashed to the ground where they were pummelled into the mud by hoof and hammer. The retreating Saints dashed at the incredible sight. A chase ensued and soon the lighter cavalry caught up with the cataphracts, as Nephrim pushed his forces picking off one knight after the other in the rear with just a slash of the Shard sword.

"They caught our tail, Commander!" yelled the lieutenant.

"Hold strong! Faster! Hyah!" Elias cursed and whipped his beast harder.

"Sir! Incoming cavalry dead ahead!" yelled another knight as a group of six horsemen approached from the front.

"They're just six!" Elias yelled back, but suddenly, an arrow flew straight into the eye of the lieutenant, tipping him over and disrupting the column behind him. "Watch out!" yelled Elias as another arrow flew right past him, striking another knight in the throat. "We'll smash through them! All lancers at hand wedge forward!" ordered Elias as the few knights with an intact lance formed a wedge at the head of the column.

The Saints ran fast and true into the oncoming group, but the oncoming horsemen split around and sped on as the Saints' column continued to narrow into a tail at the end. Elias watched as the horsemen, though clad in Carthosian colours, showed wisps of white hair and dark silver skin. "Drae'shï? Here?" he whispered to himself.

"It's here! Vuriel! It's here!" yelled Tenet as the Moirai raced towards chasing Carthosian cavalry. "It's in the sword! There!" he pointed towards Nephrim, who held the shining weapon high above his head.

"It's the sword! It's in the sword!" yelled Adam to Sirra, who was seated behind him as they rode past the last cataphract and towards Nephrim.

Sirra took a deep breath then drew her bow, struggling to keep her aim steady.

"Hit him, Sirra! Before he hits us!" yelled Lurith as Nephrim drew his arm back.

"Hit him, Sirra!" barked Vuriel. "Fire!" he roared as they were about to collide.

Sirra let go.

The arrow flew and stuck Nephrim in the shoulder. His strike waned, but his grip held strong. Seconds later, the Moirai crashed into the horses, and chaos ensued. Carthosians could not tell friend from foe. Nephrim turned, and the retreat was sounded, breaking the chase of the Saints who were now far behind their once threatened lines.

The Moirai rode side by side with the Carthosians, trying to reach the head of the column. Lurith jumped from one horse to the next, unseating riders with his daggers as their companions tried to kill the apparent traitor. Dreskar pulled one man after another off their horses whilst Adam held his gallop, and Sirra took aim once more at Nephrim through the rumbling cavalry. Sirra fired but missed as Adam parried the incoming scimitar of a horseman. The clash of swords continued as the cavalry drew closer to the main gate.

"Kill him!" yelled Sirra in frustration as the two could not shake the horseman.

"I'm trying!" cursed Adam as the horseman became more forceful and more horsemen came forth.

Tenet rode up closely and drew his bow.

"Watch out!" called Adam, but Tenet's arm met the swing of a Carthosian sword, and the ranger soon flew off the back of his horse.

"No!" yelled Sirra as she winced at the sight of her defeated comrade tumbling to the ground.

The Carthosians soon took a right turn towards the ramparts as Nephrim took refuge amidst his bodyguards.

"If they go over the ridge, it's over!" yelled Sirra as she struggled to take aim once more. "I'm losing him, Adam! Faster!"

"Grab the reins!" yelled Adam. "Grab them!" he ordered.

Sirra took hold.

"To hell with it!" he whispered before throwing himself onto their assailant, causing him to tumble to the ground.

Freed and now faster, Sirra sped closer to the Carthosian commander. She took aim and fired, striking Nephrim in the arm and loosening his grip. The sword fell in the middle of the field. "Yes!" she exclaimed as the Carthosian cavalry sped on to safety.

Adam soon rose to his feet as he caught glimpses of the sword sticking out of the ground as it intermittently disappeared behind the silhouettes of advancing troops and retreating horses. He narrowed his eyes, focusing past the sword onto another silhouette he suddenly recognised.

Lilith dashed towards the Shard sword with all her might, abandoning her other weapons as the space cleared before her.

"Lilith!" yelled Zain as he struggled to catch up to her.

She ignored him.

The Moirai began their gallop towards her as Adam also started running. Lilith ran and reached out, but her last step clashed with an advancing soldier, sending them both tumbling to the ground.

"Lilith!" cried Zain desperately.

Lilith slowly tried to come to her senses as she pushed herself out of the muck. The sword shimmered just a few feet before her, yet as her blurred vision focused once more, it revealed the incoming Moirai on horseback just a stone's throw away. She crawled and moaned as each step felt like a thousand.

Zain called out once more as he, too, found himself beset by the enemy.

"Do it," she whispered as she watched him look for another way to escape his assailants. "Do it!" she roared as her piercing red eyes stung his heart and her voice penetrated his soul.

The Moirai ahead of her raised their swords, almost at hand.

Zain's heart sank, and just as he was about to hesitate, he dug his teeth into a Carthosian soldier, shrivelling him in a matter of seconds. His eyes widened to the blackness of night, and the blood electrified Zain's body, suddenly turning the Vampire into a mist of black smoke and blood. The ethereal essence sailed through the battlefield and swung by Lilith, engulfing her and the Shard sword and soaring into the sky, leaving nothing behind just as the Moirai's horses trampled on her position.

Everyone looked above as the cloud of red and black smoke rained blood on those directly below, just before dashing back down to the ground in the middle of the field.

Lilith emerged from the smoke as Zain reformed beside her. Once more, she brandished her sword.

"Shit!" yelled Sirra as all the other Drae'shï gritted their teeth.

The Carthosians froze momentarily at the seemingly bewitched couple. They hesitated but soon rushed the two.

Zain flashed a large haunting grin as the first men approached. He dashed in a flash from one to another, coming in and out of his blood cloud and leaving nothing but shrivelled corpses behind him.

Vuriel cursed, looking at the others and nodding begrudgingly. "Hyah!" he yelled as they charged forward, and Adam followed on foot.

"Adam!" called Sirra from behind. Concern had crystallised into fear. She frowned and then shook her head at him.

Lilith ran down beside Zain as more and more troops abandoned what they were doing to try and kill them. With each swing of the Shard Sword, Lilith tore five men asunder.

Zain jumped from one cluster of men to another, picking up sword then spear, mace, and shield, slashing, stabbing, and smashing with the force of ten men. Limb was torn from limb. Heads were severed from shoulders, and soon, Lilith and Zain were completely covered in blood.

For every other kill, Zain drained another in an orgy of blood. His jaw grew bigger, and so did his razor-sharp teeth. Each kill formed part of a crescendo of bestial evolution as he grew larger, stronger, and more vicious. Arrows peppered him, and spear and sword cut through, but his wounds lasted no longer than a few seconds. As the terrified horde desperately tried to pin him down, he soon climbed upon a siege tower, clawing his way to the top. He dangled and swung until his monstrous size pulled the hulking tower down upon the panicking legions beneath.

Meanwhile, Lilith soon found herself before the rush of the Moirai's horses. She stood fast, fearless, drawing her sword for the strike. Vuriel and Ellior looked for an opportunity, but Lilith cut through their horses, flinging them to the ground.

Dreskar followed and dismounted before her, heavy mace at hand, ready to crush the puny girl before him. He struck, and she blocked, but the Dratesh Khan's might forced her back.

"You remember black steel, don't you, Ilvaresh?" asked the Dratesh Khan.

The two fought as the other Drae'shï dashed forward, yet Sirra held back as she watched Zain tear everyone to pieces.

"We have to help them!" barked Adam. "We can't leave them!"

"No. We have to go!" she said with pursed lips. Adam began to head forward, but Sirra turned the horse in front of him. "Don't let your stubbornness kill you."

"It's my duty! We can't leave her with the Shard!" he shouted back angrily, watching the desperate scene unfold before him.

"Right now, it's your duty to warn everyone," she said as she extended her arm to the Eldassari.

He continued staring at Lilith as she fought ceaselessly against the Moirai, gritting his teeth.

"Adam! Don't let your convictions blind you. We have to go!"

He cursed.

Sirra extended her grip once more.

He cursed and took her arm.

Lilith fought and parried the slashes, strikes and swings of Vuriel, Ellior, and Dreskar, who slowly pushed her towards a burning siege tower that was still standing. Each of their hits landed on the sword, which, though made of steel, carried like a feather in her hand. In the meantime, Lurith scaled the wooden structure, coming upon the sole standing platform above the fight and holding his daggers. Lilith soon found herself with her back against the tower as Dreskar spun his heavy mace like a battering ram. Lilith bided her time, dodging without striking back, concentrating clear and cold.

In what felt like a second, Lilith raised her sword and the Shard right before her eyes, and the maw of darkness filled the shard instantly.

As each weapon of the Moirai landed on her, they burst into a thousand splinters, sending Vuriel and Ellior to the ground in agony. Dreskar staggered back as blood started dripping from the hundreds of holes punctured through his thick plate armour. Lilith screamed and charged him, throwing the metal goliath to the ground, climbing upon him and stabbing him incessantly with her sword. She rose before the horrified Carthosians with her dress in tatters, exposing half her body as it gleamed in blue and red blood.

"Now or never," spat Lurith as he leapt off the platform, daggers in hand.

Lilith turned.

Lurith flew towards her but was immediately caught in mid-air by the throat. He choked and gurgled as the vampiric abomination tightened his grip. Barely a whiff left Lurith's wretched look of terror as Zain squeezed, crushing his neck, and then tossing the Drae'shï ten yards away. Zain turned to the troops. He was now four metres tall, broad as a bear and with a sharkish mouth that ran almost from ear to ear. He roared, and the crowds before him turned tail.

"Zain!" called Lilith from below him. The beast looked back without recognition. Zain grabbed her by the throat and lifted her to his gaze, leaving her sword stuck in Dreskar's armour. The Vampire watched closely as she held on without a struggle. "Do it," she gasped. "Take me," she taunted deviously.

Zain slowly released Lilith. His hand still loosely held her neck that was covered in blood. His eyes returned to their normal hue as he gazed into the ruby eyes of the Drae'shï before turning his attention to her bloodied lips. His grip tightened once more, and the Drae'shï released a soft moan. She sneaked a deviant smile, and the Vampire forcibly pulled her to him, bringing her lips to his.

She moaned once more as they locked in a bloody embrace. Their tongues met each other's with violent passion as their sharp nails sank into each other's skin. He licked her from neck to ear, nibbling on her smooth skin that was drenched in the honey-like taste of Drae'shï and human blood.

He lifted her from her waist and slammed her back against the wall of the broken siege tower, ripping off what was left of her robes. Their eyes locked, and he penetrated her as she released a loud uninhibited moan. They heaved and gasped as they consumed each other with every hard thrust that pushed the Drae'shï into the hot wood at her back. Their skins smouldered with the heat of the burning tower, and their bodies ran drenched with blood, sweat and soot.

She held his chest back as she watched the true Eldaresh fuck her. His eyes darted from hers down to her supple body before focusing on her pulsating neck. She held herself against the wooden boards with one arm whilst the heat coming through scalded her back. She turned her neck to him. "Take me," she whispered, and Zain sank his teeth into her neck.

Her blood was exquisitely electrifying. An intense rush of adrenaline filled his chest, and his thrusting increased. She moaned and wailed as she slowly felt her senses leaving her. The apnoea of her submission was almost as delightful as his final domination. He thrust, and she held on until he neared his release. He let go of her neck as she reached the brink of unconsciousness and climaxed in chaos and ecstasy.

The field had cleared around them. Chaos was rampant, but soon, the call of the Royal Guard of the Shirral came from above the ridge. The golden standards had arrived. The Shirral watched as the army was in disarray. Some still rushed the walls where the siege towers had finally breached. Others drew away from their lines. The ship masts hiding in the port also appeared to be getting ready for retreat.

"Your Grace, the fort is ours, and the Valendrians are retreating," said the commander of the Royal Guard.

"Destroy it," said the Shirral, almost growling.

"What? Excuse me, Your Grace, but—"

"You heard me," said the Shirral, deadly serious.

"But, Your Grace, we have the fort."

In a stern look, the Shirral turned to the rest of his men and called out above the roar of war. "Wipe this fort off the map. There will be no spoils to claim from this treachery. Any who claim but a single stone of this fortress will do so on pain of death!" The blare of the Shirral's horn caught everyone's attention, and they quickly abandoned the area around the gate. All siege engines fired at the walls and portcullis, raining hell on anyone still there. In a matter of minutes, the entrance was nothing but a pile of rubble, and the walls were crumbling at every hit

Zain and Lilith soon realised none of their allies were left on the field. The Valendrian vessels gradually sailed out, thrashing through the blockade. "Lilith," he said hesitantly as he gazed at her ruby eyes.

"We can't stay here, Zain," she said as she stroked his face. "The fort is lost."

Zain nodded. "Let's hold their retreat then."

The two soon stepped into the middle of the open field, awaiting the rush of men, but none advanced.

The Shirral peered into the distance. "What's happening there? Why aren't they advancing?"

"They're scared, Your Grace," said the captain sheepishly.

"A man and a woman? Alone?" he exclaimed.

"It's the Drae'shï and a Vampire. They slaughtered a hundred men alone."

"Fire the scorpions."

"Your Grace?"

"Now!" he roared furiously.

Zain and Lilith watched the soldiers cower before them and their nakedness when suddenly a scorpion's bolt flew right between the two and into the mangled corpses behind them. Zain's eyes widened to black again, and he began to grow. A second bolt flew, and in an instant, Zain caught it in mid-air. The beast twisted and bent the iron shaft into a knot and threw it with force at the line of cowering men, shattering their shields with the impact.

The Shirral widened his eyes. "Fire! Fire all of them!" A shower of scorpions soon followed, and Zain quickly caught Lilith and flew in a mystical flurry of blood and smoke before landing upon the broken bastion walls of what was once Morren's Gate.

The Shirral stood in astonishment at the display.

"Let me go! I have to see!" yelled Adara as she dashed through the royal guard and stood beside the Shirral. Adara gasped at the sight of the massacre, covering her mouth. Soon her eyes landed on the blasted walls. "Is that Lili—? Zain!"

The Drae'shï and the Vampire looked at each other and the fort behind them. The courtyards were clear, and the last ship had sailed. "It's time to leave, Death of the Undeath," she smirked, and in a twist, they turned to mist once more and sped out of sight in a single cloud of red and black fury.

Adara watched bewildered as the ruins of bloodshed lay at her feet.

Men of all colours and creeds lay on the ground, wailing in agony as others wept. She turned to Pïshkah as the Cleriheu arrived at the scene. "Tell them to get my medicine chest!" she ordered.

"Adara," said Pïshkah, pursing her lips.

"Get it! Now!" she yelled as she darted down the ramparts, weaving her way amongst puddles of blood and mutilated bodies. The smell of charred skin christened the air like dark incense. She dove beside a man, weeping on the ground in a pool of blood. "Pïshkah!" she called once more as the Cleriheu and nurses hurried down the ridge under the sullen gaze of the Shirral.

The ailing man watched Adara as a calmness fell upon him. The Eldain brushed his hair and wiped his face with her sash. "Breathe! Stay with me! Breathe, come on!" she said as she desperately looked for the wound that injured him, but the man's gaze lengthened, and all that left him was a final tear.

Adara stood up and looked around her as the choir of cries intensified, and the carrion birds began to circle the field.

"Adara, there's too many. We can't save them all," said Pïshkah softly.

Adara clenched her bloodied fist, gazing into the battlefield. "I know," she said, her eyes watering as she forced a brave smile. "It's alright, Pïshkah. All that matters is that someone is still trying," she said, trembling. She paused for a moment but soon sank her face in her hands and fell to her knees.

Pïshkah ran to Adara, clinging her to her chest.

"And I'll be there to help you." The Cleriheu held Adara tightly as she wept, watching over Adara's shoulder as the flailing bodies of Nephrim and the other generals were slowly hung by their necks under the stern judgement of the Shirral.

The ridge soon displayed new banners for all the Shirra to see.

CHAPTER 32

VIRTUES OF LOST SOULS

"I don't know whether it was because of her or because part of me wanted to let go after so long." Zain gazed at the roof of his cell. "I don't know which answer scares me the most. I thought that in her I could find meaning once more in an endless sea of pointless solitude, but in the end, all it did was unleash the darkness within. Countless died at my feet, and I revelled in it, in the destruction of this wretched cruel world. Even if such a terribly empowering feeling was short-lived," said Zain melancholically as he fiddled with his chain, popping each link through his hands one at a time. "I've tried so hard in my life to be less of the beast I truly am, but in the end, I've brought more death and suffering than anyone who has ever lived. Perhaps this cell is truly where I belong."

Aria sighed. "Zain, the battles for our hearts, minds, and souls are not determined by any single event. It's a constant struggle, like yours, like everyone else's." Her soft voice echoed in the other room. "And there is a lot more left in you that is neither Lilith's nor that of the beast that dwells within."

Zain returned no response.

"Maybe. Yeah. The Cursed Ones they called us." He laughed to himself. "How right they were. I just wonder, had my father and I managed to lead us out of the darkness, would our corruption have died with our hunger for blood? After being so corrupt for so long, you forget what you once were in the first place."

"It is the continual pursuit of a better way in spite of our nature that redeems us. You survived the Immortal Wars for that reason, and you helped others survive over the years. Did you forget?"

"At what cost, though?"

"You can never truly know. The death of one can save millions. The birth of another can take more."

"Indeed, but I am tired of being an agent of death. For better or for worse."

"I understand, Zain. Yet, how we choose to see it is up to us. You cannot be an agent of death without being one for life as well."

Zain paused pensively. "Huh. Never thought of it that way." He smiled. "Thanks, Aria."

"You're welcome, Your Grace," said Aria sarcastically.

"Shut up!" Zain laughed.

"Hey, you told me you're the heir to the throne of Dos Narak."

"Yeah. Though I'm quite sure the blood fiends and hellions that roam there may find it objectionable."

The two smiled silently as Zain tried to sneak a glimpse of Aria through the crack in the wall. "I've never been friends with someone I've never seen before."

"Oh, so we're friends now?" she teased.

"It's in the word; cellmate, *mate*."

"Shouldn't we be sharing the same cell then?"

"They're sorting out your bed. It's on its way. I'm sure it takes them a while to get a bale of hay up those bloody stairs," he said dryly as Aria laughed back. "Anyway, why are you here? Where are you from?"

"Oh, where to begin? It's difficult to explain."

"Nonsense! I'll start for you. Once upon a time."

She sniggered. "Well, it's a long story, but needless to say, I'm here because many people didn't like what I had to say. It's strange how when telling the truth, people first tell you you're wrong, then they call you crazy, and then they try to silence you."

"It's a lonely path. I, too, was considered crazy for refusing to drink the blood of men, but after they tried to silence me, I silenced them. All of them."

"Death of the Undeath"

"Some emperor, huh? Ending a legacy of thousands of years single-handedly. In the end, the myth became reality, the curse of the Eldaresh; 'For all those that sought blood to remain with the living, would always know death so long as they did,'" said Zain sombrely. "A *crowning* achievement, wouldn't you say?" He chuckled as Aria laughed on the other side.

"Well, for all it's worth, Zain, I think you're far from cursed," said Aria. "We do not choose how we are born, but we do choose how to live, and your choices do not belong to one who is cursed. All I see is a man buried under an avalanche of guilt born of his own judgement, and guilt, your majesty, is not an affliction of the cursed. The truly cursed know one thing and one thing only: apathy. And apathy is worse than death."

Zain smiled to himself as he looked down at his sorry state. "Thank you, Aria. Your words are very kind."

ALSO BY JENS C. BÜDINGER

THE DARKNESS WITHIN

– BOOK II –

THE CHRONICLES OF LILITH SERIES

The Battle of Blood is over, but the true war is about to begin.

Pïshkah's visions herald a far greater darkness beyond the Carthosian war. A battle between Greater Immortals. One that seeks to devour the very mind, heart and soul of the world. One that comes at the hands of Lilith, the Queen of Shards.

Meanwhile, Lilith has set her sights on the Hall of Mirrors, the one place she can truly unlock the truth held within her Shard, and nothing is going to stop her from getting her answers, not the power-hungry Saints, not the threat of the Carthosian war or the Wardens who wish to harm her.

Zain reluctantly aids Lilith as her unsettling determination to reach the Hall inevitably draws them into the darkness within Mount Ussar Varys. Yet he is still intent on rescuing Adara and those he loves from the war.

Zain is now faced with an agonizing decision: follow the woman he so desperately fought for down an even darker path and turn his back on the world, or turn his back on her when she needs him the most.

Available 30.06.2023

About the Author

Jens Carl Büdinger is the author of the Darkness Within and the Chronicles of Lilith series.

In 2018, after working as a lawyer for almost 7 years, Jens decided to leave his legal career to pursue his own journey. From start-ups to UX design to crypto and writing, Jens has a wide range of experience and interests making him a nomadic wanderer in a sea of infinite opportunities.

Jens' love of writing and telling stories began at a tender age but was always put on the backburner. This was until November 2019 when Jens finally decided to embark on the dream of writing and completing the Chronicles of Lilith series.

The Chronicles of Lilith's inception began around 15 years ago. Many books were started and never finished, largely due to time and commitment issues apart from lack of experience. However, this long road brought him back to the writer's desk with the commitment and resolve to see this through, whatever it takes.

Jens currently resides in Malta, a little island in the middle of the Mediterranean. He spends his free time gaming, belting it out, scraping guitar and cuddling his cats.

About the Series

The Chronicles of Lilith is a Metaphysical Dark Fantasy / Sci-Fi series that explores many deep existential themes and ideas as well as the nature of reality. It is a story within a story within a story.

At its core the Chronicles are a series of books about the origins and end of creation, the meaning of life and whether it ought to continue. It is story witnessed through multiple realities and timelines by a host of supreme deities known as the Greater Immortals who together uphold the very fabric of existence and reality, whether they're aware of it or not. As this deep narrative slowly unfolds the reader joins each character as they slowly discover themselves and their roles in the mystery that is life as well as their own humanity, or lack thereof.

Readers who embark on this long journey will travel across realities following a various complex and interesting characters as both endure a riveting, heart wrenching adventure about finding hope, meaning, love, courage and beauty whilst facing the struggles of life, death, suffering and the true face of nihilism.

<u>The Chronicles of Lilith Series</u>
The Queen of Shards – Book I
The Darkness Within – Book II

Thank You Note

Thank you for your support and for purchasing this book. I truly hope you have enjoy this adventure and are looking forward to the next. If you did so enjoy it, please do leave a review on Amazon and Goodreads. It is a small act that helps authors like me tremendously and makes our efforts worthwhile.

To keep up with news and updates on future publications visit www.jensbud.com and subscribe to the newsletter.
Follow @authorjensbud on instagram.

Heartfelt thanks,
Jens C. Budinger.